α

London Blood

A Benjamin Franklin Mystery

London
Blood

Further Adventures of the
American Agent Abroad

by
ROBERT LEE HALL

St. Martin's Press
New York

A THOMAS DUNNE BOOK.
An imprint of St. Martin's Press.

Library of Congress Cataloging-in-Publication Data

Hall, Robert Lee.
    London blood : further adventures of the American agent abroad : a Benjamin Franklin mystery / Robert Lee Hall.
      p.   cm.
    "A Thomas Dunne book."
    ISBN 0-312-16908-6
    1. Franklin, Benjamin, 1706–1790—Fiction.   2. Americans—England—London—History—18th century—Fiction.   3. Government investigators—England—London—Fiction.   I. Title.
PS3558.A3739L66   1997
813'.54—dc21   97-18813
                                                  CIP

First Edition: October 1997

10 9 8 7 6 5 4 3 2 1

In memory: Diane Cleaver

London Blood

𝕏 1 𝕏

IN WHICH One Man Tells of Lightning, Another of Murder . . .

Thunder shook our house in Craven Street hard by the Thames. It rattled over all London, so that even King George, in his great state bed in St. James's Palace, must have felt it too. It had been preceded by lightning, a flash so near the hair on my arms stood erect, though whether from an excess of the electrical charge or from fear I could not say. A sulphurous stink invaded the room.

I turned to Benjamin Franklin.

He stood on one side of the long wooden bench in the center of his workshop, Mrs. Margaret Stevenson, his landlady, and I on the other; she smelt of nutmeg and freshly baked bread. It was past 10:00 P.M. We had come up at Mr. Franklin's bidding; now we waited for him to speak. He stood alertly in his customary plain brown coat and blunt-toed shoes, the hair from his balding crown tied back with a simple black ribbon. His eyeglasses sat far forward on his nose, so he could peer over the tops if need be. Candlelight gave his sturdy form a nut-brown glow. He was mild-looking, no threat, yet his demeanor belied a remarkable nature, for he was famed amongst philosophers as far as St. Petersburg for demonstrating that lightning and electricity were one.

Glancing toward the window, he smiled at the lightning, as if Nature had pleased him. *Never fear, Nick,* his gray-brown eyes assured.

Gesturing toward the storm, he addressed Mrs. Stevenson:

"Imagine the consequences if the bolt had struck your house, dear lady. We should be dead in the instant—though if by some chance we survived, we should awake to a shambles. Why, I have known a flash to fuse the pewter spoons in a cellar. Should you like your finest china shattered? Your bedclothes aflame? Your best lodger, Ben Franklin, roasted like a pig on a spit?"

Mrs. Stevenson was a plumpish woman in a white housewife's cap. "Indeed I should not," averred she.

"Why, then, you must have a lightning rod, ma'am."

Her eyes narrowed. "A lightning rod?" Lifting her hand, she tapped at a mole by the side of her nose; she did this when she was doubtful, which was frequently—though her skepticism had not prevented her serving Mr. Franklin well since he came to London in the service of the Pennsylvania Assembly.

He had thought to stay only a few months, but his business had proved onerous, and it was now the twelfth of November, 1759, more than two years since he landed at Falmouth.

"You shall not regret it, ma'am." Mr. Franklin waved an arm toward the window. "Why, by its means we can disarm even a storm!" Together they peered at black clouds above the southward curve of the Thames, whilst I gazed about the workshop at the implements with which Benjamin Franklin probed the world: his pitted workbench, the calipers, the lenses, the "Philadelphia machine," as he called his electrical apparatus, which could kill a man by its charge. Specimens that had provoked his musings rested on a shelf: seashells, the fossil bone of a mammoth, a stalactite of salt from a Norwich mine, which he had collected on a recent journey to Edinburgh. There were more sinister mementoes, too: a Bible with a hidden pocket in its cover, the vial of opliss-popliss drops which had done in Roderick Fairbrass, Wedgewood chess pieces given by David Garrick in return for ridding Drury Lane of murder.

I thrilled to the latter items, for whilst he waited upon the Board of Trade, Benjamin Franklin had turned to solving crimes, and I, Nicolas Handy, aged fourteen, was privileged to be his helper.

Mrs. Stevenson turned away from the storm. "I *may* have a lightning rod, sir," said she, "—if you will tell me how such a thing can protect my house."

"Indeed, that is why I asked you to come upstairs after supper. Hearing the churchbells ring to warn of a storm, I determined to demonstrate my 'doctrine of points,' so that you might be amongst the first to reap its benefits." Beckoning us near, the gentleman set upon his workbench a glass bottle. Then he produced two round balls. "This is of iron," said he, balancing one on the mouth of the bottle. "The other is cork." Mr. Franklin never stood on ceremony, so climbing upon the table he tied a silk thread to a nail affixed in the ceiling. From this he suspended the cork ball directly above the iron so that the cork rested lightly against the other's side.

He got down. "Let the experiment be made!" Taking up a metal rod, he withdrew a charge from his Philadelphia machine. This charge he transferred to the iron ball by touching the tip of the rod to it.

As if affrighted, the cork ball flew outward and remained in a bobbing orbit six inches from the iron.

Mrs. Stevenson's eyes thinned in suspicion. "What, sir? Magic?"

Mr. Franklin made a face. "Not magic. Nature! Have I not told you that 'magic' is paltry trickery? Look you, the glass bottle, the silken thread, and the cork are all nonconductors of the electrical fluid. But iron takes a charge exceedingly well, and it now has been 'fed' an excess of it; that is, it is electricized 'positively,' as I have taught the world to say. This positive charge drives the cork from it. But, now, see this." Taking up a long, sharply pointed metal pin, he moved its tip slowly toward the iron ball. As the pin neared the iron, the cork's orbit began to falter, and when the pin was yet three inches from the iron, the cork suddenly fell back to its former position.

"Goodness!" exclaimed our landlady.

"See, the electrical fluid is drawn to *points*," said Mr. Franklin. "That is why the cork fell back. (Note that the point need not touch the iron to draw its charge.) Put another way, the charge from the iron ball has fled into the metal pin's sharp end."

"But might not a . . . a what-d'ye-call-it, a 'charge' be drawn by any shape of metal?"

Mr. Franklin beamed. "We shall make a philosopher of you yet! Let us test your idea." He electrified the ball again, sending the

3

cork into its orbit as before—but this time he approached the iron with the blunt end of the rod. Nearer and nearer it came as we watched, waited.

He had to touch the iron before the cork ball reluctantly fell back.

Mrs. Stevenson's mouth flattened. "I see what you do, sir," said she, "and perhaps I even understand a bit of it. But—"

"But what signifies philosophy that does not apply to some use, eh? A lightning rod is the use—or a 'Franklin rod,' as they insist upon calling 'em. We shall attach it to the chimney of your house, eight or ten feet high, sharpened to a point like a needle. Thus we shall draw the electrical fire out of the storm."

Mrs. Stevenson gaped. "You wish to put upon my rooftop a spire to *attract* the lightning?" She shook her head so hard the lace on her starched cap jiggled. "I respect you greatly, sir, but I shall never allow that."

"Tut, I see that in my zeal I have left out an important detail." He turned. "Tell it, Nick."

I knew my catechism: "A wire shall be attached to the spire, ma'am. It will run down the side of your house into the ground. Thus the charge will be diverted where it can do no harm."

Mrs. Stevenson frowned from me to Mr. Franklin. Truth to tell, his "doctrine of points" was by no means universally accepted— it was disputed even by the Abbé Nollet of France. Would Mrs. Stevenson dispute it, too?

We were spared contention by the rap of the housemaid. Thin and shy, Nanny slipped in with downcast eyes. "Beg pardon . . . but there is a man come to speak to Mr. Franklin."

"Do I not teach you to say what man?" chid Mrs. Stevenson.

Nanny blanched. "I d-do not know what man. I only know he says he is sent by Justice Fielding."

Mr. Franklin glanced at me. John Fielding, the "Blind Beak," London's most feared crime-fighter, sometimes called upon Craven Street when puzzles vexed him. Did the arrival of one of his men on such a night bode trouble?

Mr. Franklin removed the iron ball from the bottle. He untied the cork from the string. "I shall go down at once. *We* shall go down. Bring your writing book, Nick."

Rain licked the windowpanes.

"Yes, sir," said I.

In less than a moment we had descended to the front parlor, a neat, orderly chamber on the ground floor, facing Craven Street. Embroidered sayings of Poor Richard hung upon its distempered walls. Comfortable furnishings sat about. It was chill, without a fire, for no one had been expected, but Nanny had had the presence of mind to light candles; three flickered upon the mantelpiece. Mrs. Stevenson hovered just outside the parlor door. She was naturally curious, but though she was sometimes privileged to hear what passed betwixt Mr. Franklin and callers, the louring look on the face that awaited us portended ill, so Mr. Franklin firmly shut the door.

Turning, he made a bow. "Billy."

Our visitor offered a curt bob of head in return. "Mr. Franklin, sir." Clutching a dripping tricorn hat, he wore heavy boots and a voluminous coat. His gaze briefly acknowledged me, for I knew him, too: Billy Banting, one of Justice Fielding's men, a "Bow Street runner," as Fielding's minions were called, after the street from which they were dispatched. Banting was broad-shouldered and red-faced, with sinewy hands and hooded eyes under a brow topped by curling brown hair. He was a man of few words, but I had seen him crack the head of more than one brute; cutpurses and footpads had best not trifle with him.

"Justice Fielding sent you?" prompted Mr. Franklin.

"Yes, sir."

"Murder, is it, then?"

Banting squinted from under his heavy brow. "You already know of it, sir?"

A gesture. "The night, the storm, the hour—yet you are sent nonetheless. It is something dire, then—and what more dire than murder? Too"—Mr. Franklin motioned—"the blood upon your boot."

Thunder rumbled as Banting peered down. "But I took great care—"

"Not care enough." With his bamboo stick Mr. Franklin tapped

5

Banting's right heel, where I discerned an irregular brownish stain. It was hardly distinguishable from the filth of London's ways—the horse dung and other leavings that begrimed ten thousand shoes—but Mr. Franklin had spied it. "The rain has just begun, so it has had no chance to wash off." The gentleman pursed his lips. "There must have been a great deal of blood to come upon your boot." He cocked his head. "Was there a great deal of blood, Billy?"

A moment of silence greeted this. Banting had seen many terrible sights, yet he shuddered. "A great deal, yes, sir." He licked his lips.

"Not a recent murder either? The stain upon your boot is scraped from dried matter. The deed is just discovered, then?"

"By a linkboy."

"And it has . . . unusual features?"

Banting shifted his feet. " 'Twas a young woman, sir."

A tiny frown marked Mr. Franklin's brow. Did he think on my mother, who had been young when she, too, was murdered? "Many young women die ev'ry day in London," said he evenly.

"This one's heart was cut from her chest!" Banting burst out. He mastered himself. "She . . . she is not the first such victim." His voice was barely audible.

Another stillness filled the room, as if London held her breath, whilst the tick of the case clock in the entryway came to us like the impatient tap of a finger. The smell of ginger biscuits lingered in the air.

Mr. Franklin nodded. "I see. And your master sends for me to come?"

"If you please."

"I shall, then, for no woman must be dishonored in such a fashion." He turned to me. "Nick?"

"I am ready."

"We shall need our boots. And our long coats. Lightning rods must wait. Lead on, Billy Banting. We are with you."

6

❧ 2 ❧

IN WHICH We Greet a Blind Man, a Dead Woman,
and a Stranger . . .

Fielding's man had come prepared, for we found one of Bow
Street's black-leather coaches waiting in the storm. Heads
ducked, we dashed to it, Mr. Franklin settling on the right,
Billy Banting left, I squeezed tight between. With his hat streaming, our driver huddled atop. A flick of reins, a scrape of wheels,
a clop of hooves, and we were off. I rid with mixed feelings. I had
embarked on journeys before with Mr. Franklin, dangerous ven-
tures. Another such?

Yet I should envy any boy who took my place.

The rain blew fiercely, pounding our rooftop, lashing the cobbles. In the Strand shop signs rattled, whilst lead spouts gushed,
and black shapes bent against a blustering tide. Past Charing Cross
we turned west into the Haymarket. "Toward Pall Mall, then?" inquired Mr. Franklin.

"Yes, sir."

"I am surprised. A whore may be found beat to death beside the
Fleet Ditch or in Cheapside—but what woman has been murdered in Westminster's finest precincts? Others have perished
likewise, you say?"

"One."

"And both their hearts cut out?" Mr. Franklin shook his head.
"Most strange."

We splashed left, past the Royal Opera House. Here rose the
grand facades of houses of the great and wealthy, and I peered at

them in the hissing night. Had the storm not prevented, we should have glimpsed the red brick of St. James's Palace, but we turned into St. James's Square, vast and deserted, swept by swaths of silver light from the sentinel lamps. Mr. Franklin had taught me much about the city in my two years with him, so I knew that St. James's had been laid out a century ago by the Earl of St. Albans, who had meant it to be the most fashionable address in town, and perhaps it was, for it lay very near the king. The rain briefly relented, and I gazed at the square's thirty or so fine houses. One especially caught my eye, at the northeast corner: number 18, its upper stories spilling light. Much wax was burnt there, and a great carouse went on, for we heard laughter as we passed, men's and women's: the privileged at play.

Exiting north, we plunged into darker ways. Piccadilly lay ahead, and Burlington House. Before we reached them, however, we swayed into a side street, so narrow and dog-legged that I rocked against my companions as our coach scraped its rain-wet walls. Then we slowed, and I made out what appeared to be a disused stableyard, close and gloomy. Our mare was pulled to a halt, and I found myself looking round a forlorn rectangle of broken cobble where an old waggon lay on its side as if it had been tipped by some violent hand, its wheel-spokes stark as bones.

Under a draggled thatch roof three or four men huddled in heavy coats, holding bull's-eye lanterns.

"So it is here," said Mr. Franklin.

" 'Tis," replied Billy Banting.

We got down. As if it bowed to the drama of death and the solemnity of the law, the rain abruptly ceased, though the indifferent eaves still splashed. I pulled my scarf tight round my throat. What a melancholy place! The air smelt of iron, offal, stone, and the brick walls were like the backs of giants turned on unspeakable sights. A narrow way exited the mews at the other end.

Feet scraping, we scuffed toward the men. A staring, hatless lad, his damp hair plastered to his head, stood nearby, the linkboy who had discovered the body, no doubt. He gaped in dumb fascination.

"Franklin," came a peremptory rumble, and a bulky form separated itself from the circle of men. The shine of Billy Banting's lantern showed it to be John Fielding, Chief Magistrate for Westminster.

Fleshy and huge, Fielding stamped toward us, snorting in his slow-breathing way. "Your boy is with you, eh?" Though he had been stone-blind since a misadventure at age seventeen had destroyed his sight, he knew more than a thousand London felons by their voices alone, so I was not surprised he surmised I was here. Wearing a black band across his eyes, he bent toward me as unerringly as a hawk. "Do you keep to the right side o' the law, boy?" came his hot breath. "Do you say your prayers?"

"Al-always, sir," said I.

He straightened. "Make sure you heed your master." A grumbling sigh. "Well, Ben, you are come. My man told you what we have found? Horrible! I cannot see, but it is dreadful. And it has happened before—madness! I must know what you make of it, for my men have eyes but not Ben Franklin's eyes."

"I shall do what I can."

A curt gesture. "To it, then."

The huge man led us to the group of men, whom Banting had joined. One, kneeling, rose at our approach, and they all stepped aside, fixing their lanterns upon the crime so we might take it in.

I must look.

I did.

A woman lay on her back upon a patch of bare, wet earth, just under an overhang of bedraggled thatch. She wore a simple dress, touseled, with two slim legs sticking out of its hem, two slim arms akimbo. Her face: it might once have been pretty, though its stiff waxen grimace—lips parted, forehead covered by tangled hair, eyes naught but empty hollows—made it ugly now. The sight wrenched my soul. What vile artist had drawn this ignominious scribble of horror?

Billy Banting had told true: a great gore-smeared cavity opened in the woman's bosom, and her heart was gone from her chest.

My legs near gave way, and I must have uttered a moan, for a hand gripped my arm, and I found Benjamin Franklin's brown eyes upon me.

"Nick?" said he.

9

I swallowed my gorge. "I . . . I will be all right, sir." I steadied myself with a bravery I did not feel. "Truly."

"You must step aside if you wish."

"No need." Bunching my fists, I found courage. I would not step aside. One of Mr. Franklin's principles was that I must know the bad as well as the good of life, and this terrible death was as bad as one might see. Yet as I looked more, I saw worse, for bits of flesh had been nibbled from the arms and legs; the rats had been here betimes.

This explained the black hollows of her eyes. Rats always ate the eyes first.

Mr. Franklin turned to John Fielding. "Dreadful, indeed. When was she discovered?"

"The linkboy—Skivvens is his name—informed the watch just after eight-thirty. A constable was called. He posted a guard and came straightway to Bow Street."

"This constable knew such a death had occurred before?"

"Did."

"Where was the first found?"

"In St. James's churchyard."

"Not far from here, then. How long ago?"

"Two weeks."

"Why, then, have I not heard or read of it?"

Fielding drew himself up. "We do not rush to the newspapers to report all we find, sir. We needed time to make inquiries."

"I see. And what did your inquiries reveal?"

"Nothing, damn it."

"So you do not know who she was?"

"No."

"What of this one?"

"Nor her, though it is early days. The murders seem by the same hand, so I may've been wrong not to tell London of the first. In any case we must prevent more of the same."

"I agree." Mr. Franklin gestured toward the staring linkboy. "How did he come to find her?"

"This is a disused way, but if you know it you may use it to get quickly to the clubs and gaming dens to the south. That is why the lad passed through tonight: He had lit a gent along Jermyn Street and was heading for Pall Mall. Going to piss against a wall, he fell over the body. Another boy might've run off, but Skivvins has scruples."

"Praise scruples. Yet others must use this way; she would have been found soon enough. That abandoned waggon—her murderer might very well have dragged her behind it, but he did not. Was the other body hid?"

"Canon Briggs came upon her before the blood had dried."

"The murderer does not mind 'em being discovered, then. Does he *want* 'em found? Was he disappointed not to see his first in the newspapers?" Mr. Franklin turned to me. "Nick, your pencil."

Having helped before, I knew what he wished; so taking out the small octavo volume I always carried in my coat, I drew a rough map of the stable square, locating the ways in and out, the waggon, the body. I added the pump, too, rusted iron; the half-dozen stark, empty horse stalls.

Mr. Franklin turned back to the dead woman. "And so . . ." By the pitiless glow of the lanterns he knelt and began to feel about the body. It had lain here long enough for its rigor to have passed, so he could move the limbs easily. He wore a quizzing glass on a cord round his neck. Most such glasses were fops' toys, but he had had his specially ground. With it he squinted at the bruising on the skin. He peered especially close at the shoulders, plucking some invisible thing from them. He looked at the gums and teeth, too. Last he investigated the hands, which were clenched like claws. I thought I caught a glint of metal in one, but if he found something there he chose not to reveal it. He knelt a moment more, very still, whilst eaves dripped mournfully and the voice of the watch wailed from a nearby street: "Twelve o'clock and all's well . . ." I flinched. A human soul lay in ruins; and cut up as she was, I could tell she had been young. Pretty too? Had she laughed? Taken pleasure in life?

All was not well.

Mr. Franklin stood with the aid of his bamboo stick.

"Some whore, done in by her gin-soaked pander, then?" muttered Fielding.

"Much denies it. Her dress is simple, but it is of fine Holland stuff, lace-trimmed. Her skin, too, has the fashionable pallor. Did you feel of her teeth?"

11

"No."

"They are beginning to rot; she would have worn ivory before she was thirty. She must be of the gentry, then, for only the rich can afford the sweets to ruin their teeth so young. And her shoulders—I found strands of hair upon 'em, not her own." Mr. Franklin held these up. "They show traces of powder. And they are not her color. They are of excellent quality: human, I believe. She wore a fine wig, which none of your fireships do."

Fielding spat. "The daughter of some gentleman, then. What trouble!"

"Or the wife. Or the sister."

"But why—?"

"She does not seem to've been robbed. The lace is not cut from her dress; no thief would let that go. Too, she has a gold ring upon her right hand; any receiver of goods would pay dearly for it. I have examined the finger. The ring fits snugly. There is no chafing, no bruising, no attempt whatsoever to pull it off."

"What, then—?"

"What, indeed? And we have not talked on the most notable feature: the hole in the poor woman's chest. No thief would bother to cut her so—unless he were a madman. Yet even in that there is something, for though the wound spilt a great deal of blood, it did not spill as much as it might have done."

"Meaning?" the justice prompted.

"Meaning that the carving was expert." I shuddered at the word, whilst Mr. Franklin turned his gaze into the night, as if the answer to this new and monstrous puzzle lurked like an incubus in its gloom. He bestirred himself. "Who examined the first victim?"

"Billy Banting."

"I should like to speak with him."

Fielding summoned the man. "Tell Mr. Franklin all we know about the other woman."

The lieutenant began to speak, but my attention was drawn elsewhere, for I glimpsed an unknown figure in the yard, a shadow half-hidden by the tipped waggon. I could not make out his face, and he stood preternaturally still. Did others note him? He had not been present when I sketched the area, so his presence now made me frown. Had he been in time to watch Mr. Franklin examine the body? To overhear his report?

Uneasily I turned back. The first victim had been young as well, Banting was saying, ". . . found by the vestry door. But she was no fine lady. Her clothes were common. She wore no fancy rings."

"Was she bruised, like this one?" Mr. Franklin asked.

"A bit. She'd been knocked about. Fought, p'rhaps. But now I think, there *was* something . . . a mark that was not a bruise. Under her hair, here, see?" Banting pointed by his left ear. "Mulberry colored. A birthmark, I b'lieve."

Mr. Franklin thumped his bamboo. "*Someone* knew the poor creature. Must have. And that person—or persons—may be able to tell us what led her to that dreadful pass. Nick?"

"Yes, sir."

"Mr. Banting, describe the birthmark to my boy, its shape and size. Nick shall draw it. Tell the victim's height. Her age, to your best guess. Her shape. The color of her hair. He will write that down as well."

"Do as the gentleman says," Fielding commanded, and Banting spoke near my ear whilst I drew.

"Was the first victim by any chance with child?" asked Mr. Franklin meanwhile.

Fielding scowled. "Not to our knowledge. What, you have found that this one was?"

"No."

"I understand. You seek motive, reason. But you know what was done to these women! Is that reasonable? Why, the murderer is a monster! There can be no reason in him."

"The serpent reasoned exceedingly well with Eve. Nay, sir, the most dangerous villains are the cleverest, and this one may be clever. Done, Nick? Your lantern, then, if you please, Mr. Banting."

Banting handed it to him.

He swung it upon the stranger by the waggon. "Good even, sir."

The man caught in its beam was thin and ferretlike. He blinked but made no attempt to flee, drawing himself up as if he were pleased to be discovered. A low hat covered his brow, but as he glided toward us in a long snuff-brown coat, he pushed it back to reveal eyes that burned cynically beneath deep bony ridges.

His head reminded me of a skull.

"Good even to you, Benjamin Franklin," came his insinuating voice.

"Pah, Scratch," John Fielding muttered.

"I have not had the pleasure," Mr. Franklin said.

The stranger growled. "Take that light out of my eyes and I will give it you!"

Mr. Franklin lowered the beam, though not so far that we could not still see the taut, lean face. It made a smirking mouth, as if the man had won something of us.

He carried in one hand a small octavo book very like mine. The tip end of a bitten pencil peeked from his scruffy wig.

"*I* have had the pleasure, if it can be called that," muttered Fielding. "The man is only a scribbler, a Grub Street dog."

The stranger made a mock-elegant bow. "Christened Pyecroft, but you may call me Jack Scratch."

Mr. Franklin bobbed his head. "I *do* know you, then, after a fashion, for I have seen 'Jack Scratch' appended to many a tale of scandal."

"In the worst newspapers," puffed Fielding.

Scratch sneered. "Scandal is news, and the city is news-mad. Thus I sniff its air, and thus I know Benjamin Franklin. O, you are not news yet—who cares that you have come to raddle the Pennsylvania proprietors?—but I tuck you in a corner of my brain nonetheless, for perhaps you will shoot one of 'em one day, and then I shall have a tale to tell."

Mr. Franklin smiled. "Thomas and Richard Penn shall be made to do as they ought without shooting."

"What *you* think they ought."

"What is right, then, if you please."

"O, right!" Scratch made a face. "As to that"—he flung an arm toward the pitiful body—"is *that* right?"

We looked at the torn, pale flesh. "It is terribly wrong," replied Mr. Franklin.

"But what do *you* in the matter? Why does the Blind Beak call

14

upon Benjamin Franklin?—that is what I ask. There is something here, I know that there is, and I shall nose it out, for a scribbler must fill his belly."

"I have been a scribbler, too. I have labored 'til my back ached to pull the press."

"We are brothers, then? Ha! But you have risen above Jack Scratch's station." His features contorted in fury. "O, I should have had more than this! I am an Oxford man. I set my sights upon the law. I had hopes to pass the bar, all blasted, and he who spoilt 'em—!" He dragged a hand across his mouth, as if he had said too much, and a sneaking light lit his eyes. "There may be more of interest in this than you know, Benjamin Franklin."

"Tell it, then."

"Not yet, sir, not yet. But a question for a question." Scratch leant near. "How do you know there were but two with their hearts cut out? Why not"—he tilted his head—"three?"

"What do you mean?"

Scratch retreated. "Nay, sir, read the *London Courant*. Read Jack Scratch. Good eve." A quicksilver doff of his hat, one last wry twist of lips, and the mocking man was gone.

"Pay him no heed," grumbled Fielding when Scratch had vanished into the night. "He is one of those devils who turn bad into worse."

"Yet he was very particular. 'Three'—do you know aught of three?"

"No."

"And how did he come to be here?" Mr. Franklin pondered. "How bitter the fellow was." Sighing, he turned to the body. "A pity we have no clue to this woman's name either. And yet—Nick?"

"Sir?"

"I should like you to draw the dead woman's face—but to draw it as it might have been in life. Do you think that you can?"

I gazed at her remains. The features were frozen, the eyes gone—and yet I had limned many a London countenance. Might I reconstruct this one?

"I shall try, sir."

"Brave lad. Meanwhile . . ." He took from his coat a small tin box, specially made. In it lay a pad of printer's ink with which he had brought more than one miscreant to justice.

Whilst I struggled with my drawing, he knelt and began to press each of the woman's fingertips onto the inked pad, then onto small sheets of foolscap. He marked each carefully—"right forefinger," etc.—before he blotted it and tucked it away. Fielding's men frowned at the unorthodoxy, but Mr. Franklin knew what he did. "New methods have hard births," he often said. As a boy in his brother's Boston printing shop, he had observed how the patterns of lines left by the inky fingers all about him were never alike. From this he had devised what he called finger-printing. The Blind Beak could not see what Mr. Franklin did, but the wrinkle of his nostrils said he smelt the ink, and he waited patiently; he knew Benjamin Franklin was no fool.

Meanwhile I did my best to draw the woman, guessing how her smile had looked, putting light back into her destroyed eyes. The face that emerged was delicate and faintly smiling. Was it somewhat hardened, too? Did I resurrect her well?

Finished with finger-printing, Mr. Franklin stood and examined my work. "Good, Nick." He pointed to one of the buttons on the dress. "Draw this, too." I did. Titled folk sometimes had their buttons stamped with particular designs: heraldry, a coronet, a family crest. This, which seemed to show a ship's sails, might lead to useful knowledge.

Done, I stood amidst the creak of night, the scuttle of vermin. Fielding's men still huddled nearby with their bull's-eye lanterns, but the linkboy had slipped off. A cry of laughter started up from some unseen alehouse, and thunder rattled faintly, far away. The great city hovered, bent, listened. "Done all?" Fielding inquired.

"For the present," replied Benjamin Franklin.

"Home, then. You have earned your sleep. Shall we confer in Bow Street tomorrow?"

"As you please."

Billy Banting stepped to the coach. He held its door, but Mr. Franklin shook his head. "Nay, it is not far. The rain has stopped, and I wish to reflect. Your cold night air is an excellent stimulant to thought."

"I prefer a warm fire and port." The Blind Beak turned his back. "Good night."

His men closed once more about the body, to carry it away. It was but a thing now and must be buried soon. Worms did not wait upon the law.

❧ 3 ❧

IN WHICH Rakehells Prance and a Dead Woman Reveals a Secret . . .

Rain never stifled the city's stench for long, so the dog-legged alley by which we returned to St. James's Square reeked of decay. Rats scurried—I heard their squeaks—and I was glad when a three-quarter moon slid from fretful clouds to light our way.

Mr. Franklin walked wordlessly amidst the drip of the storm's aftermath. What did he make of what we had seen? I was untroubled by his silence, for we were often companions in private thought, and I had my own turmoil to sort through: horror, bewilderment, dismay. Poor woman! I had led a hard life as a printer's boy-of-work 'til Mr. Franklin found me. I had been ill-used and often beaten, and I had seen my share of the life of the streets, where gin and poverty bred death as easily as dung breeds flies. But I was not inured to mayhem. It was always a blow, as if the victim, however remote, were somehow dear.

Ah, London, what has washed up on your black shores now?

In York Street lamps flickered like cats' eyes. Inky puddles gleamed. A watch-box stood on a corner, and I thought we should walk past, but Mr. Franklin drew me to it.

A grizzled old Charlie huddled within. "Dear God!" cried he, flinching, when Mr. Franklin roused him. His rheumy eyes bulged. "Do you mean harm?"

"None, sir, I assure you."

The fellow sighed in relief. "Blest be to God, I thought you was the bloods, acreepin' up again." The bloods were much talked on lately, young rakehells who amused themselves by pushing over watch-boxes and cutting up unwary travelers.

"They plague you, do they?" inquired Mr. Franklin.

"They tip me over, sir. Sometimes kick me, too. Twice in the fortnight." The man rubbed a leg in rueful remembrance. "Wot may I do for ye?"

"Were you on the watch last night?"

"O, aye, sir. Eyes peeled ev'ry moment."

"Did you see anything, then? A man and a young woman, perhaps? Going into that alley? Show your drawing, Nick."

I opened my book, but the light was dim and the old fellow's sight plainly none too good: "I do not reckernize the face," said he.

With thanks, we walked on.

Mr. Franklin shook his head. " 'Eyes peeled ev'ry moment'? Peeled on dreams, most likely. Yet the fellow is old; he deserves his rest. What folly that the watch are not vigorous young men!"

This took us into St. James's Square. It lay deserted, no light in any window now. The cobbles gleamed like a convocation of tiny tombstones. A cat darted like a streak of oil into a drain. Overhead the clouds shifted and parted like tremulous hands, and I felt a pang of ill-ease. Glancing at the corner house, number 18, which had rocked with carouse, I saw that it lay dark and silent, though I thought I heard laughter somewhere, a muffled snigger, and I glanced at Mr. Franklin.

I could not make out his eyes under his round beaver hat, but he must have caught my look, for his pointed lips pursed. "Remember Buck Duffin, Nick?" murmured he.

Buck Duffin, the bullying apprentice at Inch, Printer, from which Mr. Franklin had rescued me. Buck had been taller and stronger than I, cruel and sneaking—but Mr. Franklin had taught me just where to strike him to lay him low. He had taught me other tricks of fighting since.

Did he suggest I might have to use them now?

I stayed close by his side as we entered Charles Street, narrow and ill-lit. I jumped as a hand pawed my arm, but it was only a beggar, reeking of beer. Mr. Franklin slowed. His small round lenses caught the moonlight, head cocked to listen, and I, too, heard the scrape of a boot, a muffled *hst*.

19

"Quickly, Nick." The gentleman pulled me round a corner, in the direction of Pall Mall. We began to run—but too late.

They set upon us in St. James's Market.

They came out of the dark—stumbled, rather, from behind a shuttered stall. There were no streetlamps here, but the moon was bright enough to disclose their looming shapes. There were five of them—no, six, for one swaggered behind the others. All wore half-masks over their eyes, and like the beggar they reeked of drink, though unlike him they sported fine clothes: ribbons and silk, the latest in foppish fashion.

Bloods.

I had no doubt. They had drunk their fill, and now they looked for mischief. They had no grudge against Benjamin Franklin or Nick Handy—they did not even know our names—but inflicting pain was their pleasure, and pleasure they would have.

They closed in a circle round us. One pulled out his sword—the sound went up my spine—and the others followed suit; sharp steel glinted. They wore haphazard grins, and they made little *Ohos!* and *Ahas!* One had lost his hat but seemed not to know it. Another wore his wig awry. They would have been comical were it not for all I had heard of their antics, for they would cut men's hamstrings for fun, they would stab 'til blood came, and if you did not submit, one of their favorite tricks was "tipping the lion," in which they crushed your nose against your face whilst they gouged out your eyes.

These were the pastimes of the spoilt rich.

Mr. Franklin wrapped an arm about me. "Steady, lad." He stood watchfully as the cavorting circle tightened about us. "Well met, gentlemen. What may we do for you?"

"Dance!" cried one.

"Aye, a jig!" slurred another.

There was a chorus of *Yea*s—from all but one. "Nay, a sweat," said he, and his voice was frigid as ice. It belonged to the last to emerge, and it was not drunken but rather commanding, as if he were the captain of a regiment. I quavered, for I had heard of the "sweat," in which one of the brigands stuck your backside, and when you spun round to flee, another stuck you, then another and another, 'til you sweated indeed.

The others took up the cry. "A sweat, a sweat!" Nearer now,

they formed a six-sided figure with their swords, a prison of steel.

I huddled against Mr. Franklin.

"Come, sirs," he demanded, "Englishmen must have the freedom of the streets. Desist, or we shall be forced to scour you."

They guffawed. What delicious bravado! What sport it would be to prick this braggart's rump! They rounded closer, nickering, and at last one of the band made his essay. He lunged—but he did not wait 'til Mr. Franklin's back was turned.

Almost faster than I could see, the gentleman's bamboo danced up, striking his assailant's weapon so hard the steel flew out of his hand.

"What!" cried the blood as his sword crashed in the dark. Then the bamboo drove into his gut, and with a great deflated *Oof!* he clutched his belly and sat ignominiously upon the ground, where he proceeded to spew his supper in wretched moans.

There was a faltering. A bewildered buzz. The captain's mouth, strangely red, twisted in fury: "On, cowards! They must not get away!" At his words two of the besotted bravehearts took their chance, making to run Mr. Franklin through. But again his bamboo did its deed, deftly smacking their swords, sending them ringingly awry, before he set amongst their heads—*swack, swack!*—so that in less than a moment three sat in surprise and pain upon the ground.

Three remained. Again there was pause. The captain stood apart, hands on hips, silent, watchful. The other two, however, seemed sure they took the measure of their mark. Placing themselves on opposite sides of him, they began to bait him with their points.

"Coo, coo," taunted one.

"O, you will be a stuck pig!" his fellow drunkenly agreed.

I was only a boy, and in the melee I had fallen to one side, apart from Mr. Franklin.

"Nick, do you care to take a hand?" called he.

"Gladly." Stepping beside one of the swordsmen, I inquired, "Sir?" He turned, stinking of port and brandy. He was near insensible, I guessed, but he threatened my master with a sword, so with only the smallest of regrets I struck his throat with the side of my hand, just under the left ear, as Mr. Franklin had taught me.

With a strangled grunt he dropped upon the ground.

By then I began to think there should have been eight or ten to match us, and what befell next near made me laugh. The fifth fellow stared, blinked, dropped his sword, and without bidding plumped down in a filthy puddle beside his companions, where he began to whimper amongst some discarded vegetable ends.

St. Martin's rang the quarter hour. The wheels of a nightsoil cart creaked, whilst a gust of wind tugged scraps by our feet. Mr. Franklin and I turned to the remaining blood. He was tall and lean, and his stance and the slow smile beneath his mask said he knew how to use his sword. All my confidence leaked away as he drew near. *Which shall I run through first?* his sneer coolly asked. Why was his face so strange? A moonbeam hit it, and I saw with a chill that the skin was painted white. The lips had appeared red because they too were painted, red as blood. He looked some ghastly phantom.

Abruptly he straightened, sheathed his steel, vanished. The shadows swallowed him like a mouth. I heard no retreating footfalls.

Mr. Franklin lowered his bamboo. He met my confounded stare. "I do not think he departed because he was afraid." Together we surveyed the litter of bodies. "Trouble springs from idleness," murmured the gentleman as he clapped my shoulder. "What would have befallen a poor, lone wayfarer without such an excellent boy to help him? Let us home."

In ten minutes we were in Craven Street, the Thames sliding sluggishly by at the bottom of the way. The sleepy Nanny unbarred, and we crept upstairs with a candle. The house lay quiet; peace reigned, thank heaven. Reaching the upper landing I made to go into my little chamber opposite Mr. Franklin's, but he beckoned and I followed into his room.

He lit a lamp. "Well, Nick?"

"It was a terrible death, sir."

"We have seen many terrible deaths."

Silently I thought on Ebenezer Inch, scalped; Roddy Fairbrass, poisoned; Abel Drumm, crushed between the gears of one of the great winches at Drury Lane. There had been others. Was death everyone's companion in the great, cruel city?

Mr. Franklin held out a hand. "I should like to see your drawing."

Silently I relinquished it, and he traced the features with one of his blunt, practical fingers. "I see you have given her a troubled air. Hum, alive only a day ago." He shook his head in the stillness. "Is not death a mystery? And her murder—'tis most strange, perhaps the strangest I have seen." He shut the book. "Why was her heart cut out? And the other's?" With a vexed look he sank into his chair. "Yet there is more mystery." From a pocket he drew forth a small metal disk. "This was clutched in the dead woman's hand." I had been right, then, in surmising he had found something— though I was not surprised he had not revealed it, for he often kept things to himself till he could make sense of them.

Stepping near, I examined it with him as he turned it to and fro.

It shone dully. Pewter? It was perhaps an inch and a half in diameter, about the size of a crown piece but with six evenly milled edges. One side was blank, but the other had a raised rim, inside which appeared four words in a bold script: *Fay ce que voudras.*

"French, sir?" asked I.

"French."

"What does it mean?"

" 'Do what you will.' " He rubbed his jaw at the words. "A motto? Who had it minted? And why did the victim clutch it in her hand? The words may also mean 'Anything is permitted.' Is murdering an innocent woman permitted? Carving a poor, helpless creature's heart from her body?" Rising, he placed the medallion upon his desk. "I do not like it, Nick." Beyond his bow window London sighed as if it dreamed bad dreams. "Tomorrow we must put our heads together with John Fielding."

❧ 4 ❧

IN WHICH I Draw London and Spy a Scribbling Man . . .

Tuesday dawned cold but clear: no rain. Outside the window of my little room November etched the sky; London was limned in grainy gray as a wan sun roused her. Though we had been out late, I rose betimes. The belowstairs stir of Mrs. Stevenson waked me, but I would have climbed from bed at cock's crow nonetheless.

"Early to rise," Mr. Franklin had often adjured, and I strove to obey.

Slipping into shirt and breeches, I crossed to his chamber door. "Come," sounded the gentleman's voice when I rapped.

I found him in his calico bedgown and flannel sleeping-trousers by his bow window, the casement open. Beyond it the Thames unrolled vast and gray. I loved Mr. Franklin's room; it had become my home, so I looked with affection upon the horsehair chair, the side table holding yesterday's *London Chronicle,* the broad desk littered with inkhorn and pens for writing correspondence to men who might help in Pennsylvania's cause, the bookcase spilling with works from Locke's to Mr. Franklin's own philosophical essays, the dresser with the painting of his daughter, Sally, and his little son Francis, tragically dead of the smallpox before he was five; the featherbed, the old oak wardrobe.

I shut the door. At fifty-three, Mr. Franklin was watchful of his well-being. Thus he held heavy iron weights, his "dumb-bells," which he swung in great arcs as he greeted me. "Morning, Nick *(puff)*. By use of these *(puff)* I have in forty swings *(puff)* quickened my pulse from sixty to one hundred beats a minute. Ah!" Setting down the weights, he held out his arm. "Take up my watch—it is upon the night table. Feel of my wrist."

I did so (I had done it before), counting by the second hand of the instrument. "One hundred six beats, sir."

"Better than I believed!" He waggled a finger. "The disused pot rusts, Nick. The untilled field runs to weed." At a rapping he called, "Enter!" and Nanny scurried in, her little cap askew. She hugged a basin of steaming water, but at sight of the man in his bedclothes she clattered her burden on his washstand and fled.

Mr. Franklin made a face. "Am I such a monstrous sight, Nick? Surely there are more villainous apparitions." Pulling off his nightshirt, he proceeded to shave, which he nearly always did himself (he did not care for barbers). Meanwhile, shutting the casement, I went about my tasks: laying the fire, setting odds and ends in order. I envied the clean stroke of the blade through Mr. Franklin's soapy lather; and catching my gaze, he paused and began to study me. "You were twelve when I found you, but you are decidedly taller, with a manly look about your chin. Fourteen, eh? You must soon learn to shave. Should you like a razor of your own?"

"Why . . . very much, sir."

"Then you must have one." A pang suffused his gaze. I seemed to read his mind, and without thinking I felt for the locket on its cord beneath my shirt. Inside was a silhouette of my mother, all I had of her save fitful memories. He nodded, and a mixture of sadness and pride overwhelmed me.

Rose Handy formed a bond betwixt the gentleman and me, for I was his natural son, whom he had discovered shortly after coming to London.

He too grew grave at the memory, his look softening, and I felt all over again how grateful I was that he had found me. I never minded that the truth of my parentage must remain secret—neither of us wished to distress his good wife, Deborah, nor his daughter, Sally, nor his twenty-nine-year-old son William, who had come with him to London to read law. It was enough that he had loved the young woman with whom he had talked of books in Philadelphia and who had taught me to read before poison snuffed her life.

Was that why Benjamin Franklin helped souls in distress? Did bringing criminals to justice in some measure recompense him for his love, whom the great and terrible city had ground to ruin?

Seven o'clock bells rang out. Turning to his glass, the gentleman finished shaving with a few quick strokes, dried his face, slipped into shirt, breeches, and morning coat; he went promptly to his desk. Since Wolfe's victory—and tragic death—on the Plains of Abraham in September, everyone debated whether England should restore Canada to defeated France. Mr. Franklin opposed the idea—"Madness!"—but his way of speaking out was often humorous, so he writ arguing that England should annex minuscule Guadalupe instead. He smiled as his pen scratched, his legs curling about his chair like a schoolboy's, whilst I studied my Latin by the fire.

How happy I was in company with my father, hearing Mrs. Stevenson stir reassuringly below.

Yet we had witnessed a terrible crime last night, and I could not get its memory out of my mind. Nor could Benjamin Franklin, it seemed, for after half an hour his pen stopped. I glanced up. The light seeping through the window made his balding brow gleam, and I saw he held the medallion he had discovered last night. "*Fay ce que voudras*," muttered he. "Whatever you wish, eh?" He made a fist. "Nay, not what you wish—reason, law, humanity must guide us!" His chair creaked as he turned. "I have much to do—the hearings of the Board of Trade are near to ending this wretched business of the Penns—but John Fielding waits. I will call on him this afternoon. Shall you come with me, Nick?"

"Yes, sir."

"We must do something about these murders."

Breakfast was served belowstairs in the snug little room off the kitchen looking out upon Mrs. Stevenson's back garden; already the earth had been turned for winter vegetables. We were four this midmorning: Mr. Franklin, I, William, and our landlady, who cus-

26

tomarily joined us whilst her maid served. Mr. Franklin preferred simple fare: bread soaked in buttermilk, a bowl of gruel, but William had conceived more splendid tastes since he came to London (eligible and presentable, he began to be invited to Northumberland House, home of the Tory Percys, which did not entirely please his father), so Mrs. Stevenson had warmed a veal pie. There was marchpane, too, to pleasure me, and small beer.

Mrs. Stevenson chattered happily about her twenty-year-old daughter Mary, whom we affectionately called Polly. In the spring Polly had gone to live with a rich maiden aunt, Mrs. Tickell, at Wanstead in Essex, but she would return this day for a fortnight's visit.

"I shall be delighted to see her," Mr. Franklin replied to our landlady's effusions, for she was a bright, lively girl who understood electrical matters well. "What a loss to the world that intelligent women are restrained by custom. Why, your Polly would make as fine a philosopher as any man!"

Frowning, Mrs. Stevenson tapped her bellwether mole. "Can a philosopher capture a husband, sir?"

"Tut." Mr. Franklin was too wise to pursue this; he had other matters in mind. "I regret that our talk was disrupted last night. Shall you have a lightning rod, ma'am?"

Mrs. Stevenson drew in her chin. "The storm has passed."

"A storm always passes; another always takes its place. Come, lightning is a dangerous thing. 'Tis said that in Bucks County a flash came so near a lad as to melt the pewter buttons off his breeches."

" 'Tis well nothing else thereabouts was made of pewter," William put in, and we laughed, though Nanny blushed as red as a rowanberry.

We finished eating with no resolution, although I saw that Mr. Franklin was determined to make his landlady's house safe. As I got up, my eyes fell on the framed drawing of a hand on one wall. I had sketched it in the murdered painter James Cavitty's house, and it gave me pause, for it reminded me I had been in grave danger there.

Let not this business of the destroyed women lead to such a pass, thought I.

27

Mr. Franklin and William went up, I following. Plainly they thought I stayed behind—I often did, to help Mrs. Stevenson—for as I reached the top of the first stairs I found them in the entryway, heads together, murmuring. They did not note me, and their peculiar air made me stop, though not with any intent to spy—I simply preferred to be elsewhere. How secretive they acted, but I could tell some dispute was in progress. William appeared chagrined, his father angry.

Suddenly William glimpsed me. He could smile gaily, and he loved the life of the town, but a spiteful scowl twisted his features now. Truth to tell, he had never cared for me. Why did his father keep "a poor street boy"? I had heard him ask. Mr. Franklin's customary reply was that William needed time to study law—"Nick gives you that"—but this no longer applied, for William had been called to the bar a year ago. Still, I had become a fixture in the household, so for the most part he ignored me.

He could not ignore me now, and with an angry start he placed a finger to his lips as warning.

Mr. Franklin turned. "Why, Nick, we did not hear you upon the stair."

"I . . . I just came up."

The case clock clucked its tongue at this. Mr. Franklin returned his eyes to William. "We must talk on the matter later, for I have promised to call upon Straney." Straney was William Strahan, Mr. Franklin's old friend, publisher of the *London Chronicle*.

"But, father—"

"Later, I say! The thing is not of my making."

I started at this flinty reply, whilst William glowered at me as if I had caused it. His fingers fidgeted, but clenching his jaw he bowed his handsome head. "Very well." He thundered up the stairs.

Mr. Franklin and I followed. We were in time to see William push past a tall blackamoor as he slammed into his room. This man was Peter, Mr. Franklin's servant, just come down from his attic chamber. His dusky eyes seemed to register little, though I knew they missed nothing, for he had often helped Mr. Franklin in his investigations.

The gentleman gave Peter instructions, and only when his man was gone did he turn to me. "Pay no heed to what passed between William and me, Nick." He drew a hand across his brow. "Curse it that a man must be a father 'til he dies! I must go out until three. Then we shall call upon Justice Fielding."

The knowledge that I should have several hours to myself filled me with joy, so I was happy to forget the exchange between father and son, happy to forget the murdered women, too, for I could now go about, explore, observe, write and draw in my book. I could set some types, as well, and earn some money, for I had contracted with the printer Jacob Tisdale.

There was Birdy Prinsop, too.

Duty first. One of my tasks was to keep Mr. Franklin's papers in order, so I remained after his coach bore him off, arranging his latest correspondence. He liked to have copies of the letters he writ, so I copied one to his wife, Deborah, and one to William Pitt, the latest of many he had penned in an attempt to lay Pennsylvania's case before the minister. I was pleased to earn my keep this way, but I had begun to wonder what would become of me. Where would my life go? Mr. Franklin might have sent me to grammar school—William had attended one in Philadelphia— but he preferred to keep me with him: "You will learn better by my side. Besides, I despise the rule of the birchen rod." I could not complain; I was taught well. But what then? I had talent in drawing—or I was told that I had (William Hogarth himself had once said I could sketch a line)—and Mr. Franklin had trained me after Addison's model, so I could write decently, too. But I could not become an artist if I were not apprenticed to one; and as for becoming a writer, most (like Jack Scratch) led a catchpenny life, measuring ink against food.

My greatest worry was this: when Mr. Franklin returned to America, as he must, what would become of Nick Handy?

Yet London! The city awaited, and all my doubts flew to heaven as I tucked my book and pencil in my pocket at eleven and set out. Fourteen years old—near fifteen—a bold, adventuring lad! Eagerly I turned east at the top of Craven Street. Behind me rose the equestrian statue of Charles I, ahead unreeled the city's great ribbon of commerce: the Strand. Mud clogged it, but an undeterred throng pushed, bustled, milled under countless hanging signs.

I joined them. Carriages and coaches, hackneys, drays, great groaning waggons clattered over the cobbles, whilst chairs bumped and swayed amongst the din of a thousand tongues. Fishmongers cried their wares: "New mack'rel, six a shilling, alive-O!" The tambourine of a mountebank rattled in my ear, and a scramble of dirty-faced boys danced a jig by Somerset House, thrusting out grubby paws for coin. Alert for cutpurses I stopped to draw them, then pushed on. I gazed in shop windows. Bred in poverty, I never ceased to be amazed at the goods such windows displayed: clocks, swords, engravings, fans, candles, India silk. There were viands as well: pies and sweets, oysters, geese, joints of beef hanging in raw, red rows.

Men hung too. Near Covent Garden dangled a poor stinking knave chained to a gibbet. He had been executed at Tyburn but (according to custom) had been brought to rot where his crime was done. I held my nose as I crept by.

And then I was past Lincoln's Inn and Temple Bar; I stood in Fleet Street, in the great and ancient City.

I glanced back. Four heads adorned the pikes atop Temple Bar, shriveled, blackened purses that had had their coin shook out. A bird sat on one, pecking at sightless eyes. A street vendor offered a spyglass—"On'y a penny to see"—but I waved him off, though a chill November mood moved me to me draw the heads under the unforgiving sky. Who had they been? Traitors, for only perpetators of crimes against the Crown were piked so high.

Death again. You could not escape it in London's ways.

Fleet Street was where books and newspapers were printed, so I passed many printing shops. Near Butcher's Row I came to Mr. Tisdale's. He had kept a modest establishment in Craven Street— it was where Mr. Franklin and I first came to know him—but a year and a half ago he had set up in partnership with Mr. Worsley. Newspapers were a great thing now—you could not go into a coffeehouse without finding four or six (a gentleman *must* have his newspaper)—so you might make a good living by catching the public fancy, and Jacob Tisdale had removed to a larger shop, where he was now master of three presses and a dozen ink-stained minions. The *London Post* had grown to over two thousand numbers twice a week, at twopence ha'penny each.

Mr. Tisdale himself greeted me when I walked in. He was lean and sandy in an ink-smeared apron, with shrewd, gimlet eyes. "You are here. Good. There are types to be set. Here are the words." He handed me a sheet of foolscap. "Take no more than an hour, hear?"

"Yes, sir." I never minded his blunt manner. He turned heel, and I went to the composing bench—but I took a moment, to smell, to hear, to see. The odor of ink, the creak of the presses, the sheets drying upon the lines, the apprentices and boys-of-work washing types, pulling the screw, cleaning friskets—how it pleased me! I had had little consolation at Inch, Printer, but its master had taught me to love his craft; thus I had learnt to set types near as fast as Mr. Franklin. A year ago he had bade me show off my skills to Mr. Tisdale. The printer wished to apprentice me at once, but Mr. Franklin had said nay, he would not give up his boy, yet as a compromise I was allowed to do piecework on those busy days before the *London Post* went to press. It earned me money, which I was free to spend as I liked.

This brought to mind a pair of milk-white breasts. My heart thudded, and sweat burst out on my palms, but I forced the thought aside.

Later, Nick. You must work now.

I took up the composing stick, my eyes darting from the words I must set to the little squares of type in their box. Then I began to arrange the letters, the little wooden shims. It took a moment to find the rhythm, but soon I went without thinking. Pluck the proper letter, place it; pluck, place. Mr. Tisdale had other men to set types, but they did the advertisements that made up three-quarters of the newspaper; the rest was left for me: odds and ends of gossip that was meant to be wit. Believing I could write as well, I had thought of proposing doing so to Mr. Tisdale. Had not Benjamin Franklin, as Silence Dogood, writ for his brother's Boston newspaper when he was little older than I?

I was just securing the rows of types in their form when Mr. Tisdale returned. He ran his eyes over my work, reading backward as printers must. "No *errata*. I should still like to 'prentice you, Nick, but if your gentleman will not allow it—" Regret briefly stiffened his features. "Here is your hire, then." He counted a shilling six-pence into my palm. "Return o' Friday, if you wish more."

"Thank you, sir." I walked out.

One o'clock bells were ringing upon Fleet Street. I gazed east, at the dome of St. Paul's. How grand! I liked to wander in the shadow of the great church, to draw the denizens of Paternoster Row, but I would have to pass the crime-infested alleys of Fleet Ditch to do so, and I did not mind forgoing that. Too, I must meet Mr. Franklin.

And she who owned those milk-white breasts.

I had just turned back toward Westminster, when who should I spy but Jack Scratch. Ducking my head, I watched the ferretlike man. He clutched his little book, his pencil stuck in his scruffy wig. He looked even sourer by daylight, eaten by bitterness, so I was glad his cynical eyes passed over me as he darted into the offices of the *London Courant* like a spider into its hole. I walked on.

Yet my mood was changed, for Scratch brought back all our mystery—the woman murdered in the drab, dripping stables, the other as well—and a moment of dread shook me.

Three. Why had Scratch proposed three women? Who was the third, and where was her body?

I did not think on this long. Desire overcame me. Would Birdy Prinsop be at her lookout by the Shakespeare Tavern?

All afire, I set out to see.

❧ 5 ❧

IN WHICH I Make Love to a Woman and Test My
Knowledge of Men . . .

I walked quickly and in ten minutes, crossing by Southhampton Street, found myself in Covent Garden. What a hubbub! One of the great open spaces of London, Covent Garden was a far cry from the elegance of St. James's Square, for by day it was a bustling market: rows of stalls where you could buy everything from marrows to cockles, thronged by a milling crowd and a hundred voices crying their wares. At one end rose the dignified facade of Inigo Jones's church; at the other, Covent Garden Theater. In between taverns abounded. Coffeehouses, too—Tom King's, Davies's, The Bedford. Under the piazza ladies of pleasure beckoned to willing gents.

The Shakespeare Tavern was on the north side. Jostling past a juggler and a drove of geese, I came under its famous sign, a full-length painting of the bard in a carved and gilded frame, but I hardly noted it for the urgency that moved me. Pushing beyond the square, I made my way to Cork Alley, a quiet lane leading to Longacre. Shadows filled its narrow stretch. A pig rooted amongst scattered leavings. Was Birdy Prinsop here? My breath came quick. Yes, there, beside a flight of narrow stairs.

I hurried to her.

"Birdy," said I hoarsely.

She wore a dress of yellow linen cut low to show her charms. She turned her face up to me. She was pretty in the way a thousand girls were pretty, yet her hair was the color of summer straw and she had a way of swaying her body that twisted the knife of desire in me. She offered a sidelong smile, her voice reedy. "I have not seen you in a week, Nicolas. Do you not like me?"

"I like you very much, Birdy."

"But not so well as other girls?"

"I like you best of all."

"So there *are* other girls?"

"Nay, do not torment me!"

A tiny laugh. "How funny you are, Nicolas. I do not wish to torment anyone." She peered about in her sly, provoking way. "Shall we go up?"

O, yes, let us go up.

With no more ado we mounted the stairs.

I had found Birdy three months ago—or she had found me, in midsummer, in the early days of Mr. Franklin's long journey to Scotland. William had gone with his father; they had stopped by their ancestral home, at Ecton, and in Edinburgh Mr. Franklin had received an honorary degree from St. Andrews. Left behind at loose ends, I had tramped each day to Covent Garden to draw its sights. Where else was there so colorful a scene? It had been a thick, airless forenoon, a mazy heat gripping the city, and standing by a flower stall, I had felt half dazed as I sketched a flock of fishwives carrying baskets of pike and eel upon their heads. A voice had curled into my thoughts: "How well you draw, young sir."

I had turned, and there stood the girl whose name was Birdy Prinsop.

She seemed little older than I, and at first I took her for some merchant's daughter—though not for long, for no respectable daughter would speak to a boy in the street. She praised my work—and me: "What a handsome boy!" allowing a tip of pink tongue to protrude from her teeth. (How practiced she was!) Should I like to draw her?

Yes.

She had a little room nearby. "I shall show you the way."

I had followed her into Cork Alley and up these same stairs we mounted now. At the top had opened a narrow corridor with many doors. Pushing one, she had led me into a tiny chamber containing no more than a bed and a washstand. "T'will do," said she with another sly look. "Artists like to draw a girl with her clothes off, eh? Oh, I have served artists in my day. Shall I take off my clothes, Nicolas? I do not mind."

I watched her disrobe. She was not the first girl I had seen so, for I had lain with the maid in James Cavitty's house. But that had been more than a year ago, a moment stolen in the dusk, whilst this was bold, the light from the window revealing every freckle on Birdy Prinsop's nose, a mole upon her right shoulder, the scar of a burn upon one childlike hand. She slipped out of her shoes, undid bodice and blouse, stepped from her dress; it was done in a moment whilst I watched breathless. And then she stood before me as God had made her, slender and pale, save for cotton stockings smudged by the dirt of the town. Her breasts were rose-tipped globes, her waist a tender tuck. How old was she? Sixteen? She watched me. "Shall I take off my stockings, too? You would be surprised how many gentlemen prefer a girl in her stockings." Climbing upon the bed, she held out her arms. "Nay, it is not drawing that you desire. Come to me, and I shall give you what you wish."

Birdy Prinsop smelt of sour milk. She tasted of salt, and I lost myself in her.

Since then I had met her in this same place a dozen times. She was not always waiting, and then I was angry and vowed that I would not come again. But I never kept my vow, for when I found her we always mounted the stair. We did so again this day, to the same tiny chamber. She offered her breasts to my hand. She felt of me. "What a fine tool you have, Nicolas! How it stands! Armor?"

I nodded; I did not wish to be clapped.

She slipped the sheath of sheepgut upon me, tied its ribbons, and we sank upon the bed.

Afterward I paid her two shillings. The first time had cost but one, but her price had risen, so that she took most of what I earned from Mr. Tisdale. The coin was well spent, but as I made my way back along the Strand I wondered: did Mr. Franklin guess how I used my hire?

He did not ask; he himself had been a lusty lad.

As for Birdy, did she despise what she must do? I wondered, as a chandler's boy bumped by with his barrow of tallow, and I kicked a pebble. She spoke like a lady. What had happened to turn her to the street? And who was her bawd, for someone must keep her? How long would her prettiness last? And when her looks were gone, would she become just another hardened jade who sold herself against the wall of a stinking stew for a dram of gin?

London was a buy-and-sell city, I told myself; Birdy Prinsop merely sold whilst Nick Handy bought, but this thought did not console me.

An unpleasant incident followed: two haughty rakes in shiny boots and the latest fashion in wigs pushed me so hard I near tumbled into a horse trough. They merely wished to pass, and they swaggered on. "Count yourself lucky we do not duck you!" Bloods. Their arrogance angered me. Two of last night's swordsmen? But it was unlikely they were the same fellows, for London held many of their kind. I followed for a time. They thought it a great joke to lift ladies' dresses with their ebony sticks. They dashed a blind man's cup into the road, and with wanton blades cut down a string of birds from a poulterer's shopfront. The poultryman bellowed in protest—but he ceased bellowing when they backed him against the wall and twisted his nose 'til blood ran down his chin.

A throng gathered to watch. London loved diversion, and some laughed. No one made any attempt to stop the outrage, and reflecting on lawlessness I trudged on.

I arrived at number 7 at three, just as Mr. Franklin was returning from New Street Square. He was in a jolly mood, for he had been to see his old friend William Strahan, who besides publishing the *Chronicle* had printed Adam Smith's works on economics and Samuel Johnson's dictionary too. Mr. Franklin loved any man with printer's ink under his nails, but especially Straney. They had writ letters across the sea for years, and Straney had even proposed that his eldest son wed Mr. Franklin's daughter.

Luncheon was a cold bird with carrots and peas, Mrs. Stevenson hardly able to eat knowing her daughter would arrive before nightfall. She clasped her hands eagerly. "I wonder what news she will bring!"

Mr. Franklin had not forgot John Fielding, so he and I climbed into a hackney at a quarter to four, but at the top of Craven Street he gripped my arm. Following his glance, I glimpsed a man in a long brown coat in the shadow of an upholsterer's. His hat was pulled low, but I knew him.

Jack Scratch.

Mr. Franklin met my eyes. "What does he do here? Spy on Ben Franklin?" The gentleman settled back. "I have not forgot that he said three."

As our coach moved on, I told Mr. Franklin I had seen the scribbler in Fleet Street.

One brow lifted. "You did a little smouting for Mr. Tisdale, then?"

"I did."

"Did he pay you?"

"Promptly."

The gray-brown eyes narrowed. "And do you spend promptly, Nick?"

I flushed, but Mr. Franklin merely patted my arm. "Take care, lad, for you would not enjoy the arsenic cure." He hummed "The Honeysuckle and the Bee" as we joined the traffic of the Strand.

Though I had walked here this morn, our coach gave the Strand a new and different perspective, so I gazed at its river, at elegant and tawdry, high and low: a deacon in blackcloth and bands, a crippled boy with his hand outstretched for coin. A throng held us up near the Savoy, and Mr. Franklin pointed. "There goes a tailor," said he.

I looked at the rail-thin man he indicated. "You know him, sir?"

"I have never set sight on him."

"Then—begging your pardon—how do you know he is a tailor?"

"His humped back."

His shoulders were indeed rounded. "But may not other men have humped backs, too?"

"But with scissors poking out their pockets? And, look close as he passes, there are tails of red and green thread upon both sleeves. A tailor, surely."

"Why . . . you are right."

His finger jabbed. "That bearded fellow behind him? What is he?"

I examined this new object. He wore fustian stuff. "Surely no lord."

"It is a beginning."

"But as to more—"

"Come, he is a tanner. See his coffee-colored hands? Observe more carefully. Let us try again." The traffic began to clear. "Quickly, there, just coming out of that grog shop. Look sharp, tell how he earns his bread."

By now I was determined to prove I could read a trade as well as Benjamin Franklin, so I squinted hard. The man was thick-shouldered, with a beetling brow and alert eyes, but his clothes gave no clue that I could discover: heavy boots and a greatcoat. His hands? They were as raw and strong as his face. He walked with some authority. Used to command? Yet he was common. What common fellow issued commands? He strode toward us; soon he would pass, and my chance would be gone. Had I lost the game?

Then a pretty maid crossed his path. The man leered, and as his thick lips parted, I knew. "He is a coach driver, sir!"

"How do you know?"

"His teeth are filed. Many coachmen file 'em, to hold their whipcords in their mouths."

Freed of the crush, we jounced on. Mr. Franklin winked. "You are indeed Benjamin Franklin's son."

In sight of New Church we turned into Drury Lane; from thence we made our way to Bow Street, arriving by half past four. The day remained gray. Three-quarters along the street stood a green-shuttered house on the west side, number 4. It was unprepossessing for the abode of the chief crime-fighter for London, but woe betide any cutpurse, highwayman, or bludgeoner who fell under the Blind Beak's hand.

A motley crowd was dispersing as we drove up; sessions were over for the day. Plaintiffs, witnesses, relations, petty barristers, beadles, constables, and hangers-about trailed from the door under an iron sky. Pushing past, we went in. First the narrow entryway, then the Justice Room: a high-ceilinged chamber with a raised bench at one end and a portrait of His Majesty, George II, glowering with Hanoverian displeasure, at the other. The chamber was deserted save for Joshua Brodgen, sitting at a tall desk in a corner scribbling warrants and writs.

Brogden was the Blind Beak's clerk; he hopped promptly from his stool as he spied us. "Mr. Franklin, sir! Nicolas!" His bulging eyes popped. "Murder, eh? Hearts cut out? You shall have your hands full. His worship awaits you. You know the way?"

"We have traveled it many a time," replied Benjamin Franklin.

In a moment we had passed through the door behind the bench, into the inner sanctum of the man who stood betwixt London and anarchy.

🦋 6 🦋

IN WHICH the Investigation Begins . . .

The Blind Beak wore his black band across his eyes. He was plucking off his full-bottomed wig of office as we entered, his voice its customary growl: "So, Franklin, you are come. And your boy." His chamber was a crowded rectangle with a worn Turkey carpet on the floor, a broad desk in the center, a tall bookshelf, three foxed prints of racehorses, and a narrow window looking toward Great Hart Street. It smelt dry as dust. There were no papers on the magistrate's desk—what use had a blind man for papers?

Fielding had memorized every corner of the room, for he placed his wig unerringly upon a stand before he trundled to the desk. Sinking down behind it, folding his fingers across his belly, he regarded us as if he had eyes. In truth he "saw" with his ears, great, curled shells that seemed to hearken with alertness as we took the two straight-backed chairs before him.

There was no preamble. "Well, what to do about this second murder? I count upon your counsel."

Mr. Franklin peered. "Surely you have already begun. Your good fellows have nosed about?"

"O, they have nosed." The good fellows were "Mr. Fielding's people," his force of trained men. The magistrate gave a disgruntled snort. "Croft and Smith. Billy Banting. They have scoured the area where the woman was found. They have asked questions, too: of whores, nightsoil men, beggars, chimneysweeps. They have gleaned nothing."

"Are you surprised?"

One prickly eyebrow lifted. "You mistrust 'em, sir?"

"Nay, you have trained 'em well. But our quarry is clever. He would not leave so easy a trail. Too, you were unable to discover anything about the first." Mr. Franklin mused: "Two hearts cut out in the same fashion. And both women young. Have you read accounts of the far parts of the world? Pagans sacrifice virgins in like fashion, I have heard. To bloodthirsty gods."

"Pagans? In London? What do you propose, man, that our killings were some rite?"

Mr. Franklin pulled at his lip. "I do not know. But the clean nature of the carving. Cold. Inhuman. Pitiless. The women offered up to . . . what? It is suggestive."

Fielding twitched. "You make me shudder, sir!"

"And were they killed where you found 'em or done in elsewhere?"

"If elsewhere, not likely far."

"Our compass is narrow, then. From Green Park to the Haymarket, let us say. But your men must inquire higher than beggars and chimneysweeps. They must apply to the titled and wealthy, as well."

Fielding's features bunched. "Asking fine folk about murder is a delicate business. It will raise an alarm."

"So be it."

The magistrate sighed. "True, the main thing is to prevent more murders." In fact prevention was the justice's main aim. Just last year he had published *The Asylum of Orphans and Other Deserted Girls of the Poor*, a scheme to keep abandoned women from crime by employing them. "London will rejoice to see her downtrodden barrow-sellers and miserable prostitutes converted to respectable service," he had writ, and recalling the words (which had provoked much dispute), I could not help thinking on Birdy Prinsop, who sold herself because she had no better means of earning her bread.

"The two murders will be no secret anyway," Fielding puffed. "That cursed scribbler, Scratch, has likely writ of 'em already, so

41

it will make no matter if I also put word in the *Public Advertiser.*"

"Do so at once," agreed Mr. Franklin. The *Advertiser* was where Bow Street sought information about crimes. "You will spread word amongst your informants, too?"

"I shall."

"And alert your patrols?"

"They have already been given orders."

Mr. Franklin sat silent a moment. He did not look hopeful, and I understood: London was a sprawling maze, with hundreds of hidden places like the disused old stables where a woman's mutilated body had been found last night. How to prevent anything in such a warren? Though the Blind Beak had prised funds from Parliament to support his trained force, the funds were still too little, the men too few.

Mr. Franklin was not one to remain discouraged long. "We must also find the murderer," said he. "To that end we must learn the identity of his victims. May I look through your *Bow Street Register*? There may be some detail which Banting neglected last night."

"You are welcome to it."

"Meanwhile I have asked Nicolas to make half a dozen sketches of the design on the murdered woman's buttons. We have brought 'em, so your men may use 'em in their inquiries. There is something more. Your men will also find at the bottom of each sheet a drawing of a medallion, with some French words upon it."

Fielding stiffened. "What medallion?"

"That which I found grasped in the victim's hand."

Fielding's jowls shook. "What? You have withheld evidence?" He bent forward. "Why did you not reveal it last eve?"

Mr. Franklin rarely showed chagrin, but he did now. "I wished to think upon the thing. I have brought the medallion now. Here." He placed it on Fielding's desk.

The magistrate made more displeased rumbling, but he contained his ire as his fingers found the thing, "read" its stamped letters. "*Fay . . . ce . . . que . . . voudras.* French. My French is poor."

" 'Do what you wish.' "

"What the devil does that signify?"

"If we knew, we might know all. You have not heard the phrase before? In the street?"

"No."

"A pity. Ask your men to inquire about it, too. Meanwhile I have another idea. Nick's drawing of the second woman is excellent. Let us employ an engraver to copy it, to show it about with the rest."

One of Fielding's rare smiles flashed: a wolfish show of teeth. "Capital!" He thumped his desk. "Why, a true policing force, which I dream on, would have just such a man on hand, to put faces on postbills ev'rywhere."

"I shall see to it, then. As to the first victim, do not neglect to have your men describe the birthmark behind her ear. Her trail is cold, but it may lead somewhere."

"As you say."

The pair sat in thought a moment, Mr. Franklin rubbing the head of his bamboo, John Fielding fingering the medallion as if he could squeeze secrets from it. A clatter of iron wheels sounded, the cry of a coster, a clamor of bells to say it was five. Though I was troubled by our new mystery, I felt privileged to observe these two men at work. Different in temper, they were alike in despising lawbreakers. They longed to tame the great, mad metropolis, and I was proud to know my drawings might help.

Mr. Franklin bestirred himself. "I shall make inquiries, too." He adjusted his breeches about his knees. "For now, I should like to know more of Jack Scratch."

A curled lip. "Pah, I can tell you little. I have done what other magistrates have not: admitted newspapermen to my court; I have even supplied 'em with pen and ink, in the hope that broadcasting news of crime may begin to diminish it. Alas, they have proved a mixed blessing. Many are honest, but others conflate or lie, and Scratch is among the worst; he loves to fan a spark to a flame."

"He suffered some disappointment. At Oxford, did he not say? Thus he seeks revenge against the world? So, he is in your court often?"

"Creeping. Wheedling information from prisoners and witnesses."

"Begging your pardon—" I put in.

"Nick?' Mr. Franklin turned.

"I only wondered if his honor had thought what to make of the number, 'three'?"

"Make of it?" Fielding waved dismissing hands. "Why . . . there is nothing to make of it. Scratch is a liar, I tell you. He only wishes to lead us on." Mr. Franklin and I exchanged a glance, and as if he had seen, Fielding added, "Nonetheless I shall swear out a writ of evidence if you like. Shall I collar him for questioning?"

Windowlight glinted from Mr. Franklin's small round spectacles. "Nay, not yet. Give him rein. To another matter: London's 'bloods.' "

Fielding's mouth flattened. "Plague take the troublesome rakes!"

"Nick and I had a sally with half a dozen last night. They wished to make us dance, but they danced to our tune instead. And ended in the mud."

Fielding chortled. "Franklin, you are a wonder! I should like to've seen it."

Mr. Franklin did not laugh. "Other innocent citizens are not so fortunate. They are tipped into rainbarrels, their property is broken, their backsides pricked. Can nothing be done?"

"Very little, curse it. The bloods are sons of title, near impossible to bring to task. Their fathers have hundred-year-old names; they sit in Parliament or on the King's Bench, and like as not they got up to the same antics in their youth, so their sons think they may do likewise."

"*Fay ce que voudras*, eh? One law for them, another for the rest?" Mr. Franklin shook his head. "Justice weighs with an uneven hand. Your *Bow Street Register*—may I examine it now?"

"As you please. I must confer with Brogden."

Rising, the huge man thumped out, whilst Mr. Franklin and I went to his bookshelf. John Fielding was the half-brother of Henry Fielding—novelist, pamphleteer, playwright—who had held this post before him. One of their reforms was punctilious record-keeping, so dozens of thick, leather-bound ledgers, their famous *Register,* sat on the shelves. Taking down the most recent volume, we thumbed through it, seeking the entry for the young woman who was so dreadfully discovered in St. James's church-

44

yard. We found it: Monday, 29 October, 1759. There seemed nothing new, a tale of horrible butchery with a deposition from the canon who had found the body. But Mr. Franklin did not stop there; he searched through the two previous months as well.

Had there been a number three after all, not cut up like the others, perhaps, but with some similarity that might link the crimes?

But the pursuit proved fruitless, save to trace an appalling history of thievery and violence. The English dread of standing armies meant that bludgeoners and bloods terrorized the city with shameful impunity.

Mr. Franklin sighed as he closed the book. "Will John Bull ever reform?"

It was half past five when we stepped out into Bow Street, dusk beginning to blur the day, but Mr. Franklin still was not done. He directed our coachman to deliver us to Charterhouse Street.

We were there in a quarter of an hour, before a trim yellow-brick house. A sign with a graver and burin hung above its fanlight door; the words *M. Ravenet, Etching and Engraving* headed it. We got down and rapped, and Monsieur Ravenet himself, a thin, sprightly Frenchman with eyes as bright as new-minted coins, opened.

He greeted us warmly, for we had visited a year ago in the matter of the Shenstone diamond, and I had called several times since, Mr. Franklin believing my artistic skills might be sharpened by practice at the printmaker's craft; thus I had learnt to cut and etch a copper plate, to prepare the press, to pull a print.

Explaining our purpose, Mr. Franklin showed my drawing, at which monsieur paled. "*Nature morte*—you give new meaning to the words!" But he saw clearly what we wished. "*Oui, c'est possible.*" His bright eyes fell on me. "Let the boy engrave the plate. I have taught him the craft."

We repaired to his workshop.

For the second time that day I sat amidst the smell of ink. I had learnt to love engraving: the incising of the lines, the calculating of light and dark, trimming the burr with the fluted scraper. A square of metal was placed before me, and Mr. Franklin and Monsieur Ravenet took places at my shoulder. "To it, Nick." I felt uneasy under such scrutiny, but Benjamin Franklin had taught me bravery, so I took a breath, gripped the burin and set to, and in half an hour I had incised the woman's face.

"*Voila.* Did I not say he could do it?" asked monsieur with his brittle smile.

"I never doubted," replied Benjamin Franklin.

Next, to the press. It was different from book presses with their powerful screws. This one worked by roller and, inking the copper, I produced in another three-quarters of an hour a dozen impressions. As I hung the last to dry, Mr. Franklin asked Monsieur Ravenet about *Fay ce que voudras.* "Do you know the phrase?"

"*Mais, oui.* It is Rabelais, from *Gargantua and Pantagruel.* Why do you ask?"

"It was on a medallion in the dead woman's hand."

"*Formidable!* But what does it signify?"

"I had hoped you might say."

Ravenet thought. "It is permission for license. But Rabelais was a monk. Surely he did not mean . . . murder?"

"Surely not. I thank you, sir." I cleaned my hands of ink and we went to the door. Mr. Franklin bowed. "My manservant, Peter, will fetch the prints when they are dry."

"*Si'l vous voulez.*" But Monsieur Ravenet kept appraising eyes on me. "You have skill, Nicolas. You draw well. Some men earn their living by engraving. There is a whole class of merchants and tradesmen who cannot afford paintings but who like to hang something on their walls—a sign of respectability, position. You and I together—"

"We shall think on that," replied Mr. Franklin.

We descended to the cobbled way.

It was well past seven when our hackney returned us home, the sky dark. We got down. At the bottom of Craven Street the Thames was a black swath lit by the lanterns of the barges and wherries in lonely sway upon it. The air bit.

Indoors was warm and welcoming, however, and Mrs. Stevenson was as merry as ever I saw her, for her Polly—our Polly—had arrived. We greeted the young woman in the front parlor, she kissing Mr. Franklin on both cheeks and pressing a kiss upon me, too, with a hug that took my breath. Though she was older than I, twenty-two, I was smitten with Polly, so her frank affection made me blush.

She fairly danced as she said she must tell us all about her adventures in Wanstead; she must hear our tales, too. "Do the stubborn Penns still trouble you, Mr. Franklin?"

"As fleas trouble the dog, my dear."

Mrs. Stevenson beamed. She had prepared a fine supper in hopes her lodger dined in tonight, she said; but, alas, the gentleman regretted to inform her that he and I were engaged otherwhere. It was the first I had heard of any such engagement.

Mrs. Stevenson bit her tongue—she had learnt not to question her lodger's business—but Polly was nothing if not forward. "Where do you go?" demanded she.

"Out," Mr. Franklin replied.

"But can you not stay on the day I return? I am told you wish to put a lightning rod upon our house—I *must* hear of that."

"I regret that we must talk of lightning another time."

Polly was as shrewd as John Fielding. Her blue eyes glinted. "You are on one of your investigations, I see that you are." She grasped both Mr. Franklin's hands. "Dear Mr. Franklin, tell me of it. O, let me help." Stamping her foot, she whirled upon me. "You, but a boy . . . how I envy you! Why was I not born a man?"

"Polly Stevenson!" exclaimed her mother, and I averted my eyes. It was an old scene, for Polly always chafed under the restrictions imposed by her sex. She was quicker of mind than most men, spirited too, and Mr. Franklin encouraged her however he could. But his good landlady would never have forgiven him—nor he himself—if Polly had fallen into danger, so he promised he should devote three hours to her on the morrow, and we escaped upstairs.

There Mr. Franklin took great care with his person, combing back his fringe of brown hair and tying it with a new ribbon; he changed into better clothes, too: velvet breeches and a red figured waistcoat. He hummed as he slipped into his best coat, so I had no trouble guessing where we went: to Mrs. Comfort Goodbody, of Wild Street.

She was his intimate friend. Remarkable, too. Might she help us to resolve murder?

7

*IN WHICH We Learn Scandal from a Knave and
Discover a Dead Girl's Name . . .*

Before we set out, Mr. Franklin instructed Peter to fetch my
engravings from Monsieur Ravenet; they would be suffi-
ciently dry. Ten were to be delivered to the Chief Magistrate, two reserved for Craven Street. As Mr. Franklin gave orders,
I stole glances at the blackamoor, tall and still, his hands by his
sides, his deep-set eyes buried in a covert of a face. Peter was a
mystery, and as always I wondered what he thought. Whatever it
was, he seemed to have made peace with his life, for he never
complained; and there was dignity about him, as if he had a firm
grip on his soul. He sent me one of his sly, watchful smiles, and I
could not help smiling back. *We are alike,* our secret exchange
seemed to say, and it was true, for I had been a slave at Inch,
Printer, as he had been a slave before he served Mr. Franklin. I
felt a bond with Peter—he had once saved my life—and I liked
to hear the songs he sung in his attic room at night.

Nodding at orders, he set off.

Mr. Franklin and I departed, too.

Wild Street wound east of Drury Lane. It was a precinct of the city
Mr. Franklin knew well, for it lay near the spot where more than
thirty years ago Watts's Printing House had employed a nineteen-
year-old lad just crossed the Atlantic on his first bold visit to England.

49

That lad was Benjamin Franklin.

Mrs. Comfort Goodbody lived at number 52, a three-storied red-brick house in a terrace of similar dwellings. The night was chill—an icy wind lifted our collars as we stepped down from our coach—so the cheery light spilling from her windows drew us welcomingly.

We knocked. The maid admitted us, and in a moment we stood in a parlor where a fire crackled merrily. Prints of *Drury Lane Theater*, *Covent Garden, Sadler's Wells* and the *Haymarket* hung on pale yellow walls. The room was furnished neatly and well.

Mrs. Goodbody knelt by the mantel. She was in deep converse with a small, thin girl of perhaps ten, who stared at her as if she were a fairy or goddess. At our arrival the woman looked up. "Benjamin." Rising, she came forward, skirts rustling. He took her proffered hand, kissed it, and they gazed at one another a moment before she turned frankly to me. "Nicolas, I am glad to see you." Her voice was warm.

"Thank you, ma'am. I am very happy to see you, too."

She took me in with her light blue eyes. "How handsome you grow. Very near the height of your father, too." (She was the only person in London privy to my true relation to Mr. Franklin.)

"I am happy to be like him in any way I can," answered I.

Her full lips curled. "You grow a politic tongue."

"Nay, ma'am, an honest one."

She glanced at Mr. Franklin. "Also like your father—except when it suits him to be dishonest for some purpose."

"I am never dishonest with *you*," replied Benjamin Franklin.

She smiled. "You had best not be. Some men have attempted to play me false; they suffered for it." Logs spat sparks. Candlelight fluttered with an orange glow. Mrs. Goodbody was of Mr. Franklin's age, somewhat over five feet tall, her figure plump in a dark green dress with a white satin underskirt. She wore a little beribboned cap on backswept hair that was just beginning to show traces of gray. Her face must have been exceedingly pretty when she was younger, for I thought it beautiful now, marked by wisdom's stamp. Comedy, tragedy—life had tried her and found her game. Mr. Franklin had met her more than a year ago, when he helped David Garrick rid *Drury Lane* of trouble (she was head wardrobe mistress there). They had formed an alliance, Mr.

Franklin sometimes spending the night in her company. Mrs. Goodbody knew the gentleman had a wife in Philadelphia, but she was accustomed to taking life as she found it; and truth to tell, her house had been secured for her by another married gent, who had kept her before he died. As to her relationship with Mr. Franklin, she had confided to me one afternoon that she should not be pleased when he returned to America. "I have not met another like your father, Nicolas."

I well knew what she meant.

"You do not know Susan, do you?" said she now, smiling at the girl by her side. "Susan, curtsey to the gentlemen."

The girl, who wore a plain starched dress, made a shy obeisance.

"Good child." Something passed behind Mrs. Goodbody's eyes, a shiver of both pain and anger. "She was begging in the Whitechapel Road, near frozen, when I found her. We have just washed the lice from her hair." She touched the child's cheek. "I shall find a place for her—or she shall stay with me. Betsy and Mrs. Nunn will help me to train her if necessary." Betsy and Mrs. Nunn were the maid and cook.

"I should be happy to inquire after some good woman to take her in," offered Mr. Franklin.

"You have helped in the past. I should be grateful if you do so again."

"Your servant."

Moved, I looked into the girl's eyes. How often had I seen the same stunned expression above filthy begging children's hands. Had this one enjoyed, before tonight, a single moment of kindness in her short life? She continued to stare at Mrs. Goodbody; plainly she did not know her fortune, for her savior had herself come near being lost to the streets. She had survived by wit and will, and now that her nimble fingers earned her a living, she helped other women. Two were her maid, delivered from the impecunious, whoring life, and Mrs. Nunn, who had once sold marrows—and herself—from a small stall in Cockburn Street. The three of them now formed a household dedicated to rescuing a few of the legions destined to die of the pox or gin before they were thirty.

"Betsy," called Mrs. Goodbody. The maid returned. "Some

broth, I think. And good, clean bedclothes." The mistress gave her charge of the child. "Thousands," murmured she when they were gone. "Thousands . . ." She looked down, then up, and when she did all her rue was gone. A warm sparkle replaced it. "Come, gentlemen, sit by the fire and warm your hands."

Drinks were brought, and we settled in, Mr. Franklin crossing his legs. A cheerier mood prevailed. He must hear all the gossip of the playhouse, for he knew Mrs. Cibber and Mr. Woodward and the other actors who entertained London when the green curtain flew up at six, so Mrs. Goodbody regaled us for twenty minutes with tales of backstage scandal. She praised Mr. Franklin's *Historical Review of the Constitution and Government of Pennsylvania*, published in June. "Does it help to resolve your dispute with the Penns?"

"I am hopeful."

"Does William attend the hearings with you?"

"He does."

Mrs. Goodbody had never met William (he might not approve her relationship with his father), but she always wished news of him. "How do things go with him?"

"O, excellently," replied Mr. Franklin, but there was something about his manner, a fleeting disgruntlement, that made me recall the cloudy moment in the entryway this morn, when father and son had conspired and sparred. A flicker in Mrs. Goodbody's eyes said she noted the alteration, too, but she only brushed her lap. "Here is Betsy. Time for supper, sirs."

We repaired to the dining room, where bone china was laid on a smooth white cloth. A vase of dried roses completed the table. As we began with one of Mrs. Nunn's excellent roasted birds, talk turned to me, and I told our hostess how I set types in Fleet Street twice a week. "I study engraving with Monsieur Ravenet, too."

"And he has learnt his Latin so well that he can read Horace *stans pede in uno*," Mr. Franklin added proudly.

"*Mirabile dictu,*" replied Mrs. Goodbody.

He gazed at her across the table. "*Mirabile visu.*"

"Tut," said she, but I saw her blush.

Our knives and forks clicked. Over salmon and peas Mr. Franklin introduced the affair of the two murdered women. He began as if it had just come to mind, but I guessed it was one reason we were here. In other company he might have proceeded more gingerly, but Mrs. Goodbody had been privy to more than one murder at *Drury Lane*, so he spoke plainly, describing the butchery we had witnessed, the medallion, the steps he had taken.

When he was done, Mrs. Goodbody sat quite still, her little house still, too, as if it had been struck dumb. The candles sent up spiraling wisps of smoke. Somewhere a clock ticked like a tiny heart. "Do you, then, seek my help?" she asked at last.

"I do."

"I offer it, then."

The gentleman turned to me. "Nick?"

I had my sketching book in my pocket. Pulling it forth, I opened to the drawing of the murdered woman.

Mrs. Goodbody perused the face. "Another . . ." murmured she, touching the page as if she touched a human soul. "Another victim of London."

Mr. Franklin shook his head. "Beg pardon, but London did not do her in. Some villain did—and we must find and stop him." He related all Billy Banting had told us of the first woman: her height, the color of her hair, her likely age. "She had a birthmark behind her left ear." He described this too. "We seek to learn who the victims were. We are much in the dark. You know various women about the city. Will you spread word amongst 'em? I will deliver an engraving of Nick's drawing, to help."

"I shall begin this very night."

I was surprised. "Tonight, ma'am?" It was near ten. What could she do so soon?

"London is alive at night, Nicolas," replied she. "Eyes watch. Voices whisper. Many women do not sleep 'til dawn. Mrs. Nunn knows 'em. Betsy too. Betsy!" The maid returned. "Tell Mrs. Nunn we have work to do."

Betsy smiled. She understood, and a light sprang into her eyes, as if she liked the prospect of soldiering. Curtseying, she hurried out.

Mrs. Goodbody turned back to the drawing. Her face grew grave. "Discarded in the West End? They are usually not found there, but no matter. I quite agree. The beast who did this must be stopped."

53

. . .

"*Is* he a beast?" murmured Mr. Franklin as we rid home an hour later to the hollow clop of hooves echoing from night-black walls. Out upon the Thames a ship's bell clanged, and a gin-maddened cry flew from a tavern. "If so, he is not of any kind that I have met."

I had no answer, and in Craven Street we retired promptly, I sleeping fitfully amidst dreams in which a thousand impoverished children—a thousand Susans—begged with supplicating arms.

I found Peter with the gentleman when I went into his chamber next morn. Beyond the bow window the sun was barely up, but it shone bright; a rattling wind in the night had dispersed the city's fog. In measured tones Peter was informing Mr. Franklin of his labors: he had delivered ten prints to Bow Street; he held the remaining two in his strong hands.

"Take one to Wild Street, then," Mr. Franklin replied. "Mrs. Goodbody has need of it. Keep the other yourself. I have told you the details of this matter. Show the face amongst your acquaintance. You know what I seek."

The blackamoor bobbed his head. "Yes, sir." Peter knew servants, workmen, St. Giles blackbirds. They might stand low on society's scale, but they saw and heard what privileged souls did not.

Peter set out.

When he was gone, Mr. Franklin bobbed his head at me. Already shaved, he wore his morning coat; early to work, then, thought I. But I was surprised. I was used to seeing only the *London Chronicle* upon the table by his horsehair chair—he perused other gazettes at the coffeehouses—but there was a pile of many different newspapers now. "Peter brought 'em round." He plumped down in the chair. "I mean to school myself in scandal."

I lit the morning fire whilst he began. At his desk I toiled at ciphering, parsed some Virgil, studied John Locke's *Treatise on Government*, much praised by Mr. Franklin. But I was distracted by the rustle of the newspapers, quarto-sized, formed from double-folded folios: the *Spectator*, the *Tradesman*, the *Courant*. I was distracted by Mr. Franklin, too. He read aloud: news of the war; a letter by Dr. Johnson on the design for Blackfriar's Bridge; notices of deaths, marriages, preferments; party clamor; a shipwreck off Hull; the latest comedy with Rich at *Covent Garden*. I listened especially alertly to John Fielding's notice about the murdered women in the *Advertiser*. It told where the victims had been discovered, their manner of death. The words were matter-of-fact, the tone unsensational—its purpose was only to seek information—but the magistrate had been right: it was sure to alarm. Hearts cut out, a butcher loose in London—it must make the great city shudder.

And then, Jack Scratch. His column in the *Courant* was called "The Scandal Club." Mr. Franklin read a sample:

> *"An assignation at the White Hart at St. Albans between Lady G. and S.W., Marquess of B——— was disconcerted by the forcible intrusion of the outraged husband. A suit is likely to commence . . ."*

"Scratch is not the only knave to write thus," said he, "but he does it expertly: sticks in the knife, twists; those who deal in the small wares of scandal will never want subjects. But this is to the point. Listen:

> *"His Majesty's men have heretofore sought to hide two murders, for fear the populace will panic, but they are now known: women with their hearts violently cut out near Pall Mall. The constables are baffled—and even an old bird from America, who is supposed to see keenly, proves as blind as a Bow Street magistrate. But Jack Scratch is not blind. Why sniff low when you should peer high? Seek in St. James's Square, Mr. F———."*

Mr. Franklin frowned. "St. James's Square?" He snapped the paper. "Does the fellow know as much as he pretends? What a hodgepodge! He rails against the bloods, too: 'The Dionysus Club is the vilest den of them,' he says. What is this 'Dionysus Club,' Nick?"

"I do not know."

"Ev'ry man in London seems to belong to some club. Scratch hints at a name, too: 'C.R., the most profligate of the Dionysians.' Who might that be?"

· · ·

The day was a quotidian one. I studied, copied letters. I fetched a loin of pork from the butcher for Mrs. Stevenson, whilst Mr. Franklin and William attended sessions at the Board of Trade. I watched them confer before they left: grave looks, an uneasy truce, then out to their coach; plainly there was something betwixt them, which was all the more unsettling because Mr. Franklin was used to confiding in me. Why exclude me now?

Polly noted their discord, too—her keen eyes noted everything—and awaiting her chance, she drew me into the deserted parlor after the father and son were gone. Her nose twitched like a terrier's. "Now, what is this between 'em?" demanded she.

"I do not know."

"Wha-at?" Backing me into a corner, she began to tickle me. "You will tell, Nick, you will!"

I writhed. I hated being tickled—I could hardly bear it—but I could not strike a girl, and having grown as tall as she, and stronger, I feared that if I fought too hard I might hurt her. She persisted, giggling, digging her fingers hard whilst I grasped at her wrists. Finding ourselves locked together, we tumbled upon the sofa. My face ended an inch from hers, and I stared into her eyes, mischievous, merry. Her hair was awry, her breath hot in my face, her mouth moist and pink. Suddenly she stopped tickling, and we lay still, whilst a bemused smile grew on her lips. "Well, Nicolas, what would Mama make of this?"

I leapt up, brushing my breeches. "You tickled me!" I burst out.

She rose, still smiling, coolly adjusting her honey hair. "So I did. You did not dislike it as much as you used." With a saucy look she strode from the room. "I am not done with you, Nick Handy."

I panted. I had escaped—but was I was glad to be free?

I did not see Mr. Franklin 'til after ten. He had supped with friends, then attended a meeting of the Royal Society, he told me when he came in from the night, flinging off his cloak. He tossed his hat on a peg. "Fothergill was there. John Pringle. I was presented to Francis Dashwood as well." He conferred with Peter, but the servant had nothing to report; there was no word from Wild Street, either.

But the day was not done, for round about eleven there came a soft rap on my door. I had gone to bed and was reading my favorite book, *Tom Jones*, when Mr. Franklin poked in his head. I sat up at his triumphant smile. "I am glad to find you awake." He waved a paper. "From John Fielding. I thought you should like to know that your drawing has already done the trick! We have learnt who the second victim was: Hester Ward, niece to a marquess. We call on her bereaved uncle tomorrow."

IN WHICH a Magistrate Talks of Riot, an Uncle of Murder . . .

After two days of fitful sun, Thursday dawned to rain once more. Slipping from bed, I peered out my window. Droplets bleared the panes; beyond them London lay damp and drear, the masts of the great ships far down the Thames like the fingers of drowning men. I crossed to Mr. Franklin's chamber, where an anticipatory silence shrouded us. What would we learn from the murdered woman's uncle?

Around nine Richard Jackson—"Omniscient Jackson," a friend to Pennsylvania—called, and he and Mr. Franklin conferred about the Board of Trade, though there were no hearings today. William was not to breakfast—he slept late—but Polly Stevenson raised her eyebrows at Mr. Franklin over her porridge. "Have you and William had a falling-out?" asked she innocently.

"Why do you ask?"

She showed a tip of pink tongue betwixt her teeth. "You seem not so in accord as before."

"Fathers and sons are often at odds," replied the gentleman in a tone that said the subject was closed.

Polly made a face. "You promised me three hours' talk yesterday. Why, you did not give me twenty minutes!"

A relenting smile. "As I should not like any falling-out with *you*"—Mr. Franklin squeezed her hand—"I shall find time today." He glanced at Mrs. Stevenson. "We shall discuss lightning rods, eh?"

John Fielding arrived at half past ten, a surprise, for he rarely called at number 7. Mrs. Stevenson made a great ceremony of installing him in the front parlor, but as Mr. Franklin and I went to him, she frowned. Was her favored lodger engaged in some dangerous pursuit? She never liked that.

The Blind Beak did not bother to sit, nor did he take off his hat. His black band hid his eyes. "I must away soon," grumbled he. He had meant to go with us to the dead girl's uncle, but he had been called to put down a riot in the Tottenham Court Road. "Some disgruntled market sellers near Whitefield's. Soldiers have been ordered from the Tower. I must attend. See the uncle without me. It is for the best. You are more politic, and the man may need handling. He is Silas Ward, Marquess of Bathurst. One of his servants recognized his niece by the engraving, but when Bathurst learnt his lackey had spoke to us, he beat him about the head. That gives some measure of the man! His note agreeing to see me was barely civil. He is one of the city's great rakes, a lecher, a gamester—if he is not in some dicing hell, he is tumbling one of Mother Cockburn's whores."

"I will go," replied Benjamin Franklin.

Jamming his tricorn hat upon his head, Fielding barked, "Billy!" and Billy Banting darted in to lead the magistrate to a small waiting chaise, which was lashed summarily up Craven Street.

We set out shortly after, I more puzzled than ever. I had thought to meet sorrow, outrage, even a vengeful cry from the uncle—but what to expect now? Why should Silas Ward be angry that the law had discovered his niece was murdered? We walked, for the rain had stopped and the distance was not great. Amidst the gush of gutters and the clack of pattens, I gazed into an overcast sky.

The Marquess of Bathurst lived in St. James's Square. Mr. Franklin and I exchanged a glance as we arrived before his fine brick house, number 6, for we both recalled Jack Scratch's words in the *Courant*: "St. James's Square, Mr. F——." But my gaze was also drawn to the northeast corner. There stood an equally fine house, which had rollicked with men's and women's drunken cries as we rid to view the dead girl Monday eve.

That same house had lain silent just before we were accosted by bloods. Had our attackers issued from it?

Mr. Franklin rapped, and a servant answered, a gray-fleshed, drawn-looking man. Was it he who had been beat about the head? I saw no signs of injury, however, as we were led to an elegant drawing room with a marble fireplace. Chinese wallpaper adorned the walls—drooping willows and bridges—whilst chairs in the latest style sat round. The servant withdrew.

At once a man strode in, tall, in a somber maroon coat. He was perhaps fifty, with a look of iron and vitriol. His nose and chin were sharp, his eyes black, his mouth a restless line. Coming to a halt, he took in Mr. Franklin with a mixture of impatience and contempt. His voice spat, "I am Lord Bathurst, sir. You are John Fielding? I have not much time. This is bad, very bad, but I do not see how I can help you. I am certain I cannot."

"I am Benjamin Franklin, my lord."

"Not the magistrate?"

"No."

Bathurst's fingers fidgeted. "I was led to believe . . . Damn it, what do you do here, then?"

"Begging your pardon, but the justice was called to put down a riot; he has sent me in his place. He hopes I may do." This was said in the mildest way, but Bathurst continued to glare at Mr. Franklin. (He did not seem to think I was worth noting.) He puffed, he scowled. He might have tossed a more obdurate man into the street, but Mr. Franklin seemed to strike the right placating note, for he flapped his hands.

"Very well." His eyes warned. "Do not take much time."

"Thank you, my lord. May I say, first, that I am sorry for what has happened to your niece."

An acknowledging growl.

"Her name was Hester Ward?"

"It was."

"She lived with you?"

"Did."

"How old was she?"

"Twenty. Twenty-one. I am not certain."

"Not certain?"

"We had little to do with one another."

60

"Where are her parents?"

"With the worms. Her mother died in childbirth."

"She was your brother's daughter, then. Was he the eldest son?"

An eyebrow twitched. "How can that signify?"

"Pray, was he?"

"If you must know, he was."

"So you gained your title by his death?"

The marquess rose on his toes. "Damn it, man, I gained my title *upon* it. What the devil do you suggest?"

"Nothing, my lord. Pray, how did he die?"

"Bludgeoned in the street. The robber who did it was caught and hung. Come to the point or begone."

"Beg pardon, I am certain the justice himself would inquire better. How long did your niece live with you?"

"Six years."

"Nick?" I held out my book. "Is this she?"

Bathurst snatched the book; he gazed at my drawing. How to interpret his expression? Annoyance? Distaste? He stiffened, his broad mouth worked, his jaw tightened; and when his voice came it was a low, controlled murmur. "Not exactly like her, but near enough." He thrust the book back at me. "Yes, it is she."

"And when did you last see her alive?"

"She breakfasted with me on Saturday."

"Did she speak of any particular plans?"

"No."

"She did not say she meant to go away for a time?"

"No."

"I do not quite understand. You did not know her whereabouts from that morn until your man recognized the engraving which the constable showed at your door four days later? You were not alarmed? You made no inquiries?"

"Why should I? She led her life, I mine. I will not be judged upon it."

"I assure you, my lord, I intend no judgment. And yet . . . did she often disappear for days?"

"She always returned."

Mr. Franklin pondered this. "To the crime. Do you have any idea who might have done it?"

"Some thief. Some cutthroat."

" 'Twas not her throat that was cut."

"Do not quibble."

I thought a heart carved from a breast was hardly a quibble, but Mr. Franklin merely bowed his head. "O, indeed, the murder may have been chance: if not she, another." He shifted his feet. "And yet you seemed to hesitate before you replied. Are you certain someone did not come to mind?"

"Come, my niece is dead, and there's an end."

"Not for Justice Fielding. He is persistent; why, he can worry a man to the grave! He has the weight of the King's law behind him, too. Even a peer must bow to that. Surely you do not wish to be questioned again, your grief provoked?" This was said with no appearance of guile, but a narrowing of my lord's black eyes said he began to see he dealt with a shrewder man than seemed.

"Very well." He spoke betwixt his teeth. "I do not know who might have murdered her, but she ran with a bad crowd. She was a wild girl. Headstrong. Impossible."

"You could not constrain her, you say?"

Bathurst flared. "I can constrain anyone I choose! Damn it, I did not ask to have the creature put in my care. She was thrust upon me, so I did what I ought. I hired the best dancing-master. I paid a fop to teach her French. I bought her silks. I installed her in a suite of rooms."

"And let her go her way?"

"She had a companion for a time, a *duenna*, but they did not get on; it lasted six months. Meanwhile, I had business to attend to."

"What was this 'bad crowd' you name?"

"Others of her like. Daughters of rank and title, but with the same rebellious spirit. A vexation to their fathers. A blot on good names. They went about with a gang of idle young men, in a perpetual round of routs and squeezers. I am no Puritan, sir. I think even women, within bounds, may live as they like—"

"*Fay ce que voudras?*"

"What?"

"French, sir."

"I despise the tongue. Hear me, even a woman may live as she pleases, so long as she knows how to do it without scandal. But my niece could do nothing without scandal; she flaunted her affairs. Her reputation sullied my name."

"A name so respected as yours! I am sorry to learn it. But who were these rebellious young women?"

"Lydia March, Viscount Dean's daughter, for one. She bedded a dozen footmen before she was twenty."

"And the idle young men?"

"Members of the Dionysus Club."

I started, but Mr. Franklin put on an innocent face. "The . . . Dionysus Club? What is that?"

"A nest of riot and bloody mischief. They meet at Ravenden's, across the way."

"Across St. James's Square, you mean?"

"The corner house." Bathurst pointed out the window.

I stared, whilst Mr. Franklin rubbed the head of his bamboo. The peer's finger indicated number 18, the house that had rocked with carouse Monday night, the house from which the bloods that attacked us may have issued.

"Who is this Ravenden?" Mr. Franklin asked.

"Charles Ravenden," Bathurst replied.

C.R., thought I.

"The sixth Earl of Chalton," Bathurst went on. "Surely you have heard of him?"

"No."

"A devil of a man! All London calls him that."

"Why?"

"Because of his dev'lish practices. Rumors of wicked rites. And his face—he looks a devil, too, with his painted features."

"And your niece?"

"Women were allowed to be members of his club. I shall leave you to guess their duties."

"Dear me! But ev'ry woman has a heart. Was there no particular young man she was interested in?"

"Any man who wanted her." Bathurst relented. "Very well, there *was* one she might've liked more than any other—or pitied. Tom Elstree. His father is only a knight, but he has money. I half hoped the damned young rake would win Hester. That would have settled things, and I would have been rid of her. But Elstree is a fool—young men are all fools these days—so nothing came of it." Bathurst snatched a watch from his brocaded waistcoat. "Enough. I have said all I care to, and you must tell the magistrate

63

there is no more. I shall send men to collect what is left of my niece. I will spare no expense. I shall see her buried with a fine marble stone and the blessings of the clergy. Then I will have done my duty, and there's an end." He clicked his heels. "I have affairs to attend to. My man will see you out." He wheeled and was gone.

Mr. Franklin and I stood in ringing silence. "Charles Ravenden," mused he. "Tom Elstree. Put the names in your book."

I did.

The drawn-looking servant crept in to show us out. In the hall we passed a row of portraits, the Bathurst ancestors, looking chagrined at having produced so egregious an heir. "Your master told us of Tom Elstree—but he neglected to say where he lives," said Mr. Franklin to the servant as we went.

"Soho Square, sir," replied the man.

"Tell me, did Miss Ward's friends call here sometimes?"

"Sometimes, sir."

"Did one—a young woman—have a mulberry birthmark behind her left ear?"

"It is not a servant's place to note such things, sir."

"Servants always note the things they should not. Come, did you ever see such a mark?"

"No, sir."

"Did Tom Elstree call here, too?"

"Once or twice. He was the only man of Miss Ward's acquaintance whom her uncle would suffer in his house."

"And was he presentable?"

"He loved Miss Ward, I believe."

"And did she love him?"

"She allowed him to call. Then she ceased to be 'in' to him."

"Why?"

"I do not know. Perhaps she liked him too much." A thin smile. "Only the view of a servant, sir. Miss Ward had odd ways."

"I am told your master was not pleased you told the constable you recognized the engraving of her."

"I did my duty. As to my master's feelings, sorrow can unman even a peer." He opened the door.

Mr. Franklin persisted. "What was Miss Ward like?"

A long look, as if the man were deciding whether to reply. "She was a poor, pitiable creature, sir. I liked her very much. Good day."

We walked out, and the tall door closed behind us.

On the pavement Mr. Franklin spanked his bamboo stick against a horse-post. "A wanton wench or a poor, pitiable creature. Which, Nick? As to Bathurst's 'sorrow,' he is thoroughly glad his niece is dead—the man is stuffed with vanity! Yet we have learnt something." He squinted at the house across the way, number 18, three stories of elegant red brick under a murky sky. It lay silent, its windows closed to scrutiny. Horses' hooves clopped wetly, and a finely dressed couple, she with parasol, he with moustaches, stepped from a nearby door, peered at the day, darted back in alarm. Mr. Franklin tilted his head. "The Dionysus Club, eh? And Charles Ravenden is a devil? But we shall begin elsewhere, I think." He drew me toward the Mall, where hackneys abounded. "Is not the river of human concourse as surprising as Nature's? One catches unexpected things in it. Let us see what sort of fish Tom Elstree may be."

❧ 9 ❧

*IN WHICH We Question a Dead Girl's Suitor and Are
Watched by a Lord . . .*

As we clambered aboard one of the last available hackneys in
Pall Mall, the rain started up again. It fell in rods, slashing,
whipping, churning London's gutters into turgid brown
rivers. Dead rats floated by our wheels, alongside hats, a tattered
cabbage, a lady's fan. We had a struggling time—it took full half
an hour to reach our destination—but at last we pulled to a halt in
Soho Square. I gazed about. As large as St. James's, this square was
subtly different, genteel rather than elegant, with a more grateful
appreciation of the tokens of wealth which new money could buy.
I knew because I had been here before, and I could not help
glancing at the the former residence of Roderick Fairbrass. Two
years ago his daughter had come to Benjamin Franklin with a tale
of ghosts, which had led to a battle upon the icy Thames, where
I nearly drowned.

Going about with Mr. Franklin could prove perilous.

But it was another house whose marble stoop we dashed to
now: number 12. Would Tom Elstree prove in? A second time this
day Mr. Franklin rapped upon a fine fanlight door, and a second
time a manservant opened, though this one was of a far different
stripe: short and stoop-shouldered, with a rough, weathered face.
But he knew his business, saying, yes, he would see if young master Elstree might speak to us. "It is about Hester Ward," Mr.
Franklin added, at which a light seemed to flare and die in the servant's watchful eyes.

When he had crept off, we looked about. This was not so grand a house as the Marquess of Bathurst's, but there was an air of prosperity about its rich wood moulding. The knobs of the stair rails were as massive as cannon balls, and pictures of ships with billowing sails adorned the walls.

Abruptly a young man burst upon us, wild-looking, with a mop of tangled brown hair, untied. He was pulling on his coat, as if he could hardly wait to greet us. He stared frantically into Mr. Franklin's face. "Hester Ward, sir? You come about Hester?"

"I do."

The young man glanced about, as if he did not wish to be overheard. "In here." Gesturing, he urged us into a parlor with a large window looking upon the drenched gray light of the square. Heavy furniture sat about, and a set of brass ship's bells gleamed somberly on the mantel. The young man shut the door, his breathing loud. "Now. Who are you, sir? What do you have to tell?"

"You are Tom Elstree?"

"Yes, damn it."

Despite this impertinence Mr. Franklin took a moment to examine him. He was twenty-five years old or so, of medium height, and sturdily built: thick of calf, with a farmboy's heavy shoulder. He had a blunt, square face, handsome but with something weak about the chin and the small, peering eyes, which watched us with a wary stare, as if they were in the habit of mistrusting the world. His brow was pinched, and he was pale, as if he had arisen betimes from a night's frantic revels.

A shine of perspiration dampened his lip. He jerked impatiently at his sleeves. "Well, I say?"

"My name is Benjamin Franklin. This is my boy, Nicolas Handy. May we sit?"

"Yes, yes." We did so, Mr. Franklin and I on a sofa, the young man flinging himself into a red plush chair, where he perched expectantly at its edge.

"To be brief," began Mr. Franklin, "I come in behalf of John Fielding, the Bow Street magistrate. He is investigating the murders of two women. They were not murdered at the same time, but both were done in alike, their hearts carved from their breasts. They were found within a quarter mile of each other."

Elstree's little eyes seemed to shrink into his face. "Dear God, not the women I read of in the *Courant*?"

"The same."

"But you do not say that Hester—?"

A nod. "I am given to understand by Miss Ward's uncle that you had some interest in her; at the very least she was your friend. I am sorry to inform you that she was one of the victims."

Elstree ground his hands in his lap. His mouth worked.

Abruptly he staggered up, fell to his knees on the parquet floor, and vomited onto the hearth.

Ugly coughing sounds filled the room, and the stench of his vomit curled my nostrils. Mr. Franklin rose, went to the convulsing man. "My dear sir, a very great blow." Bending, he offered his handkerchief.

Elstree snatched it, wiped his lips.

Mr. Franklin helped him to his feet. "Shall you sit?"

Pale as chalk, Elstree stumbled to his chair. Sinking into it, he stared out of red-rimmed eyes.

Did only sorrow fill them? Fear, too?

Mr. Franklin resumed his seat. Footsteps sounded somewhere in the house, the closing of a door, the creak of boards. Out upon the street a harness jingled. "You cared for her very much?" inquired the gentleman.

Elstree's mouth worked before any words would come. "I . . . yes. No. That is . . . I did once, but she would not have me. I was reconciled to that. And yet . . . and yet, to learn she is so horribly dead, when I once . . . dear God . . ." He clutched the handkerchief. "When was she . . . found?"

"Two nights ago, in a mews near Pall Mall." Mr. Franklin gave details. "Do you have any idea why she might have been in that part of London?"

"N-no."

"It is a very terrible thing, and I would not trouble you. But we seek her murderer. You read the *Courant*? The *Advertiser*? You already know, then, that her death was the second in that vile manner. That suggests it was not haphazard—there may be some plan, which we must stop. So I should like to learn as much about the poor girl as possible. Will you tell me all you know?"

Elstree stared. "B-But you said you spoke to her uncle. How should I, then—?"

"Her uncle says he had not much to do with her."

"The selfish scoundrel!"

"Yet he is not why I am here. I ask again, will you—can you—tell us of Hester Ward? It may help save other lives." Mr. Franklin waited for a reply, his hands crossed over the top of his bamboo. I watched him. His manner with Silas Ward had been the bumbling inquirer, but in his plain brown suit he seemed avuncular now, his gaze solicitous. Did he truly sympathize with Tom Elstree? I mistrusted the young man though I could not say why. Not that he was not shaken; he trembled all over. But the reason was obscure; and as he continued to wring the handkerchief, a look of cunning seemed to creep into his little eyes.

"I . . . I suppose I may tell of her," murmured he.

"Bravely spoke." Mr. Franklin sat back. "First, how did you come to meet her?"

"We ran with the same crowd. Surely Bathurst told you that?"

"You pleasured yourselves thoughtlessly, he said."

"Ha, he is one to cast stones, the old libertine!" Elstree thrust out his chin. "May one not be a *young* libertine as well?" His eyes burned as I slipped my book from my pocket. Looking about the parlor, I saw that the massive furnishings and ostentatious draperies, were signs of hard-won prosperity. Recalling the secrecy with which Elstree had urged us out of earshot, I wondered what his father thought of his "crowd." Was the rich merchant, who had worked long and hard to achieve his status, pleased with his wayward son?

Quietly I began to draw Elstree as Mr. Franklin shrugged. "The young have as much right to be libertines as the old—if any have the right. But did you mean earlier that you would have married Hester Ward?"

"I proposed to her, if that is what you ask."

"What prevented your engagement?"

"She would not have me." Elstree dragged a hand through his tangled hair. "But even if she had consented, my father stood in the way."

"Objected?"

"Forbid."

"But she is a peer's niece, a good catch."

"She is Silas Ward's niece, and my father despises Silas Ward."

"Why?"

"His Tory politics. His whoring. But it was not only the uncle. Hester, herself—" Elstree ground his teeth.

"Her character?" Mr. Franklin prompted.

"Damn her! Damn her!" Tears burst from the young man's eyes.

"Was she truly so bad?"

Elstree's mouth twisted. "Bad, sir? She was light, lovely, gay! But she was wanton and selfish, too. O, my father was right, much as I hate to confess it: she was a cheat, a liar. And how her lies could make you burn, before you discovered she'd whispered 'em to a dozen other rakes who did not care a fig what she professed, so long as she gave 'em what they wanted. Afterward they winked as they told me of it." He buried his face in his hands. "Dear God . . . Dear God . . ."

I thought on the picture I had drawn of the dead girl. She had smiled at Tom Elstree, she had taunted him, she had broken his heart. Motive for murder?

"Our hearts rarely know what is best for 'em, sir," said Mr. Franklin. "This 'crowd' of yours—they encouraged her wantonness, then?"

"Yes, curse 'em—though I do not paint myself any better than they. I am wanton, too." Elstree's voice dripped with self-loathing. "We are all vile wantons."

"Come, you are too hard on yourself. Who were these others?"

"Does it matter?"

"One of 'em may lead us to our murderer."

Or be the murderer? thought I.

"The Earl of Chalton was one, her uncle said," Mr. Franklin persisted.

Elstree bit a lip. "Charles Ravenden, yes," answered he carefully, whilst something equivocal seemed to stir in him. He flung up his hands. "He is bright, handsome, clever! No stink of the pulpit about him—or of my damned father, either."

"You do not like preaching?"

"I despise it."

"And Ravenden was your leader?"

"Was. Is."

"He did not preach? But perhaps you liked his lessons better. How did you come to know him?"

"We were at Oxford together. St. John's College."

Oxford . . . Jack Scratch, thought I.

"You are of an age, then?" asked Mr. Franklin.

"He is somewhat older, but . . . yes."

"I am told he is a devil."

"Ha, I have never met the devil."

"I also hear of the Dionysus Club. What is it?"

Elstree's eyes in his square, blunt face seemed to retreat. "Why . . . only my lord Ravenden's conceit. A game, that is all. 'The Sacred Society of Dionysians,' he calls it. We drink, we dress up, we have our ceremonies."

"What sort?"

"Nothing to speak on. Foolishness."

"Molesting Londoners after dark?"

Elstree started. Did he begin to see he had met Mr. Franklin and me before? In any event, I suddenly felt certain he had been one of the six drunken bloods who had lurched at us out of the night. I frowned. Six bloods. Six sides to the medallion: *Fay ce que voudras*. My pencil moved on, seeking the true Tom Elstree.

"Are women allowed as members of your club?" Mr. Franklin asked.

"They are allowed to attend meetings."

"To participate, too?"

"After a fashion."

"To dress up with you?"

"Sometimes."

"Or not dress at all?"

"We are wanton, as I said."

"Hester Ward took part?"

An unhappy nod.

"When did the Dionysus Club last meet?"

"Monday eve. But Hester was not amongst us," Elstree added quickly. That meant Mr. Franklin and I had rid past the young man in Charles Ravenden's house, perhaps heard his drunken laugh, whilst the woman he had loved lay dead in the rain.

71

"And when did you last see Miss Ward?"

"A week ago. At Ranelagh. She was with another man. I did not know him, and she and I did not speak."

"So you do not know what she had been about in recent days?"

"No."

"I should like the names of the members of the Dionysus Club." Mr. Franklin looked at me. "Nick?"

Turning the page so he would not see my drawing, I passed the young man my book and pencil, and he scratched grudgingly before handing it back.

Mr. Franklin cleared his throat. "I thank you. Now"—his chair creaked—"do you have any thought who might have murdered Hester Ward?"

"To cut out her heart—" Elstree choked. "Only a madman would do such a thing."

"Or a clever man with no scruples." Mr. Franklin rubbed the knees of his breeches, whilst I resumed my drawing. I could limn the young man's face, but his character proved elusive. Should we pity him or shake him by the scruff? "By the by," Mr. Franklin put in, "amongst the women of your crowd, did one have a mulberry birthmark behind her left ear?"

"The other murdered one had such a mark, you say?" Elstree replied.

"She did."

"None of our crowd had one."

"Then tell me, do you game?"

"Game?"

"For I thought I saw you at the Hazard. Perhaps it was White's. In any event, you were in deep play—faro, *vingt-et-un*, the French ruff."

The young man was plainly disconcerted. "I . . . I . . ."

"What if your father should learn of it?" Elstree blanched, but Mr. Franklin held up a hand. "Do not fear, I do not mean to tell him. But a young man owes something to his father; he ought to keep within bounds." His earnestness brought to mind William and the troubling conspiracy in the Craven Street entryway. Had William got out of bounds? "Come, you are a good fellow. Give up all that leads you astray."

This was preaching indeed, and Tom Elstree crossed and uncrossed his legs, and puffed his cheeks, whilst his conscience seemed to wrestle with a deeply wavering will.

"*Fay ce que voudras,*" Mr. Franklin whispered into his silence. "Do you know the phrase?"

Elstree's Adam's apple leapt. "What do you say?"

"Hester Ward had a coin in her hand with those words stamped on it. They are French: 'Do whatever you please.' Do you know it?"

"I—"

But at this moment the stoop-shouldered servant shuffled in, proffering a letter on a salver. "Just come, sir. It is urgent, I am told."

Elstree snatched the letter, broke the seal. He read and read again. "I see." He looked up darkly. "Tell the bearer, 'Soon.' "

With a cool glance at the stinking effluvium upon the hearth, the servant crept away.

Elstree leapt up. "I must go. In any case, I have told you all I can, and . . . and you have told me the worst, so we are quits."

Mr. Franklin rose, too. "I am sorry to've been the one—"

"Yes, yes . . ."

Elstree hurried us to the chamber door. Glancing back I peered one last time at the room with its dark furniture, like a captain's cabin on some prosperous sloop. A very demanding captain? Elstree had opened the door, but Mr. Franklin stood a moment gazing into his face, and the young man reddened. I could see he wished to turn away, but he appeared unable under the piercing stare that seemed to know his soul. Some deep probity met him, some offer of understanding, and it wrung surprising words from him.

He passed a trembling hand over his brow. "I do not know, I do not know . . ." His mouth worked wetly. "Did *I* murder dear Hester, after a fashion?" With that he rushed from the room.

Mr. Franklin and I stared at each other—but we had no time to speak, for the manservant was back. He showed us to the front door, and in a moment we stood upon the pavement of Soho Square, rain drumming about us as if heaven wept. Our carriage waited, its broad-hatted driver hunkering on his perch like some Stoic philosopher who took all weathers equally. Dashing, we scrambled in, the hackney's springs rocking—but amongst the

73

odor of damp leather, Mr. Franklin did not give orders; instead he squinted out the window. "Did you observe the waxen seal upon the letter Elstree received, Nick?"

"No."

"It was imprinted with the letters *C.R.* Charles Ravenden, I guess—though if you doubt, glance across the square."

I did. A curtain of rain swept it, but I discerned another carriage twenty yards from ours, on the east side. It was a fine equipage, with a coat of arms on the door. Did a face peer out the window? If so it was gone abruptly, leaving only a chilling impression of white, like the memory of a ghost. My eyes found the coat of arms—an ornate C, gold on black enamel—and I sucked breath. "Chalton," said I.

"Aye," said Mr. Franklin, "Charles Ravenden, the earl himself. Does my lord observe us, too?" His bamboo thumped our hackney's roof. "To Craven Street, driver."

❧ 10 ❧

IN WHICH We Talk on Murder and a Corpse Finds a Name . . .

It was past four in the afternoon when we arrived home; the rain fell steadily. We had not eaten—neither of us had missed food, but Mrs. Stevenson, whose god was huswifery, must lay out ham, bread, and cheese belowstairs and sit to assure herself we partook of it. "You are the finest landlady in London," said Mr. Franklin as he wielded his knife.

"O, sir!" said she.

The day had darkened considerably. The storm surged. There came a flash and a rumble as we rose from the table, and I saw by Mr. Franklin's look that the matter of the lightning rod was not forgot.

How to get round the finest landlady in London?

As we mounted to the entryway, Polly dashed in from shopping. She had gone out with Nanny and despite the rain, had purchased a hat and a bag of sweets. As she set aside her wet cloak, Mr. Franklin drew her into the front parlor for the talk he had promised. I watched her figure precede him; and glancing back she sent a flash of white teeth that reminded me how she had tickled me in the selfsame room. Her nose wrinkled. Her pink lips smiled.

"Write our day from your book, Nick," adjured Mr. Franklin, and I went upstairs.

To the murmur of the storm I settled at his desk amidst his papers; I like sitting here. Would I have my own fine desk when I

75

was grown? After lighting a candle with a coal from the grate, I took my book from my pocket. I had set down much during our day's two interviews; it was an old habit, and I had learnt to do it discreetly—"Invisible Nick," Mr. Franklin sometimes called me—so that people rarely noted the jot of my pencil. I used the "short-hand" the gentleman had invented—he was always devising new ways of doing things—and, having mastered it, I had amassed more than three dozen books of sketches and observations in my two years with him.

It is from such notes that I tell this story.

Dipping ink, I set down a fuller account of our encounters, adding the details: Lord Bathurst's iron brows, Tom Elstree's twisting of the handkerchief, the face half glimpsed in the Earl of Chalton's carriage window. I added speculations, too: *Jack Scratch, Tom Elstree, and Charles Ravenden—at Oxford together?* I was pleased to be of use, for the gentleman always perused what I writ. "Four eyes are better than two, four ears hear more," said he, and I was proud when I spied details he had missed.

In truth I had conceived the idea of writing a life of Benjamin Franklin, so I took pleasure in obtaining any little anecdotes. As my pen moved, I thought on Mr. Tisdale, too: ought I to try some amusing sketch of city life, *à la* the *Idler?* Could I be "Clever Nick"?

Mr. Franklin came up at six to the tolling of a score of churchbells. I could tell by the way he sank into his chair, rubbing his knees, plucking at his brows, that one of our talks was imminent. The storm continued to murmur as shops were shuttered against the night. "Let us see what you have writ and drawn." A gust of wind shook the house as I held out my book, and reading with pursed lips, the gentleman emitted an *Mm* and two soft *Ah*s whilst I perched at the end of his bed. He met my eyes over the tops of his spectacles. "Excellent. Well observed." He rubbed his balding brow. "We are led into something deep, are we not?"

"Yes, sir."

"Very bad."

"Those murders—"

"But we shall discover truth?"

"I hope so, sir."

He waved my book. "To it, then. You have got Silas Ward and

Tom Elstree well—as far as they can be got. Indeed, either might have murdered Hester Ward, one because she was inconvenient (she spoilt his name, as if he had not already spoilt it), the other because her infidelity drove him mad. But if one of 'em did do her in, why did he do in the other?"

"If he did."

"True, we have no proof."

"Sir, I have thought—" I broke off. Droplets struck the panes like flung pebbles.

His inquiring gaze told me to speak.

"What if the second murder was done by a man who knew of the first and copied the method when he did in Hester Ward?"

"It is possible, but to what purpose?" Mr. Franklin patted my knee. "Yet we shall keep the idea in mind. Meantime there are two additional names: Jack Scratch and Charles Ravenden. Scratch wrote some scandal about 'S.W., Marquess of B——.' Silas Ward—Bathurst—surely. On the same page he railed against the bloods of the Dionysus Club, particularly against 'C.R., the most profligate' of them. Charles Ravenden."

"Sir . . . is there more to connect 'em? That night in the mews—Scratch said he was at Oxford."

"Just like Elstree and Ravenden, eh?" A quick smile. "You have a good memory, Nick. Hm. Bathurst, Elstree, Scratch, and Ravenden, then. The four are linked. What do you make of 'em?"

"Three knew Hester Ward."

"Did Jack Scratch know her as well? That would make four. But, still . . . the other murdered woman—how does she fit in? Did they know her too? Who was she? Curse it that Peter has discovered nothing. Nor Bow Street. No word from Mrs. Goodbody, either, and all we learnt from today's visits is that she was likely not of Hester Ward's circle—no peer's wayward daughter." Mr. Franklin tapped his fingers before his chin. "To this 'three,' which Jack Scratch so tantalizingly dangles before us. Scratch's real name is Pyecroft, he said. His bitterness troubles me. His words seemed to suggest that a particular man was the cause. Who, I wonder?"

"Might it be a woman, sir?"

"Women may cause men much sorrow—think of Tom Elstree. Which leads us to Silas Ward. What do you make of the marquess?"

"Mean-spirited. Self-centered."

"Undeniably so—why, he did not even know his niece's age!" Mr. Franklin stared into the night. "I think on the poor girl, Nick. Perhaps she *was* wanton—a failing winked at in men—but could she have been as bad as she is described? And if she sought love in many arms, I cannot fault her, raised as she was by that unconscionable rake. If Bathurst did not carve out her heart—or hire someone to do it—he is still to blame for much." Our candle guttered as the gentleman's features darkened. "Men of rank, Nick— there is an arrogance in many. Why, they believe they are above the laws of king and God!"

So that even murder is their right? thought I.

"To Tom Elstree," said he.

"One of the bloods who waylaid us?"

"Surely."

"Yet he did not seem to know us today."

"It was dark in St. James's Market. And he was thoroughly drunk. Six against two gave him courage that night, and he made some show of defiance today. Prompted by . . . what? What does he hide? Yet at bottom he seems decent. Not that he is not weak—but I find I pity him."

"So he did not murder Hester Ward?"

Mr. Franklin shook his head. "I do not say that. Weak men have been known to do terrible deeds, to save worse trouble."

"And he admitted he *might* have murdered her."

" 'After a fashion,' were his words. Damn him, what can he mean? Murdered her by neglect? By proxy? Could Tom Elstree bring himself to carve out the heart of a woman he loved? We know him too little."

"Sir, did you really see him gaming?"

"Ha, no! But like Jack Scratch I cast out bait, and our fish took it. Alas, cards and dice do not speak well for him, for when a man has parted with his money like a fool, he generally sends his conscience after it. Yet if he is a villain, he should learn to lie better. He stared at *Fay ce que voudras*, did you see? And he did not tell all he knew of the Dionysus Club or Charles Ravenden."

"Ravenden—" A realization struck me. "St. James's Market, Monday night—then we have met him, too?"

"The captain of the bloods."

I recalled the tall, slim figure in the black mask: his careless air, his pale jaw, his blood-red mouth. He had not been drunk, for he had swung his sword with cool skill, and a sudden fear made me shudder.

What if he had gone for Benjamin Franklin?

We sat silent a moment, whilst the storm moaned. "Tom Elstree gave but a quarter of the truth, Jack Scratch an eighth," murmured Mr. Franklin, "yet something begins to take shape. Do you see it, Nick? Is Scratch right? Does the secret of the matter lie in St. James's Square? We shall call upon Charles Ravenden soon."

William returned just past seven, when the storm was beginning to die.

Mr. Franklin beckoned his elder son into his chamber.

The young man was dressed very fine, in black breeches and a blue merino overcoat, with a canary waistcoat and a ruffled linen shirt. His boots were mud-spattered, but I could see they had been waxed 'til their tops shone like glass. He was in a jolly mood, smiling, humming, for he had been at tea at Northumberland House, the Tory stronghold. He described its peers and politicians, its judges, bishops, dames. There had been much high-flown talk. "I must marry a young woman of quality, they say! I will surely advance in rank!" Rising and falling on his heels, he beamed with the pleasure of a young man flattered by folk whom flattery costs nothing.

I could tell that Mr. Franklin was not pleased, for he mistrusted the Percys. Yet they could prove a good thing—William might profit from their patronage—so he bit his tongue and asked about Tom Elstree instead.

William flicked a finger carelessly along a chair back. "I don't believe I know the fellow."

"Charles Ravenden, then?"

"O, I know of him!" A sly wink. "Very wicked!"

"A devil?"

"So they say—and a very strange devil, at that. He paints his face, he patches. I have seen him at the theater. He loves a show, and some call him a show himself, though not to his hearing, for it is said to be unhealthy to cross the man (Francis Light, Roxbury's son, has a scar on his cheek to testify to it). Ravenden was sent down from Oxford."

"Why?"

"Immoral behavior."

"What sort?"

"Whatever you like; he's a master of sin, they say. He is also master of the 'Dionysus Club,' I believe it is called." William tapped his nose. "Diabolic revels are rumored to take place there. Secret ceremonies. The black arts. Its members have a reputation as the worst bloods in London—though I know many a fellow who would be glad to join 'em. Not all are eligible, though, for come to think of it, its members—except for Ravenden—are less than first rank. They are merchant's sons, and when they are not, when their fathers have a title, they are the second or third son, the 'Honorable,' never 'My Lord.' None will inherit. Ravenden seems to like it that way."

"Odd."

"What is this about?"

It was Mr. Franklin's turn to draw a finger carelessly along a chair back. "No great matter—you know how I like to learn about London." He smiled. "I am obliged for the information. As to the matter between *us*"—at this William's own smile fled, and he frowned at me by the bow window—"Strahan has said he will take a hand." Mr. Franklin's mood seemed to have turned sour, too. "Do you sup at home tonight? I, myself, dine out."

Thursday was Benjamin Franklin's evening with the Honest Whigs; they convened at St. Paul's Coffee House. He had often described their meetings: the wine, the punch, the pipes, the discourse, the sideboard at nine, with Welsh rabbit, apple puffs, porter, and beer. Tobacco smoke flew up in a haze, and talk grew genially disputatious. The Honest Whigs had no "secret ceremonies" or "black arts," only conversation, which Mr. Franklin loved.

I was left alone to think on our mystery—and on the mystery betwixt him and William.

I resolved neither.

Mr. Franklin brought Dr. John Fothergill home at eleven. They disposed themselves in the front parlor, legs out by the fire, drinking a brew stirred up by Mrs. Stevenson; I was allowed to join them. Fothergill wore a suit of sober gray. He was a Quaker, lean, with high cheekbones and piercing eyes. He had helped Mr. Franklin's *Experiments and Observations* to be published in England; he had writ its preface, too. He owned in Essex one of the finest botanical gardens in Europe, and his postal address was simply "Dr. Fothergill, London."

Skilled at botanical drawings, he thumbed through my sketchbook. "You observe well, Nicolas. Even the heads upon Temple Bar, I see. But what is this?" Coming upon Hester Ward's face, his eyes narrowed. "Copying from the dead?" Seeing by my expression that he had guessed aright, he glanced over my most recent notes. "So," said he to Mr. Franklin. "Off on another of your investigations, Ben?"

"I confess it."

"They have not been good for your health."

"They are good for my soul. When I do right, my soul prospers."

"Just so long as your body prospers, too. Is there danger?"

"Not yet."

"An equivocal reply."

"A true one."

Fothergill closed my book. "Dear Ben, your safety . . . our friendship . . ." He smoothed his breeches. "But you will persist. You are a hound, a woodborer. It is this business of the women with their hearts cut out, eh? I read of it in the newspapers."

"London will buzz."

"But how were you drawn into the thing?"

Mr. Franklin told him.

"The Blind Beak again."

"A remarkable man. Speaking of which, you are remarkable, too. A clever investigator, do not deny it. Tell me, could you determine if a dead woman were with child?"

"An autopsy could. Why?"

"Motive for murder. I do not say it is a motive in this case—likely not. But I find women cut down in the streets appalling. Damn it! A proper policing system should prevent such crimes—make 'em harder to commit, at any rate. The constables and the courts ought to have a doctor at hand, to say if a man has been poi-soned, to say if—"

"Medicine in the service of law?"

"Perhaps I may write on it someday."

"Pray, wait 'til your Penns are vanquished."

Mr. Franklin smiled. "I shall."

Fothergill drew in his legs. His cool eyes glinted. "Meantime, take care. Better draw flowers, a Michaelmas daisy if any are left, Nicolas, rather than dead women's faces." He departed shortly, Mr. Franklin and I stepping out upon the stoop to see him off. Above the rooftops the moon was a half-circle of gold. Jostling clouds crowded it, and the city stirred in the night. As our guest vanished to seek a hackney, a chair carried by two strong bearers passed him coming down Craven Street.

It stopped before our door, and a woman got out: Mrs. Comfort Goodbody's maid.

"Betsy—" Mr. Franklin stepped upon the cobbles to greet her.

She met him in an earnest rush. "The mistress sent me with this, sir." She held out a paper. "She wished you to have it at once. We have discovered who she was—the girl with the mulberry birthmark."

❧ 11 ❧

IN WHICH We Are Summoned by an Earl and Call
on a Woman of the Game . . .

Friday I woke to a wan sun beating back the last of the rain. I stared out over the city: Hungerford Market, Villiers Street, the Workbuilding Stairs, Southwerk across the broad swath of the Thames. The river was scattered with golden coins of light, whilst a lone lighter pulled toward Westminster like an ant on a sheet of glass. I tugged on my clothes. The other woman, the first murdered—we knew who she was.

Would that lead to answers to our mystery?

Yet there was more, for at midmorning another note arrived, this on fine linen paper with an imprint in its red wax seal that we had seen before: *C.R.*

Charles Ravenden, the sixth Earl of Chalton.

Nanny brought it in her shy way, and Mr. Franklin stood by his bow window frowning over it whilst a workman's hammer sent a rat-tat up from the street. When he looked round it was with an expression of deep mistrust. "Ravenden has heard of my struggle with the Penns, he says. He asks me to call on him in St. James's Square at four. He wishes to help me in my cause." He held out the paper. "Find a place for this, Nick."

I took it. "In the box marked 'devil,' sir?"

A wry smile. "Is there such a box? If so, many a letter must fly into it. But what does Chalton truly have in mind? Surely not the Penns." Mr. Franklin rubbed his jaw. "So, he makes the first move?" He plumped down at his desk. "You must accompany

83

me, Nick, for I must know what you, too, make of our 'devil'—speaking of which, have you copied the Dionysus Club list that Tom Elstree writ?"

"Just finishing, sir." Penning the last of the names, I noted that there was indeed none better than an "Honorable," as William had said. All men of lesser rank than the earl, then. Did that sig‑nify?

At eleven, his morning's work done—his ruminations, his read‑ing, his correspondence—Mr. Franklin summoned Peter. He gave him my copy of the club list, to deliver to Bow Street. "Fielding may wish to look into these men." He added a report on our progress. "Tell the magistrate I pray his riot was quelled without bloodshed, there's a good fellow." He sent Peter on his way.

We set out in the opposite direction, to a whorehouse in the Haymarket.

"Providence has not given carriages to ev'rybody, but it has given ev'ryone a pair of legs," pronounced Mr. Franklin, as his muscled calves in their white stockings carried him over ditch and dung alike; he was nimble for fifty-three. The sun continued to strug‑gle against the November bluster as we passed the equestrian statue of Charles I on its huge stone plinth in Charing Cross. A poor, befouled miscreant hung in the pillory there, whilst a band of urchins hurled apple cores at him. How they jeered at his mis‑ery! Passersby ignored them, but Mr. Franklin shook his bam‑boo—"Away, you boys!"—and they scattered like rats.

Mrs. Goodbody's message had informed us that word had gone out amongst her "great army of women," as she called it, from chars to costers to the saintly ladies of St. Martin's and St. Anne's, who did charity work amongst the poor: *Who was the young victim with the mulberry birthmark behind her left ear?* I imagined a great sea of whispers rolling across London, a tide of murmurs, an ocean of news. Word had come ashore at last, at suppertime, from a whoremistress who kept a dozen girls at the sign of the Golden Guinea in the Haymarket.

"Apply to her in my name," Mrs. Goodbody's note had said. "She will tell you what she can."

Mr. Franklin had surprised me by pulling from behind Willem

Van Gravesande's *Mathematical Elements of Natural Philosophy* a copy of *The New Atlantis*. This was London's infamous guide to brothels, but he made no apology as he consulted the volume. It gave the location of each temple of love, the name of its lady abbess, and the services a gentleman might enjoy in its cells, from beating to sodomy. "The Golden Guinea." He tapped the entry. "Mother Cockburn is its mistress. Her establishment caters to the usual tastes. One of the finer, I see, at two guineas a tumble."

As we strode west over the greasy cobbles, I could not help reflecting on the two shillings I paid Birdy Prinsop for a quarter-hour's pleasure in her tiny crib off Covent Garden. Two guineas—what delights might that lordly sum buy?

We turned into Cockspur Street. Only one block west lay St. James's Market, where we had been set upon by bloods. St. James's Square was but one short street from that, and the mews where Hester Ward had been found not far beyond. St. James's churchyard, which had discovered the other dead woman, lay nearby, too.

Let not another body be discovered horribly mutilated hereabouts!

We pushed past the throng in the Haymarket: butchers carrying legs of mutton over their shoulders, a pudding vendor, a knife-grinder spitting sparks. The Golden Guinea stood at the top, near Coventry Street. It appeared from its hanging sign and white plastered front to be merely a chop house and tavern—and it was, on the ground floor, for as we entered, the smells of roasted meat and ale met our nostrils. But the serving wenches were all provocatively dressed, and the rollicking gents who sat about felt of them freely. Sallies were made, terms agreed upon, and I watched a buxom jade lead her "beau" to a set of narrow stairs, where he pinched her as they mounted out of sight.

We approached a slim dark girl. A mulatto? (Many London gents loved the brown-skinned beauties.) Mr. Franklin asked for Mother Cockburn, and the wench directed us to a door in a narrow corridor at the rear of the taproom.

Approaching, we knocked.

A throaty voice called, "Come," and we stepped into a surprising chamber.

This was worlds from John Fielding's austere office, for we

seemed to be in the drawing room of some titled dame. Figured carpets lay on the floor, fine French paper lined the walls, and elegant, spindle-legged furniture sat about. Against the far wall a bust of a Roman gazed incongruously upon a marble-topped writing desk, where a woman sat with a quill pen. She wore costly blue satin edged with lace for which any thief would have risked a strangling at Tyburn. She wore a dainty lace cap, too—though that was all of daintiness about her, for she was prodigiously fat, with pink globes of cheeks and three pendulous chins. Stays creaking, she turned to fix upon us a gaze as old as time—the hawker measuring her gull—and all her elegant surroundings were belied by her coarse rough voice: "What're ye after, gentlemen? Is't cunny ye seek? None in the taproom will do, eh? Shall Mother Cockburn show ye the wares upstairs?" Puffing, she heaved her bulk from her chair. "Ah, me! Come, then, we'll find what ye desire."

"We do not seek the usual wares," replied Mr. Franklin.

The woman's eyes were like an old sow's. "What?" She chortled a laugh that made her belly shake. "Ye cannot want the mother!" An admonishing finger. "Nay, ye cannot have her, for though she is mistress of the game, she does not play it."

"I am Benjamin Franklin."

"Who?"

"Mrs. Comfort Goodbody sent me."

A long look from the fat-englobed eyes—"Ah . . ."—and the woman sank slowly back into her chair. " 'Tis about poor Tuesday Marrowbone, then."

"That was her name?"

"She with the mulberry mark. The dead 'un."

"She was a foundling, then."

"How d'ye know?"

"They call the poor abandoned creatures after the day they were discovered. And the place. She must, then, have been found on Tuesday, in the parish of Marylebone."

"Sad, a'nt it?" Mother Cockburn flung down her pen. "But she found a home here. Very cosy. Sit ye, sirs." Two chairs faced her desk, and we took them. Mr. Franklin presented me. "Oho!" The whoremistress took me in as if I were a piece of veal for supper. *I must draw her*, thought I, slipping my sketching book and pencil from my pocket. Her squinting eyes saw Mr. Franklin's glance at the thick leather-bound ledger in which she had been scratching numbers. "Aye, I keeps the accounts myself. I do not trust no one else."

"And do your accounts say you prosper?"

"Look about you, sir."

"Very fine." A woman's muffled laugh came from the floor above. "Tuesday Marrowbone was murdered, you know."

"Alas, poor chick!" Mother Cockburn rolled her eyes. "The Goodbody's maid told me. One o' them awful murders with the heart cut out. Who would want to do such a thing?"

"That is what Justice Fielding seeks to know."

Mother Cockburn's jolly eyes congealed. "Here, now, the Bow Street magistrate?"

"He."

A curtain of displeasure fell over her. "I were not told you come from Fielding."

"I come in his name. I have no interest in anything other than Tuesday Marrowbone, however. I shall not report your house, I mean. I seek only to prevent other poor creatures from a like fate. And to find who murdered your girl. You must help in that."

Mother Cockburn snorted. Mr. Franklin had not mentioned John Fielding by chance, she knew, and she had not risen to mistress of so prosperous a house without knowing which way the wind blew. "I did not say I would not help you, sir." She formed a treacly smile.

"Tell of the dead girl, then."

As she spoke, I sketched Mother Cockburn's fat, beringed fingers and her sharp little nose.

"I know little of the poor girl's hist'ry," she began, "but, then, they are all much alike." Tuesday Marrowbone had been procured for the Golden Guinea when she was sixteen. "She'd been on the game at Ludgate Hill, asellin' herself on a street corner. But she were a pretty thing—I saw her more'n once—so I made her a offer one day, and she jumped at it. I took her in: a room and a warm bed and a better sort o' custom. I never regretted it. She were good with th' gents, and some of 'em liked that mark on her, the mulberry. Gents is funny."

"Any particular gent? One who asked for her often?"

The woman smoothed her voluminous lap. "None in partic'lar."

"How long was she with you?"

"Two year. Thereabouts."

Mr. Franklin rubbed the head of his stick. "Dead at eighteen, then . . ." There came another sound from above, a man's cry, followed by a steady creaking, like a ship's yard in a wind. "She was found some way from here, in a churchyard," Mr. Franklin pursued. "You must keep a close eye on your girls. Why was she gone from your house?"

"A twang took her."

"A procurer?"

A jiggling nod. "He got girls from me. For clients of his own. It is no strange thing," the huge woman added quickly. "Many houses lets twangs take girls."

"So he collected Tuesday Marrowbone?"

"More'n once."

"How often?"

"Five or six times. Since half a year ago."

"Who did he want her for?"

"I never knew. He were close-mouthed, though there is nothing odd in that (gents does not always want theirselves known). But I can tell you the twang's name—if you will not tell 'im you got it of me: Enderby. 'Long John Enderby,' they calls 'im, found at the Blue Dog, in Longacre. But I warn ye: he's a bad 'un. He hit one of my girls once, broke 'er jaw. Still, whoever he works for pays well."

"This Enderby came for her himself?"

"Did."

"And delivered her to his client?"

"So he said."

"How long was she gone each time?"

"Now that *were* odd. Two nights."

Mr. Franklin frowned. "It is not customary to keep a girl two nights?"

"Ha, 'tis customary to use 'em and be done! That's the way o' the game."

"And she herself never said where she had been? With whom?"

"I asked—I takes an interest in my girls—but she hung back and would not talk. She seemed afraid, as if she'd been warned not t'spill her craw. Well, I did not press her. After all, she'd done her work—that was what was wanted."

"Other than seeming afraid, how was she when she returned?"

"Why"—Mother Cockburn looked shamed now—"she *may*'ve been beat a little. A bruise or two. Some marks."

"What sort of marks?"

"As if she'd been whipped. Some men likes t'be beat, and some likes to beat, if you know wot I mean. 'Tis part o' the game, too. But it were not dire. Nothin' Dr. Arnot's salve could not fix."

Mr. Franklin looked grim, whilst beyond the window the light abruptly dimmed, as if clouds had strangled the sun. "So when the poor girl left here for the last time, she went with this twang?"

"She did—but never tell 'im I told ye so."

"And you did not report her missing?"

A guffaw. "Who should I tell? The constable? He would laugh, then clap me in gaol for runnin' a bawdy house!"

Mr. Franklin shook his head. "A hackney driver can report a stolen horse, but when a girl goes astray we must say nothing. Surely you asked this Enderby why Tuesday Marrowbone was not returned?"

"I did. But he give me one o' his looks. 'None o' my business—nor yours,' says he. I did not want my jaw broke, too."

The woman's cloying perfume began to make my head swim. What had happened here? A net had caught Tuesday Marrowbone, and Mother Cockburn feared it would catch her if she did not watch out. It might catch us, too, and I recalled what Mr. Franklin had said of men of rank: "Too many think themselves above the law." Had one bought a woman so he could cut out her heart?

Mr. Franklin gazed at the woman in the costly garb that could not disguise her coarse origins. "Is there any more that you can tell?"

"Seek Long John, sir. That is wot you must do."

"Yet one last question. What was Tuesday Marrowbone *like*?"

I understood, for I, too, wished to put a face on the destroyed young woman for whom we sought justice.

Mother Cockburn thought. "O, she were a little thing. But shapely, comely. Bright eyes. Hair like flax—after I'd cleaned her up. She sang little songs. She liked rings and things, too. Truth t'tell, she were born to be a whore. She could please th' men, I mean. Not all that's in the game is born to it, some just do wot they must, but Tuesday"—a low laugh—"how she could lead the gents a dance!"

"Like Hester Ward," murmured Mr. Franklin.

"Who, sir?"

"No matter. Have you found another to replace your lost girl?"

"O, there is always another."

"More's the pity." Windowlight reflected from the gentleman's small round eyeglasses. "Come, Nick." We stood, whilst the woman creaked to her feet, too. She put a hand on Mr. Franklin's arm. "But do not go without refreshment. Joy awaits ye, gen'lemen. Pleasure yerselves b'fore ye depart?" She gestured toward the upper floor, and her eyes gleamed. "Mother Cockburn offers the best wares in London."

"Nay, we must find a murderer, ma'am."

"As ye will."

We turned. *We must find a reason, too*, thought I, as we walked to the door, *some sense*. I felt lost. What did a young whore with a mulberry birthmark have to do with a marquess's niece? What had entwined them in murder?

Mr. Franklin opened the door—but as he did so, a young woman leapt back as if she had been listening, and we found ourselves staring into a thin, startled face. She was slender, with skin so pale it was almost blue. A timid air, reddish locks, nervous hands. She made to creep away, but Mother Cockburn spied her. "Nelly, what . . . ?" Her little eyes squinched. "Upstairs, child!" The girl scurried off, but not without a glance back at Mr. Franklin. Fearful? Hopeful?

"By the by, is the Marquess of Bathurst amongst your clients?" Mr. Franklin asked the whoremistress.

Mother Cockburn smiled her treacly smile. "Giving the name of a gent is against the etiquette of the trade."

"John Fielding does not give a hang for etiquette. Shall he ask you himself?"

"Very well, my lord Bathurst has pleasured himself here."

"Ever with Tuesday Marrowbone?"

"With many another, too."

"So he took no special interest in her?"

"No."

"Does Tom Elstree also come here?"

"I do not know the name—though a man does not always say who he is."

"What of Charles Ravenden? Do you know his name?"

"O, I knows the Earl of Chalton. He is wicked, they say, but he had never blessed Mother Cockburn with his custom. He likes another sort of house, I am told."

"That is all, then. I thank you."

Mother Cockburn tilted her round, pink face. "And yet—"

"What?"

"My girls come to me with little. I clothe 'em, and the gents buy 'em trinkets, if they like. I turned out Tuesday's room when she did not come back—well, it is my right. There was things: rings, a brooch, ribbons, lace, odds and ends she got as favors—she could please men well, as I told ye—but there was something more. I have kept it with the rest. It's not worth a groat, so you may have it if you wish." Going to a cabinet, she withdrew a japanned box, from which she took a small, dully shining object. She dropped it into Mr. Franklin's palm. "There, sir. Make of it what you will."

Together we gazed at a six-sided medallion with the familiar adjuration in French: *Fay ce que voudras.*

❧ 12 ❧

IN WHICH We Meet a Painted Man . . .

A moment later we stood under the sign of the Golden Guinea in the Haymarket. The sky was pewter gray. Housemaids carried buckets to a nearby pump, and a woman shook powder from a wig at an upper window. Mr. Franklin rubbed his jaw. "Both murders were done by the same man, then? Does the French coin prove it?"

"Indeed, sir—" But my throat closed on my words, for I suddenly spied Jack Scratch. The thin, cloaked man stood only a dozen paces away, peering from a stonecutter's doorway, and though he scurried off amongst drays and chairs, he made no secret of his presence for he glanced back. *We meet once more,* said his mocking stare, and I almost expected him to doff his hat. A coach blocked him from view, and when it had passed he was gone as if London had swallowed him.

I turned to Mr. Franklin. "Did you see—?"

"I saw. But was he in Mother Cockburn's? Did he lurk outside her door? Did he hear what passed—or speak to one who did?"

I had no answer, yet as we moved on I began to wonder if we were pawns of the strange, scribbling fellow. He had said to seek answers in St. James's Square, and the very next day we had done so. And in four hours we would call in that same square again, upon a man Scratch harried in print.

What did it mean?

We stopped in the King's Head, in Pall Mall. Over dishes of coffee we perused the newspapers. Amongst gossip, party squabbles, word of the latest negotiations with France, we found more stories of the bloods' pranks: they had cudgeled a silversmith's apprentice in Chandos Street, they had scattered a chandler's wares in Wharf Lane, they had fired pistols at 1:00 A.M. outside the deanery of St. Paul's. "And the law truly seems unable to touch 'em." Mr. Franklin sighed. Opening the *Courant,* he discovered more of Jack Scratch's venom. "He rails against C.R. yet again: 'the most villainous rake in London.'" He slapped the paper. "Does he hold some grudge?"

Was he at Oxford with the earl? thought I.

Out into London again. Mr. Franklin was to dine this afternoon with his old friend James Ralph, with whom he had sailed to England thirty years ago, so we parted where St. Martin's Lane crosses the Strand. Turning our mystery over in my mind, I hurried to Mr. Tisdale's to set my portion of types, pushing against toffs and swells, fishwives, beggars, soldiers, porters, and the ubiquitous dung-boys with their brooms, but I hardly saw them for thinking on Mother Cockburn, Tuesday Marrowbone, Long John Enderby. Where did our trail lead?

As I strolled back toward Westminster an hour later, my mind turned to baser matters. It pictured the girls I had seen at Mother Cockburn's: their low-cut dresses, their provocative smiles, their laughter whose silver sound made me shiver. Only a bit of coin stood between a fellow and the fulfillment of his wishes at the Golden Guinea, and as Covent Garden drew near, I felt the tug of desire.

In the shadow of the Savoy, jostled by foot traffic, I struggled with lust, and lost.

Breathless, I took but five minutes to reach the narrow lane where Birdy Prinsop kept her watch. I longed to feel her breasts in my hands, smell her, taste her. But she was not there, and a violent kicking at a horse-post did nothing to deliver her. Was she upstairs with some gent? Thwarted, I wheeled away, seeking comfort in reason. Did I not still have my pay, which had not been lost in some low fashion? The bard on his tall board outside the Shakespeare Tavern seemed to agree: *An expense of spirit in a waste of shame*, he chid, but I was unconsoled. I had wanted Birdy Prinsop. I had longed to expend myself upon her, shame or no shame, and I cursed the itch that had plagued me since I was twelve. A man never lost it, I heard—I was sentenced for life.

I was calmer by the time I reached Craven Street. In Mrs. Stevenson's kitchen, I gnawed a leg of cold bird, and when Mr. Franklin returned at half past the hour I set out with him.

We arrived in St. James's Square promptly at four. Horses' hooves clopped. Somewhere a shrill whistle blew, and a man with a cage of canaries pranced by. Standing with the little park at our backs, I peered up at the Earl of Chalton's fine brick house, but though its white shutters were open, its windows were blank eyes that gave nothing away.

Mr. Franklin rapped the brass knocker. A servant in a white powdered wig opened. He was the third servant of our pursuit. The first two had been old, but this one was young, no more than twenty; his livery fit his slim frame snugly. His eyes were a drained pale blue, as if the soul behind them had been leached away; they took us in with a cynical air. His face was soft, callow, unformed, and he wore a small black dot by the corner of his mouth. I had never seen a servant patch before—patches were the affectations of fops (what master would let his servant wear one?)—and it gave him a peculiar air, as if he were a player in some strange artifice.

"The master will meet you in the library, sirs," said he with languid punctilio. "This way."

Our feet whispered on carpet that seemed designed to muffle secrets, as we mounted a curving stair to a spacious chamber overlooking the square, from which I could see the Marquess of Bathurst's house across the way in sullen afternoon light. The walls were lined with books. When I turned, the manservant had withdrawn.

Mr. Franklin eyed the long shelves. "I should like me a library like this, someday." Strolling, he examined the bindings. The smell of paper and leather, the fine morocco and calf; I should like a library, too. Could a man so cultivated as the Earl of Chalton be as wicked as London said?

94

He could be singular at any rate, for though we found Dr. Johnson's dictionary, Rowe's Shakespeare, the *Biographia Britannica* and Plutarch's *Lives*, there were books of a more arcane sort: *De Occulta Philosophia, Paleographia Sacra, A Theory of the Black Arts.* Mr. Franklin pulled out the *Conjectura Cabalistica* to peruse it. "Dr. Ardwell opines here that the Dionysus of the poets is Jehovah himself. He makes much of the Cabal, a system of hidden wisdom. (If it is hidden, can it be wise? If it is hidden, how does he write of it?) Listen to this: 'The sixth emanation represents the divine force that compels life to continue.' What mumbo jumbo!"

"Six emanations, the six-sided coin?" proposed I.

Mr. Franklin met my eyes. "And six bloods in the night? Do we come near something?" Replacing the book, he took out another with a less refined subject: *The Nun in Her Smock.* He glanced at it but a moment before handing it to me. The title page announced: "The Amours herein are not paralleled for their Agreeable Entertainment in any Romance. Price: two shillings." But it was the engraving accompanying this promise that drew my attention: a bishop, naked save for his miter, performing unbishoplike acts upon two nuns before an altar. My eyes started up to find Mr. Franklin gazing coolly over the tops of his small round spectacles. "My lord is plainly a fellow of varied interests." He gestured to a whole collection of such works: *Fanny Hill, The Maid Debauched, Men amongst Boys.* "But what of Rabelais?" He scanned the shelves. "Aha! *Gargantua and Pantagruel.*" Lifting the heavy, gold-embossed volume, he turned it in his hands. "Mm." He gave it me. "Do you note anything, Nick?"

"It is heavy. Fine bound." I peered inside. "Printed in Paris."

"The edges of the pages."

I examined them. "Some are smudged. They have, then, been read more than others?"

Taking the book, he opened to the smudged section. He found there a red leather bookmark stamped with the Chalton coat of arms. "See." He pointed to a line on the page.

I guessed what it would say before I read it: *Fay ce que voudras.*

"Do you like my library, sir?" came a commanding voice.

I started whilst Mr. Franklin deftly slipped the Rabelais back in place. We turned. By the door stood the man of Monday night, the captain of the drunken bloods. He was not masked as he had been then, but I was certain it was he.

He wore no sword, yet swordflash seemed to glint in the air.

"I admire it exceedingly, my lord," replied Benjamin Franklin with a deferent nod.

The man strode toward us. "I am pleased that so notable a gentleman does. I have your work, too." He pulled a pamphlet from a shelf. *"Experiments and Observations on Electricity Made at Philadelphia in America*, by Benjamin Franklin. See?"

Mr. Franklin bowed. "I am flattered. Are you, too, a student of Nature?"

The earl laughed. "I am a philosopher of a different stripe." He came nearer, into the light cast by one of the tall windows. He was perhaps thirty, with the grace of a cat. He had a cat's wariness, too, as if he liked to know just where he placed his elegantly attired feet, and I thought on William's description of him—how he loved the theater. He wore flamboyant clothes: a scarlet coat over a corded-silk waistcoat embroidered with little pink flowers, claret-colored breeches, clocked white stockings, pointed high-heeled shoes, lace at wrists and throat. A silken handkerchief flowed from the end of one fine sleeve. He did not wear a wig, and his hair, long and strangely black, was not tied back after the fashion but flowed in a thick, rich billow about his shoulders. What sort of fabrication was he? I thought of mummers in masques. His most startling feature was his face, which he had painted dead-white. His eyes were oil-black smudges in this pallor, and his mouth was rouged to a lewd bow. Like his servant he wore a patch, though his perched at the corner of one eyebrow, giving him a quizzical look. His nose was large, his jaw abrupt.

"I present myself," said he in his peremptory way. "Charles Ravenden."

"Benjamin Franklin, at your service, my lord."

Ravenden's eyes found me. "But who is this pretty boy?"

I flushed with ill-ease.

"Nicolas Handy," replied Mr. Franklin. "My indispensable helper. I hope you do not mind my bringing him. He is useful. Discreet, too. I assure you that though he hears all, he tells nothing."

Ravenden glided near, and I smelt his clove-scented breath. His bizarre, whitened face floated before me like a ghost's. He poked my shoulder. "A boy who tells nothing? Just what I like." He made a snatch at my head. I felt his hand upon my ear, tick-ling—one of his fingers actually poked inside—and when the hand withdrew it held an enameled snuffbox. "Now that I have removed this, you will hear even better." Smiling, he tossed the box onto a table.

Mr. Franklin applauded. "Bravo, my lord."

Ravenden wheeled away. "To business. Come. Sit." We took places upon a richly embroidered sofa whilst he perched on a bro-caded chair. Pulling the flowing silk from his sleeve, he dabbed at the corners of his mouth. "Thomas and Richard Penn—pah! I met 'em once. Impossible boors! You are come to persuade 'em they must pay taxes on their proprietary lands in Pennsylvania."

"You are well informed, my lord."

"London is informed about *me*—or thinks it is—so I inform myself of it."

"Very wise, my lord. Yet, I am hardly of London. I come from America, seeking redress. Ministers shun me, and as for the Board of Trade, I am but one more flea upon its back. In short, I am no one; so, I do not see why you say you wish to help me."

Ravenden twisted a ring on one of his fingers. "I shall tell you, sir: because you are despised. Do not think that because Sir This or Lord That refuses to see you, they do not know who you are or what you aim for. People in the best circles discuss you, like a bad port or a stinking cheese. The 'Devil Dogood,' you are called, and, 'Franklin the Fart.' You are an upstart, they say, and so is America for presuming to question any noble privilege."

Mr. Franklin bowed his head. "I know all this. Thus I am all the more bewildered. You side with my detractors, you say?"

"They are prating fools, and I long to tweak 'em!"

"Because they prate of you, too?"

Ravenden's rouged lips broadened. "You understand well." He tapped Mr. Franklin's knee. "O, we are of a kind!" He flung him-self back. "How dare they prate against *me*, who live openly the life they hide. I would do much to see 'em squirm."

"You desire to help me discomfit 'em, then?" Mr. Franklin

rubbed the legs of his plain brown breeches. "I do not wish to seem overscrupulous, my lord, but I would rather you aided my cause because you believed in it."

"That *is* overscrupulous."

A small smile. "But since Pennsylvania cannot afford scruples, I give you leave to help how you can."

Ravenden rocked with laughter. "Ha, excellent! I admire a fellow who sees his interests. I know just where to begin, too: with Rupert Anstey, the puffed-up toad! He looks down his nose at me, but he will vote on your side."

"He has long opposed me. How will you persuade him?"

"I will tell you: I am privy to certain acts the creature would not have known." Ravenden crossed his well-gartered legs. "A word in his ear will suffice."

"The Scots call it blackmail."

"Damn the Scots; it is tit for tat."

"And shall I thank you in Pennsylvania's name?"

"Thank me in the name of routing all the pompous asses in London." Ravenden pursed his lips. The business of the meeting seemed done, but neither gentleman moved, as if some other business must come. Ravenden's gaze examined Benjamin Franklin. How cool my lord was, how ironical, leaning back flicking his pale, thin fingers, like some Roman emperor debating the fate of a slave. I slipped my book from my pocket, wanting to draw the man, to capture his icy confidence. But I was uneasy as his look strayed to me. *How do you really serve your master?* it seemed to ask. The sing-song of a street vendor bubbled up from the street as I glanced at Mr. Franklin. His plain, round face was calm, apparently content to be observed.

"You know a great deal of me, my lord," said he, "but I should like to learn more of you. If't please, will you tell your family's history?"

"Better, I shall show it you." Rising, Ravenden strode to an elegant reading stand, where he opened a volume of the Peerage. Joining him, we read in flowing script how the family had first settled near York in Elizabeth's reign, making its fortune in wool. It had earned its title in 1622 from King James for military services; to accompany the honor the Chaltons had been granted an estate of land. "It is near Richmond, on the west reach of the Thames," my lord told us. "The house is a pile—it is a former monastery—so I am abuilding a temple to please the eye."

"A temple?"

"To Dionysus."

"Dionysus, my lord?"

"Temples are the fashion, do you not know? I dedicate mine to the greatest of the old Greek gods. As to myself, I came to my title at twenty-six, when my father died. There being no other issue— none who survived, that is (I had two stillborn brothers)—the name was mine. My mother lived a few years longer."

"You went to school—?"

"At Eton, with boys as pretty as yours. Nearly all were the sons of title, but the masters beat us nonetheless. Some liked to have their rosy buttocks smacked, and we had secret flogging parties, where we played the masters and beat the smaller boys." He told this blithely. "Then Oxford."

"What did you pursue there, my lord?"

"Vice. O, we all studied vice, but I was 'caught with the book,' as they say, and away with me, sent down in my last year, so I never took my degree. Father railed. Then he packed me off on the Grand Tour, as far as Turkey, where I lay about in the hum-mums and saw the antiquities. (There is a splendid temple of Dionysus there.) When I got back, father was dead of an apoplexy and I was earl."

"In America we have no earls."

"Ha, you must get yourself some. But, I forget, you are a republican. Nonetheless, I like being one; I like doing what I please—save for the expense. I counted upon three thousand a year, but when the books were toted after father died, he proved to've been a wastrel, so I must now scrimp." His library did not look like scrimping, nor did his clothes. He winked at Mr. Franklin. "I should love one of His Majesty's royal preferments— Lord of the Something, with little work and a tidy sum to buy what I need, eh? I lobby for it now."

"And what should you buy?"

"Pleasure." Ravenden led us back to our seats, still observing with his ironic smile. "Does your scrupulous soul reproach me?

Tut, do not prove a hypocrite like the rest—you like pleasure, I know that you do." His black eyes gleamed. "With your 'friend' in Wild Street, eh?"

A tightening of Mr. Franklin's jaw told me he did not like Mrs. Goodbody to be known. "Do you spy upon me, sir?" But he mustered an answering smile. "No matter. I confess, I like pleasure as well as the next man."

"Capital! And *all* men—and women—like it exceedingly, eh? But do not think I care only for the pleasures of the flesh. I love music, plays, dancing. I am a great patron of art." He pointed to a painting across the room. "That, for example."

We turned. The picture hung in an alcove, so I had not noted it before. It was about three feet by five, framed in gold, showing a young man with only the flimsiest of cloths about his loins rising into a bronze-colored sky. There was blood about his body, marks, wounds, as if he had been bit, scratched, flayed, and I thought of the marks on Hester Ward's body, those Mrs. Cockburn had said were on Tuesday Marrowbone, too.

"A Christ?" asked Mr. Franklin.

"Am I some Papist? I banish Christ from my house! Nay, it is Dionysus, the beautiful god, reborn after the death of the year. Is he not splendid? See the grape vines? And the Maenads, the wild women, who have just tried to tear him apart?" A band of frenzied female figures writhed at the bottom of the picture, bloody-fingered. They unsettled me, but not as much as the god's face, for its expression, half agony, half joy, seemed to say pain pleased him. The work was well executed, but the effect was unwholesome, and I glanced at Mr. Franklin, who sat very still.

Ravenden's eyes glowed. "It is a Reni."

"Very fine."

"I bought it in Rome. I am having my own portrait done to match it: *The Earl of Chalton as Dionysus.*"

"You are fond of Dionysus, then?"

"The god of gods!" Ravenden leant forward. "Tell me, what do you do in London, sir—other than seek taxes of the Penns?"

"I gather with friends."

An impatient flick of fingers. "Your Honest Whigs. The Royal Society. But, come, I mean the Blind Beak. The Bow Street justice. Do not deny you visit him."

"I do not deny it, my lord."

"But *why* do you call? That is what I should like to know. Is it about the murdered women, those with their hearts cut out?"

"It is a subject we have talked on, my lord."

"Only talked?"

"I have agreed to help the justice in discovering who murdered 'em, then."

"Why?"

"Because he asks me. I have helped him sev'ral times in the past, and he asks again."

"So you begin to make a name as a solver of crimes, do you? And how do you progress in the latest?"

"May I inquire, first, why my lord takes an interest?"

"Because I *like* murder, sir! I am fascinated by death. You are drawn to it, too, confess." Ravenden's mouth puckered. "Is there not something *delicious* about death?"

Mr. Franklin poked his spectacles higher on his brow. "I am 'drawn' to death only to bring its vile perpetrators to justice, my lord. Or to prevent more murder. But I assure you I have no interest in it because it is 'delicious.' " He gazed into the white-painted face. "But . . . you are a connoisseur of death, you say?"

Ravenden shrugged. "I merely mean I like death as well as London does, and she likes it exceedingly. It is her meat and drink. She reads about it, she talks about it. She shivers and shakes over it in the safety of the coffeehouse before she crawls home to bed. We all love death in just the same way, and you lie if you say we do not."

"I do not deny that the mob is titillated by the subject, though I am not pleased that it is. But how do you know I visit John Fielding?"

"I learn of men in whom I take an interest."

"You take an interest in me? I am flattered, my lord. I take an interest in you, too, so may I ask . . . did you call upon Tom Elstree yesterday?"

"I did. I saw you come out in the rain. 'What does Franklin here?' I asked myself."

"That is no secret. I inquired of the young man. He told me you were at Oxford together."

"He spoke true."

"He was sent down also?"

"Poor fool."

"For the same 'studies'?"

"We were rotten apples in a barrel. We left by the selfsame coach."

"Were others sent down at the same time? A man named Pyecroft, for example? Who now calls himself Jack Scratch?"

"The gadfly who harries me in print? He is a creature, sir, nothing, and I do not know him."

"Not at Oxford, then?"

"No."

"What of Silas Ward?"

"Another toad! I know him only to shun him; we cut one another dead."

"Because of his niece?"

"Ha, *I* did not debauch the wanton Hester."

"She is one of the women whose hearts were cut out."

Ravenden peered. "Now I see why you called upon Tom Elstree. He loved her, she would not have him, so he killed her, is that it?"

"I do not say—"

"What a waste his passion was! Women are good for but one thing, and if they give it to a regiment of men, it is good economy, I say!"

The words welled from some deep place, full of scorn, but as my pencil sought to draw more than Ravenden's shell, it could find nothing in that place.

"Forgive me, my lord," said Mr. Franklin, "but if you had a sister would you say the same? Would you say it of your mother?"

"My mother was a whore!" Ravenden burst out. He brayed a contemptuous laugh. "O, I *have* offended your scrupulosity, but I do not give a fig. My dear mama spread her legs for lords and footmen alike. She groveled with my father's manservant. I had the habit of hiding amongst her clothes, in her silks and satins, and I watched 'em secretly half a dozen times in her chamber. She let Silas Ward at her too, if you must know—I saw that as well—so if I had a sister, I would expect no better of her." His whitepainted face lifted triumphantly, as if he had proved his case

102

against women, and I clutched at the silhouette of my mother in the locket on its chain round my neck.

"I am very sorry to hear it, sir—" said Mr. Franklin.

"She did as she pleased, and so do I." Ravenden licked his red lips. "To Elstree and your investigations. Did he kill the girl?"

"I called upon him only to inform him of her unfortunate death and to ask if he might help us find who did murder her. He was distraught at my news. All he said was that Hester Ward sometimes came to your house, to meetings of your Dionysus Club."

"Many women have attended our revels."

"Women of quality, my lord?"

"Especially they."

"But women of the game, as well?"

"Some."

"Tuesday Marrowbone?"

"Who is she?"

"The first victim with her heart cut out. She had a mulberry birthmark upon her neck. Was such a girl ever here, my lord?"

"Ha, the next thing, you will be saying *I* murdered the sluts. I know no girl with a mulberry mark." Ravenden leered. "But what a mystery for you: a marquess's niece and a doxy." His smile grew. "Are you all at sea?"

"I am puzzled. You knew Hester Ward. Can you tell me about her?"

"She did as she pleased."

"Her uncle called her wild."

"I should call her free."

"Do you know anyone with reason to murder her?"

"No one who did not get what he wanted of her, for she was any man's for the asking."

Mr. Franklin stared. "Forgive me, my lord . . . but you do not appear sad that a woman you knew is dead."

"I believe in resurrection, sir—in Dionysus' name."

"So she will live again? Remarkable! I should very much like to hear of your Dionysus Club."

"Our sacred society. A band of merry fellows who gather to drink toasts."

"To the devil?"

"Tut, you have been hearkening to gossip. To devil*ry*, sir. To harmless fun."

"Gossip says you topple grandfathers in the street, slit noses, bring the sweat upon men."

A shrug. "It is harmless to us."

"*Fay ce que voudras*, eh?"

Ravenden merely smiled. "You know your Rabelais. Come, the Dionysians meet here tonight. Join us. Then you may see us for yourself."

I felt great misgivings: *Do not go, Mr. Franklin!*

He looked down, rubbed the head of his bamboo, looked up. "I thank you, my lord. I should be pleased."

"And bring your boy." Ravenden's eyes found me once more. "You must bring him."

"I fear Nick has duties to perform."

"I should find duties for him here." The earl rose. "But I shall be pleased to see only you at nine."

Mr. Franklin stood. "And I you, my lord."

I put away my book as five o'clock bells rang out. Beyond the tall windows the thin light of afternoon began to leak away to dusk. His black hair floating in its cloud about his shoulders, Ravenden led us to the library door. The young manservant with the pale blue eyes stood in the corridor, but his master waved him off. "I shall show 'em out, Simkins."

"Very good, sir."

We descended the curving stairs. Hearing a yapping, I saw a small salt-and-pepper terrier baring its teeth at the bottom. There Ravenden scooped the dog up, stroked it, but it continued to growl; it wore the Chalton arms on a silver collar round its neck. By the door a turbaned black boy perhaps ten years old held Mr. Franklin's hat; he, too, was collared with the Chalton arms. I peered into his face, thinking of Peter, but the stoic features told little. Was he afraid, resigned? I could not help recalling my lord's story of secret flogging parties where small boys were beat.

"By the by, may I inquire if some of the girls who joined your revels were got by Long John Enderby?" asked Mr. Franklin as we were about to go.

"I do not know the name, sir. How strangely you press me."

"Habit, my lord. Good day." The gentleman bowed, took his hat, and the door shut behind us.

Out upon the cobbles a chill November wind blew; it was nearly dark. Mr. Franklin paused a moment, pulling his lip. "Did you see his look, Nick? He knows Enderby, though he wished me to believe he does not. Does the brute procure girls for his routs? Did Enderby deliver Tuesday Marrowbone into my lord's hands? What has occurred in that house?" He turned up his collar. "Curse the cold! I pray it does not rouse Mrs. Gout. Come, to a warm fire in Craven Street, lad."

❦ 13 ❦

IN WHICH Mr. Franklin Carouses with Bloods and Parries with an Earl . . .

Huddled by the fire with *Tom Jones*, I waited late that eve for Mr. Franklin to return from the Dionysus Club. The coals sank to ash as midnight pealed across London, whilst night pressed like an intruder against the panes of the bow window. One o'clock drew on. The cry of the watch quavered, "All's well . . ." and I pitied the poor soul who must trudge the frigid streets below.

Unable to read further, I reflected on our day. I knew some stories of the Greeks, but little of Dionysus save his name, so I had asked the gentleman about him.

"He is the god of wine and revelry," I had been told. "The ancient Celts of England worshipped such dieties, too, I have read, as do the Algonquin and other tribes of America—gods of the death and rebirth of the year."

"The women in the painting were terrible, sir."

"The Maenads. Frenzied by wine from Dionysus' grapes, they run wild and tear men apart. His worship can be joyful—wine brings delight—but it can breed black deeds, too, for wine makes men mad, and I have read tales of bloody rites performed in the god's name. He himself is said to have been torn apart by the Titans."

Did this relate to the deaths of Hester Ward and Tuesday Marrowbone? Uneasily I recalled today's visit to St. James's Square: the pale-eyed manservant with the patch by his lip, the blackamoor boy, the dog, the library with its bawdy books and bloody painting. I saw again the frenzied women in that painting, reveling in the god's ecstatic wounds.

The Earl of Chalton had sneered at much but not at his god.

I pictured Charles Ravenden, too: his ghost-white face, his red mouth, his extravagant gestures and oil-black eyes that roved and watched like an actor spying upon his audience. He was a cat-and-mouse man, playing a role—but what? And why did he play it? Plainly Mr. Franklin mistrusted him, for immediately upon arriving home he had sent Peter to Mrs. Goodbody with a note urging her—and all the women of her house—to look behind them when they went out.

Like Jack Scratch, Charles Ravenden was capable of spying. Was he capable of mayhem, too?

Some sound woke me. Blinking, I saw by dying fireglow that my candle had burnt down. A man was in the room, a shadow, approaching, and I jumped up.

Thank God it was Mr. Franklin, bending to light a new wick by a coal from the grate. I rubbed my eyes. "I am glad you are back, sir."

"Happy to be back, Nick." He shed the chill night air as he flapped his arms. "It is past one o'clock. These young bloods hold late revels! You need not have waited for me. Shall you to bed?"

"O, but may I not hear your evening?"

"At this hour?" A thin smile. "Very well, it shall be your reward." Raking ash and laying on more coal, he pulled the wooden chair from his desk. "Write it in our short-hand, as customary."

I drew my book from my pocket. "Yes, sir."

This is his tale:

The windows were ablaze when my hackney pulled up [said Mr. Franklin]. Ravenden's manservant opened to me. What an odd fellow! Simkins is his name. He cannot be more than twenty, but there is some secret knowledge in his eyes. He watched close, he examined me as if to set me down in his book. Would I could unlock his thoughts.

I was shown into a fine parlor, where four young fellows stood by the mantel with a bored, foppish air. Quizzing glasses hung round their necks, and they peered with 'em as if I were some tawdry thing. They held great bumpers in their hands. Port and sherry and other fruits of Dionysus' inspiration sat on a sideboard, with another servant to pour 'em. The little blackamoor was there, too, in his turban. He stood as still as a statue. What has he seen in that house?

The young rakes sniffed at me, and it was only when I assured 'em I was come at my lord's invitation that they loosed their tongues.

"O, if Ravvy himself has bid you, it is all right!"

"Yes, if Ravvy says you are one of us, you are!"

One tapped his nose. "Indeed, we always follow Ravvy's rules!" They brayed, as at some secret jest.

I soon learnt of 'em, for they liked to talk. There were two sirs, the son of a knight, a wealthy landlord's son. They were all on Tom Elstree's list. All well below Chalton's rank, too. Does he chose 'em thus, so he may be the best of the lot? Their conversation was antic, all cleverness without wit—no tribute to breeding. They postured and posed, playing one-up, yet they kept glancing at a far door. Waiting for their Lord of Misrule?

Another young fellow joined us, Bubb Bixby, and in the spirit of the game I broached the subject of the women with their hearts cut out. "I have learnt the women's names," said I.

"O, tell 'em!" said they.

I did.

"But they were both at club meetings in this very room!" Bubb Bixby exclaimed, before another shut him up. I might've learnt more, but just then the door flew open, and Charles Ravenden—Ravvy—strode in.

How he glittered! He wore more of his finery: a black velvet coat, scarlet breeches, a waistcoat as red as hellfire. His shoes gleamed. The rest of us were bewigged, but he wore his black hair free about his shoulders. His face was painted white.

"My lord!" and "Ravvy!" cried his fellow club members.

He strode to me. "Franklin, you are come." He gestured at his sycophants. "You have met my noble Dionysians?" A stern look. "Mr. Franklin thinks we are wicked devils, so I have asked him

108

here this eve to show him we are not. We have our pleasures, but they are innocent, are they not? Harming no one?"

"O, yes, Ravvy! Innocent! Harming no one." The noble Dionysians laughed, though with an edge, as their dim eyes goggled.

Tom Elstree came in. Number six.

He looked much as before, with his blunt, unhappy face. He wore a wig, but his pinched little eyes had the same affrighted cast, and his shoes scuffed glumly. He made a show of cheer—"Hullo, you fellows!"—but when he saw me, he stopped. "What—?"

My lord beamed. "You have met Mr. Franklin, have you not, Tom?" He herded the young man to me. "Do not hang back; it will look bad, for Mr. Franklin thinks you cut out Hester Ward's heart."

There was a general stir: "What . . . what?"

"I think no such thing, my lord," protested I.

He raised an eyebrow. "No? And yet"—he thumped Elstree's chest—"the bitch cut out *his* heart, or might as well have done, for it bleeds inside him still. Do you not tell us so, Tom? And is not tit for tat fair play?" He stuck out his lip. "But I am mistook, Mr. Franklin; you do not think Tom did it, so I beg your pardon." He sent his gaze round. "Did any of you other fellows murder her?"

A gasp. "No, no, Ravvy, never!"

He shook a finger. "For if you did, Mr. Franklin would be right that we are wicked indeed, so I am glad to hear you did not." He smiled broadly. "Shall we go in?"

"Yes, Ravvy, yes!"

Tom Elstree kept as far from me as possible whilst our host led us through a door into a long room, where logs flamed in a vast fireplace. A table stretched down the center, gleamingly set for supper, in the middle: a plaster figure of Dionysus, naked, with grapevines about his head and fat, ripe grapes at his feet; his cod stood joyfully erect, and someone—Ravenden himself?—had twined vines about it, too. There seemed some fixed order of seating, each man having a particular place, with Ravenden at the head, so I took an empty chair halfway along. Bottles of burgundy and Rhenish appeared, and two more manservants, young like Simkins, with his same debauched air, liberally poured.

Ravenden raised his glass. "To Dionysus, the sacred god of joy!" We drank deep, and more scandalous talk burst out, the Dionysians taking delight in reporting any gent or dame who had been brought low: "Lady Fane's lover was caught tupping her daughter—capital!" "His grace, the Bishop of London, had a bucket of slops tossed upon his head in Fetter Lane—what fun!" "Sir Richard Biggs lost all on the turn of a card at White's and hanged himself afterward—huzzah!" Lewd stories flew about as well, and I told one, too, though I preferred to listen and watch, as did my lord in his chair, leaning back, wearing his curling little smile. Did his noble Dionysians amuse him?

As for Tom Elstree, he huddled across from me fidgeting and sweating. Plainly he wished nothing but to drown his demons in drink. Ever and again he squinted at me from his tormented eyes. Did he long to confess, like some Roman to his priest? He gulped wine as if his host's store had no end.

We lifted our glasses to appetite as the food began to arrive: a soup, stewed fish, pigeon pie, roasted capon, a leg of veal, eggs in vinegar, peas, a flummery. We drank yet more as we ate—or they did; I husbanded my glass—and soon the table was a roar. The Dionysians tossed Bubb Bixby's wig about. They argued the merits of tobacco from the Spanish Indies at ten shillings a pound against tobacco from Virginia at half a crown. They bet upon how long a candle would take to spill. One had brought two black-beetles in a cunning little case, and they raced 'em along the table-top, poking and prodding and crying *Ho!* 'til one drowned in a bumper of wine and the other fell to the floor and was crushed. Ravenden watched all this with his mixture of amusement and contempt. Did he enjoy their shame? Our eyes met; we seemed to understand one another: *What fools they are.*

But why do you encourage their foolery? thought I.

There were half a dozen empty chairs at the table—was that where women sat, when they were allowed to be present? What happened then? Was Ravenden serving up only half a meeting, to deceive me? Now and then puzzled glances were turned upon our host. *Why do we not proceed as usual?* they seemed to ask.

Gooseberry tart and Stilton arrived. Port and Madeira. There was a sliding panel at the bottom of one wall, and now and then one of the young men stumbled to his feet to stand before the

110

panel and piss into the chamberpot within. I glimpsed a servant's legs behind this panel; plainly it gave onto another room, so the pot might be emptied. Whatever passed in the dining hall must be overheard.

Tom Elstree rose unsteadily.

"Nay." Ravenden stopped him with a flutter of his handkerchief.

Elstree turned.

"Let Prince do your duty for you."

"Prince! Prince!" cried all the fellows, besottedly banging their glasses.

Who was Prince? It took but an instant to discover: the blackamoor boy. He had stood by the sideboard in his turban and dog collar, and my heart sank. He gave a little start at being summoned, but his expression remained fixed as he stepped forward like a mechanical toy; plainly he knew what he must do.

He unbuttoned Tom Elstree. He took him out, he held him as he pissed. He buttoned him up again.

"Hurrah!" all cried, and one by one they marched up so Prince might serve 'em too. I gripped my chair arms, and it took all in my power to keep from striking each man as he passed (only the need to spare more victims from murder stilled me). It was vile degradation, but those who used the boy so ill only yawped, as if he were another species of beetle that might be drowned or crushed, with no regret.

As for Charles Ravenden, he observed coolly. If this was what the master of the Dionysians let me see of their habits, what did he keep hid?

When at last all the young men were done, my lord's eyes found me. "Franklin?" prompted he.

"After you, my lord."

He held my eyes a moment. "As you say." He rose in his languid way.

"And yet—" said I.

He stopped, turned.

"—and yet I think I shall not follow you, for when a man requires a child to do what he ought to do, he is not a man but a child, himself, a tyrannical infant. It is not manly, sir, but"—I gestured—"do it, if you must."

Silence shuddered through the room. The young men gaped, and I could almost hear the candlewax melt. Ravenden remained quite still in his inky coat and scarlet waistcoat, his narrow face fixed like an adder's upon me. Heretofore his gaze might have been thought genial, seeking some true connection betwixt us, but I saw now that he had asked me to dine only to prove he could toy with Ben Franklin. Had my boldness prevented me discovering a murderer? Yet I could not have helped myself; and if I might have stolen that poor black boy from Ravenden's house, he should be with us now.

A tremor moved my lord's jaw, a twitch fluttered his eye. He was plainly furious at my challenge, for I had flung it whilst his lickspittles watched. Would he lose the game and thus lose them?

He mastered the moment. "You are scrupulous, sir," said he evenly. "I judged you so this afternoon, and I find you even more so now. But damn your scruples! A man who is truly a man does as he pleases, and I do what I please now." Whirling, he snatched the boy's ear, twisting his head. "I wish to piss, boy." He jerked the ear again. "Help me to piss."

With a helpless mew, the child unbuttoned the Earl of Chalton and did as he was bid.

When he was done, Ravenden tumbled the boy upon the floor. (How I hated knowing I had provoked this cruelty!) Then he sent a fierce gaze round the table to rally his Dionysians, and they gulped and fell in line. One began to beat his glass upon the table, "O, well done!" and the rest took up the chant, bleating like sheep: "Well done! Well done!"

Only Tom Elstree did not join in. The young man drew his head into his shoulders, pale with revulsion.

As for myself, at that moment I would happily have shot the Earl of Chalton.

He returned to the table as the small black boy picked himself up and crept back to his place. How stoic the child's face! Simkins stood by. Going to the boy, the manservant gripped his shoulders to steady him. *You must obey the master, you must not cross him,* he seemed to command, before his pale blue eyes found me. *There is nothing you can do,* they seemed to say. A rebuff or a warning? Abruptly he turned and slipped from the room.

The pounding upon the table stopped, and the Dionysians called frantically for drink as if to benumb themselves. Meantime their eyes would only half meet mine. As for my lord, he appeared coolly amused once more, an unusurped king, but he regarded me with a narrower look, twisting a ring upon his left hand as if he should like to twist me, too.

What punishment did the tyrant contemplate?

I longed to escape the stifling air of the place—how hot it grew, the fire blazing!—yet I remained, forcing a mask of submissive idiocy upon my face. Our host proposed gaming, and we all rose and filed into a further room, heavily draped and thickly carpeted, where baize-covered tables waited with cards and dice. Paintings hung upon the walls—naked men and women in debauchery— and the candles smoked with a sickening stench. The ubiquitous Simkins waited with an inlaid box from which he sold counters. More drink was laid on, and we sat and dealt cards and rattled the cup. I played desultorily, husbanding my money, but Tom Elstree was reckless; he lost great sums. Shouts of excitement flew up, yet an air of expectation grew, as if gaming must be a prelude to better pleasures. Hopeful glances again searched our host—did women customarily appear now?—but he proposed nothing, not even a sally into the streets to tumble some poor old Charley or cripple a hapless beggar.

I stayed to the end. Did Ravenden think I would not? But I did, subject to his displeasure, his contempt. Past midnight he rose and waved his handkerchief, proclaiming he was tired of us all.

"But tomorrow, Ravvy?" his Dionysians cried like children, crowding round him as we made to go.

"Yes, yes." As we stood in the entryway, he fixed his deep, ambiguous gaze upon me. "But Mr. Franklin does not know of what we speak. Tomorrow, I unveil my completed Temple of Dionysus, at my estate near Richmond. It is to be a grand ceremony, sir. Shall you attend?"

The Dionysians grumbled—they did not want Ben Franklin to dampen their pleasure—but I did not give a damn. "Thank you, my lord. I should be honored to see what you serve up."

"You must leave your scrupulosity at home."

"I make no promises."

"Nonetheless I shall send instructions. To Craven Street, is't? Where you stay with Mrs. Margaret Stevenson, her daughter, and your son. I congratulate William on passing the bar."

Was this intimate knowledge meant to warn me? I confess I did not like it.

Winking, Bubb Bixby exclaimed, "Ravvy knows ev'rything!" and there was giggling all round. *What does he know about you that keeps you his slave?* thought I.

My lord yawned. "Bring your pretty Nick as well, promise me that. Good night."

We departed, the black boy handing us our hats by the door, Simkins recording me one last time with his unreadable eyes. The night was chill, the cobbles damp, the moon a silver shape above the square. Mists rose about our feet. Tom Elstree came down the steps after me, his form lurching in the dark. He hesitated, then tottered toward me. He opened his mouth to speak.

A commanding voice prevented him. "Tom!" It cut the night, and the young man made a moan, the cry of the slave called back to captivity. He retreated like a puppet into Charles Ravenden's house, and the door shut like iron . . .

". . . and that is my tale, Nick. have you writ it all?"

"All, sir." A dog barked forlornly from the Strand as I set down my pencil. Beyond the panes starlight lit the angled roofs of London, and laughter spilt from some night-bound door.

The gentleman rose heavily. "The deaths of those two poor women have to do with the Dionysus Club, I am sure. But what *is* the Dionysus Club? I must travel to Richmond tomorrow, to learn more." He peered at me. "You are asked, Nick, but you need accompany me only if you wish."

"I do wish, sir." I did not want him to go alone.

"I near forgot—" He reached into his coat pocket. "The counters which were used for gaming—here is one." He withdrew a six-sided coin. "See?"

He dropped it into my palm. Two o'clock tolled over London as I read the words: *Fay ce que voudras.*

🦋 14 🦋

IN WHICH We Brave a Whoremaster, and a Servant Strikes Three Blows . . .

I slept ill that night, though it was past two when I crawled into bed. My dreams were haunted by Charles Ravenden, white-faced, red-mouthed, threatening Mr. Franklin. Stars glittered evilly in that nightmare sky; then they turned into coins with *Fay ce que voudras* on them, dashing upon the world in a vengeful rain. I shot upright. The earl's white face seemed still to hover, and blinking it away, I shook with anger to recall the poor blackamoor boy. Too, I could not forget Monday night when five drunken puppets and their captain had set upon a pair of lone souls in St. James's Market. One had been Benjamin Franklin—but what if it had not? Would the rakes have done grievous injury?

Saturday waked beneath a fitful sun. London murmured to life. At breakfast Mr. Franklin was uncharacteristically silent, pursing his pointed lips, tracing little circles on Mrs. Stevenson's crisp white tablecloth. Her squint fixed on him. She was a vane to his weathers, and she hated a wind she could not read.

Did she long for him to renew his sallies about the lightning rod? That would be the Ben Franklin she knew.

As for Polly, her eyes observed William, who had joined us in fine clothes, eager for a day with his Tory friends. He tucked a cloth at his neck, he sat with his nose high. He could be overfine, full of himself, and he met Polly's look coolly. He had seemed smitten with her once, but she had rebuffed him; and now that he had passed the bar and was asked to balls at Northumberland

House, he paid her no court. How did she feel about that? I did not know, for she was clever enough to hide it.

I found her long-lashed eyes upon me, her saucy mouth pursed. *I watch you, Nick,* she seemed to say, *and I shall tickle something out of you yet.* Then she turned to Benjamin Franklin. She loved him like the father who had died when she was young; thus she hated to be treated with mistrust. She toyed with her dish of tea, she tugged at a curl of golden hair, but behind her gay mask I saw that she schemed.

Would she try to tickle news out of Benjamin Franklin, too?

After breakfast he drew her out of earshot of her mother, onto the back stoop. "Tell me, child," I heard him say as I passed, "since you returned, have you observed anyone watching this house . . . ?"

"I had to tell the girl some of our mystery," the gentleman informed me when he joined me in his chamber ten minutes later. He sank gravely into his chair. "Charles Ravenden knows too much about us."

I agreed. In the affair of Roderick Fairbrass's poisoning, enemies had broke into number 7, turning things topsy-turvy, so I knew our walls were breachable. "What did Polly say?"

"She has observed nothing untoward, though she promises to keep watch. She is quick, clever. My only misgiving is that she laughed when I said there was danger—the affair titillates her, Nick—so I was forced to press upon her that she is the same age as one of the murdered women. She did not laugh at that."

Take care, Polly! thought I. Mr. Franklin and I spoke on our mystery, reviewing the actors in our play: the scribbler, the dissipated marquess, the heartwrung swain, the whoremistress, the earl. The two murdered women were talked on, too, "Hester Ward and Tuesday Marrowbone sat at chairs at Dionysus' table." Mr. Franklin rubbed his blunt-fingered hands. "Is that why they died?"

A knock came, and Nanny darted in. Presenting a note, she fled as fast.

Mr. Franklin glanced at me over the tops of his spectacles. Outside his window the sun struggled in a smoke-bound sky. The note was a smudged sheet of foolscap, and unfolding it he perused it with a furrowed brow before he passed it to me.

> Dere Mr. Franklin,
>   I am Nelly Skindle. I be one of Miz Cockburn's girls. I seen you at her house t'other day. Fergive me, I did not mean to, but I lissent outside her door. You talked on murder. Tuesday Marrerbone were my friend. It were horrible wot happent to her, and I wish to help find who kilt her, the bloody man. I will wait for you in the Mall, by Malbro House, tomorrer arternoon, for it is Sunday and I have three hours. Pleese come.

Nelly was affixed at the bottom in large awkward letters.

Taking the note, Mr. Franklin examined it. "Penned by one of those scribes who write letters in the street, no doubt, of no great literacy himself though she seems to have signed it; at least she knows how to write her name." He tapped the paper. "Does luck turn our way? May we learn something of profit from this Nelly Skindle?"

Whatever the young whore might reveal, Mr. Franklin had not forgot Long John Enderby; thus he had set Peter to spy upon the Black Dog, the twang's haunt, and at half past ten a second note arrived by street boy. It was in Peter's hand, for Mr. Franklin had taught his man to read and write: "He is come," it said. "I shall keep him in sight."

Mr. Franklin pulled on his coat. "Make haste, Nick."

Moments later, we were in a hackney, rattling up St. Martin's Lane under a sluggish sky. Bells rang eleven o'clock as two bedaubed apprentices trudged by carrying a painting, no surprise, for St. Martin's was the haunt of painters. Shops selling pigments and oils lay about, framers, an auction house. The area reminded me of my adventure a year ago with Mr. Franklin. As workboy in the house of James Cavitty, the murdered painter, I had helped Mr. Franklin investigate the theft of the Shenstone diamond, a deep affair. That was when I had met William Hogarth.

Five minutes later our destination loomed at the top of Longacre, not far from the whorehouses of Covent Garden. Birdy Prinsop's crib lay but three minutes away, and I was stirred, but I thrust the girl from my thoughts. *You have other business, Nick.*

Peter slipped from a doorway at the corner of Drury Lane. He had been invisible—he was expert at sinking out of sight—but he was suddenly beside us, tall and solemn in his long, dark coat. Beckoning, he led us to a shabby, tilting building with a slavering hound on a signboard above its door: the Black Dog. "At a back table, sir. You will know him by the scar on his jaw."

"Good work." Mr. Franklin pressed his servant's arm. "Stay, if we should need you."

Peter bobbed assent, and the gentleman and I pushed aside a greasy leathern flap and entered the tavern.

It proved the basest of grog shops, a long, low-ceilinged room reeking of beer. A fireplace burnt fitfully at the far end, and tobacco smoke hung in the air; the smudged plaster walls were near black with time. Several rude tables sat about, flanked by peglegged benches where gatherings of men murmured over their pints. A pickpurses' lair? Yellowish eyes followed us, but Mr. Franklin paid them no heed as he made boldly for the farthest table, tucked in a back corner. It was so dark that an old tin lamp barely revealed the two figures seated there in a ghostly glow, one large and hunkering, the other, across from him, small and wizened, with thin pinched features. Two tankards of porter sat betwixt them. The small one saw us first, an old man, I thought. A boy, made ancient by the streets? With a start I realized it was a girl, with a dirty face and hair as white as ivory.

"Who be you?" she squeaked when she saw us. At her words the hunkered man seemed to unfold like some undersea thing, and I sucked breath, for he was enormous in a shapeless, duncolored coat. His fists were as big as puddings, his hair a black thatch upon a head like a boulder, and his ears lay flat against his temples, as if they had been driven there by furious blows. A pale scar ran along his blocklike jaw from lip to neck. Had someone tried to cut his throat? A flat nose. Raw, red cheeks. A maw of a mouth. But his eyes were his most frightful feature, round, black holes with nothing behind them: no soul, no notion of right and wrong. He would cut out your heart and eat it, too, I saw, and I understood why Mother Cockburn had feared to cross him.

He emitted a peevish growl.

"I am Benjamin Franklin," said Mr. Franklin. "You are Long John Enderby. I wish to speak to you about a girl you took from Mother Cockburn's."

"Nunnavit," the brute spoke.

"Sir?"

"He says he'll 'ave none of it," the wizened girl piped up, wiping her nose on a ragged sleeve. "Yer'd best clear off."

Mr. Franklin met her slitted gaze. "Nay, he *shall* have some of it, for that girl has been murdered, and he will speak of what he knows to me, or he will speak to Justice Fielding at his court in Bow Street. I have the justice's authority for that." He spoke with no fear; here was a man who meant what he said.

There followed a silence, in which the hairs at the back of my neck told me that every denizen of the Black Dog heard all. The fire sighed like a dying man. The old beams creaked. Long John Enderby fixed his black holes of eyes upon Mr. Franklin.

"Smiggs!" he rumbled suddenly, snatching the girl by the collar and dragging her across the table, where she ended nose-to-nose with him. He hissed something into this Smiggs's ear; she nodded furiously. Then he flung her from him, as he might fling a cat he had strangled for pleasure, and she ended with a clatter against the coal scuttle. Finding her feet, she made a face at me before she swaggered off into the gloom.

Enderby's huge hands beckoned. "Sit," muttered he, and we did, opposite him.

Pulling out my book, I sketched the monster by the dim glow of the tin lamp.

"Wot?" said he, a species of consent, and Mr. Franklin began to put questions, which he answered with guttural growls. Did he take girls from the Golden Guinea in the Haymarket? Did. Was one of them named Tuesday Marrowbone? S'posed so. I drew his thick head, the thatch of hair, the pale scar. He was a brute but not entirely brutish, for he had guile; those black eyes were not so dead as I had thought, and I grew wary. He was answering too readily. What orders had he given his wizened minion?

"Where did you deliver Tuesday Marrowbone?" Mr. Franklin asked.

"To a gen'leman's gen'leman."

"His name?"

"Simkins."

"The Earl of Chalton's man."

"If yer sez so."

"Did the earl ask for her in particular?"

"Ha! A whore? He wanted a pretty piece o' quim wot could keep 'er mouth shut, that wuz all."

"Keep her mouth shut about what?"

" 'Ow should I know?"

Mr. Franklin peered. Had Enderby been warned to keep his mouth shut, too?

"Did you obtain other girls for him?" the gentleman pursued.

"Wotever 'e liked."

"When Tuesday Marrowbone was taken by Simkins, she was kept for two days. Why?"

"None o' my bizness. And none o' yers. A piece o' goods is a piece o' goods—no matter 'ow long 'tis used, 'twill not wear out." Enderby sucked at his porter.

"Did you know a woman named Hester Ward?"

"Never 'eard of 'er."

"Do you carry a knife?"

Here was a question Enderby liked. He formed a ghastly smile—and suddenly a wide-bladed knife slammed with a great *thunk!* into the oak before Mr. Franklin's nose. It stood there, quivering.

I jumped, but Mr. Franklin never stirred as Enderby leaned across the table into his face. "Aye, I carries a knife. Can use it, too. But"—opening the fingers of both hands on either side of his face, he waggled them like a bogeyman—"I don't nivver need it, for I got these. They can squeeze yer neck to a straw."

The knife might have been another glass of porter for all the heed Mr. Franklin paid it. "You say you got the Earl of Chalton whatever he wished. Was it sometimes boys?"

"P'rhaps. But he has his young men now, don't he? So he don't need boys no more." A scowl. "Now, no more talk."

"But Justice Fielding—"

"The devil with Justice Fielding!" This burst out with such violence that spittle flew. The twang jumped up, jerked his knife from the wood, and stood warningly, whilst poison seemed to leak from the terrible, black orbs in his face. A shiver shot through me, and jamming my sketchbook in my pocket, I glanced round. Watching eyes. Shadowy men whose hands crept inside their coats. There were safe places in London, but this was not one.

The wizened girl had not returned, and Mr. Franklin drew me slowly to my feet. "Enough for now," said he.

"Much good it'll do ye," growled the hulk, and I could hear his thick catch of breath, like the groan of some ghost ship's yard.

Mr. Franklin peered. There was no wresting truth from a stone, and he took my arm. "Come, Nick." Turning, I went with him, but as he drew me toward the door, the cavelike room seemed far longer than when we crossed it. More men seemed to have arrived, stirring in shadowy bunches, though no one spoke, no tankards clinked. I heard only my own raw breath and the scuff of our shoes on the beer-soaked planks.

Then I saw the girl. She leant against the jamb, her young-old face mocking beneath her ivory hair. Wiping her nose, she nodded to three burly men beside her. "Them," I heard her grate, and with an ominous shuffle the men formed a wall to block us. We stopped. They were determined-looking brutes, and I recalled how the bloods had come at us in St. James's Market. We had beaten them, but they had been drunken toffs, whilst these men looked thoroughly sober, and used to cracking heads. The middle one, in a wide, flat hat, held up a long, thin blade.

I trembled. No wonder Long John Enderby had not minded giving Mr. Franklin what he sought.

"Nick—" I heard the gentleman's murmur. He placed a hand on my chest, as to push me behind him, but I would fight by my father's side. We glanced about, but there was no escape, no other door, only four soot-smudged windows that would close their eyes to any blood spilt here. I heard grunts of satisfaction as pint pots were set down and benches scraped back. Slow smiles spread. There would be a lively dance to pass the morn; later two gore-slimed bodies would be fished out of Fleet Ditch. Was this how we would end?

But not without a fight. Recalling how at Bath Mr. Franklin and I had fought similar enemies back-to-back, I set my feet, whilst he gripped his bamboo. He raised it—yet I cannot tell what would have happened had he been forced to use it, for there came a thump, like a muffled knock, and one of the three men emitted a moan.

Tottering, he crumpled like a sack of flour upon the floor.

"Here—!" came Smiggs's sharp protest.

Peter stood behind the two remaining men.

I near cried out for joy; never had I been so pleased to see him. He stood very still, waiting. Plainly he had felled the man with a single blow, and Flat Hat—he with the knife—turned. He stared. "You dare?" With a snarl he swung his blade.

This proved great error, for Peter gripped his wrist in an instant, twisting with an upward jerk. There came a *snap!* like a branch breaking, and Flat Hat's knife clattered upon the floor, he with it, holding a strangely bent arm. He writhed, he whimpered, he kicked. His pain-wracked eyes pled to God.

Smiggs's sharp eyes glinted in the gloom. She looked ready to dash for the knife, but I clapped my foot on it.

"Just so, Nick," I heard Mr. Franklin say.

I scooped it up as the remaining man turned to face Peter. "Wo-ot?" said he, as if he could not believe a blackamoor had done what he had. "Blast you!" He made a lunge.

Peter's fist flew at his face like a length of oak. It struck the nose unerringly, and there came a crunch, an explosion of blood, and the man staggered back, bounced off a bench, embraced the floor. He did not move.

Silence rang, whilst triumph tingled inside me. Hoorah, Peter! I glanced about. Grumbles and growls sounded, but no one else looked like challenging us. Had we won?

Yet there was danger at our backs, and I spun to face it. Mr. Franklin did, too.

Long John Enderby stood like some huge toad. He took three heavy steps toward us, his long knife seeming to gather all the light in the room. "I'll finish ye meself," muttered he.

Mr. Franklin pressed the tip of his bamboo into the man's chest. "Tut, sir." Something in his tone made Enderby stop. The brute looked down at the bamboo. He squinted at Peter, who had come to stand beside Mr. Franklin. He looked at the knife in my hand. He chewed his pendulous lip. "The devil with ye, then." He brushed the stick away. "Beer!" he shouted at the pot boy, who leapt to serve him. "I want more beer!" He clumped back to his table.

We retreated through the gloom. The wizened girl spat at my feet as we passed, and I was glad I had not had to fight her. Outside I glanced back before the greasy leather fell. Was it my imagination that Long John Enderby picked Smiggs up and flung her like a missile across the smoky room? I tossed the knife in a gutter.

❦ 15 ❦

IN WHICH We Worship at a Temple and Creep Into a Cave . . .

Though I was shaken by our encounter at the Black Dog, I had little time to reflect upon it, for we returned quickly to Craven Street, to prepare for our journey to the Earl of Chalton, at Richmond. Mr. Franklin thought aloud as our small hired coach rattled toward the Thames, I tucked betwixt him and Peter: "Tuesday Marrowbone was hired by Ravenden just before she died. That does not mean my lord did her in. Or the other poor woman. Enderby would've twisted the knife without a thought. And, taking Hester Ward as a separate case, her uncle wished her out of his way and might have gone as far as murder." He sighed as we turned into Craven Street. "Then there is Tom Elstree. He seems to wish to blame himself for the crime—what the devil does he mean by it? He is young, foolish, but folly is not evil; we all drink our dram. Yet, blast him, could he have drunk so much of it he carved out a woman's heart?"

"If Charles Ravenden commanded him to?" proposed I.

"He does seem in some strange bondage to the man."

A letter on fine vellum paper waited in Mr. Franklin's chamber when we arrived. It was from the Marquess of Bathurst. He scanned it, snorted, handed it to me.

> You said the law would not call upon me if I answered your questions, but it *has* called, in the person of the blind magistrate. Damn you, sir, for lying; and damn the

world for casting that girl upon my doorstep—she is more trouble dead than alive!

Mr. Franklin and I exchanged a look—what brass! Taking the letter, he flung it upon his desk. For my part I was angry to know the iron-eyed old lecher thrived in his St. James manse whilst his young niece was food for worms. Secretly I thanked John Fielding for troubling him.

The Earl of Chalton had promised to send directions to his estate. They waited, sealed with the Chalton crest, and we made ready for our journey.

It took an hour and a half by hackney coach, along Piccadilly, then out upon the Knightsbridge Turnpike. It might have taken less, but the road was deep in mud, so our wheels slipped and skidded whilst we tipped and veered. I liked escaping the city nonetheless. Past Hyde Park the fields and hills of England opened welcoming arms. Little farm steadings stood out like toys: hedgerows, stiles, sheep folds, autumnal copses shedding their last crumpled gold. What a change from London! In that great, smoky house one crept under beetling rooftops and inhaled reeking fog. Here one gazed at an unsullied sky and smelt sweet air.

Was this the true hand of God?

But the way was also notorious for footpads—you might be murdered for your purse (just a year ago on our way to Bath Mr. Franklin and I had faced a highwayman's pistol). Too, I could not forget that we traveled into Charles Ravenden's realm, so I wanted distraction. "Tell me of Rabelais, sir?" I proposed.

Mr. Franklin drew his long woolen scarf tighter about his throat. "Rabelais. A French monk, a doctor of medicine. He died round about Shakespeare's birth. France embraces him today, but in his time he was reviled for his unorthodox views—Catholics and Calvinists both despised him." A small smile. "Does this mean Ben Franklin may be beloved in England one day? His great work is *Gargantua and Pantagruel,* the story of a giant and a son so prodigious that six hundred cows must be milked to feed him. The son goes on many journeys, and near the end he sails to the Island of the Sacred Bottle, where he comes upon a mosaic in a cave: the story of Dionysus (*nota bene*, Nick), where he is instructed by a priestess to 'drink'—to taste all life has to offer."

"*Fay ce que voudras?*"

"Perhaps. Yet we must not blame Rabelais for the way some misuse him. He despised most restraints on freedom—yet the people he satirized were hypocrites and pedants; surely he would not have countenanced unrestrained license."

I thought on that. A giant. Adventures. A cave. Our coach careered into a trough, we tipped precariously, but our driver righted us. "I should like to read this Rabelais, sir."

Mr. Franklin adjusted his tumbled beaver hat. "I shall see that you may."

We arrived at the Chalton estate near four. Though it was still light, the day was already dissolving into shadows that spread upon the swards like blight.

The death of the year drew near.

The sharp cry of a vixen met us as we topped a rise. Rooks flew overhead like ash in the wind. We passed a deserted gatehouse, followed by a long drive amongst stark elms whose tattered leaves twisted fitfully. *Jing-jing* went the horsebells, whilst our wheels crunched on the chalk-and-gravel road. Mr. Franklin and I fell silent, searching for our first view of Chalton House, but all we saw was thorny wood. Yet something could be glimpsed now and again, glinting in the distance: a tower surmounted by a gleam of gold. What could it be?

And then the trees parted, and Chalton House appeared below. I recalled the distaste with which the earl had described it, and I understood: it was an uninviting manse. Hills ringed it, but instead of being built on some fortunate promontory, it had been dug into a hollow amongst an army of oaks that seemed to surround it like marauders. Pointed arches, lichened stone, rows of crenellations like crones' teeth—the place had been an abbey before it was a home. Had its long-dead monks chosen to burrow like moles?

Our coach descended to the broad gravel circle before the house. Laughter could be heard—yet it did not come from the forbidding pile but from uphill, to the west, and we stared at a Greek-looking building on a far slope, gleaming in the declining sun.

This must be the Temple of Dionysus whose completion we had been invited to celebrate.

It was columned and pedimented, and as we debouched on the graveled circle, we also spied "Greeks" before it: men and women in long white robes such as I had seen only in books. Some wore powdered wigs, as Greeks never did, and many carried goblets. Dionysian wine? Disporting themselves on the sloping lawn, they showed glimpses of leg and breast which would have sparked scandal in any London drawing room. Flute music fluttered. Drums sounded a pagan beat.

But there was more, for the tower we had glimpsed on our approach rose beside the temple, a spire of marble reaching a huge height. At its apex stood a golden medallion as tall as a man. The medallion had six sides.

Fay ce que voudras was embossed upon it.

Mr. Franklin looked at me, I at him, and an ominous wind seemed to sweep across the darkening hills. The column produced an unsettling effect, as if obscenity had unsheathed its member here, for the thing was swollen and ill-proportioned compared to the temple, which it overshadowed. What did it mean? In any case it was plain that with his love of theatricality my lord had built a sort of theater here, and we were all actors in his masque.

A manservant approached. He asked our names, we gave them, and he peered at a list. As blithely as if giving directions to Whitehall, he gestured. "Pray, ascend, sirs." This we did, by a curving path. Halfway up we were beckoned to an intermediate building, also in Greek style: a "robing house," we were told, where we were bade to remove our outer clothing—it would be kept for us—and to put on flowing white garments, "chitons," a servant said, which were pinned about our shoulders. I found a pocket in mine—for snuffboxes, timepieces, love toys? Whether or not true Greek chitons had pockets, I was glad to have a place to tuck my sketching book and pencil.

Our hats were taken, too. Mr. Franklin was given a crown of laurel—"Socrates, eh, Nick?" proclaimed he—and we proceeded uphill.

The succeeding hours were amongst the strangest I have spent, surpassing even swimming in the King's waters at Bath, where the ladies' patches bobbed in black spots upon the waves. As we mounted, I observed statuary amongst the trees: satyrs ravishing maids, the swan deflowering Leda, Zeus despoiling Ganymede. Great priapic monsters lurked there, too, and I glimpsed a flesh-and-blood couple thrashing in amorous frenzy.

At last we reached the temple, a great, colonnaded rectangle many times my height. I gazed up at its pediment: a naked Diony-sus and Ariadne, leading a procession of profligates. Mounting, we passed betwixt fluted columns to a polished floor set with mar-ble hexagons. Also inspired by the "sixth emanation" that reju-venated life? Three scantily dressed young men poured wine amidst the hubbub of a banquet laid out on long tables: fruits, rabbits, boar, goose, salmon, pike, sweetmeats. One reveler gnawed a chicken leg, then flung it from him, whilst another, on his back, opened his mouth so a woman might pour wine down it. The temple did not stand free. Three sides were columned, but the back wall was built against the upward slope of the hill, adorned with paintings of debauchery. Yet there was a door in its center. Where did it lead?

"Let us see all, Nick." Taking cups, we pretended to drink as we gazed down the green sward. The members of the Dionysus Club whom Mr. Franklin had met yesterday were scattered there with dozens of others; he pointed them out: foolish-faced fellows careering after maids. Were some of those shrieking women well-born girls like Hester Ward? Many were likely whores, hired for the occasion, and I watched them jig and turn.

Were some Mother Cockburn's girls? This must be where Tues-day Marrowbone had been brought. Did the answer to our mys-tery lie here?

There were older men as well, lecherous-faced. Peers? Parlia-mentarians? Priests? I saw painted boys, too, hardly older than I. Some of them pranced lewdly (had they been instructed to do so?), but others appeared lost, even frightened, as if this were their first time at the game.

Tom Elstree sulked nearby.

I caught sight of his slumped shoulders and small unhappy eyes at the foot of the temple, his brown hair atangle above his chiton.

Seeing us, he seemed to struggle in torment, and for a moment I thought he would join us, but with a sudden defiant gesture, as if he damned hope itself, he lifted his cup, drank it off, and flung it from him.

He charged into the temple to get another.

"Poor soul," murmured Benjamin Franklin.

We strolled the grounds as the sun lowered, I with my book, drawing. Where was the Earl of Chalton? Watching? Sneering at the farce he made? If so, he did it secretly, and I shivered to think of his shadow hanging over us like a great black wing. No one seemed to miss him; they were too well occupied as the merriment rose to a pitch. A lake had been dug at the bottom of the lawn. A barge with *Charon* painted on its bow plied it, a bent old fellow in a woolly faced mask at its helm ferrying rioters back and forth. Some fell in, but they floundered ashore, for the water was not three feet deep. In the darkening woods at the edge of the lawn other figures flickered amongst the leaves in a lewd frolic. A goatish old man leapt from a bush to tug at my garment, but Mr. Franklin rapped him sharply with his bamboo.

The man only blinked, grunted, clapped his brow. "Your boy, eh, sir? I wish you good use of him." Leering obscenely, he reeled off.

Was I surprised? No. I had been raised in a parish where I met depravity daily, and of late I had had my own lascivious thoughts. Yet this was no round I cared to join, so I was happy to obey Mr. Franklin's adjuration: "Stay close."

As dusk sank toward night, two great bonfires flared at the edge of the lake, and all the revelers were herded there. They milled, they fussed with their costumes, repinning what had been pulled or torn, buzzing with anticipation: what would come? I glimpsed the earl's man, Simkins, at the edge of the throng. Greek-garbed and patched as I remembered, he seemed at home amidst these strange revels, and catching Mr. Franklin's eye, he nodded in his cynical fashion. Yet was he all scorn? Did something deeper kindle behind that languid look? He seemed to measure us. Why?

Then music burst out, and we gazed uphill. At the top of the sward rose the temple with its incongruous tower topped by the golden medallion that caught the last rays of the sun: *Fay ce que voudras.* Torches blazed at the sides of these mismatched structures, and despite my misgivings I was stirred. What would Charles Ravenden set spinning now?

My lord, the earl, appeared at last.

He swept out from between the tall columns of his temple, dressed in flowing robes: Dionysus personified, vine leaves entwined above his brow, a cluster of grapes in one hand, a golden goblet lifted for libation in the other. His face was as before, painted white, his mouth a red scar, his cloud of black hair hanging free. I sucked a sharp breath, though Mr. Franklin appeared calm, observing in his quiet way so you would never guess his mind read every detail.

The fire of the torches seemed to spark from his small steel-rimmed spectacles.

There was applause, shouts of *Huzzah!* at which my lord pranced. He twirled a hand, he made a speech: "Ladies and gentlemen, fops and whores"—a wink—"(you know which you are), we dedicate this eve to Dionysus, the god of joy, who bids us cast aside all restraint and live as we please. His temple is built again. It is here, in England. He has planted his foot on our shores, and he offers you a better life, so join with me in following his rule." He lifted his cup. "Hail, Dionysus!"

More cheers greeted this, raised glasses: *Hail Dionysus!* Our rabble was plainly drunk, but not so drunk that it could not be formed by footmen into a rollicking procession, which proceeded by torchlight around the lake, headed by the earl himself, who came down to command us. As we went, more pagan horns wailed, whilst small boys dressed as fauns gamboled and tootled on some kind of pipes. Night fled before the glowworm of our march. *What a pretty sight we make!* thought I, beginning to feel the bonds of restraint slipping free. Why not give myself to the moment? Bare-breasted nymphs danced alongside us—surely I could lure one into the dark verge, if I wished.

But though I longed to be a libertine, I could not. *Fay ce que voudras* was well and good, but like Mr. Franklin I was cursed with scrupulosity, and I could not help wondering: did the scantily dressed women and boys, hired to decorate the lawn, live as *they* pleased? Did the chill night air delight them? And when some gross lecher dragged them into the wood, did they enjoy being tupped? I found pleasure in making a drawing, reading a book, strolling London, peeling carrots for Mrs. Stevenson in her warm kitchen on a biting winter's morn, but Charles Ravenden would sneer at all that. For him, pleasure must be cruel: debauching fops, tipping Charleys, abusing boys.

Cutting out women's hearts?

Our procession ended inside the temple, where we bumped and jostled, rocking the tables of food so hard that one crashed to the floor, spilling meat and drink. Mounting a dais at one end, Ravenden uttered more fol-de-rol about death and life, with solemn, ritualistic passes of his cup. He was aided by the members of the Dionysus Club, some of whom could barely stand. He curled his lip at the fools—but he appeared to believe what he said, for a fervor lit his white-painted face as he proclaimed his faith in resurrection: "There *is* life after death, for those who do not fear to do as they please!" The torches hissed and spit in a whipping breeze. "The Maenads may tear a man or woman to pieces, but that man or woman *can* live again!" I glanced at Tom Elstree; he trembled at the words. "Hail, Dionysus!" our host cried. He raised his cup, and like sheep we raised ours—all save Mr. Franklin.

Ravenden saw the apostasy, and rage seemed to start up behind his extravagant stare.

Afterward he came to us whilst the rest resumed their mad carouse. We stood at the edge of the temple, the great shaft of the tower looming nearby. The wind cut like a knife. "You are come," said the earl to Mr. Franklin. He looked at me. "And your pretty boy." Fingering the edge of my chiton, he gestured into the night. "There are many would enjoy you. Some wealthy young ladies of the town should be pleased to teach you their tricks. Gents, too."

"Nick shall remain with me," pronounced Mr. Franklin.

"As you will."

Mr. Franklin gestured. "You make a great display here."

"I like display."

"All for Dionysus' sake?"

"For *my* sake. And yet, I believe in the god."

"Forgive me, my lord, but why not Apollo, if you must have a Greek?"

"What? This is no whim. I despise Apollo! He is the god of order. He was my father's god, damn him; he spoke through him.

131

Always 'Nay, boy, nay.' I can hear him now, nattering like a parson: 'Govern yourself, boy; follow my rule!' Did his rule keep his lady from groaning under his manservant? She did not follow his rule; she pleasured herself to the end. That is my way. Dionysus was her god, and he is mine, and I take joy in spending my fortune in his name."

"I thought that fortune had dwindled greatly."

"This, you mean?" Ravenden gestured at the temple, the tower. "It cost a pretty penny, but I shall recoup. If not"—his red lips curled—"there is always death."

Mr. Franklin peered. "With resurrection to follow?"

A curt nod. "For the chosen."

I had no idea what he meant. Was the man mad?

A hint of storm flickered far off, and Mr. Franklin glanced up at the tower, its top lost in the gloaming. "You must have a lightning rod, sir, or the true God will blast what has cost you so much."

"The God of Abraham, you mean? Why, you believe in him as little as I. Confess, you are no man of faith."

"My lord, I am a man of reason."

"Pah, reason is no better! The world is not governed by reason. It is not even governed by the heart—it is ruled by this." He clutched between his legs. "The cod, sir. And the quim. They are what rule."

Mr. Franklin smiled thinly. "I do not say they do not—in some quarters. But they are not perforce best or right. Reason tells us that."

I thought the earl might burst out in anger, but he only clapped Mr. Franklin's shoulder. "You would reason me out of my humor, but do not try to change my mind. I am ruled by Dionysus, who bids us drink and be merry, so whilst you are here you must let yourself be guided by my god. Follow me." He led us back into the temple, where two panting old men pursued a young girl of no more than fourteen round the long, spilt table of food. "You see?" said the earl. "The rule of Dionysus."

"Nay, the folly of lechery." The child was plainly terrified, and Mr. Franklin stuck out his bamboo, tripping one of the men, who brought down the other. Both tumbled amongst the broken crockery and greasy bones.

The nymph fled into the night.

"You are expert with your stick," Ravenden said, and I recalled the moment in St. James's Market when Mr. Franklin had faced the earl and his sword. My lord kicked one of the fallen men. "You must practice the chase better, Dunstable! You shame the race of men." Stepping coldly past, he led us to the door in the back wall. Taking out a key, he unlocked the door, plucked a bull's-eye lantern from the darkness within, and lit it by one of the flaring torches. He bade us follow.

A tunnel stretched before us into dank and inky depths. " 'Twas dug long ago, to mine the chalk used to pave the roads," my lord said. "I have put it to other use. We are greeted, I see." Pausing just inside, he directed his beam upon a marble statue. It leered with a satyr's face, holding in its hand, like an offering, its enormous member.

"Priapus," murmured Mr. Franklin.

"You know him, I see." Beneath the statue was a legend: *Peni tento, non penitenti.* My Latin was inexpert, so it took a moment to translate its lewd joke: "A penis tense, not penitence."

"Priapus knows the rule of Dionysus," said the Earl of Chalton as he led us on.

The tunnel was approximately ten feet wide, eight high. Heavy wooden timbers supported its roof. The floor was packed earth, the iron tracks for the trams which had carried the chalk still in place. We followed our guide in silence, the torchbeam wavering, the rustle of our long garments whispering. Where did we go? In any case the noise of revelry was left far behind, and I began to hear a lisp of water in the flickering gloom. After a moment we came upon a stream, spanned by a narrow bridge. Crossing this, we continued, at a downward slant. As the tunnel curved, I liked it less and less. We were in earth's intestine. I shivered at the mouldering walls, a nightmare trap; I felt ice in my bones.

Abruptly a form loomed ahead, resolving into another statue, also naked, with a flower in its hair, a finger at its lips. The eyes were closed, but the lips smiled knowingly, the expression seeming to warn: *Tell no one.* "Harpocrates, the god of silence," murmured Ravenden, patting the statue's bare flanks. Another curve, and the tunnel opened upon a broad, circular chamber. Its ceiling rose thirty feet, and there were six torches in its walls, which my lord lit. By their spitting light we gazed upon a mosaic floor, intricately designed, thick with detail.

The mosaic in Rabelais, thought I.

Its theme was Dionysus.

Ravenden watched as we examined the thing. One aspect of Dionysus brought joy, but this celebrated the mad, inflamed side, the irrational—for here were frenzied dancers, there fornication; here rape, there buggery. All manner of vice was depicted in unflinching detail, and everywhere the Maenads ran wild, tearing at human flesh with their clawlike hands.

In the center of the mosaic, like the hub to its wheel, stood a broad hexagonal block of marble about three feet high, its edges decorated with leafy fillets. An altar?

Upon it ran faint, dark stains.

The torches sent up oily smoke, but currents of chill air carried it deeper into the cave. The Earl of Chalton gestured proudly. "This is where the Dionysus Club has met 'til now, waiting for my temple to be done. Does it like you?"

"I like a chophouse in the Strand better," replied Mr. Franklin. "I am a simple man."

"I do not think that you are simple."

"Then, my lord, we mean different things by the word. Your mosaic is executed with great skill."

"Italian craftsmen did it."

"How long has it been completed?"

"Two years."

"So you Dionysians have met here that long?"

"We have."

"Out of sight of the world."

"We thumb our noses at the world!"

"And what do you do when you meet?"

"Drink to the god."

"No more?"

The earl tapped his jaw. "Perhaps you will one day see for yourself."

Mr. Franklin stepped to the altar. "But you have spilt some wine. Look."

Ravenden fixed his lantern upon the stains. "Someone has spilt something, sir."

Out in the world my lord's celebration limped to an end. The torches sputtered. The tables of food made a scattered jumble. Empty goblets lay about. Ribbons. Clasps. Slippers. The faun-boys had commandeered the barge, poling it to the middle of the lake, where they jeered and hooted. A silver moon raised twin horns over the tower. The threatened storm had passed, but a bone-cold wind ruffled the lake, tumbling cast-off garments across the green.

Though my teeth chattered, I felt a warm burst of relief when we walked free of the cave. Mr. Franklin followed me out. The Earl of Chalton came last, locking the door before he strode off as if we did not exist, and I heard him bark orders to his servants to extinguish the torches.

All done, then? Bedraggled souls began to trail downhill, though some lay snoring. One fellow bayed at the moon, whilst another danced a strange, lone dance, as if phantom music played. Exchanging a look, Mr. Franklin and I trudged to the robing house, where we retrieved our garments.

No longer Greek, we descended by glinting starlight to the graveled circle before the crenellated house.

I felt as if I waked from a feverish dream; I had drunk nothing, but there was a sour taste in my mouth and a queasiness in my gut. Shadows lay about, pools of black. Our carriage was drawn up with several others past a stand of oaks, and as we crunched along the road to it I could not help picturing those stains upon the altar. Only spilt libations?

By his expression Mr. Franklin seemed to reflect on them, too, and I was about to ask what he thought, when we came upon Tom Elstree, sagging against a tree. He appeared green in the moonlight, with sweat upon his brow and trembling hands. We stopped. Leaves rustled. The grass seemed to bend its ears. "Dear God, dear God," the young man wailed as if he were damned, and I flinched at his cry.

Was it Dionysus he appealed to?

Mr. Franklin touched his shoulder, at which he shrank back. "I should like to help," murmured the gentleman. "You recall me, Benjamin Franklin? I reside in Craven Street. Seek me there."

The young man's mouth opened, closed. Tears wet his cheeks. What demons tormented him? Whoever they might be, he broke away. Twigs crackled, and in a sudden mad rush he was gone.

I felt my hair prickle. Turning, I saw a shape in the shadows. I took it for one of the grimacing statues until it glided near, looking as if an arched eyebrow and a curled lip were the only talismans against the world. It was the servant, Simkins. An owl hooted. Leaves fluttered as night exhaled a breath. There was a long silence; then Simkins said mournfully, "He is innocent, sir. I tell you, he is innocent." Abruptly he wheeled off.

Mr. Franklin emitted a cry. He tugged my arm. "He was not here by chance. He stood watch over Tom Elstree. By his master's orders? Or did he follow Elstree for reasons of his own? Come, we must speak to him before he escapes, for it was he to whom Tuesday Marrowbone was delivered." We followed his broken crackling through the undergrowth, but it faded, and we became lost amongst night and trees: our quarry was gone.

Nothing for it but to make our way to our coach, where we unfolded a traveling rug over our legs. Glancing at the gloomy manse hunched in its hollow, the temple on its hill, I shivered. *"Haw!"* cried our driver, jostling his steeds into motion. He was a short, burly fellow with a formidable wart upon his nose, and a well-primed pistol by his side. He had boasted he knew how to use it— "I c'n shoot a fly off yer noses, sirs!"—but he had no need, for highwaymen laid low on our weary way home.

✥ 16 ✥

IN WHICH We Interview a Whore and a Dionysian
Drinks Deep . . .

I fell asleep on our return. The rocking sway of our coach, the jingle of reins, the cold night air on my face. I jumped at Mr. Franklin's gentle shake to say we were home. By dim lamplight I glimpsed fog curling up from the Thames. I heard the night watchman's bleak call. Then: Nanny peering at us in a glow of candlelight as she unlatched the door. A groggy stumble upstairs, a mumbled good-night, and I sank upon the narrow bed in my little chamber across from Mr. Franklin's.

No dreams—Chalton House was dream enough—and when I woke next morn I discovered I had not even took off my stockings.

Daylight fell through my window. Sitting upright, I listened. Churchbells rang eleven sonorous strokes, and I groaned in dismay. We had returned at one, so I had slept ten hours? Scrambling into shirt and breeches, I tied back my hair.

What would Mr. Franklin think of so lazy a boy?

I hurried from my room to find the house quiet—no surprise, for Mrs. Stevenson and Polly would be at services, at St. Martin in the Fields—yet this morn's stillness seemed deeper than usual. Mr. Franklin rarely went to church—"At the last day we shall not be judged by our hours at worship but by what we did," he was fond of saying—so I expected to find him in his chamber; yet when I entered after a brief knock, I discovered the room empty,

137

the fire low in the grate. I frowned. The gentleman was down-stairs, then? Gone out?

His bow window stood open, and I was about to go below to see what I might find, when a murmur of voices drew me to its case-ment. Peering out, I discovered the top of Mr. Franklin's balding crown just below, William beside him. A trim gig had drawn up, its occupant just stepping down, and I recognized him, too: the printer William Strahan. I was puzzled. He and Mr. Franklin or-dinarily met in back-slapping joy, yet they were restrained this morn, glancing about as if they feared to be observed.

I drew back so I could watch unseen.

"She will arrive soon," I heard Mr. Strahan pronounce in his strong Scots burr.

"Let us wait in the parlor, then," replied Benjamin Franklin, tugging both his friend and William toward the door. The three vanished—though before they did, I saw Mr. Strahan pat William's back.

"Courage. Many a man before you . . ." said he.

"I shall face it bravely," William replied.

The latch clicked behind them.

I stood whilst a three-legged dog hobbled over the grimy cob-bles and gulls wheeled above the Thames. Withdrawing from the window, I listened to the steady tick of Mrs. Stevenson's case clock from the landing. Sunday. A day when the shopfronts of Craven Street were closed. A day when Craven Street customar-ily lay deserted, with few if any to observe a caller. Eleven o'clock, too. An hour when the mistress of the house, her daugh-ter, and her maidservant would be away. The men had chosen the time carefully, then—but who was "she"? And why did William need bolstering?

What part did the publisher of the *London Chronicle* play?

Despite an inner chiding that said I ought to mind my business, I could not. I was the son of Benjamin Franklin; he loved secrets. Too, it was one thing not to know a thing and another to know it discreetly; thus I stayed by the window, keeping far back out of the light so no one in the street might see. The clock ticked more. The three-legged dog snuffed nearer the Thames. Moments passed—and then I was rewarded, for here came a woman down from the Strand, tentative, peering. She wore a simple dress, though her bonnet was much beribboned. How old? No more than thirty, her face small and thin, with dark brows and a delicate chin. She toyed with something in her right hand: a thimble. Her fine hat—had she made it herself? Was she a milliner? She paused to wipe a tear. Plainly she was unhappy. Shaken, too; her hands trembled. Her arms were slender—she was fine-boned—yet her figure grew stout; the gathers at the front of her dress could not conceal it, and she walked with particular care.

Her belly. She was with child.

William? thought I as she tucked the thimble in a bag and rapped solemnly at the brass knocker below. *William is the father?*

The three-legged dog gazed mournfully at the Thames.

The Mall was London's most fashionable promenade, broad and well-paved, lined with double rows of trees. It was bounded by Whitehall, the Admiralty, and Treasury at one end, Buckingham House at the other. The red brick of St. James's Palace proclaimed royalty to the north, whilst St. James's Park spread its green swards south, where cows grazed, and anyone could buy a cup of milk for twopence. The gentry strolled the Mall in fine weather, to see and be seen, and though they did so less as winter came on, the sun shone bright this afternoon, unfettered by cloud, so a swelling throng had gathered.

Sunday was a day of rest, so why should not the inheritors of wealth and title—and the rest of London, too—step out?

As Nelly Skindle had asked, Mr. Franklin and I waited by Marlborough House, observing the scene 'til she appeared. Splendid dresses and fine velvet coats passed, but we also saw clerks with inky fingers, maidservants lightly afoot, skylarking underbutlers. Stern burghers strolled too, and even a clergyman showed his face above his white bands, though his pinched look said he took the air only to disapprove. Women of the game plied their trade as well, striking bargains; commerce flourished.

I only half saw, thinking on this morn. A woman with child by William? She had remained but a quarter of an hour, fled in plenty of time to avoid Mrs. Stevenson's watchful eyes and Polly's clever ones; Strahan had spirited her away. Crouched on the second landing, I had heard only the buzz of their parley behind the closed door at the foot of the stairs. The woman had sobbed—I pictured a handkerchief pressed to soft, leaking eyes. What had they talked on? What accommodations made? I heard no loud voices, no recriminations; all seemed reasonable—and why not? For the most reasonable man in the world, Benjamin Franklin, chaired the meeting. Yet that reasonable man had also fathered an illegitimate child—me, Nick Handy—and I hoped I, too, would not father a bastard and he one after that.

Mr. Franklin and William had discovered me on the landing after Strahan left. Relieved-looking, William seemed hardly to note me, but Mr. Franklin had fixed a gimlet eye. "I see you are up."

"Just risen, sir." Hating my lie, I had apologized for arising so late.

The gray-brown eyes narrowed. "Late? Yet I glimpsed you at my bow window twenty minutes ago, as I stood upon the stoop."

My face had flamed red.

Now other business must be done, so I blinked away the memory, though I still hoped Mr. Franklin would tell me what had passed this morn some day. Must it be secret? Was my theory correct? Meanwhile the throng came and went, parted, surged, eyes searching for form and fashion. London on parade. Did anyone spy upon us? It would be easy to do so without being seen. Jack Scratch? One of the Earl of Chalton's minions?

Nelly Skindle arrived just past one. I recognized her blue-white skin, her reddish hair, her wanly pretty face. She wore a simple green dress and clutched a little purse to her bosom, a shy maidservant on her afternoon off, it seemed. Few would take her for a girl of the game.

She approached with wary eyes, and Mr. Franklin grasped both her hands. "Miss Skindle. You were right to write to me. Very brave."

His kindness seemed to settle her, though a furtive wildness remained in her look. "Th-thank you, sir," quavered she.

"Let us walk." He offered his arm. "We shall be less conspicuous that way."

She accepted, and we set out in the direction of Buckingham House.

Nelly Skindle had a chary manner but she needed little prompting to speak now; talk poured from her like water from a pump. She was discouraged from talking at Mother Cockburn's, she told us—she had not been hired to talk, and the whoremistress punished girls who became too friendly with one another. Yet they whispered late at night or in the early morn, "when the gentlemen are not at us," Nelly explained. Thus she had made a friend of Tuesday Marrowbone. Sorrow mingled with pleasure on her simple, scrubbed face as she recalled that time. "Dear Tuesday! She were a good girl. Fell into th' game like me, b'cause there weren't nothink else for 'er, I s'pose." At Mr. Franklin's prompting she told her own history; it was heartrending. The daughter of a costermonger's widow, she had been debauched by a brutish cousin, a wheelwright's apprentice, then by the wright himself, who kept her in back of his shop amongst the shavings, like some beast. She felt lucky to have found a place with Mother Cockburn. Her smile fluttered like a ha'penny candle. "A little room o' me own. Food. That's wot I need." What matter if she earned it by giving herself to any man who paid for her? Mr. Franklin asked what she might do in years to come, but she seemed hardly to comprehend the future. *Now* she was safe, that was what mattered.

She began to tremble, her hands to chafe. "Yet *am* I safe, sir? Wot if Long John Enderby comes for me? Wot if he takes me to th' earl?"

"The Earl of Chalton?"

"That were where Tuesday were took. Long John give her to the earl, and he carried her away, out o' London, to some big house in the country. She tol' me when we whispered at night. It were dreadful, she said. There were a cave, and men who wore masks and drank and danced and had 'er and the other girls, which was made to wear white sheets that were only tore off. The cave were like church, she said, with candles. The men prayed and worshipped—only not the true God." She rolled her eyes. "The earl were their priest, and their god wore leaves. There were a altar, too, where they done terrible things with a knife."

Mr. Franklin squinted. "A knife, child? What things did they do with a knife?"

"Bloody ones. There were lots o' blood, but I don't know more. 'Twere too 'orrible, Tuesday said. She would say nothink else."

"She was afraid, then?"

"They swore her to secrecy. She must never tell what she saw, or—" Nelly began to sob. "O, O, she never revealed it!"

We stopped under a sycamore, its branches stark against the broad, clear sky, and Mr. Franklin took both her hands. "You are a good girl, Nelly. You are right to tell me these things, for they may help bring your friend's murderer to justice." Had Tuesday ever spoken of Hester Ward? No. Tom Elstree? Not that she recalled. Did Silas Ward, the Marquess of Bathurst, frequent Mother Cockburn's?

"I dunno, sir, for we almost never learn a gen'leman's name. Most does not care to give 'em. O, Mr. Franklin, I wish t' tell more, but I do not know it. I asked Tuesday, but she said she had talked too much. She were terrible afeared o' th' earl. Long John, too. I have never seen the earl, but I have seen Long John. I have heard how he blacks your eye or cuts your lip." The girl began to sob. "She had a good heart, but it was carved from her. O, please, please find who murdered my friend, sir! Please make him pay!"

Mr. Franklin tightened his grip on her small, thin hands. He wore an iron look. "I mean to make him pay, Miss Skindle. If it is in my power, I shall make him pay."

We turned back toward Charing Cross, and when we reached Marlborough House, Nelly Skindle darted off as she had arrived, peering over her shoulder as if someone might watch. I did not like this. She was of no importance, yet she had been Tuesday Marrowbone's friend; she had spoke to Benjamin Franklin of it, too. Did that put her in danger?

Let her not be found with her heart cut out!

Whilst Mr. Franklin and I continued down the Mall, I reflected on the city's merciless nature. My heart was wrung at the thought of the two young whores whispering together, seeking friendship in a friendless world. I, too, had once been helpless under London's thumb, so I knew the city's ruthless caprice, and my fists clenched. We must discover why a wealthy ward and a penniless whore had been murdered in the same dread fashion!

Yet as I pictured Charles Ravenden's cave, its flickering torches, its lewd mosaic, its stained altar, a vision of disorder rose before me, where men acted without reason—*Fay ce que voudras*—and justice was a sham.

I must have looked grim, for I found Mr. Franklin's eyes on me. "Not wine upon that altar, then, eh, Nick?"

"Did Tuesday Marrowbone die because she dared speak of what she saw?" I asked.

"To Nelly Skindle? How would her murderer know she had done so? Yet did she speak to someone else? Oho, here is good fortune!"

He had halted in the thick of the throng. "What, sir?" asked I.

"Bubb Bixby, one of our Dionysians." Mr. Franklin accosted a foppish fellow in a burgundy coat and a gold-trimmed hat. "Mr. Bixby, sir!"

A puffed young man halted, lifting his quizzing lens in a manner that might have been practiced before a glass. His voice was a callow drawl: "Beg pardon, sir, but I do not believe—"

"Benjamin Franklin." A crisp bow. "We met at my lord Ravenden's Friday eve, and then at Chalton House yesterday. We were differently dressed at Chalton"—a wink—"and I think that, for a while, you were not dressed at all."

The young man started. He was little more than twenty, but already he ran to fat, with blubbery jowls and eyes encased in pockets of suet. He looked unwell, the color of a fish's belly. Still recovering from the Chalton revels, no doubt. Taken aback, he made mouths, and his dim eyes puckered. "I . . . I recall you now, sir," sputtered he, "but—"

"O, I am happy for it," Mr. Franklin said, beaming, "for I should like the wit of your company—if you have the time." He cocked a thumb. "I know for a fact that the Crown serves a fine French brandy to those who know to ask for it and are willing to pay; and as I know to ask and am happy to pay, I invite you to imbibe some with me."

This was better. Bubb Bixby licked thirsty lips, and I read his mind: drink had sent him awry, but more might right him. This gentleman would pay?

"I have half an hour to spare, if you please," agreed the fellow with bloated condescension.

. . .

The Crown was in Warwick Street, near Whitehall, a genteel establishment. It had a fine brandy, indeed—or so Mr. Franklin informed me, for I drank only a syllabub at the scrubbed wooden table by the window, where we sat ten minutes later. Pint pots clicked as serving girls swept to and fro in aprons and long skirts. Our libations were brought and, sinking into a corner, I sketched a portrait of Bubb Bixby whilst Mr. Franklin fished his waters.

They were not deep. Sucking his cheeks and quizzing the room, Bixby boasted that he was the son of one of His Majesty's upholsterers. "My father was knighted for a set of dining chairs!" he drawled, puffing like a pigeon. "As for me, I am the Earl of Chalton's bosom friend. Ravvy loves me. He knows a pearl beyond price."

How did Mr. Franklin keep from laughing? But he was expert at "enacting the humble inquirer or doubter," as he said, so he mastered his features, and after some desultory chat—all Bixby, Bixby, Bixby—he broached the Dionysus Club in his best manner.

Well oiled by a second brandy, our guest loosened his tongue: "Why, I have been a member more than a year," he proclaimed.

"Attended many a meeting, I'll wager?"

"Ev'ry one."

"In St. James's Square?"

"A jolly place!"

"At the cave, too?"

Bixby frowned. "You know of that?"

"My lord showed it me himself. Why . . . I may join your club!"

A smirk. "But you are too—"

"Too old? Do not fear to say it. Yet surely age is a matter of spirit. Why, I am as young as a babe!" Mr. Franklin bent near. "And yet . . . what exactly *is* the Dionysus Club? I am not clever. I cannot not quite make it out."

Bixby had begun to flush as he drank more, his words to slur. "Ha, 'tis Ravvy's fol-de-rol, that is what. Silly stuff, but great fun. Larks and girls—plenty of girls! He procures the finest, the cream o' the London brothels." Another long sip. "He likes to watch us at it, d'ye know? It is part of becoming a Dionysian: you must de-flower a virgin before him, before all of 'em, upon that stone in his cave. You must show the measure of your member." The fellow giggled.

Mr. Franklin smiled. "And how was your measure, sir?"

"I am an ox! A very bull!"

"Did you make your virgin bleed?"

"Like a stuck pig. But that was nothing to . . . You would not be-lieve . . . There are gouts of blood, for—" At this Bixby thought better, and thumped the oak. "I must have another brandy, sir!"

Mr. Franklin beckoned to the serving girl. She brought Bixby his third, and he drained half.

Mr. Franklin persisted. "Gouts of blood, eh? Not only from de-flowering? Come, man to man, what else do you Dionysians do?"

"There are other rites . . . wonderful . . . awful. They stir me to my soul. But I cannot tell 'em. I have spoke too much already." A belch. "You can learn more only by going through the initiation yourself. Are you up to it, sir? Can you muster your member?"

"Not as well as you, I am sure. How bravely you swallow your drink! But surely you can tell me this: my lord talks of death and resurrection. What does he mean by 'em?"

Bixby's eyes were fading, but a knowing smirk played about his lips. "He means that one may die and not die. I have seen the evidence, myself."

"Seen what?"

"He is a great sorcerer, y'know."

"How?"

Bixby waggled a drunken finger. "Nay, that is one of the secrets you will learn only if you become one of us—which you will never do, for you *are* too old, I say. And too fat." Plainly drink began to make him insolent, but Mr. Franklin only smiled.

"You grow stout yourself, sir. By the by, did you attend Ox-ford?"

"Did."

"At the same time as my lord?"

"Nay, but do not talk to him of Oxford. He struck a man who spoke to him of Oxford." Bixby barely got his glass to his mouth before he spilt the last of his brandy down his chin, belched once

145

again, and slid from view like a sinking ship. His head thudded on the bench. We heard prodigious snores.

Mr. Franklin looked at me. "I should like to've asked more, but this must do. Oxford again, eh? Let us waste no more time, for this bladder will not wake 'til six."

❦ 17 ❦

IN WHICH We Confer with a Magistrate, a Daughter
Turns Spy, and a Lord Sneaks Out . . .

The afternoon remained crisp and fine. A breeze had ban-
ished much of the coal smoke, and the sky was spanking
blue above the rooftops. It being Sunday, the streets were
uncrowded. A puppeteer danced his dolls by Spring Gardens. A
blind fiddler sawed a merry tune.

But there was murder to think on. And the Dionysus Club.

"It grows more strange the more we learn of it," said Mr.
Franklin, his brow furrowed, as we skirted puddles. "Debauchery
occurs there—but debauchery is one thing, murder another.
Gouts of blood? From deflowered virgins only, or is there worse
upon Charles Ravenden's altar?" He swung his stick. "My lord is
a sorcerer, is he? So is Ben Franklin—would I could magic the
truth out of him."

I thought on Mr. Franklin's magic as we passed Charing Cross.
There were many species of it: his "magic squares," as he called
them, by which he made interlocking rows of numbers add to the
same sum; his card tricks (he had defeated the master criminal
Quimp by trickery at London's most notorious gaming den); his
calming of turbulent waters by making solemn passes over them.
I had thought this truly magical 'til he revealed his secret: oil in a
glass knob at the top of his stick; his passes sprinkled the oil upon
the water's waves, and it was this which did the job. "There is no
true magic, Nick, only ignorance," he had often said—a pity, for
I wished some magic could reveal the truth of the Dionysus Club.

147

We came to Craven Street yet did not turn down, continuing instead to Covent Garden; in ten minutes we reached the great square. What a change from its wonted clamor! Faced by Inigo Jones's fine church, the piazza seemed hardly itself this Sunday at three, deserted of victual sellers, though tavern doors stood open, with the usual denizens hanging about. Glancing past the Shakespeare Tavern, I peered into Birdy Prinsop's alley, but it lay deserted, and a pang shot through me. Birdy's day of rest, too?

Our destination was number 4, Bow Street, the offices of Chief Magistrate John Fielding, just round the corner

The maidservant who opened fetched him from his good wife upstairs, and he joined us in his Justice Room, as bereft of drama as Covent Garden. The portrait of His Majesty, George II, kept its customary watch. Joshua Brogden was absent.

"Hullo, Franklin." Thumping unerringly to his bench, Fielding assumed his seat of honor, whilst we sat before him in the place where arraigned souls were judged. What must it be like to be accused here? I prayed I never learnt. Fielding customarily wore his black band in public, but he did not wear it now, and I examined the eyes in his great doughy face The flesh about them was puckered, yet the milk-white orbs within seemed to kindle, and I shifted uneasily upon my chair. I knew he was blind, yet I always had the impression that he saw as keenly as I.

"Do you stare at my eyes, boy?" demanded he, as if to confirm my thought.

Magic, indeed.

Mr. Franklin patted my shoulder. "Nick bears you great respect, sir." He had come to compare notes with his fellow justice-seeker, he said. "I pray no more women have been discovered with their hearts cut out."

Fielding's head was like a great cauliflower squashed upon his shoulders. "Murder always troubles London, but no more like that, thank heaven."

"I am glad to hear it. And your notices in the newspapers— have any discovered information? Culled witnesses?"

"No—though if they cause women to keep watch and take care, they have served good purpose."

"And Banting and the rest—do they learn anything?"

"Again I am sorry to say no. This affair is but one amongst many, damn Parliament for withholding funds! Our murderer is canny. Perhaps he has left London."

"Flew away, eh? Nay, I do not think so." Mr. Franklin related our past week: the encounters with the Marquess of Bathurst, Tom Elstree, Charles Ravenden, Mother Cockburn, Long John Enderby.

"Enderby?" Fielding slapped his bench. "You bearded Long John in his den and escaped with your skin, you say? I know the bloody brute. He is violent and capricious—he would crush your skull for a farthing. He has stood before this court more than once, but I have never been able to bind him over. He is protected in high places."

Mr. Franklin looked sharp. "By whom?"

"I have never been able to discover, though he provides more than one grandee what he fancies; they do not like their panders gaoled. Do not cross him, sir."

"Next time I shall be sure to take Peter." Mr. Franklin rubbed the head of his stick. "Yet you see my drift. Both murdered women were connected with Charles Ravenden and his Dionysus Club. What do you know of him?"

"Little. I do not pry into the gentry—cannot. Bludgeoners and riots are the Blind Beak's province, whores and cutpurses; my plate is full of 'em. Yet I do hear of Ravenden. There are complaints of his bloods."

Mr. Franklin reminded him of our encounter in St. James's Market.

Fielding's mouth flattened. "Take care, then. Most of the city's bloods are catch-as-catch-can; they act on caprice. Not Ravenden's. They are an army, which he uses for bad ends. They all have well-to-do fathers, so it is near impossible to touch 'em, though if I did lay hands on one, Ravenden would toss him to the dogs; he demands loyalty but never gives it. He knows how to avoid getting caught, too. Rumors of his debaucheries come to my ears: flogging houses, houses of boys, dens of poor abused beasts. Ravenden's name continually surfaces in regard to 'em, like gas above a cesspit—but there is nothing to get your hands on. He creeps. He lurks. He gets what he wants and skips free."

149

"Can murder be one of his debaucheries?"

"I would not put it past him," Fielding grumbled. "A temple deep in the country? A bloody altar in a cave? Dear God!" He lifted heavy hands. "Yet it is out of my jurisdiction."

"Perhaps not out of mine. To Silas Ward. He writ me a letter saying you paid him a call."

Fielding snorted laughter. "Aye, I harried him—he is an arrogant dog! You were quite right, he is thoroughly happy to have his niece dead."

"Did *he* murder her? Or pay someone do it?"

"Yet why cut out her heart?"

"Well taken. What of our scribbler, Jack Scratch?"

"He attacks both Ravenden and Silas Ward in print these days—Brogden reads me the papers."

Mr. Franklin thought. "That rainy night I came to view Hester Ward—how did he know you would be there? Did you see him hanging about Bow Street?"

"I *see* nothing, sir."

"Hear him, then. Did one of your men spy him?"

"No. But what do you propose? That he already knew the body was there? That *he* murdered her?"

" 'Tis possible."

"Too much in this affair is possible. Scratch might've murdered the other woman, too, you say? In the same fashion? What could be his motive?"

"Alas, what motive could any of 'em have? Yet I cannot forget he was at Oxford. He was driven out before he got his degree, he said; it eats at him like bile. Charles Ravenden and Tom Elstree studied at Oxford, too. They are of an age with Scratch, and they were sent down together—though I do not know why. Was Scratch sent down at the same time? For the same offense?"

Fielding's fingers drummed. "A trio of bad boys, eh? You may be onto something—but that was long ago. How can it relate to two murders years later?"

"Tom Elstree may yet tell me. There is something about the young man . . ." Mr. Franklin let this hang. "Failing Elstree, I shall ask Scratch himself. If neither proves fruitful . . . well . . ." The gentleman turned to me. "What of a journey to Oxford, Nick?"

. . .

We strolled home as four o'clock bells rang out. Shop fronts were closed, but beggars plied their trade. A huddle of cloaked figures rattled dice by a chandler's, whilst a bill-poster slapped up the latest at Sadler's Wells. Kicking dirty cobbles, I felt more bewildered than ever: what might have happened at Oxford years ago to provide the answer to our mystery? Still, I should like to see the great university town.

Mr. Franklin's thoughts lay elsewhere. His look remained fiercely fixed ahead as he walked with his hands behind his back. "Titled folk. My lord. My lady. Tosh! I do not care for titles. Do they confer merit? Adam was never called Master Adam. We never read of Noah, Esquire, nor the Right Honorable Abraham, Baron of Canaan. They were plain men, honest country graziers who took care of their familes and their flocks. One day we shall dispense with inherited privilege and all the arrogance it breeds, Nick."

"I hope you are right, sir," said I.

As we approached Craven Street I could not help recalling how masked men had once breached Mrs. Stevenson's walls, so I was relieved to find all well. The odor of roast beef wafted from the kitchen below, whilst the bannister and newel posts gleamed with polishing. Mr. Franklin took Polly quietly into the front parlor, to ask if she had observed anything; I went with them. Her eager blue eyes said she longed to impart some dread news, but she had to confess she could not. "But I shall keep watch, sir, I shall!"

Mr. Franklin spoke to Peter, too.

This occurred in his chamber. He had set his servant to discover when the Earl of Chalton returned from his estate. His lordship had drawn up before his St. James house just past two, Peter reported.

"Alone?"

"A young man arrived with him." Peter described Tom Elstree. "He stayed a short while, no more than a quarter hour. A sadlooking fellow. Unhappy."

"Good work."

When Peter was gone Mr. Franklin stood by his bow window gazing into the gathering dusk. "Does Ravenden keep an eye on

151

Elstree? Does he advise him? Does he warn him off Ben Franklin?" He turned. "Does he fear Tom Elstree, Nick?"

I had the remainder of the day to myself. At his desk Mr. Franklin writ to his good wife Deborah; and to David Hall, William Strahan's former apprentice, who had become Mr. Franklin's partner in his printing shop in Philadelphia. I sat in the chair by the fire examining my drawings, adding a line here, a detail there. Faces peered back: Tom Elstree, Mother Cockburn, Long John Enderby. I had sketched the revels at Chalton, too: the white-garbed forms amongst the damp black trees. My pencil added the fleeting storm. I read my notes as well, setting them in order so Mr. Franklin might peruse them, so I also might peruse them when I wished, to recall this troubling time.

Yet though I could say what we had seen and heard since that rain-drenched mews, even draw pictures of it, I could not fathom what it meant.

Mr. Franklin had many Scots friends. Sir John Pringle was one. He had been professor of moral philosophy in Edinburgh before he became physician general to the British forces in Flanders; his *Observation on the Diseases of the Army* had made his name. A Fellow of the Royal Society, he held convocations of learned men at his house on Sundays. One met this eve, and Mr. Franklin departed for it at eight.

This left Mrs. Stevenson and Polly and me.

William joined us at supper.

I examined him by the warm glow of candlelight as we spooned potato soup. He looked chastened but hopeful. Because the issue with the woman was settled? Polly watched him, too. Did she suspect his crime?

After supper I felt restless, longing for . . . what? I half wished Polly would tickle me; I even waited where I knew she would pass, by the parlor door. But having been made privy to our affair by Mr. Franklin, she did not need anything of me, it seemed, so she merely ran her fingers through my hair as she passed.

I flamed, I burned.

Upstairs I fretted over murder.

· · ·

Monday I was up betimes. *A week since we learnt of Hester Ward,* thought I as I dressed. Across the landing I found Mr. Franklin in his nightshirt, just setting down his dumb-bells before his bow window. A shine of perspiration said he had swung them vigorously. The casement lay open, and he sucked great gusts of brisk, chill morn.

"Good day, sir." He loved his air-baths, but this was done, so I made up the fire, raking banked coals to kindle new ones.

The sky was cloudless again, and London stirred cheerily; a coster sang his wares below our window. Yet the weather was sure to change. Did pursuits and danger lay ahead? Not today, for Mr. Franklin was to attend the Board of Trade, whilst I must remain mired in ciphers and Latin (*"Usus promptos facit,"* said he: practice makes perfect). But plans changed when Richard Jackson poked in his head to say that the proprietary question had been postponed another week. "Damn." Mr. Franklin tossed down his pen—he had worked more than two years to see the question resolved. But then he glanced at me. *All the more time for our mystery,* his look said.

Polly rapped upon his door only moments after Richard Jackson departed.

All breathless, she darted in. "O, I have seen him, Mr. Franklin! I have seen him!" She pressed her back to the door.

He rose from his desk. "Who, child?"

Her breast heaved dramatically. "The man you set me to see. I have watched and watched, and then this morning I forgot to watch, for Nanny was doing my hair whilst I read a book. But I looked up—and there, out my window, I saw a man in the street."

"There are many men in the street. I am myself quite often there."

"Do not mock me. It *must* have been he. He was dreadfully suspicious. He glanced at the house as if he did not mean to, but I saw him, I did! Then he slipped into that little alley across the way. You would have missed him if you had not been quick, but I knew he was there, so I hid behind the window curtain and spied, and there he was. He watched us, I tell you. He fixed his eyes on this house—on your very window. He took out a paper and writ upon it."

"Is he there still?" Hurrying to the casement, Mr. Franklin and I peered out—but the alley lay empty.

Mr. Franklin turned with a furrowed brow. "You are certain of what you saw?"

"Can you doubt me?"

"What did he look like?"

Polly's description was unmistakably of Jack Scratch.

Mr. Franklin rubbed his jaw.

"You know him, I see that you do!" Polly cried.

"I know *of* him. A creeping fellow. He prints scurrilous stuff in the *Courant* and learns more about me than I like." Plainly he had not told her of Scratch, much less that we had seen the scribbler the night Hester Ward's body was found.

"But why should he spy upon you?" Polly demanded.

"I do not know—but listen carefully." Mr. Franklin looked at her hard. "You have done well, yet this may not be the only man who spies upon us. You must still watch out."

He could not have commanded anything better. "I will, I will!" Polly clasped her hands to her breast. "O, it is wonderful!" she cried.

At breakfast Mrs. Stevenson looked gratified when Mr. Franklin broached the subject of lightning rods—here was the lodger she knew—but she would not come to terms without a fight. "You said such a rod might attract the lightning."

"And will carry any charge harmlessly into the ground."

"I still do not like the idea."

"Come, you would like it less if the lightning visited you in your bedchamber, dear lady."

"O, sir!"

At this moment there came a crash from the kitchen, and Mrs. Stevenson jumped up. "Will your lightning rod cure clumsy housemaids? Nanny!" She bustled away.

William customarily accompanied his father to the Board of Trade, but learning he need not today, he set out to Ranelagh, to look at the Chinese bridges, he said. His father watched him depart.

At eleven he and I repaired to Goodlow's Coffee House in the Haymarket.

Monday continued near as fine as Sunday, bracingly chill. We saw fleeting shadow as shreds of cloud fretted the sun, but London still enjoyed a respite from rain. Mr. Franklin wished to examine the newspapers, he said, settling on a bench amidst all the others who drank their coffee and smoked their pipes and burst out in curses at what they read. There were not many papers Monday morn, but the *Courant* was one; in it, Jack Scratch spewed yet more scandal.

Mr. Franklin read him, then passed him to me. The typesetting was disgraceful, not near as exact as I—or Mr. Franklin—would have done (there were seven *errata*), but that was beside the point. I was surprised to discover that Scratch knew all about the ceremonies at Chalton House. Surely he had not been there, yet he had impeccable sources, for he described the debauchery accurately—the temple, the lake, the torchlit procession—though he only hinted at who had been present: Sir ———, Lady ———, the dimwitted Dr. F——— of Craven Street. His worst barbs were saved for the earl himself. "A painted whore," he called him.

Mr. Franklin met my eyes. "There is no love lost betwixt 'em, it seems."

As noon bells rang out we strolled west—not by chance, I guessed, for our steps took us into the orbit where the two mutilated bodies had been found. Did Mr. Franklin hope some detail might set him on a better path? I found myself wondering about the moment of the womens' deaths. Had they known what end came to them, or had it been a surprise? And the places they were found: a mews and a churchyard—did they signify?

I prayed the women had been in God's arms before the knife cut their hearts.

We came to St. James's Square: thirty-one elegant red-brick facades fronted by horse-posts. The park at its center was symmetrical, neat, trim, proclaiming reason and order, but it lied; chaos lurked here. At the southwest corner rose Silas Ward's house, at the northeast, Charles Ravenden's. Both were bastions of privilege—but privileged men could be fools, and the two peers despised one another. Did they sneer as they left their doors? And when they met in the House of Lords, did they snarl, or did freezing politeness reign?

Mr. Franklin stood very still, leaning on his bamboo. His eyes measured the distance betwixt these two houses, and mine did, too. How easy it would have been for Hester Ward to slip across to Charles Ravenden's door. She had, sometimes. Why? Though he claimed to have liked her, he did not care for most women, he said. Because boys pleased him better? His mother had whored under his father's nose; he had seen it himself. He had spoke proudly of her—he and she were, alike: defiant. Yet how had he really felt when he discovered her with his father's manservant? Had he been proud of her then?

I could not help thinking on my own beleaguered mother.

Ah, London.

Mr. Franklin's hand abruptly fell upon my shoulder; it drew me into Charles Street, and from round its corner we peeped back into the square. The door of number 18 lay open. A shabby hackney passed us, stopping there just as Simkins appeared on the marble stoop, followed by Charles Ravenden, glancing sharply round.

But this was not the Charles Ravenden I had met. His face was not painted, and he was dressed far differently from his usual fashion. He had on a drab coat some twopenny tinker might have owned, and his black hair was hid under a tatty wig, upon which he wore a battered tricorn hat.

I should hardly have known him.

Simkins bowed him down the steps, whilst a blackamoor boy in a turban held the door of the hackney. Ravenden gave a second glance round, then darted in and the driver snapped his reins.

"Quickly, Nick!" Mr. Franklin set off back down Charles Street.

I scrambled after him.

"Let us secure conveyance; there are many in the Haymarket. We must follow the man."

🏵 18 🏵

IN WHICH We Witness a Lashing and Follow a Lord . . .

We were fortunate within a moment to come upon one of the ubiquitous London hackneys. We leapt in, and Mr. Franklin directed our driver posthaste to St. James's Square—yet he need not, for as we were about to wheel round, the earl's hackney rattled along Charles Street. We sank back so as not to be seen, though I glimpsed my lord's profile in the shadows of his coach, marked with a hungry look.

He careered by. Mr. Franklin thumped our roof. "That one, sir. Follow—but not too close."

Our driver called *"Haw!"* and we set off.

Past Leicester Fields to Hemmings Way, then into Chandos Street. As we jounced along, Mr. Franklin fidgeted. "My lord leads a strutting life of show—he is no hypocrite like other men, he says. Yet he disguises himself, too, and hires a common carrier, of which there are hundreds in London. To take him where? Does he often go about this way?"

As we wheeled right into Bedford Street, I thought on Simkins. Did he know his master's destination? *He is innocent,* Simkins had said of Tom Elstree, during our strange encounter at the Earl of Chalton's estate when the tormented young man flung himself away amongst the night-black trees. What had Simkins meant? Innocent of what? Why tell us?

At the bottom of Bedford we turned left into the Strand, speeding toward the City of London, where money was banked and huge, dank jails imprisoned those who stole it. The day dimmed as a coal-fire fog began to drift like a shroud over the great thoroughfare; our respite of clear skies was done. For a quarter hour we stopped, started, veered—once our wheels crashed into a dray's, and once we near tipped into an ironmonger's yard—but our driver kept our quarry in sight. Fleet Ditch neared. St. Paul's huge dome loomed.

But before we could cross Fleet Bridge, Ravenden's coach veered south into Salisbury Court. As it passed the church of St. Bride's I frowned. Dorset Street lay ahead, a timber yard, some water stairs, and then the Thames. What should he do here? His coach drew up at the corner of a narrow alley, Wilderness Way. Opposite this lay a burying ground, and beyond that the walls of some forbidding palace.

Mr. Franklin gazed at them. "Bridewell," said he.

I knew it. It had been built by Henry VIII for the emperor Charles V on a state visit, but, poorly sited, it had been presented to the city soon after as a workhouse; it had been a workhouse ever since.

One of the great prisons of London.

Its infelicitous bulk seemed to fill the sky. A grog shop, the Broken Stave, stood on a corner, and Charles Ravenden got down by it. "Hm," Mr. Franklin grunted, rapping the roof, and our own coach pulled to a halt at a distance. Peering out, we watched our quarry pay his driver. Then his hackney rattled off whilst he stood as if sniffing the wind. A one-legged pieman hawked misshapen little rounds of dough from a stand. Two carriers wheeled tottering piles of clinker-bricks. A drunkard huddled against a wall cradling his head in his hands. Fingers of fog snatched at the sun. Still, though my lord was well-disguised, he kept his head low, his hat well down. Plainly he did not care to be noted.

Crossing past the burying ground, he slipped through the gate of Bridewell Prison.

At this Mr. Franklin started; he struck a fist into a palm. "Monday," murmured he. "That is why he is here."

"Monday, sir?" I peered into his bespectacled face.

"You shall see—though I wish you need not. Come."

Leaving our coach, we crept past the burial ground to pause before Bridewell's mawlike gates. Other men were entering as

Ravenden had, some well dressed, some in plain garb, though an air of feverish anticipation hung about them all. I had sneaked into a cockfight once, in Moorfields, before Mr. Franklin had rescued me from Fish Lane; I had been ten years old, a new-fledged boy—what adventure! But the vicious den had frightened, me, its noise and urgency, the earth sprayed with blood. I had felt the same stirring in that sweating arena that I sensed in the men hurrying into Bridewell now: a hot, wicked excitement, not of joy but of something shameful.

We entered the prison, too.

Inside I felt even more the dread of the place; its great weight seemed to press down so I could hardly breathe. Prostitutes were remanded here, to pay for selling themselves by deprivation, abuse, rank air, and tainted food. Our noses wrinkled at a stench of must, sweat, excrement, despair, and Mr. Franklin brushed a hand over the cold stone walls. "I despise such places, Nick. John Fielding is right: these women need useful work, not imprisonment—and they need it *before* they are locked up."

Charles Ravenden was nowhere in sight, but we hung behind the other men; we did not want him to know we followed. At the end of a narrow corridor we stood in line at a Keeper's Office, where Mr. Franklin paid two shillings. For what? His expression grew grimmer, and the grizzled man who snatched his coin cocked a knowing look. "A quarter hour, gen'lemen," said he. "That is all you must wait. Do not be impatient, for there are three today to please you."

We and the others—seven in all—followed a bailiff up a winding stair. On the second floor the air grew worse, and I saw that some of the men in our group held vinegar-cloths or poncets of herbs before their noses; plainly they had been here before. Cockroaches scuttled into cracks. The air was like ice. I began to hear a steady *thump-thump*, like a march of leaden feet, and pausing at a doorway I saw a line of women beating hemp on great sawn logs with heavy wooden mallets. A few were old, but most were young, Birdy Prinsop's age, and some of these could hardly lift their tools. *Thump-thump. Thump-thump.* Every face showed a plodding exhaustion, as if all hope had been extinguished. Could this be the fruit of English law?

"Aye, Nick," murmured Mr. Franklin, "yet there is worse . . ."

Our destination proved the flogging room.

Twenty paces more, and we turned right, into a large, dungeonlike chamber. Straw was strewn upon its rough wooden floor; otherwise it was unfurnished save for a rope dividing it in half, behind which we stood. Two narrow windows let in bruised light, and a pair of manacles hung from iron chains stapled to the far wall.

Dear God, thought I.

An earlier group of men already stood in front of the rope, opposite the manacles, Charles Ravenden amongst them. We ducked behind others of our party so he would not note us, though there seemed little chance, for he was deeply preoccupied. I peeped at him. His tongue oiled his lips, and he seemed to tremble in anticipation, his long-fingered hands opening and closing at his sides. I recalled John Fielding's words: *Rumors of his debaucheries come to my ears . . .*

No more witnesses arrived, and the silence grew ominous whilst we waited. *This is wrong,* thought I, holding my breath, *dreadfully wrong.*

Of a sudden a heavy door banged open in the other half of the room, making me jump, and I glimpsed three women beyond it, their faces wretched with fear. Snatching one of them, two strong warders dragged her in, slamming the door behind them. She was pretty, little more than twenty, her copper hair in disarray about her shoulders, her eyes swimming with terror. "No, sirs, I repent!" cried she, twisting pitifully. "Have I not told you, I repent?"

The men only leered. "Too late, Moll," growled the taller, a brutish fellow who forced one of her small white hands into a manacle high on the wall and snapped the iron shut. "Yer must have yer due. Here're some nice gents to watch it." He winked at us. "Yer would not want to disappoint 'em, would yer?"

The woman's other hand was entrapped too, so she hung with her back to us, her arms above her head. "O, O!" cried she, writhing, sobbing.

Could I bear this?

A bailiff strode in. From a stamped paper he droned the charge against the miscreant: some infraction of Bridewell law having to do with a scrap of bread. So little a thing? The bailiff had a chalky face. His eyes were as dead as spent coals, and gazing at us blackly, he growled, "Here's wot yer come for."

Turning to the woman, he stripped her shirt from her.

He did it so quickly, in one swift motion, that I gasped. How vulnerable was the woman's back, an ivory triangle tapering to a narrow waist. It was a white and perfect back, an innocent back—everyone in this room must see that—and I trembled. This must not be! The poor woman had lain with men only because she must; surely she would not be violated for more men's pleasure. Her twisting showed her breasts, and I could not watch more. I peered at Mr. Franklin. Never had I seen him so gray, so appalled. I turned to the other men—surely they would protest the thing! But no, their boots stirred in the straw, their lips puffed, they muttered like beasts. They had come to see a beating, not to stop one—and Charles Ravenden was the worst. He leant forward like some eager predator.

I long for your pain, his look said.

The bailiff stepped aside, and the tall, brutish warder took up a scourge with a dozen leathern thongs. He flicked them, they made a sharp *snap!*, and the woman wailed thinly: "I repent, sirs, I repent!"

Her words did no good.

The warder began.

I had heard the words "blood lust." I had seen what they meant at that cockfight in Moorfields—unreasoning madness—but I had never thought to see it in a place where human flesh was made to bleed whilst men smiled to look on. The warder set his legs. He swung—and at the first terrible sound of leather upon that pure back, at the first awful red lines it made, at the victim's cry of shock and pain, feral gleams lit the faces of the witnesses. This was justice? I could not watch, and though Mr. Franklin gripped my arm to steady me, I saw that he, too, averted his eyes, fixing them instead upon Charles Ravenden.

My lord stood at the far end of the room. Plainly he saw and heard nothing but the vile spectacle for which he had paid. His face was contorted into a mask of ecstasy; he reveled in agony. I thought on the white flesh of Dionysus in the painting in his library; the flesh-ripping Maenads he worshipped; Hester Ward, Tuesday Marrowbone.

He murdered them, my mind thundered. *He carved out their hearts because it pleased him.*

I could not bear it. One man pawed at his breeches as the whip flicked. Another, a fat, well-dressed fellow, took snuff and laughed, whilst yet another began spitting abuse at the helpless woman. I saw why there was straw upon the floor: to catch the spattered blood.

Cockfight blood. Human blood.

By now the woman twisted but feebly. *Let her fall unconscious,* thought I. *Lord, be merciful.*

My head spun. I must escape. I stumbled toward the door, so near, but in doing so I bumped the fat fellow, who barked displeasure: "You clumsy pup!" My gaze flew to Charles Ravenden. His shoulders twitched, his blazing eyes began to turn—and in a panic of fear I averted my face.

I ran out, and in the corridor vomited my breakfast upon the stones.

The sour taste. The sick heaving. Mr. Franklin had followed, and I wiped my mouth with the handkerchief he lent me. "Th-thank you, sir." He led me hurriedly to the stairs. I turned to him desperately as we reached the ground floor. "But is there nothing we can do for that poor woman? Surely there is something!"

His grave eyes met mine. "What? Wrest the scourge from the warder? We should be arrested for obstructing the law, and the woman would be beat nonetheless."

We exited the prison. "This is not law," said I.

He sighed. About us coal smoke thickened the day. "Laws are made by men—how rarely they express true justice! The outrage occurs weekly, for Mondays are flogging days, and if no inmate has transgressed enough to warrant beating, the keepers find good reason nonetheless, for the gents who pay their coin must have their show."

A dray clopped by. My spinning brain had steadied. "The devil take 'em all!" I choked.

"Let him take Charles Ravenden first. I am sorry you saw this, Nick, but it has taught us the extent of my lord's callousness."

I swallowed. "He cut out those women's hearts?"

"Dear God, I believe he may." He gazed at the prison's soot-begrimed facade. "You ask what we can do for these poor inmates.

Little for the ones we have seen—but for those to come, we must change the world. It is slow work, yet one day right will prevail." His gray-brown eyes burned behind their twin lenses, and I knew why I loved him.

Yet had Charles Ravenden recognized me as I fled the flogging room? Had he spied Mr. Franklin? I peered at the Bridewell gate, like a mouth which had spit us out. Soon it would disgorge the Earl of Chalton; he must not find us here.

Mr. Franklin read my thought, for he drew me into a mercer's shop near Wilderness Way, a cramped, narrow room where a dozen dusty bolts of cloth lay on plain deal counters. A watery-eyed clerk pounced—"Fine Holland for your shirts, sirs!"—and we pretended interest whilst we lurked by the grimy windowpanes. Through them we watched the other Bridewell patrons trail out ten minutes later. The fat fellow regaled his nose with snuff, whilst another glowed pink with surfeit; plainly they had got what they wanted. My lord emerged last, in his dun-brown coat. As before he squinted about under his hat. Seeking traces of Benjamin Franklin? But his look barely grazed the mercer's, and with a vain little jerk of his shoulders, as if to say, *I have fooled 'em*, he set off.

"He walks, eh?" murmured Mr. Franklin—but no, for at a corner my lord sprang into a passing hackney, and it sped off. "Quickly." Mr. Franklin tugged my arm. He had paid our driver to wait, so we dashed for our coach. As I scrambled in, I misgave—if our quarry glanced back, he would surely see us, but there was no help for that.

Settling himself, Mr. Franklin scowled. "Whither the man now?" His bamboo tapped the roof. "Driver, follow on!"

The earl's hackney returned west. Back to St. James's Square? But no, for his driver veered north, wending to Newgate Street. Past St. Sepulcher's Church, he headed up Holborn Hill. Mr. Franklin gave me a glance. *We shall see*, it said as he settled back, and I sat back, too, fingering my sketching book, though I doubted I could bring myself to draw what I had seen in Bridewell today. The afternoon grew grayer. Bits of ash blew in our windows, and people huddled in pulled-tight coats. Boys played hoops in a mews. A hurdy-gurdy man cranked his raucous tune at the corner of Fetter Street. Reaching the wider way of Holborn, we passed Gray's Inn and Chancery Lane.

Above Lincoln's Inn Fields, we descended into the parish of St. Giles.

This was a poor parish indeed, a cluster of meandering streets where High Holborn became Broad Street. You saw its air of poverty everywhere, in sagging house fronts, broken brick, shabby garments. Dirty faces watched us pass, for few coaches came this way. "Beggars reside here," said Mr. Franklin. "You can rent crutches to help you cadge your coin. Women rent their babies, too—a man will more likely open his purse to a babe—and receivers of goods abound. See those pawnshops? Crime breeds in St. Giles. What does the Earl of Chalton here?"

I wondered the same, though by now I would put nothing past the man. We had kept a fair distance behind his hackney, but it now stopped by a tumbled wall where a dog with ribs like sticks sniffed at a pile of rubble. The earl got down, as anonymous here as he had been at Bridewell.

Paying his driver, he vanished like a wraith.

"What—?" Mr. Franklin thumped the roof, and we leapt out. I glanced round. Only one other conveyance was in sight, a small, closed coach, but it had halted so far behind ours that I thought nothing of it. Mr. Franklin eyed it, too, but he seemed to pay it no heed.

He tossed coin to our coachman, and we set off.

Our quarry had slipped into a thoroughfare whose entrance had been obscured by a shed. *Croft Lane* was painted on its crumbling wall. My lord was nowhere in sight, but we turned down it nonetheless. It proved more an alley than a street, winding into a warren of fetid ditches and decaying houses, over ground that heaved and cracked. A ragged watercress girl passed us: "Cress . . . Cress-O!" A toothless cat's-meat woman pawed my arm. A coster with a barrow of bruised and wormy apples thrust his wares in our faces. There were cheapjacks' stalls as well: stolen goods? Rough-looking fellows hung about, and I worried. Though plainly dressed—Mr. Franklin wore his customary brown—we were still well-garbed for St. Giles. Ripe for robbery? Passing under tilting eaves and hollow windows, we were marked by men who lounged in the doorways of gin houses that spilt with the banshee wail of despair.

Yet I never hesitated. Though St. Giles reminded me of the dispiriting streets of my boyhood, I could not forget those two destroyed women. Hester Ward and Tuesday Marrowbone were not names we had read in a newspaper. We had met people who knew them, we had learnt of their lives, we had seen the body of one, and we must avenge their murders. As for the man we followed, we did not know for certain that he had cut out their hearts, but if he had not wielded the knife, he had been instrumental—I felt it in my bones. I stayed by Mr. Franklin's side.

A dirty-faced urchin lugging a bundle of faggots trailed past. A woman flung slops from a door. Mr. Franklin touched my arm. "There," said he, stopping by a rusted pump; I stopped, too. We stood in a little widening of the way, muddy and unpaved; tatters of laundry fluttered on a line nearby. Ahead rose a house larger than most, though it was still a melancholy place: three stories of begrimed plaster topped by mossy slate. A pair of painted women gazed out a second story window, smiling lewdly. They waved and beckoned—no surprise to find whores in St. Giles.

Yet I was puzzled. "The earl is here?" murmured I to Mr. Franklin.

The gentleman gestured. "Look closer, Nick."

I squinted at the women in the window. They were boys.

It was unmistakable in spite of their paint. *He is here, indeed*, thought I.

Nearer than I knew, for he suddenly emerged six feet from us. I started, though Mr. Franklin did not appear surprised. My lord had slipped from a doorway; he now stood, hands on hips, smiling but with a knife-edge of displeasure on his long, strange face; and I saw what I had not before: that his white paint had masked poxy skin. His cheeks and chin were pitted, as if some dread poison had eaten him from within.

He reached out to finger the lapel of my coat. "Did you enjoy Bridewell, boy?" I smelt his clove-scented breath. "Yet I think not, for I had to step over your stinking vomit. Tut, you must learn to take things as they are. The woman was nothing; she deserved a beating. Learn to be stoic. It is best not to be discommoded by another's pain."

"The true stoic is not discommoded by his *own* pain," replied Mr. Franklin.

Ravenden turned. "You will be a philosopher, will you? Well, I am in no humor to fence." He gestured toward the painted pair at the window, wearing cat's grins. "Do you come to have a tumble? O, delicious! I like a boy's buttocks—there is nothing like 'em for pleasure. Or do you come to introduce your Nick to the game?" He rocked on his heels. "We are alike, Mr. Franklin. I knew we were the minute I saw you."

"I introduce Nick to better things. And I hope we are very little alike."

Ravenden only smiled. "Tush, not even in cleverness? Surely you think you are a very clever fellow. As for myself, I am the cleverest fellow in the world. I know it is the fashion to demean cleverness—it is no true virtue, the wits say—but damn fashion! I despise virtue. Cleverness for me. Was I not clever to know you followed me? (You are clumsy, sir.) And to await you here?" He tapped Mr. Franklin's chest. "But your cleverness is tainted by scrupulosity. I saw that when we met; I warned you of it, but you did not heed me. You will spend your life being scrupulous, Mr. Franklin, and then you will discover you have lived no life at all."

"I shall have lived the right way."

Ravenden spat laughter. "And I the wrong? Damn me, sir, you *are* impertinent. But perhaps your 'right' way will not last as long as you think."

Mr. Franklin ignored this threat. "Why were you sent down from Oxford, sir?"

"And why did you speak to that little whore in the Mall on Sunday?" My lord snapped his fingers. "You see, I am well ahead of you. But I have vowed not to fence, and I will not. You have spoilt my day; I shall not have a boy, after all, for I must go home to think about Benjamin Franklin. What shall I do about him?" He eyed me with dark speculation. "And his pretty boy. Good day."

With that he strode off.

I stood there hardly aware of the painted faces in the window or the gloomy street, the crowding afternoon. *Take care, Mr. Franklin, take care!*

He did not look afraid, however, nor as if he had any intention of taking care. Some other matter was on his mind as he watched our enemy's retreat. "Is he clever enough to know that *both* of us were followed?"

I blinked. "Followed? By whom?"

"Let us see." Ravenden had departed by an intersecting lane, as if he knew these precincts well, but Mr. Franklin led me back along the path we had come. We approached a grog shop, the Skull and Bones. At its low door he darted in, and I scrambled after.

Jack Scratch hovered just inside.

❧ 19 ❧

IN WHICH We Question a Scribbler, and a Servant Delivers Dire News . . .

The Skull and Bones proved an even lower den than the Black Dog: a cramped, ill-lit lair like the burrow of some animal. Beneath its smoke-blackened ceiling four squat tables were occupied by hunkered forms muttering over their gin. The floor was beaten earth. A fug of musty thatch and sour clothes assailed my nostrils.

How much further could a soul descend from here?

The light was poor, but the man who faced us was unmistakably Jack Scratch. Had he hoped we would pass? Whether or no, he faced us defiantly, and he was as I remembered: ferretlike in a snuff-brown coat, with a belligerent look in his yellowish eyes.

"Good day, Benjamin Franklin," pronounced he in his insinuating way.

"Good day, Jack Scratch. Or should it be Pyecroft? I am glad you have followed me—glad, too, that I spied your coach and glimpsed you creeping behind us—for I have questions to ask."

"I did not follow you." Scratch's head jerked. "I followed the other one."

"But you watched outside my lodgings this morn."

"You have sharp eyes. You ought scribble for the newspapers—ha!" He wiped his nose. "But I make no apology. A man who takes an interest in the Earl of Chalton earns Jack Scratch's regard."

"Why?"

"Because I hate the man!" His venom took me aback. What angers and secrets did he harbor?

"Again, why?" pursued Benjamin Franklin.

"The world will know soon enough." Scratch shook a righteous finger. "I will see the devil done for!"

"How? By abusing him in print?"

"I write the truth."

"And what *is* the truth?" Mr. Franklin made a placating gesture. "Women have died. Perhaps we may work together, to—"

"Nay, sir. I have read *The Way to Wealth*. I know what Poor Richard says—'Three can keep a secret if two of them are dead'—and I shall hearken to that advice, else I might also—" He bit the words off.

"Likewise be dead?" Mr. Franklin finished.

"I survive, sir. I watch my back. I lock my door. I shall live to keep this secret, 'til I have evidence enough to lay before the court."

"Of sodomy?"

The bitter mouth twisted. "Sodomy? Why, it is not a crime worth spitting on! Men may be tried for it, but murder is worse—and far better, for it is more certain to lead to a hanging, and I want to see damned Ravenden hang. I want his eyes to pop, his tongue to swell, his boots to kick. I want to stand at the foot of Tyburn and cry, 'See, sir, see!' "

The man's hands trembled, and I trembled, too. There was madness here. Madness in Jack Scratch. Madness in St. James's Square. Madness in a cave dug into the Richmond chalk.

"Three, sir." Mr. Franklin pressed him. "What signifies the number three?"

"Nay, I have told you enough. You must make of it what you will."

"Yet if you mean a third woman may be murdered, you must help to prevent it."

The yellowish eyes glimmered as Scratch weighed these words. Then, as if to tease—as if he could not resist flaunting his secrets—he said with sly cunning, "Very well, I give you this: murder may happen in London, and it may happen in other places, too."

"What can you mean?"

169

Silence.

"Do you speak of Oxford, sir? You are of an age with my lord. And with a young man named Tom Elstree."

"O, I know Elstree, a weakling, a pup, one of my lord's things. I see him in St. James's Square often."

"The three of you were together at Oxford."

"Who says so?"

"I do, sir. Damn it, what happened at Oxford?"

Scratch pushed past us. But in the low doorway he spun round. "Enough, sir—except for this: Charles Ravenden is a fiend; he crushes men's lives and laughs at 'em. You are a clever boots, but I pray you fail to bring him to justice, for when he stands in the dock, I want him to know 't was *I* who put him there. Good day." He pushed into the street.

Drunken laughter rattled at our backs. The crash of a dice cup. Outdoors we were in time to see a snuff-brown coat whip round a jog in the twisting lane; then Jack Scratch was gone.

Mr. Franklin rubbed his jaw. "What a deal of malice! It is the second time today I have been called clever, but I do not feel clever. Must we travel to Oxford to find the answer?" He turned up his collar. "Brr, how ill the day grows! How murky our pursuit! If I had known—" He broke off to chuckle wryly. "Well, if I had known, I would have done the same, for I am a hound, Nick." He clapped my arm. "Home, lad, to Mrs. Stevenson's ministrations."

I was happy to depart St. Giles, happy to reach Craven Street before four.

Nanny opened to us, but we entered to disarray, for a shipment of comestibles had just arrived from Pennsylvania: dried venison and bacon, cranberries, smoked beef, pippin apples. They sat in just-opened boxes in the entryway smelling of a foreign land. A letter had come, too, saying that Mr. Franklin's wife had sent the goods, and he perused it with a small, pleased smile whilst Mrs. Stevenson poked though things to see how they might fit in her larder. "What a fine woman your Deborah must be!" pronounced she. "An excellent wife?"

"A paragon!"

Our landlady frowned. "But surely we have better pork in Eng-

170

land?" She felt of a ham. "I wonder she sent it." Biting her tongue, she sorted quietly through the rest, and I saw that on these shores Benjamin Franklin was *hers* to care for, so she did not like foodstuffs from a stay-at-home wife.

Mr. Franklin beat a retreat.

In his chamber he stood wrapped in thought. A fishmonger cried her wares in the street. A ship's bell clanged out upon the Thames. The gentleman's gray-brown eyes found me. "We have much to talk on, Nick. But first, the woman who called yesterday morn—"

I started. "Woman?"

"Do not deny you saw her from my window."

"Yes, sir, as she came down Craven Street." I felt my face flame.

"You were up earlier than you claimed, then." He peered hard. "What did you make of her?"

"Thirty years of age. Her hat and thimble made me think she was a milliner."

"She a milliner indeed: Miss Slurry, of Portugal Street, near Lincoln's Inn."

"Not far from the Middle Temple, then? Where William studied law?"

"Why do you bring William into it?"

"Because I observed more, sir. Her belly was swollen. Is she with child? Forgive me, but . . . is William the father?"

A sad, wry look suffused Mr. Franklin's face. "I have trained you to observe well—to think well, too—so I must not be surprised when you discover what I would rather you did not." Going to his desk, he sank down. "Aye, she is with child, William is the father, and the babe will be born within a month of the new year, 1760." His eyes puckered. Picking up his featherpen, he let it drop. "It is impossible he should marry her. She is not a bad woman, but she is uneducated, and a man seeking a career must have a better wife." He faced me. "It is hard for me to say these things, Nicolas, for my good Deborah was near as ignorant as Miss Slurry when I took her to wed. And yet it is different for William. When I married, I was no one. I was ambitious and hardworking, but I had no idea life would lead me to England on behalf of the Pennsylvania Assembly. Why, I myself should like a wife who . . . but William . . . and, then, your mother, Nick . . ."

It was a hard moment. Rarely was Mr. Franklin at a loss for words, but he faltered now, his eyes moist, the last rays of day lighting his balding crown palely, as if the skull showed through. I read his thought: as he had fathered me, his elder son had fathered a child out of wedlock, and I recalled my own similar fears: bastard out of bastard. I felt a pang for him, for William, for the milliner and her babe, for all erring souls—but especially for my dead mother. Mr. Franklin had told me how he had fallen in love with Rose Handy long after he wed Deborah Reed. He had regretted that Rose could not be his wife, and I regretted it, too, though it made me feel disloyal to Deborah Franklin, whom I had never met. Yet if Rose Handy were Rose Franklin, she would be with us still, and I could tell her how I loved her. She could answer me. She could stroke my hair. A turmoil shook me.

No wonder Mr. Franklin looked troubled. Taking off his spectacles, he peered into them as if they might answer some deep question. Then refitting them over his ears, he said, "Well, Nick," drawing himself up, forcing a smile. "Things must be seen to. This one has been. Straney has been of great help. Mrs. Goodbody aided him, and together they have found a place for the mother whilst she is confined, and when the babe is born she will give it into other hands; then she can resume her life. Never fear, I do not intend to abandon the child. I shall watch it grow, I shall send it to school. I shall represent it as the issue of some distant relation. It is the best I can devise, for no one must learn that William is the father." He regarded me. "So . . . you shall have a little niece or nephew, Nick. What do you think of that?"

My words came out in a rush. "I think you are the best father any son could have, sir!"

He blinked. "O, tut." But he was moved, I saw by his trembling mouth. Day by day we had talked on my studies, on his correspondence, on the damnable Penns, on lightning rods, on all manner of subjects, but I could not let pass this chance to tell my father that I loved him.

But there was still murder to talk on, so as dusk drew its curtain we turned to it once more. William Strahan might help further, for he was the publisher of the *London Chronicle;* he knew the scribbling world. Thus Mr. Franklin writ him a note and sanded, folded, sealed it. It asked his old friend whether he knew Jack Scratch. Had he heard tales about the time Scratch was at Oxford? Was there some connection betwixt Scratch and the Earl of Chalton?

Mr. Franklin summoned Peter. "Straney may know where Scratch lives," he told the tall manservant, giving him the note. "If so, go to his lodgings, for I should like to hear all you can discover about 'em. Hang about awhile as well, and if Scratch goes out, follow him—though you must keep your eyes peeled in case others watch and follow, too."

Peter nodded, and I knew that if anyone could do all Mr. Franklin instructed, it was he. I gave him one of my drawings so he would know Jack Scratch's face. His quiet brown eyes returned deep thanks as he slipped out into the gathering dark.

It was five by then. I liked being tucked safe in Mrs. Stevenson's house at dusk. Hers was a plain but felicitous lodging, well run and dependable. Fires were laid against the eve, and the smells of Mrs. Stevenson's cookery drifted up to us: thyme and bay. I heard Polly's hum, too. Whilst Mr. Franklin worked at his desk, I sat in the soft, comfortable chair by the grate. The gentleman had long striven to meet William Pitt—the minister's advocacy would help his cause—but he had not managed it. Still, failure never deterred him, so he penned yet another letter in an attempt to effect the meeting. He also writ to the physician William Heberden, to praise him for his pamphlet on inoculation, which he had urged Heberden to publish. And he spent a half hour gathering sets of the *Connoisseur* to send to his daughter, Sally, so she might know the fashions and the follies of the town.

I tried to read *Tom Jones*, but I could not. As coals murmured in the grate, the real world called. Two dead women were no fiction, and I turned toward the window, where an inky blackness reflected flickering candlegleams. Scratch, Ravenden, Elstree, Oxford. Stains upon an altar. Womens' hearts cut out. St. James's Square. Silas Ward. Bloods. London. Simkins. Prince. A cave deep in the Richmond chalk.

I found Mr. Franklin watching. "A dark night, eh, Nick? Good to be home?" He examined his boot toes. "Not all are at home, however. Some must walk the streets—and some are dead." We talked on today: the Bridewell flogging, Charles Ravenden, Jack Scratch. Two points stood out: one, that the Earl of Chalton was Mr. Franklin's enemy—he had wished to toy with him, but the marionette would not dance. The second was that Jack Scratch knew some significant truth with which he longed to hang the earl. What truth? And why his great enmity?

Could the number three refer to three young men at Oxford?

Night pressed against the panes, whilst London stirred in moans and laughter. My fists clenched. Still we made no sense of things, and our conversation led to but one certainty: we must watch our backs in days to come.

If we needed any reminder, it arrived that night. As the evening wore on, Peter did not return, and Mr. Franklin began to fret. He read Addison in fits and starts. He muttered at supper, and observing him, Mrs. Stevenson frowned. Polly watched, too. With her good humor she roused him for a time, so that as we ate our roasted bird, his spirits lightened: "Kitchen spits. Dogs in cages turn 'em in some houses, but though cooks and trenchermen may be pleased, the dogs cannot like it. I am an enemy to slavery of ev'ry stripe! Thus, the hot air in the fireplace must be made to turn the spit instead." He thumped the table. "What do you say, Mrs. Stevenson? Shall you make the experiment?" He tugged at her sleeve. "You shall gain great fame amongst the dogs."

"Dogs, sir? Dogs?" Our landlady sniffed. "I should prefer something to make Nanny prompt instead. O, where is that girl, with the pudding!"

We were upstairs by nine. Still no Peter. Ten arrived with an unwelcome chiming of the case clock and a deeper furrow in Mr. Franklin's brow. "I told him to watch, told him to follow," muttered he admist the papers on his desk. "Have I put him in danger?"

I grew fearful as well. At half past ten I rose to go to bed, but I did not like it. Peter had been my friend. Would I see him again?

A soft rap sounded upon Mr. Franklin's door. "Peter?" called he, rising.

It was Peter, indeed.

I breathed relief as he came in, tall and solemn in his long overcoat. Shedding chill air, he looked agitated, out of breath, and Mr. Franklin drew him to the fire. "We are glad to see you. Warm yourself."

Whilst Peter rubbed his hands, his deep-set eyes warned us of bad news.

"Out with it," prompted Mr. Franklin.

"The scribbler is dead, I am sorry to say. Murdered in his rooms."

Only then did I note the blood upon Peter's sleeve.

❧ 20 ❧

IN WHICH We Hear of Murder and Study a Dead Man's Room . . .

The blood made a rust-dark stain where Peter's sleeve poked from his jacket. Mr. Franklin appeared unsurprised at his servant's news, as if he had expected the worst. But he passed a hand over his brow as he sank into his chair. "Dreadful!" He was silent a moment. Then, rousing himself, he said, "Rest by the fire. Tell all."

Peter sat with his hands upon his knees, and as he spoke I writ in my book.

The servant had gone first to William Strahan, in New Street Square. Strahan had heard of Scratch, for he read all the newspapers. He had called one of his workmen from his shop; thus Peter was able to discover where Scratch lived. He had then traveled to Spur Court, near Bedlam Hospital, not far from Grub Street. By then it was dark, near six o'clock, the fog rising. Scratch's lodging was one of those narrow wood-and-plaster houses at the back of a cul-de-sac, "a very poor place," Peter told us. "I saw a hunchback in a box, a beggar. I gave him a penny and showed him master Nicolas's drawing. 'Aye,' says he, 'he lives in a room at the top, third up. I have seen him in the window many a time.' Scratch came and went at all hours, the beggar said. 'Did anyone watch or follow him?' says I. 'Might be,' says he.

"I waited, as you ordered, tucked in a doorway. There was a light in Scratch's window, at the very top o' the house, and now and then I saw him apacing, restless. Ever and again he peered out, as if he kept watch.

"After half an hour or so the light was snuffed. I thought he had gone to bed—but, no, for he crept out the door. I hid whilst he peered ev'ry which way. There was a bit o' lamplight in the main road, and he stopped in it and took something from his pocket, a pistol, and he waved it about plain, as if to show he was armed, though there seemed no one to see. The beggar had crawled into his box. The mist was thick off the cobbles. 'Twas bitter cold.

"Scratch looked sharp about him, so I took care when I followed. I would see him in lamplight for a blink, then he would be gone. I feared he would take a coach, and I would lose him, but he stayed afoot, as if he didn't want no one, not even a driver, to see where he went. He trotted from Monkwell to Aldersgate to Smithfield."

"West, then."

"And stopped at a tavern in Castle Street."

"The Running Footman, by any chance?"

Peter and I both blinked. "You knew he would go there, sir?" Peter asked.

"Servants have their clubs, just as gentlemen do, where they unbutton and talk about their masters. The Running Footman is one."

What could a servants' club have to do with Jack Scratch? Peter had crept near, he said. He had peered through the tavern's panes.

He discovered his quarry at a table with Simkins, the Earl of Chalton's man.

There was no mistake, for Peter knew Simkins—he had seen him when he watched in St. James's Square.

Mr. Franklin nodded. "I thought Scratch must have a spy in his enemy's camp. Simkins, then? Go on."

The pair had sat heads close for a quarter of an hour. There had been gestures, expostulations, though Peter could not guess their significance. Jack Scratch had scribbled all the while in his book.

Mr. Franklin's fists tightened. "If I could lay my hands on that book—"

The two men had departed the Running Footman just past eight. Simkins had gone one way, Scratch another; Peter had stuck to Scratch. "He went down the Fleet, then up Ludgate Hill. The fog was bad, and there were echoes and footsteps, though I couldn't see who made 'em. Shadows bumped, and hands tried to pick my pockets. I wondered if someone else followed Scratch, for I heard a scurrying now and then, but there was no way to tell. I near lost him many a time, but we came to Spur Court just the same. Scratch stopped and stared so I did too. A candle burnt in his window; you could just make it out in the fog. 'What?' I heard him say, for he had blown his light out when he left. 'My landlady snooping again?' But he took out his pistol b'fore he went up.

"I hid in my doorway. It was quiet for a time, the mists amoving, the night freezing. There was still that light in Scratch's window, so I pulled up my collar and waited. Yet no one showed. No pacing, no peering out; it did not seem right. Just after he went up, I thought I heard a cry, though I could not be sure. The night plays tricks.

"Another quarter hour passed, and I was about to give up and come home—when I heard a shout: 'Murder! O, murder!' 'Twas a woman's voice, and it made me jump. I dashed for the door, but just as I got there a man flew out and near knocked me down. I snatched at him, but he had a blade. He slashed and cut my hand, not bad, only a bit o' blood. I grabbed at him, but he was slippery. Quick as that, he was gone."

Mr. Franklin bent forward. "Did you see his face?"

"Too dark, sir. Too sudden."

"You did your best."

"I made to chase him," Peter went on, "but then I thought better of it, for the fog was thick. I'd never find him. I ran into the lodging, up two flights o' stairs. I came to a woman by a door at the very top, under the eaves. 'Murder, murder!' she was amoaning, wringing her hands. Jack Scratch was in the room on the floor just behind her, blood about his mouth, eyes astaring. He was gone, sir, no mistaking. His hands and ankles were tied."

"Tied?"

"The woman screamed when she saw me. She stuck out a finger—'You, you!' 'Twas plain she thought I had done the deed.

178

Then I heard a stirring below and knew the whole house would be roused and would take me if they could. I ran down and came back straightaway. That is all my story."

Mr. Franklin gazed at me, I at him, as a clamorous silence tumbled about us.

Next morn the fog was thicker than ever. It hung like a fleece of dirty cotton against my window, and I squinted out to little avail, for the nearest house was a ghost. Somewhere the Thames flowed invisible, though hoots and whistles came off it to say the great ships anchored in its eastern reaches would not dare sail 'til midday. Shivering, I dressed myself. I thought on Jack Scratch. We had seen him less than twenty-four hours ago. He had mocked us, but I had not hated him.

Now he was murdered. Out of fear? Vindictiveness?

I felt the deep wrench I always felt when death brushed near. Sighing, I crossed to Mr. Franklin's door. Scratch had been driven by demons, but they had given his life purpose, and now that purpose had been vanquished; we were a poor bag of humors after all.

I knocked, opened. The fire was not yet lit, but Peter was present; Mr. Franklin wasted no time.

The servant stood by the fog-wreathed window, game-looking though he had good reason to be weary, for Mr. Franklin had sent him out last night to Bow Street. He wanted John Fielding to learn of the murder from the man who (save one) might know most about it. Mr. Franklin also wanted a constable to be dispatched to the scene of the crime 'til he himself could examine it.

The gentleman was just handing Peter a folded paper as I came in. "For Mrs. Goodbody, to remind her that 'til our pursuit is ended she must take care. Afterward: to the Golden Guinea." He gave Peter a second paper. "This informs Mrs. Cockburn that I take special interest in Nelly Skindle. Justice Fielding does, too, and we will hold it deeply amiss if anything happens to her. Nelly must be watched and protected—no more hearts cut out, eh? Afterward, resume your place in St. James's Square. Watch number 18, and send news of any comings and goings." He patted Peter's arm. "I count upon you."

Mr. Franklin gazed at the closed door when his servant was gone. "I do not know what I should do without him."

After a hasty breakfast, we set out to visit a dead man's rooms.

We were there by ten. Spur Court proved as glum a place as Peter had described, one of those shabby shoots that wither off many a London street. Its half-dozen tilting houses were the residences of poor, scrabbling souls who lived hand-to-mouth 'til poverty or disease snuffed their lives. The fog had thinned, but wisps still curled about the begrimed plaster and sagging shutters. A ragged boy with eyes like a whipped cur's stared from a stoop. A woman trudged a creaking bucket from the pump. A girl eyed us slyly, as if she should like to sell herself, though she was not yet twelve.

Mr. Franklin roused the crippled beggar from his box of cast-off boards, but he could tell us nothing. The gentleman gave him threepence nonetheless.

A tall, narrow house stood at the back of the court. We peered at its third-story window.

With no great relish we went in.

Mounting stairs that stank of wood smoke and poverty, we came to the top, where a large scowling woman stood by an open door. She had but one good eye; the other hid under a patch. She was the landlady of the house, she said with a suspicious growl, "Mrs. Dora Cust." Her good eye glared.

Mr. Franklin said he came from the magistrate and she grudgingly agreed to answer questions. She spat upon the floor. Aye, she was the one discovered the body. There'd been a black man, too. Her good eye rolled. O, she was sure he'd carried a knife! What of Mr. Scratch? Nay, his name was Pyecroft, and he had lodged here two years. He sometimes paid on time, and that was the best a poor, honest woman could hope for in this scheming world. He was a solitary gent. She had not liked him. He was short with her, and suspicious, always asking who had been by when he was away. "He thought people spied on 'im, the pisspot fool." No one ever called upon him that she knew, and she knew nothing of his relations. He crept in and out at odd hours, and she sometimes heard him muttering behind his closed door, though she could never

180

tell what. I pictured her at the thin pine, listening. Her good eye took us in with rapacious calculation.

Mr. Franklin asked what had brought her to Scratch's room last night.

"A cry. I hears all." She had gone up to find the door open and Jack Scratch dead. "Then that black man jumped out."

"The black man is my servant, who watched your house at my orders. He rushed upstairs when you shouted murder. I assure you he does not carry a knife."

"Hmph," Mrs. Cust blew skeptically as Mr. Franklin peered at the constable just inside the room. I was glad to see it was Billy Banting, for I mistrusted Mrs. Cust, and I knew he would have prevented her or anyone from helping themselves to Jack Scratch's possessions.

Mr. Franklin nodded to the lieutenant.

He nodded back. "Sir." He bobbed his head at me, too, and I returned a smile.

Mr. Franklin walked into the room.

I followed, and we stood gazing down. Justice Fielding had answered Mr. Franklin's request to the letter, for Jack Scratch lay on the bare boards as he must have lain when Peter glimpsed him last night. I struggled to master a sudden dizziness. The stink of death hung in the air, for the victim had voided himself, as many a dying body does. He lay face up, his back arched as if he still struggled to live. His ankles were bound, as Peter had said, his hands too, visible where he turned slightly from us, the rope digging into his thin, pale wrists. He wore no coat, no shoes or stockings either (why?), so that his long white feet stuck out. His eyes had been closed—Billy Banting had likely done that—but his mouth gaped in its last strangled cry, the yellowish teeth like fangs. A pool of blood lay on the bare wooden floor where it had spurted from his lips.

Rain, darkness, a body in the mews a week ago, and now another sent off betimes, in horrid fashion.

"Ah, Nick—" Mr. Franklin gripped my arm. "Did I press too hard. Investigate too deep?"

"Never, sir. You did what you must."

"Yet I do not like to think that this may be the result." He turned to Banting. "No one has touched anything?"

181

"No, sir. Justice's orders, 'til you got here."

"And will his honor be here, too?"

"There's other matters, y'see, sir. Arraignings in court—"

Mr. Franklin nodded. How hard it must be to be magistrate and chief investigator both. Would the city be properly policed one day?

"He told me to say he counted upon you," Banting added.

"Good of him. Have you spoke to the other tenants of the house?"

"T' save you the trouble. There're six, but all were asleep and saw nothing. I asked round the mews, too—those I could rouse. The same story ev'rywhere, sorry t' say."

"We must see what we can ascertain here, then." Mr. Franklin's methodical gaze surveyed the chamber. It was a dismal lair, slope-ceilinged, furnished only with necessities. Besides the cold fireplace there were a narrow bed, the chamberpot just visible beneath it, a rickety stand holding a basin and ewer, a cheap deal desk. One corner had been cobbled into a cupboard, and that was all. The crabbed nature of the room reminded me of my early impoverished days. Ten thousand rooms like it in London, ten thousand shabby lives. A burnt-out candle stood on the windowsill, and I glanced into Spur Court. The ragged boy still crouched on his stoop below. The girl still hung about. Scratch had had a clear view of the cul-de-sac. Had he chosen the lodging because he thought the room safe?

Not safe enough to save his life.

Mr. Franklin regarded the body. With a creak of knees, he knelt by it, whilst I stood, wondering what he thought. The cause of death was plain, for there was a wound in the chest, right through the shirt. Mr. Franklin peeled back the linen to reveal a bruised-looking puncture over the heart. "Unerring . . ." mused he. His eyes sought for the weapon, whilst Mrs. Cust glowered by the door. "No knife," he muttered. "Well, he cut Peter with it when he fled. Likely he brought it with him. Murdered with it, too—though he used it other ways first." Grimly he pointed to marks about Scratch's arms and face—prickings, gougings—and I felt ill. "There is worse." He gestured to the man's feet, and I saw what my first glance had not: the little toe of each had been severed.

The pink nubs lay on the floor.

I bit a lip as Mr. Franklin indicated something else, half-hidden by the body.

A severed finger.

"Steady, Nick."

"Y-yes, sir." Swallowing hard, I made myself look at the bound hands, and indeed where the index finger of the right should be was only a bloody gash, and I saw with sickened dismay that the nails of three fingers were missing, prised free, whilst a fourth hung by a thread.

I dropped to my knees beside Mr. Franklin, for I would swoon if I did not. Pressing both fists to the wood, I hung my head. "Lad?" I heard the gentleman's voice.

I forced myself to face him.

"But, *why*, sir?"

He shook his head. "Perhaps he took pleasure in it. But there must have been something to learn—though if I know Scratch, he refused to tell it. He was driven by anger and spite. He would never yield to his enemy."

"But he would cry out?"

"He did. Recall the sound Peter heard? It was nearly his only cry, however. See this blow upon the temple?" I gazed at a crushed-looking wound, matted with hair. "He must have been struck as he came in; that caused the cry. But the blow prevented him using his pistol; it also disabled him long enough for his attacker to bind him so he could cry out no more." Mr. Franklin pointed to a bruise about the jaw. "He was gagged." He held up a ball of cloth. "This was stuffed into his mouth, then tied with this." He showed a strip of the same plain stuff.

Imagining the soundless, writhing torture the man had endured, I paled. "But why is his mouth not tied now?"

"Because a gagged mouth cannot spill its secrets. His murderer must now and then have loosed his voice. At the end he freed it one last time—but when it was plain his victim would never reveal what he wished, he drove the knife into his heart. His death cry brought his landlady."

Scratch's pistol lay a few feet away, and picking it up with his handkerchief, Mr. Franklin sniffed the barrel. "Unfired. See?"

He held it for me to smell. "Still primed." Carefully lowering the hammer, he slipped the weapon into his coat. Then he began investigating the dead man's pockets. "Empty." Scratch's coat and waistcoat had been tossed unceremoniously in a corner with his shoes, and the gentleman searched every fold of these, too, but found only a chewed pencil and a tarnished ha'penny.

He shook the bedclothes, lifted the mattress, examined the ticking. Still no luck.

"Curse it, I hoped the book Scratch scribbled in would be here, but the murderer must have plucked it from his pocket. Why the prolonged torture, then?" Mr. Franklin looked in the cupboard, but there was naught save a scarecrow change of clothes and a frazzled wig. How little Scratch had owned. Mr. Franklin strode to the desk whilst Mrs. Cust peered and Billy Banting stood as stiff as a soldier. Upon the warped deal surface sat an inkpot and a draggled pen in need of a trimming—but also the next installment for the *Courant*. Had Scratch writ it before he went out? In any case it trailed off in midsentence, mocking a fellow scribbler's reputation in a crabbed hand, but there was nothing about Charles Ravenden or Silas Ward or anyone touching on the murders. The paper appeared undisturbed, though what other papers might have been stolen we could not say. The desk contained a single drawer. It opened with a protesting squeak, but there was nothing in it save a dozen sheets of foolscap and a spilt packet of sand.

Mr. Franklin huffed. Going to the fireplace, he knelt, passing a palm over the crumbled coals. "Still warm . . ." Taking up a bent poker, he fished cautiously. Charred curls of black lay in the grate, but I glimpsed a paler hue amongst the ebon, and with a little cry he plucked forth an edge of paper which had not entirely been consumed. Carrying it to the desk, he flattened it in the gray wash of windowlight.

It was from an old *Oxford Spectator*, the date plain: February 12, 1753, though all else was burnt. "Hilary term," Mr. Franklin muttered, poking at his spectacles. "Six years ago. Charles Ravenden must have been a student then. Tom Elstree, too. Pyecroft, before he became Jack Scratch. They were sent down, however." His lips pursed as he turned to me with the soundless question: *Why?* There was no clue in the *Spectator*, but Mr. Franklin bade me tuck the scrap in the back of my sketching book nonetheless.

There was one last thing to do, which earned Mrs. Cust's most suspicious squint.

Pulling from a pocket his little tin box that contained inked linen, Mr. Franklin knelt and painstakingly blackened each of the dead man's fingertips. These he pressed onto a sheet of paper, capturing their pattern of lines. He did this with the severed finger, too. Then blotting the paper, he folded it and returned it with the tin to his pocket.

I opened my book to sketch the drab chamber: the sloping ceiling, the body, the bleached light. Would my drawing discover some secret? But there seemed no more to learn, and pity and fear welled in me. Here a man had spent two years, but it took less than half an hour to survey all he left behind. No life should come to so barren an end.

Mr. Franklin dusted his knees. He turned to Billy Banting. "You can call the coroner's men to take him. I shall report to your master what we have found."

" 'Ere, now," Mrs. Cust protested. "This Pyecroft—or wotever he's called—had not paid me in weeks, so wot's his is mine, in fee." She thrust out her lumpen jaw.

Mr. Franklin returned a wintery look. "O, you are welcome to it all, so far as I am concerned. Inkpot. Shoes. Perhaps you should like to preserve the toes in a jar?"

The landlady gasped, but I hardly noted. Had we truly searched everywhere? My pencil drew the bed—but under it . . . ? Going down on my knees, I slid the chamberpot out. I felt foolish doing so, but Mr. Franklin watched approvingly. The pot was misshapen and chipped about the rim, a cheapjack thing. Scratch had not been alive to use it since it had been emptied and rinsed the previous day. Its brown depths appeared empty, but I put my hand in nonetheless.

And there was something: a leathern wallet whose dark color had made it near invisible. I pulled it out in surprise.

Mr. Franklin was at my side in an instant. "Excellent, Nick! Open it."

I did so. In its pocket was a single folded sheet of paper.

Together we read:

8 February, 1753

My Damned Lord Ravenden:

Your solicitations of friendship were pleasing—nay flattering—'til I learnt what they meant. Though young and without title, I know right from wrong, and I will not be led into perfidy, not even for the favor of knowing you, which I can do without. Your talk drew me on—I even affected your sneering manner for a time, it shames me to say—but then came the deeds you urged, repugnant beyond uttering: your "ceremonies," your degradations, your haughty insistence upon obedience to your will. And then your punishments when you fancied one of us had crossed you. Poor Pyecroft! He worshipped you. How could you treat him so?

But I will not catalogue your crimes. You know 'em well enough, though I fear you feel no shame. For all your airs, you are a blemish, a toad, a thing; and I am determined to do more than break with you. I shall inform the masters of the college. Take warning. If you have any honor, you will quit Oxford before they drive you out.

> In sorrow that ever I met you,
> James Tandy, Esq.

Mr. Franklin looked at me, I at him in the silence of the morn. "Who the devil is James Tandy?" murmured he.

❧ 21 ❧

IN WHICH We Talk on Murder and Peer at a Pistol . . .

Eleven o'clock bells tolled the hour as we departed that death-marked house. The sullen boy watched us. The beggar muttered at our feet. We trudged by Bethlehem Hospital—Bedlam, as it was called, though not all the madmen were inside. Mr. Franklin had tucked James Tandy's letter in his pocket; he had taken Jack Scratch's last scribbles for the *Courant* as well. The scrap of the *Oxford Spectator* hid in my book.

What might they add up to?

The fog had lifted, but the day remained chill, with a dank dripping of eaves. I longed to nip into some warm refuge where a fire burnt and light-footed girls served bread and beef: a jolly chophouse to sit and learn what Mr. Franklin thought, to unburden my own troubled soul, but I could not. "Mr. Tisdale, sir," said I reluctantly. "It is my day for him. Tuesday. He depends upon me Tuesdays."

We stopped under a chandler's sign. "So, Nick?" The board creaked over our heads. Scraps of leavings tumbled in a drain. Mr. Franklin gazed thoughtfully, a sturdy gentleman in square-toed shoes. "We must not disappoint those who depend upon us. You shall go to Mr. Tisdale, then—but by main ways. The Fleet. The Strand. And directly back to Craven Street afterward, hear?"

"Yes, sir." I was taken aback. Did he suggest I might be in danger? By daylight? He accompanied me down Cheapside, into the

187

very shadow of St. Paul's, before he climbed into a hackney by the great west doors. The scrap of newspaper in my sketching book seemed to stir evilly as he departed. What story had that scrap told? Why had the murderer wished to burn it. Had Jack Scratch died for its sake?

I looked over my shoulder often as I hurried through the throng to Jacob Tisdale's printing house.

The smell of ink calmed me. The rhythm of setting types. Pride in my skill. The camaraderie of the shop, where men conjoined to print newspapers and books. They inked the metal, they turned the screw, they hung the damp sheets to dry. It was a grave and manly dance, full of pattern and purpose, and it helped me set my thoughts in order, so that when Mr. Franklin and I spoke I could lay them out for him. I also renewed my idea of writing for Mr. Tisdale. When this adventure was over, might I pen it for London's eyes? Would the city praise Nick Handy for the tale?

Returning down the Strand, I paused by Southampton Street. The morn had given me an edge, an itch that needed scratching.

Birdy Prinsop.

Despite Mr. Franklin's adjuration to come straight home, I turned into Covent Garden as one o'clock bells rang out.

The noise and bustle of the market resounded despite the chill day, despite murder last night. Life went on. Pigs grunted in pens. Marrow-sellers cried their wares. A drover herded mutton amongst the stalls, whilst Shakespeare presided on his sign, his quill poised as if he directed the pageant that clamored before him.

I darted into the narrow lane that led to Longacre. Seeing Birdy's small, coy figure in its low-cut dress, her oval face topped by wheaten curls, her little feet in her little shoes, I felt even more roused.

She stamped one of those feet in the dust when I reached her, thrusting herself so near that her musky scent filled my nostrils. "It has been a *week* since you saw me, Nicolas," she piped. "Do you not care for your Birdy?" I did not know what to say. Her up-turned face was as dewy as a country maid's, but her eyes measured me shrewdly. Was I just a thing to her, then, mere custom?

Yet she knew to the day when I had called. Did she long for other than mere hire from Nick Handy?

We went up the stairs. I gave her coin, and she lay compliantly upon the bed.

Our coupling was mad and sweet.

Afterward I buttoned my breeches by the door. A moan burst from an adjacent crib, followed by the quick, insistent creak of lust and I felt shamed and doubtful. I glanced at Birdy. She stood in the window's parchment light, one leg on a stool whilst she pulled up a stocking. As if she knew I watched, her hands stopped, her head turned, and she gave me a gaze as naked as dawn. We stood there, whilst Covent Garden buzzed like a thousand flies. The girl's pink mouth opened. (Was she even sixteen?) That mouth would whisper some endearment, I thought—she would ask me to hold her hand, walk her by the river, take her to supper.

But the moment did not last. Birdy Prinsop could not afford sentiment, and her mouth formed a smile of pure brass before she turned away to tidy her legs with quick little movements, for they must look good for the next likely gent.

I hurried to the Strand.

I was home by two, within Craven Street's safe walls. Birdy Prinsop still haunted me. I saw it was only vanity that made me suppose I were more to her than a quarter-hour's earnings; after all, I did not visit her to please my heart but to satisfy my desires. Yet I fretted over her nonetheless: small, alone, unprotected. What did she really feel? Who was Birdy Prinsop?

Mother Cockburn, thought I. *Bridewell. Two women with their hearts cut out.*

Even Polly's smile as I trudged upstairs hardly cheered me. London was a grindstone and human flesh its grist.

I entered Mr. Franklin's familiar chamber at the top of the stairs. There were its shelves of books, its littered desk, its bow window facing south; his three wigs—the daily, the better, and the best—on their stands. The master was not in. Still at Bow Street?

He and Magistrate Fielding had much to talk on.

Sighing, I removed the burnt scrap of the *Oxford Spectator* from my book and placed it upon the desk. It lay there mute and yellowed, its burnt edge a mystery. I was relieved to carry it no more—but what should it lead to?

I set about to wait.

Mr. Franklin did not return 'til half past four. At once he called Polly to his chamber. "Now, child," said he when she hurried obediently in, "make your report."

"I saw nothing today, no spies, though I was about town with Mama much of the time."

"Ah." An under-the-brow glance said he pondered how much to tell her of our last twenty-four hours—little in the event, for he kept to himself that Jack Scratch would never be seen again. Plenty of time to convey the tale when we had sorted through the matter.

When she was gone, Mr. Franklin sank back, squeezing his brow. He looked fretful, his brown hair lank, his eyes awash with care. He told why he had returned late. He had met the Blind Beak, as I surmised, talking for over an hour—but after Bow Street he had gone to the offices of the *Courant*. "I sought news of Jack Scratch, but they could tell little. He delivered his weekly quiver of barbs, and they printed 'em. They did not know why the man was bitter. And they cared little if what he writ was true."

He had also returned to Soho Square. "I hoped to persuade Tom Elstree to unlock his tongue—how tortured he seems!— but, alack, he was gone from home."

Nanny's timid rap sounded. She delivered a note from Peter, who remained on watch in St. James's Square. Though my lord, the honorable earl, had not gone out, Peter reported, a man had gone in and stayed: Tom Elstree.

Mr. Franklin gazed at me over the paper. "Ravenden sequesters Elstree, does he? To keep him from Ben Franklin?"

"You think so, sir?"

"Curse it, I do not know what to think." The gentleman cast the note from him, and we talked awhile on Jack Scratch's murder. Beyond the panes dusk fell, feathery, slow, though the Strand still ticked and whirred like some mad machine. A clove-and-cinnamon smell wafted up from the kitchen. Jack Scratch's flesh had been dreadfully violated before he died. "Did the person who murdered those women do him in, then?" asked I.

Mr. Franklin flung up his hands. "Someone with the same brand of callousness. Someone who does not scruple at means. He wanted something of Scratch. He obtained the notebook. He got the newspaper, too, which he thought entirely to burn, though we retrieved a scrap. Bless fortune he did not discover the letter in the chamberpot—Scratch proved cleverer than his murderer after all. Was the letter the murderer's main aim?" Mr. Franklin pulled it from his pocket. "James Tandy. Hm. By the evidence, a fellow student six years ago. He knew damning things about my lord, he says. He meant to reveal 'em, too."

"What is the date on the letter, sir?"

"February eighth."

"And the newspaper is February twelfth."

"Aye, four days later. So what was reported in that newspaper?"

In any case Scratch's murderer must be Charles Ravenden, must it not? Recalling the earl's lewd smile at Bridewell, his mad fixity, his pleasure at another's pain, I was sure—and then I was not, for the scribbler's scandalous affronts must have made him many enemies.

"What do you make of the fact that Simkins conferred with Scratch?" Mr. Franklin asked.

"It was surely no chance. Was it the first time? Or had they met before?"

"I neglected to tell you I stopped by the Running Footman on my way home. I drank me some beer. The drawer is a jabbering fellow, Francis Otwell by name. He knows Simkins, he says, though Simkins is not a frequent visitor: an 'odd duck.' Yet he recalled seeing him with Scratch last night. So did a potboy. Both thought Scratch had been there with him before."

"Did either hear what they talked on, sir?"

"No."

"Did Simkins lure Scratch there so someone else could creep into his lodgings to search 'em?"

"What bait could Simkins use?"

"Some secret about a man Scratch wished to destroy?"

Mr. Franklin thought on that. "Yet there is another way of looking at it. Scratch took a roundabout way home. If Simkins knew

Scratch's habits, it would give him time to arrive at the chamber ahead of him."

"So *he* could search?" *And murder?* thought I.

"I only say *might,*" Mr. Franklin replied. "We must reflect on it. Scratch wrote what Simkins told him in his notebook. We must presume his murderer obtained that book and read what Scratch set down. If Simkins told Scratch something of peril to our murderer, and that murderer is not Simkins"—the gentleman's eyes narrowed—"who is likely to be his next victim?"

"Simkins himself?"

"It poses a dilemma, does it not? Warn Simkins, or hold our tongues? Yet he will learn of Scratch's murder soon enough. We have other business." Rising, he beckoned. "Time for finger-prints, Nick."

He led me next door to his workshop, where he lit candles against the dying day. Their yellow glow shone on his screw-barreled microscope and other devices: the calipers, the balances. It revealed his piles of notes, too, on matters from the stars' heat to how a flea's legs worked.

Through the window to the south the Thames gleamed like iron, whilst Westminster Bridge dissolved in night near Whitehall.

Mr. Franklin had brought the scrap of the *Oxford Spectator.* Placing it upon his workbench, where only eight days ago he had demonstrated the experiment of the cork and iron balls, he dusted it with a fine powder which he had specially ground of alum and talc by a punctilious apothecary in George Street. He blew upon the powder, then lifted the paper to gaze at it aslant.

"Alas, nothing, Nick." He held it so I might see. "The surface is coarse, and in any case the oils from the fingers that held it will have been volatilized by the fire's heat." Tugging Jack Scratch's pistol from his pocket he unwrapped it from the handkerchief and placed it upon the bench. "Let us hope better of this." Dusting it alike, tapping, blowing, he peered at the result in the flickering candlelight.

I peered likewise.

Faint but clear upon the barrel—upon the smooth-worn handle, too—showed signs of what he called finger-prints. "So!" His smile spread, as much (I thought) at his cleverness as at our success. "God makes us all alike, but he makes us particular, too," said he as he explained how his method of finger-printing was most useful for discovering who had held an object, or who might have been in a place, when he said he had not.

"Now, Nick," said he, drawing forth Jack Scratch's finger-prints. He held the paper near the pistol, and we bent close, comparing. "Aye." He nodded, and I was thrilled, for I could see that some marks on the pistol were the scribbler's, but some were plainly not.

Mr. Franklin stood very still, gazing into his own thoughts. "Let us imagine Spur Court in deep night. The man who murdered Jack Scratch had lit the candle to search his room. Hearing footfalls, he hid by the door and taking Scratch by surprise struck him down. The pistol may've still been gripped in Scratch's hand. In any case his attacker got it from him—but what could it signify? So he tossed it aside, little realizing that his fingers left proof of his guilt, curse justice that such proof is unknown in any court of law!" Mr. Franklin found a smile. "Would we had Charles Ravenden's finger-prints nonetheless, eh?"

"And Simkins's, too, sir?" said I.

"For that matter, Tom Elstree's, Simon Ward's, and Long John Enderby's." The gentleman stretched. "I should like to do more today. I should like to fly about London to rattle the truth from someone. Alas, I cannot. Richard Jackson confers with me about the Penns at six (the Board of Trade resumes shortly). Afterward I am contracted to sup with Peter Collinson." He gestured to a chair by the workbench. "Whilst I am gone, make drawings of these finger-prints, after your diligent fashion. As for tomorrow, I travel to Oxford." He fixed his gray-brown gaze upon me. "Shall you come, Nick?"

"I should like nothing better!"

"Oxford, then, in the early morn."

❦ 22 ❦

IN WHICH We Travel Many Miles and Learn of Old Murder . . .

Oxford lay some fifty miles northwest of London; Mr. Franklin had hired a small, swift gig. "The public coaches are out of the question," said he as we set out from Charing Cross shortly after dawn, our breaths plumes of mist, for he hoped to travel and return in a day. "They stop at every posting house and do not reach Oxford 'til four." Our driver smartly cracked his whip. We should have to halt twice to change horses, he had told us, but—God willing—we were promised the town by noon.

Past Hyde Park, we left the noise and press of London behind; within an hour we were in Buckinghamshire, our conveyance gently rocking. The road was muddy, but there had been no rain for several days and the treacherous frosts of winter had not yet set in. Too, our driver was skilled; we clipped along under a pewter sky.

As we went I thought again on the events of ten short days: the discovery of the body in the rainy mews, the attack of the bloods, visiting Charles Ravenden's town house and his temple and cave in the country, where white-clad Dionysians tumbled amongst the trees and a blood-stained altar hid in a hill. I thought on Tom Elstree, too: melancholy, glum. What guilty secret did he hide? I was still surprised to learn that Jack Scratch had been one of Charles Ravenden's followers, but the letter from James Tandy seemed to have spoke true. Now Scratch was dead. Because he had once sought the haughty lord's favor? As for Tandy, who was he, and what had happened six years ago in Oxford? Would we learn it today?

Fay ce que voudras. The phrase echoed in my head as our wheels clicked and turned. Flagrancy had perverted Rabelais' creed from independence of mind to murder.

We reached the university town in good time, Mr. Franklin's pocketwatch proclaiming half past eleven as the first distant towers and clustering spires rose out of the fields. As we drew nearer, arched windows and crenellations began to appear, and with a quickening heart I recalled my first sight of Bath, where Mr. Franklin had investigated murder a year ago. Bath was a town of far different character: a haven of gaming, flirtation, and dance amid buildings of mellow golden stone. These buildings were equally beautiful, but they were devoted to scholarship and learning. I looked forward to Oxford.

At noon we crossed the stone bridge over the Cherwell. Then came Christ Church Meadows on our left, Magdalen College on our right. The east gate of the town lay ahead. Passing under its stone arch, we drew up before a coaching inn in Cornmarket Street, loud with the crunch of iron on gravel and ostlers' gruff cries. Our driver would wait there, he said, jumping down and opening the door. "Ye must hire someone who knows th' streets." He winked thirstily, and Mr. Franklin patted his arm; he would draw upon his porter whilst we did our business.

Engaging a small, open conveyance, we set out.

Settling back, I looked eagerly everywhere—but if I expected the sobriety of scholarship to lend Oxford a lofty air, I was disappointed, for the place was crisscrossed with gutters that ran with dead rats and offal. Manure steamed on cobbles, and small, strangled creatures—capons and pigeons—hung outside a dozen shops; this was a market town, too. Not that there were not young men in gowns who appeared to be scholars, but most were larking fellows, and the few who wore pinched looks seemed to have got them more from carousing than study; rarely did I see a book in any hand.

Still, we saw the sights: the Broad, St. Aldgate's Front, the great Tom Tower. At half past twelve Oxford's bells cleared their throats like proctors admonishing would-be scholars to look to their studies.

" 'Twas founded five hundred years ago by a convocation of masters and scholars," Mr. Franklin said as we rid. Today it was organized round some twenty or so colleges, where fellows lived and studied—or misbehaved, for young men were still young men. We passed Trinity College, Balliol, All Souls. Gazing at their venerable stone, glimpsing the trim lawns of their inner quadrangles, I wondered what it was to live and study here. Yet I would not like to, for that would mean leaving Mr. Franklin. I glanced at him in his plain brown suit. What matter that—though he had received an honorary degree in laws from St. Andrews in Scotland not two months ago and thus might call himself doctor—he had never attended university? "In the end a man schools himself," he was fond of saying. "Learning is a matter of inclination." What pleasure to sit beside him, then, with his squarish face and his eyes that welcomed the world. What better guide could Nick Handy have?

Shortly we wheeled to a halt in Holywell Street, where the offices of the *Spectator* stood. Getting down, we went into a narrow building stirring with the familiar creak of printing. Making himself known to its proprietor—a lean, lantern-jawed man named Mr. Jakes, who popped up from his composing bench—Mr. Franklin engaged him in talk of presses, types, ink, and they were soon fast friends. Mr. Jakes was pleased to hear of Mr. Franklin's *Pennsylvania Gazette;* he was happy to make us privy to all the bound ledgers of his *Spectator* we might wish to see as well. He left us to peruse them in a small, dusty back room where ivory light fell through a narrow window. Two dozen leathern bindings stood on shelves: here was a history of Oxford year by year since 1740. But it was only one year we looked to, one week: that of the twelfth of February, 1753. Finding the volume, taking it down, we turned its musty pages—and here it was, the whole of the number which we had discovered near burnt in Jack Scratch's grate.

Here, too, was the story his murderer must have meant to conceal:

A bloody deed was discovered by a proctor of St. John's College, on the night of Tuesday last, February 9, at 10:00 P.M. Mr. Alfred Pike was making his customary rounds when he noted the west chapel door open, as it should not be at that hour. Going in, he saw and heard nothing, yet something, "the smell of death," he called it, drew him to seek further. He shone his lantern about and shortly discovered the body of a student, one James Tandy, in a back pew. The young man was dead. His heart had been carved from his chest . . .

Oxford's bells tolled one o'clock as we stared at these words.

We departed town just past three. There had been more to the story, though nothing so shocking as its first lines, and I pondered it as our driver urged his pair back toward London under a scumbled sky. James Tandy had been the son of Bertram Tandy, a well-to-do merchant of Leeds. He had attended Westminster Grammar School in London before being sent to university. News of his murder was already about Oxford, the newspaper account had further proclaimed. Such a bloody crime could not be kept under wraps, and investigations were under way by college and town alike. Results were promised soon.

Mr. Franklin and I had examined succeeding numbers of the *Spectator*, but whereas the next reported that no perpetrator had yet been unearthed, the following barely mentioned James Tandy, and the one after that forgot him entirely.

He had been tipped into oblivion, his murderer uncaught.

Mr. Franklin had led me straightway to Mr. Jakes, who sat in a little office, scribbling a story with ink-stained fingers, for he was his own chief news-gatherer, he said.

He peered up from under broad ginger brows.

Mr. Franklin told him his reasons for wishing to see old numbers of the *Spectator*.

Mr. Jakes pushed his inkpot and paper aside. "You think your London murders relate to the one here six years ago, eh? I have always wondered who did in that poor young man. Well, I shall tell you all I can—but for your part, you must tell me if anything comes of it. It is a story I should like to print."

Mr. Franklin agreed; thus we learnt of Oxford in 1753. It had not been so different from now. Like London it had its rakes and bloods, for the university was looked on by most of its privileged young fellows more as a way of preparing for the world of fashionable pleasures—whoring and gaming—than of learning Latin verbs. "There are scholars, but they are rare," said Mr. Jakes.

We heard also of the Earl of Chalton.

Mr. Jakes remembered him well, for my lord had been flamboyant even then, having just returned from the Grand Tour, where, amongst other things, he learnt to wear colorful garb and to practice bizarre customs, as done in the Turkish baths. Mr. Jakes scratched his ear with his quill. "He founded some sort of secret society, I recall. The masters did not like it, but they couldn't pin it to him—not at first. I cannot tell you its true nature, but many young fellows were bedeviled by it. How they love to make novelty their god! In any case, rumor said it offered new sorts of debauchery—but shortly after James Tandy was murdered it ended, for my lord was sent down with one or two others. The authorities finally got wind of the society's true nature, and they could not stomach it."

"How did the authorities learn of it?"

"It was a student called . . . Pyecroft, I believe; yes, that was his name, a servitor, a poor scholarship boy. He had been part of Chalton's crowd, very slavish (he was said to worship the man). But there was some falling-out, and Pyecroft peached on Ravenden; there is nothing like the spite of an apostate. Nevertheless, Pyecroft got sent down, too. By Easter term they were all gone."

"You said one or two others. A young man named Tom Elstree?"

"Yes, now you mention him."

"Have you any notion what 'odd customs' Chalton learnt in the Turkish baths?"

Mr. Jakes was frank. "Buggery for one, I should guess"—he tilted his lantern-jawed face—"though you need not travel to Turkey to learn that. It is taught at Oxford, alongside Greek."

"Hm," said Benjamin Franklin.

The newspaperman said that indeed the murderer of James Tandy had never been discovered. "After the purge, there were no more hearts carved out in Oxford. But there are new ones in London? I wish you well. Remember your promise."

That was the last we learnt in our hour in his shop. It was sufficient to draw conclusions, however, and Mr. Franklin sat for much of our journey back to London reflecting on them as we rattled along, the November day draining into the west. We approached Kensington just past six, the fields drowned in shadow, whilst the stony smell of night blew in our nostrils. "Three," Mr. Franklin murmured out of his silence.

"Three," echoed I.

He squeezed the head of his bamboo. "Not a third murder to come, then, but one already done, in the same grisly manner: James Tandy, a young man who wished only to do right. Horrible! Tandy threatened to go the college authorities, so as a consequence Charles Ravenden murdered him and cut out his heart. Why the heart? A punishment? A perversion of his obsession with Dionysus and his Maenads? *Fay ce que voudras*, and if someone stands in your way—" Mr. Franklin shook his head. "Likely he lost no sleep over what he did—unless he feared being caught. What irony that Pyecroft took Tandy's place, so that Ravenden was sent down despite his bloody precautions."

"Did Scratch know that my lord had murdered the young man?"

"He must have guessed—even more irony if that was what pushed him to expose the earl."

Our horses' hooves clopped steadily. The sky grew black. "So Scratch clung to his hatred of the Earl of Chalton all these years. The poison dripped in him. The earl could retreat behind his wealth, building a new following of Dionysians to flatter his ego, whilst Scratch sank to becoming an ignominious scribbler. He must have seethed whenever Chalton's fine coach drove by."

"But how did he obtain James Tandy's letter?"

"From Simkins perhaps? It is another mystery we must solve. In any case, however long he had it, it did him little good 'til those women were found with their hearts cut out. Ah, but then! The similar method, the violence, the cruelty. He must have been sure the earl had murdered 'em."

"And if he could prove my lord had murdered the women, he might prove he had murdered James Tandy, too," I said. How near he had come to revenge.

Mr. Franklin nodded. "And with their memories jogged, people like our Oxford newspaperman might begin to remember details that would further implicate Ravenden. All the suppressed scandal about his secret society would bubble up, and Oxford and London would lap it like cream. Ravenden would be scoured with shame before Tyburn hung him. But my lord is no fool. He saw Scratch's plan. If he had had reason to silence James Tandy, he had much more to shut Jack Scratch's mouth. Recall his hints about being strapped for funds? He hoped for some lucrative royal appointment. Any breath of scandal would dash that."

"And is he finished now, sir? Shall we lay our evidence before Justice Fielding?"

I worried that Mr. Franklin did not answer at once. "Would it were so simple," said he. "Charles Ravenden is titled; thus he has the privilege of being tried in the House of Lords, and the lords are always reluctant to prosecute one of their own, much less convict him (there are far too many who tremble at the thought that their own crimes might be aired). For another, what real evidence do we have? We *guess* that Charles Ravenden is a murderer; we pile rumor upon scraps of paper, but we have no witnesses."

"But the finger-prints on the pistol, sir?"

A weary smile. "Tut, the Chief Magistrate for Westminster respects my views, but even he would never admit such unproved methods in his court. One day, perhaps, but not now. And we do not even know if the other marks on the pistol came from Charles Ravenden's hands."

"We might learn it."

"Only to satisfy ourselves?"

How maddening to be convinced of truth, to know a man was a villain but to be unable to prove his guilt! Yet there was an even more troubling matter. "Sir," said I, "we know why my lord murdered James Tandy and Jack Scratch—but why those women?"

The gentleman turned in the jouncing dark. Some cry, a whinney or hoot, came to us across the shrouded fields as the first lights of London glimmered far off. "Did he have reason, Nick? Or did he cut 'em for the sweet pleasure of the knife?"

His reply gave me no solace as we swayed toward Hyde Park.

❧ 23 ❧

IN WHICH Polly Reports of a Stranger and a Dionysian Calls . . .

After the open skies of the west, London's narrow ways and reeking lanes closed about us. Pools of lamplight cut the dark, but the echoing rattle of our wheels was like a mocking rattle of bones. I drew my coat about my throat. The Earl of Chalton, with his white-painted face and scarlet lips, lived in these precincts. He crept their most debauched alleys, and he could not think on Benjamin Franklin kindly.

He had murdered men who threatened his freedom. Did he know that Mr. Franklin had gone to Oxford? If so, would he guess why?

In Craven Street the Thames lapped hungrily, whilst the lanterns of venturesome wherries winked out upon it like disembodied eyes. Seeing Mr. Franklin peer about as we got down, I shuddered. Did a threatening form hide in that doorway three houses up? Ravenden himself?

But nothing moved, and a firm hand fell on my shoulder. "Come." Mr. Franklin paid our driver, and we hurried indoors.

I slept ill that night. Amongst many troubling thoughts, my worst was that if Charles Ravenden enjoyed murder—and his cruel smile at Bridewell gave me every reason to believe he might—other women would perhaps die, too. Could we prevent that?

Longing for resolution, hating uncertainty, I woke irritably. By seven o'clock next morning I was in Mr. Franklin's chamber, stoking the fire, whilst he paced in his dressing gown, the sky a wash of sullen gray outside his window. He would go to John Fielding with what we had gathered, he said. "I doubt its efficacy, so we must make other plans." He would confront Tom Elstree, for one. "Ravenden cannot keep him from me forever."

At these words we exchanged a glance, for we knew Ravenden might do just as he pleased with Tom Elstree; so I was in no happier temper as I sank into a chair with my sketching book, turning over the scenes and faces of the past week, from Long John Enderby's brutish countenance to Nelly Skindle's fearful one. The coals sang their keening song. Mr. Franklin grumbled at this desk. Hester Ward's face was the most poignant; I recalled her eyes, eaten by rats. Tom Elstree's tormented look stared at me, too. "We have no witnesses," Mr. Franklin had said, but was Tom Elstree a witness?

If he lived to speak.

My ill ease increased as I recalled how Mr. Franklin had called Polly to his chamber upon our return last eve. She had not spied anything unusual about Craven Street in our absence, she said— but in Exeter Street, where she had gone for an hour with Nanny to purchase a new pair of shoes, she had been accosted by a man. "He was an acquaintance of yours, he said; he was certain he had met me when he called upon you in Mama's house. His name was Mr. Dean." Polly cocked her head. "Surely you know Mr. Dean?"

Mr. Franklin glanced at me. "Describe him."

Polly did.

I felt a sinking inside. Mr. Dean had not been painted, nor had he worn flamboyant clothes, but he was the Earl of Chalton nonetheless.

"I know him," agreed Mr. Franklin.

"I was sure you must," Polly went on blithely, "for he was aware you were gone from town. He asked in the pleasantest way where you traveled, so I told him—there was nothing wrong in that? He smiled at the news, though"—the girl paused—"it was an odd smile, almost displeased. He marched off, then. Perhaps he hoped to see you on some urgent business? Perhaps he will see you today."

"Excellently observed and reported." Mr. Franklin gripped the young woman's shoulders. "Now hear me: you must stay at home tomorrow." She opened her mouth to protest, but he held up an adamant hand. "You *will* stay home. And so will your mother."

"Then . . . then Mr. Dean is not what he seemed?"

"He is not." Mr. Franklin told her all about Charles Ravenden then; his tale made her blanch. "Very likely he murdered those young women who had their hearts cut out. I am on the man's trail. He is vindictive and unprincipled, and I would not put it past him to attempt to get at me through you. We must not allow him the chance."

Polly's eyes saucered. They seemed to see for the first time that danger was one thing when you invested it with romance but quite another when it came near enough to kiss your hand in Exeter Street. "Wh-whatever you say!" stammered she, but as she departed I misgave. Ravenden had been bold enough to question her about Mr. Franklin. What else might he attempt? Further, he must know the girl would report her encounter and that Mr. Franklin would guess he was not what he appeared.

What were the devil's plans?

Mr. Franklin had acted at once, sending a boy to St. James's Square to summon Peter. When the servant arrived he had stationed him in the Craven Street entryway. "No one must pass who is not a friend, hear?"

I knew Peter would give his life to obey this order.

Thus I was glad there had been no disturbance in the night. Mr. Franklin continued to write at his desk, but upon hearing William's footfalls, he called the young man in. William did not approve his father's hobby of pursuing crime, but Mr. Franklin had to tell him about the peril we might face. William listened silently, alertly, with a little flaring of his nostrils. "You must forgo other engagements 'til I can bring the matter to a close," his father concluded.

To his credit, William drew himself up bravely. "Naturally, I shall help Peter to keep watch." I recalled that father and son had campaigned as members of the Pennsylvania militia before they came to England, Mr. Franklin in command, his son an able captain with more than a hundred footsoldiers under him; here was a new campaign. "If the women must go out, I shall accompany 'em." William turned. "I shall tell 'em so now." He stepped smartly out.

We had taken precautions, then—but I fretted still. How long must we remain a fortress? Surely not forever, and when we relaxed our vigil, as we must, would Charles Ravenden seek revenge?

New developments arrived soon. Upon his return from Ravenden's house, Peter had told us that Tom Elstree was no longer there; he had seen him leave round about eight. As if to confirm this, a note arrived from Soho Square at ten, as we mounted the stairs after a breakfast at which Mrs. Stevenson's spoon had rattled restlessly against her porridge bowl, for she, too, had had Mr. Franklin's warning and grew as jumpy as a cat. "My nerves, sirs, my nerves!" was her cry. Nanny had spilt a bowl of cream.

The note was from Tom Elstree.

It was writ in a wracked scrawl. It said he should be in our part of town at eleven-thirty: "If you are at home, sir, I pray, may I see you?"

Mr. Franklin's eyes met mine over the paper. He had intended to call upon Bow Street, but his pointed lips thinned. "O, I shall be sure to be home to Tom Elstree."

An hour and a half later Nanny showed the young man into the front parlor, where Mr. Franklin and I had placed ourselves to wait. All was in readiness: drawn curtains and a fire in the grate. Behind Nanny, Mrs. Stevenson and Polly watched from the entryway; Peter too, with his deep-set eyes. Did the caller have to do with our endangerment?

Mr. Franklin murmured only that he must have privacy, and taking the door from Nanny's hand, he firmly closed it.

He turned, I by his side.

The bustle of London was muffled, and the light was dim, but Mr. Franklin had insisted the curtains be drawn. "No one can fire a ball accurately through drawn curtains," he had said.

The parlor walls showed their framed sayings of Poor Richard, embroidered by Mrs. Stevenson, and coals glowed in the fireplace. The solemn tick of the mahogany clock on the mantelpiece meted out time. Tom Elstree stood in the center of the chamber, pale and staring, his tricorn hat crushed in his hands. He was dressed in fine maroon velvet, but he was disheveled, his cravat atangle, his stockings ill-gartered, his mop of brown hair an uncombed wildness about his brow. He looked a poor, pitiable creature, and again I recalled his despair in the moonlight on the Earl of Chalton's Richmond grounds.

Simkins had been there amongst the black, stirring trees. Simkins had conferred with Jack Scratch just before Scratch was murdered.

"Your servant, Mr. Elstree," Mr. Franklin said. "You know my boy, Nicolas. Pray, what may I do for you?"

Elstree's mouth worked as if it did not know how to reply. "You are a kind man, are you not?" he got out raggedly.

"I am pleased to think so."

"You *seem* kind." Elstree's fists bunched. "Not like that monster, Charles Ravenden!"

Mr. Franklin tilted his head. "Forgive me, but I thought the Earl of Chalton was your friend."

"Pah! He has no friends! Only puppets."

"My lord does like to pull the strings."

Elstree's eyes squinted as if he had at last found someone who understood him. "Then you do see, sir, you do?"

"I should like to see more. Let us sit." Mr. Franklin gestured; and, with a great sigh the young man sank onto a chair, whilst we placed ourselves on the sofa opposite him. Slipping my book from my pocket, I writ whilst the stir of the Strand echoed from the top of the way.

Mr. Franklin placed his hands upon his knees. "Now. The earl is a 'monster,' you say?"

"A serpent. Like the one who tempted Eve—though *he* tempts men. Lures 'em." Elstree's eyes fell in shame. "He lured me."

"At Oxford?"

"You know of that?"

"You were students there. Were you acquainted with my lord before you went to university? No? You met him there, then. You were the son of a tradesman—a well-to-do tradesman, but a tradesman nonetheless—and he was an earl. Yet he chose to befriend you. How flattered you must have been. He was charming, he had traveled upon the continent, he knew the world. And so he drew you into his circle of young men. A secret society, was it not? I have heard of it, though I should like to know more of its nature."

Elstree's hands grappled with each other in his lap.

Mr. Franklin spoke kindly. "Come, you may trust me with the truth. Is that not why you are here, to trust Ben Franklin with the truth?"

The young man stared. "Yes . . . the truth . . . I wish to tell it. The nature of that secret society?" He smiled bitterly. "At first I did not see it, for at first there were women: the Oxford trulls. My lord was expert and getting the best of 'em, the prettiest, to lure the prettiest men. Not that he ever touched a woman himself. But he liked to watch us at our pleasure, in orgies, drunk, naked. It troubled me, but it enticed me, too. How different from my father's puritanical ways. It was a kind of freedom! And he . . . and he—" Elstree's eyes pinched as he saw himself as he had been, dew-fresh; saw the earl, too, his lord, whom he had blindly followed. "He made us think we were heroes. 'You are above the common laws,' he said. How persuasive, how mad." His voice fell. "In short, he came to make us believe that anything was permissible, that we ought to try ev'ry pleasure."

"*Fay ce que voudras.*"

"*Fay ce que voudras.* He led us from one debauchery to the next—and at last to, the most manly, he said: with one another, with . . . with him." Elstree flushed. "I confess to succumbing— but I did not like it! You must believe that! Yet many of the young fellows did; they preferred it. Ravenden has an instinct about such men. He would walk along the Broad to sneer at 'em, pointing 'em out—'That one, and that one'—as if he were better than they. O, I gave in, I participated, but I used to feel ill afterward. I hated myself."

"Yet you remained loyal to him."

"Because he seemed to offer . . . to offer . . ." The young man's hands struggled to carve out meaning. They failed, but I understood. The Earl of Chalton had offered Tom Elstree what Mr. Franklin offered me: a wider horizon, a deeper life. The Earl's offer was sensuality, a thing of the moment, whereas what Mr. Franklin gave might lead to a measure of wisdom one day; they were worlds apart. But I knew why Elstree had not quit his mentor. He had been afraid of the mire he would sink back into, as I feared the same if I lost Mr. Franklin. Tom Elstree was shallow and weak, but he was to be pitied; and knowing my own weaknesses, I could not judge him.

"Was there a young man named Pyecroft amongst you?" Mr. Franklin asked.

"Poor fellow."

"Poor?"

"My lord treated him vilely. At first Pyecroft was flattered like the rest of us; he worshipped Charles Ravenden. But when he saw how things were—when he saw the degrading acts he must perform—he would have none of it. He was a poor scholarship boy, but he had the courage to quit. He might have got free unscathed, too, but he was hot-tempered; he made the mistake of having words with my lord publicly—we all heard—and you do not embarrass Charles Ravenden and escape unpunished. Ravenden devised accusations, he planted evidence to get Pyecroft sent down. He ruined him at university for good."

"And now he is dead."

"What? Pyecroft dead? But how—?"

"You did not know he was Jack Scratch?"

"The scandalmonger?"

"The same. He was murdered in his lodging the night before last. He was tortured, a finger and toes cut off, all to obtain this, it seems." Drawing James Tandy's letter from his pocket, Mr. Franklin held it out.

Elstree's appalled eyes read the name at the bottom. "Tandy..." he murmured.

"He was also of your number, at Oxford?"

A benumbed nod.

"And likewise refused to participate in the diversions the earl required?"

"D-did."

Mr. Franklin sighed. "In sending this letter he made a mistake greater than Pyecroft's, then, for he promised to go to the college authorities. Swift action was necessary. Thus, murder." Folding the letter, Mr. Franklin put it away. "Charles Ravenden *did* murder James Tandy, eh, Mr. Elstree?"

Elstree hung his head again. "I b-believe so."

"Do you know for a certainty?"

"As near as can be."

"Yet why would he carve out the poor man's heart?"

Why carve out women's hearts, too? thought I.

Elstree rubbed hard at the knees of his breeches as if to erase his deep guilt. Strangled words bubbled from his throat: "Alas . . . alas . . . Hester . . ."

"Miss Ward, sir? Why do you speak of Miss Ward?"

"B-because I loved her. Because . . . because I *murdered* her, just as Charles Ravenden murdered James Tandy." Great tears rolled down Tom Elstree's cheeks, and my pencil stopped.

Mr. Franklin sat whilst the clock ticked on and the dying coals hissed. "I cannot believe you murdered the woman you loved," said he.

"I did! I did! Charles Ravenden told me that I did."

Mr. Franklin peered. "Come, sir, we must make sense of this. We must not credit what Charles Ravenden tells anyone. Answer my question: why did he carve out James Tandy's heart?"

The flesh around Elstree's eyes had gone as gray as ash. "To . . . to warn us, I suppose. His secret society . . . We played at being pagans. We flaunted the English church. We pretended at blood rites. Ravenden loved those rites—he loved cruelty and debauchery. He had devised a ceremony in which he pretended to sacrifice a girl. He is expert at trickery. He took the knife, he preached some mumbo jumbo. Then he seemed to cut out her heart. O, she was always alive afterward." His voice fell. "But before he did that, one of us would have her whilst all the rest watched." Elstree wiped his mouth. "Only sometimes . . . sometimes it was not a girl but a boy painted and dressed like a girl. Some poor boy . . ."

Mr. Franklin sat very still. "The Oxford authorities would surely disapprove that," said he. "I see now why my lord thought he must silence James Tandy. Did he cut out Tandy's heart so the rest of you would know who had done it?"

"To make us fear him. He pretended innocence afterward. 'A pity,' he said. 'Who could have done it?' But he said it with a wink. I could hardly bear the lie! I had *liked* James Tandy, and deep down I knew it was my lord who had done him in. But I am a coward. I was terrified—not for my life but that all our scandalous behavior would come out and my father would hear of it."

"So you have lived with your secret all these years."

"Years . . ."

An age of dread, thought I, gazing at the hangdog face.

"When my lord came to know someone had peached on us despite him," Elstree went on, "he was furious. But it was already too late, so he decided to flee before he could be called to account. 'You must do the same,' he said; I did not argue. What soiled him soiled me—and so we encoached for London that very night. The air was sweet! I remember, the Oxford air was sweet! Thank God the masters made nothing public."

"It would have blackened the college's name to do so. What did you do back in London?"

"We went separate ways. I told my father I had failed my studies, I was no student. It was hard—he is stern—but he made the best of it. He has attempted to teach me his business, and I try to learn the ships, the ports, the tonnage—though it is not easy. I am best at drinking and wenching."

"You want steel in your sinews, sir. You will find it."

Would he? Scores of hardworking gentlemen's sons were spoilt by their fathers' success. They frittered their days in turning a leg and lifting a bumper, and it made me grateful for my hard upbringing. It had wrung me, but it had taught me the virtue of work and reward; it had fitted me for Benjamin Franklin.

Elstree resumed his narrative: "And then my lord decided he must have a new secret society. He crooked a finger, he beckoned. 'No!' I told him. But he promised gaiety, diversion, fellowship. 'It will not be as before,' he purred, and to my discredit I succumbed. Yet it *is* as before. I sometimes think he believes he is some incarnation of Dionysus, beyond goodness, beyond reason. You know of his cave (I saw him take you to it). We began to meet there, with whores, and the old ceremonies from Oxford were resumed."

"The trick with the knife?"

"Hearts are still cut out—or appear to be—upon his altar. I do not know how he does it, but the women scream (perhaps they are instructed to do so on pain of his displeasure). In any event, their

209

deaths appear real, and I have known men who witness one for the first time to faint away. The victims writhe. There are gouts of blood. They seem to die—he even holds out their hearts! But they do not die. 'I revive you!' he cries, and raises 'em up, as if he is God himself, with God's power over life and death. Resurrection is his theme, he says, but I say blood is his theme, damn him. Only blood can rouse him."

I sat dry-mouthed, whilst Tom Elstree stared as into an abyss.

"And Hester Ward?" prompted Mr. Franklin softly.

Elstree flinched but to his credit mustered courage. Beyond the closed draperies London seemed to hold its breath. "Ravenden has kept me close to him lately. He has mocked you, Mr. Franklin, warning me against you—he knows I am at the end of my tether and might say too much. But he believes he has power over me. He revels in that. Well, I am here to prove he has no power. When he learns I have defied him, I do not know what he will do. Attempt to cut out my heart, too? But I do not care. I can live with this no longer." The young man's chin trembled. "And so, Mr. Franklin, here is how I murdered the woman I loved:

"As you know some young women of fashion were also of our number. Hester Ward—dear Hester!—was one. She was wild and untamed, but she had a tender side; I came to love her. She only wanted affection and trust, I believed; she could have been saved! She seemed to like me, too, at first; and I began to think, to hope, that I . . . that *we* might save each other. But she grew to laugh at me. She was afraid to love, I think. And Charles Ravenden prejudiced her against me. He mocked any of us who loved. 'We must never love!' he proclaimed. 'We must only *make* love.' How insinuating he is! His tongue can wrap itself round your soul. Too, there were the opiates—"

"Opiates?"

"The poppy—my lord learnt to use it in the East. There was much of it, and it made us even more his creatures, so that when we woke from some drugged sleep, sick with the headache, we hardly knew what we had done."

"But murder, sir?"

"Hear me. We were at his country house, he, dear Hester, and I, no others. We went to his cave. We drank his wine. Our heads swam. He demanded that Hester and I make love before him,

210

upon his altar. He would play Dionysus, prancing about; we would play the grateful receivers of the great god's bounty. It was an old game, but it kindled him. He wore his vine leaves, he gave us more wine, wheedling—though there was more than wine in the cup. We fell to his charms, we drank in the torchlight. How the stuff goes to your brain! We disrobed. We lay upon the altar." Elstree's voice faltered. "He placed his hands upon our bodies. He stroked our limbs, he told us what we must do and how—and we obeyed. How low I had sunk. But I loved Hester! She rarely let me touch her, but she let me touch her then; she drew me near. Because Ravenden bid it?"

Elstree's body began to rock in a creaking sorrow. "I sometimes wonder if she loved *him*. Not that she did not know what he was, but . . . ah, what a wretch I am! In any event my lord wanted more when we were done; he must have 'the sacrifice'—that would cap the thing, he said. Hester had played the deflowered virgin, and now I was to play the priest who took her life in the name of . . . what? Hester agreed. She lay back, all her lovely limbs naked. Ravenden gave me the knife. It was only a game, and never in the game had the girl died; she had always been resurrected despite the blood. I took the knife, and . . . and—" Elstree lifted his hands, as if he held a blade betwixt 'em; he stared up. "I remember how it gleamed. And how my head swam. I stood over Hester. I gazed upon those sweet breasts, between which I was to plunge the knife. I laughed, I believe." Elstree's hands sank to his sides. "And then I m-murdered—" His voice became a keening whine. His body jerked, his face swam with tears. His mouth delivered strangled gasps.

"My lord told you that you murdered her, did he?" asked Benjamin Franklin

"I . . . I . . ."

"Answer me, sir!"

Elstree stared helplessly. "I must have—"

"Do you *know* that you did it? Can you picture stabbing her in your mind?"

"N-no, but—"

"My lord told you after the fact, then."

"Y-yes."

"What *do* you recall?"

211

Elstree's eyes squeezed shut.

"Come, sir, the truth!"

The young man swayed, and his voice came as out of a terrible dream: "I c-can see myself holding the knife. Holding it above her. Thinking that my lord had often done the same, whilst I and all the Dionysians watched. Thinking how the knife appeared to do harm but never did. Surely I could do likewise. I could plunge the knife into my dear and do no harm." His eyes flew open. "But I loved Hester!" he gasped. "Yet did I hate her, too? Did I *want* to strike? Did I think to . . . to *purify* her by killing her?" He buried his face in his hands. "I do not know, I do not know."

"This will not do," persisted Benjamin Franklin.

Elstree struggled. "Ev'rything grows black. The next I can recall, I am upon the floor beside the altar. Blood is streaming down the marble. Ravenden stands beside me, looking down. 'It is very bad,' says he. 'I did not think you would strike. But you did strike. You have killed her. Hester Ward is dead. You have cut out her heart.' " Elstree shuddered. "I could not believe it, but it was true, for I looked, and there . . . and there . . ."

"Tosh." Mr. Franklin plucked at the young man's sleeve. "Look at me, sir. You may wish to think you murdered that poor girl. You may wish to punish yourself for your weakness, perhaps even for your love, but I will not have it. Cast off your guilt. It is why you have come, is it not? I do not believe you drove a knife into Hester Ward's breast, much less carved out her heart. The story is a fabrication of Charles Ravenden. I cannot prove that it is, but I am convinced that he, not you, murdered her. You would not cut the woman you loved in that cruel way, no matter how drugged you were. Think. The method by which James Tandy was dispatched cries out that it was the Earl of Chalton who did the deed."

"B-but—"

"No more, I tell you! Had Hester Ward done anything to displease my lord?"

"N-no. Yet . . . if he truly murdered her, was *I* the reason? B-because I loved her?"

Mr. Franklin's lips curled. "You will still blame yourself, eh? Ravenden killed her because she might come to love you? Because he could not bear to see the two of you happy? Very well, that may have been his motive—but you cannot punish yourself for it. Or for his lack of scruple. Tell me honestly: what was your relationship with him at this time?"

"Not as before. Nothing unnatural, if that is what you mean; I had put that behind me. Too, my lord seemed content with other game. He liked to watch his men at 'sport.' He frequented houses of boys. And he had his servants."

Simkins, thought I, *and the helpless blackamoor boy?* Had the earl murdered Hester Ward because she had won Tom Elstree's love? Had he meant to punish Elstree for flaunting his credo of unfeeling libertinism? Had he envied a fellow being who *could* love, whilst he himself found pleasure only in relentless depravity? I thought on Ravenden's mother, too. In carving the hearts from other women, was he punishing her?

The three of them at his estate, no witnesses, the drugged wine: had the Earl of Chalton *planned* the murder?

"Her murder was clever," Mr. Franklin said, "for it bound you to my lord: he is the only witness to your 'crime,' but he is also your savior, the man who helped you to cover the deed. Why did you spirit the body to London?"

"I did not wish to. I would have given myself up to the law, but Ravenden called me a fool; he would have none of it. 'We must think,' said he. Many people knew Hester had gone to his estate; she made no secret of anything. We could bury her on its grounds, but if the law began to nose about, she might be discovered. Far better she be found back in London."

"In some lonely mews, eh? Near her profligate uncle's house? Women are assaulted in London every day; thus she would be thought just another victim of the streets—except for her disfigurement. Truly I think my lord may've wanted to flaunt his handiwork."

"Dear God . . . Dear God," Tom Elstree murmured.

Was there blood in Ravenden's coach? Evidence? Who had driven the coach—Simkins? Did I grasp at straws?

"You said there were just three of you at Ravenden's estate," Mr. Franklin pursued. "Surely there were servants, too."

"At least half a dozen to manage the house. A dozen more for the stables and grounds."

"But my lord's man, Simkins—"

"He came up with his master. So far as I know, he remained below with the rest."

"What do you know of him?"

"Ravenden took him from one of the London houses of boys, trained him. Why do you ask?"

"We met him on the grounds of my lord's estate when we came upon you amongst the trees, do you recall?"

"I recall little of that night."

"Simkins said you were 'innocent.' What did he mean?"

"Innocent—" Tom Elstree tasted the word, and a wave of longing and despair seemed to wash over him. "I . . . I cannot say what he meant."

Mr. Franklin asked about Tuesday Marrowbone. The Dionysians never learnt the names of the whores Ravenden obtained for his rites, Elstree replied, but when Mr. Franklin described the mulberry birthmark, he stared. A girl with just such a mark had participated in Ravenden's rites: "She was one of the 'sacrifices' on his altar."

"She was the other young woman with her heart cut out," Mr. Franklin told him. "Do you have any idea why my lord should wish to murder her, too?"

"None."

"Is there any more you wish to tell?"

Elstree sat gray and spent. "Nay, you have heard all my shame."

Mr. Franklin rose. "Come." Elstree found his feet, and Mr. Franklin placed his hands upon the young man's shoulders. "I could tell you things that shame me. Any man could. You must forgive yourself. Regret is part of ev'ry life, but it must not prevent us learning from our mistakes. Promise you will return to your father, apply yourself, put Charles Ravenden behind you. You did not murder Hester Ward."

"How I wish to believe that!" The young man wrung Mr. Franklin's hands. "Thank you, sir. Thank you."

"Straight home, then." As James Tandy and Jack Scratch had been murdered, Elstree must take care. Marching to the front door, he clamped his mangled hat upon his head and trudged off toward the Strand.

Mr. Franklin and I watched upon the stoop 'til he vanished. A sudden shadow caused me to look up as a blanket of cloud drew over the sun. I turned to the gentleman. "Will he succeed in throwing off my lord's influence, sir?" asked I.

He examined his boot toes. "He is a wavering soul. He might still succumb to weakness, despair."

"But he did not murder Hester Ward. There is that."

"I *said* he did not murder her." Mr. Franklin met my gaze. "Yet in my lord's cave, far from any other eyes, who knows what really occurred? Damn all arrogance and folly!" He squinted up. "Will it rain?" He kicked the boot-scraper. "Let us in."

℁ 24 ℁

IN WHICH We are Commanded to the Country and Mr. Franklin Primes a Pistol . . .

Mrs. Stevenson and Polly awaited us when we stepped indoors. Our landlady's hands were knotted in her flour-streaked apron, and her squinting stare said she *would* be informed who the young man was and why he had come. Mr. Franklin obliged by telling her that he was a wealthy merchant's son, that he let us know our danger was real, and that he might help us to end it. He turned to me. "Nick, I must to John Fielding." He spoke to Peter, too. "Continue to keep watch." Taking his hat from its peg by the door, he made to go.

"What? Out?" Mrs. Stevenson cried.

"I shall be safe. My bamboo is my sword." In a moment he was gone.

It was half past noon. The day had grown even darker, London creaking under the press of an impending storm. We stood uncertainly before Mrs. Stevenson snapped at her housemaid to see that the scuttles were filled with coal; Nanny crept off. "I shall make some marchpane," Mrs. Stevenson announced. "Help me, Nick."

Glad to be busy, I followed her belowstairs. The kitchen was a large stone-flagged chamber hung with baskets of vegetables, cured meat, copper and tin. Its spice boxes stood in neat rows, and the air was warm from the oven. Mrs. Stevenson ground almonds whilst I crumbled bread. Fetching honey, she mixed the almonds and crumbs with it, and I proceeded to mould a dozen sweet, sticky rounds as she set about cutting a leg of lamb for stew. Lost

216

in thought, I paid her little heed, but no longer hearing her knife, I glanced up. Her eyes were startled-looking, as round as coins, and her lips trembled. "He will be safe, will he not?" she burst out. "Mr. Franklin will be safe?" Her fear was all for her lodger.

"Mr. Franklin takes care of himself; you know that he does," said I, though I felt as uncertain as she.

I did not know if any of us was safe.

At one I went upstairs to await the gentleman. I passed the time putting more of his papers in order. How chill his familiar room grew without him! I remained doubtful. Despite some unknown details, we had resolved most of our mystery, but the danger was not yet resolved. Though Tom Elstree had put us in possession of near the last pieces of our puzzle, they were of such a nature that we were still unlikely to place Charles Ravenden in the dock. Could Justice Fielding do something?

At two a rap came upon the door, and Nanny slipped in. She handed me a letter, just come, she said in her startled-rabbit way. It was in a fine linen envelope, but as I placed it upon Mr. Franklin's desk my skin prickled.

Its red wax seal was stamped with the Chalton coat of arms.

Mr. Franklin returned at three. Justice Fielding had not been encouraging, said he, sinking into his chair whilst I helped him off with his boots. "Our evidence is ragtag stuff. Too, if Tom Elstree is called as witness, who is to say Ravenden might not prevail, so that the bedeviled young man would hang for Hester Ward's murder instead?" The most discouraging element remained that, even should our quarry be brought to trial, it would not be at the King's Bench before Lord Mansfield, a just man, but in the House of Lords. "They are unlikely even to hear the case. Ravenden knows secrets about too many of 'em. They will turn tail for fear of him."

I set the gentleman's boots outside the door for Nanny to clean. "A letter from Charles Ravenden, sir," said I, gesturing at his desk.

He was at it in an instant, slitting the seal. He frowned over the thing a moment before he passed it to me.

I read, in a confident hand:

> Dear Mr. Franklin:
>   We have not met since St. Giles. What a regrettable encounter! I fear I was rude, and you . . . but I shall not

judge. Nonetheless, you are a busy man. You have busied yourself about St. James's Square, I see. Was that your blackamoor servant hanging about my house? He is a slyboots, but I spied him; and, truly, I believe I have seen him elsewhere. In Spur Court, perhaps? On a recent foggy night?

Speaking of Spur Court, a fellow of our acquaintance who lived there is dead. Jack Scratch, he called himself, though that is not his true name (he was always a liar). He gave me some trouble in the newspapers lately, but he shall trouble me no more. I knew him in Oxford, did you know? We were students. He sought my regard, a poor dog you would not kick to please yourself. But I was kind, I deigned to give him notice—I patted his head—and he fawned about me for a time. Then he turned against me.

I cannot abide disloyalty!

You owe me loyalty, too. You supped at my table, you were entertained at my estate, I showed you my temple, my cave; I admitted you to my philosophy. I believed we were alike, sir, despite your excessive scrupulosity, and I felt sure I might bring you round to my way of thinking. Yet you nose about Oxford, seeking . . . what? You entertain Tom Elstree, a mad, tale-bearing fool. You are friends with Bow Street, and who knows what you talk on there with that officious snoop, Fielding. To cap it, you set your servant to spy upon me.

I like none of it.

Yet I hold out the hand of friendship. Charles Ravenden forgives you. I must to Chalton today—some troublesome business—but I cannot bear to wait to make matters right. Thus I invite you to join me at my estate tomorrow. We shall talk. We shall stroll about the grounds. I have much of interest to show you.

One last instruction: bring your boy. I shall be angry if you do not.

Never disappoint me.

Sir, your most obedient, etc.

Charles Ravenden

"The impudence!" puffed Mr. Franklin when I looked up. "Yet it is no surprise."

"What shall you do, sir?" I trembled. To Ravenden's estate again? Far from Craven Street and Bow Street, our twin poles of safety?

A soft rap, and Nanny slipped into the room once more, her little cap askew, tails of mouse-brown hair flying. "Beg pardon, sir, but a servant is come to inquire if there is reply to the letter from the Earl of Chalton."

Mr. Franklin looked at me. "My lord knew the precise moment I came home, then." He gazed out at London, where a thousand chimneypots spewed coal smoke into the smudgy sky. "Well, answer must be made." Going to his desk, he took up paper and pen, whilst Nanny peered meekly round his chamber as if she had never seen it before. There came the soft scratch of his quill. He sanded and sealed the note. "Give this to the servant."

"Yes, sir." Nanny departed.

The gentleman faced me.

"You will go, sir?" asked I.

"I cannot take you with me."

I took a step toward him. "Please, sir, you must!"

He regarded me out of the gray-brown eyes I knew so well. "We have traveled many perilous ways together, have we not?" He bit a lip. "If I am persuaded to relent, we shall take the greatest precautions."

The day played itself out. The clouds continued to gather over London, but little rain fell, a mockery, for a great storm was plainly imminent. I read more of *Tom Jones*. I brought water from the pump at the top of the way. Afterward I stood by the Thames sketching two ragged boys who flung pebbles at gulls under the recalcitrant sky. All this I did watchfully, feeling a great pressure betwixt my eyes. A weight bore down on my shoulders, and fear gripped my limbs. But an exultation grew, too: resolution would come at last—action, an end.

Did a duelist, pistol in hand, feel so as he waited to fire?

I longed for tomorrow to arrive.

. . .

Arrive it did: Friday, the twelfth day since we had been called to that bleak stables to view a poor murdered woman in the rain. The sky was thunder-gray as I arose; the clouds seemed to scrape the rooftops. Richard Jackson stopped by at nine, to confer once more about the Board of Trade on Monday. Would the issue of the Penns be settled at last?

Let Mr. Franklin be there to see it.

At breakfast we gathered solemnly: Mr. Franklin, William, Mrs. Stevenson, Polly, and I, whilst Nanny served, and the warmth from the kitchen seeped into the small dining room. Peter had eaten; he stood staunchly one floor above us with a pistol Mr. Franklin had borrowed from John Fielding. There were buttered toast, curds with milk, kidneys (a treat), and some crumbs of marchpane left from yesterday. A pot of chocolate, too. We ate in wary silence, Mrs. Stevenson emitting little moans and peering in distress. What had her lodger brought on her house? A handful of rain slapped the panes, followed by a warning rumble.

"The storm," William murmured.

Mr. Franklin nodded. "Sooner or later it will break." He turned to Mrs. Stevenson. "Do you still deny my 'doctine of points'? Will you not have a lightning rod, ma'am?"

"O, I give in, sir!" she burst out, her housewife's cap bobbing. "You promise you will stick one of those whatd'ycall'ems into the ground to spare our lives? Anything, sir, anything! But what will you do about this terrible man who murders women? What will you do about him?"

We did not depart London 'til two. Mr. Franklin had consented to take me with him, though only after precautions were in place. One was Peter. William would remain in Craven Street to see after the ladies—it was thought they should be in little danger with my lord out of town, but we must not relax our vigilance; Peter could thus accompany us with his pistol.

The second precaution I learnt when Mr. Franklin beckoned me into his workshop just before we set out. The room was cold, its equipment and artifacts mute and still. Beyond the window

220

Hungerford Market crawled with buyers and sellers beneath an iron sky. Opening a drawer, the gentleman took out a small, bone-handled pistol. I started. The same with which Mrs. Jared Hexham had near shot him on our first adventure together two years ago?

"Aye," nodded Mr. Franklin. "I plucked it from that Thames-side warehouse, and I have kept it ever since, for Mrs. Hexham has no more use for it." Indeed, the wicked woman had died in Newgate of gaol fever.

Outside, winds stirred as the coming storm threatened. *Soon*, it seemed to moan. Mr. Franklin bade me watch as he primed the weapon. Unscrewing a flask's cap, he poured black grains of powder into its muzzle. Next he inserted a wad with a ramrod, then a ball from a box, which he also pushed in with the rod, tapping with a mallet. "To force the ball against the sides of the barrel, so it cannot fall out." He pointed. "This is the steel, against which the flint strikes." Opening the priming pan, he filled it with a pinch of powder from the flask, then closed it. "Done."

He held out the pistol.

"I, sir?"

A grave look. "To be safe. The Earl of Chalton murders people, remember?"

I took the weapon. It felt strangely warm after his handling, and awkward. But power came with it, too, thrilling, as if it made me larger and stronger than I had been. Yet there was a weight of responsibility as well, and I was awed.

"To fire, cock the flint and pull the trigger." Mr. Franklin mimed the motion, aiming as if at an unseen enemy. "Understand?"

"Yes, sir."

He gazed out at the louring sky. "The weather troubles me. I hope it does not dampen your powder (powder is a fickle thing). But you shall carry the pistol nonetheless. Use it if you must."

"I promise." I slipped the thing in my coat pocket. It was small enough to fit under the flap, which I buttoned.

"Now." Mr. Franklin drew me to the door. "You have your pistol, I my bamboo." He made a slash with his stick. "Let us vanquish the Earl of Chalton!"

And so we set off. Peter had been sent to engage a closed carriage; it waited by the stoop. Its interior was small, redolent with the rich, rank smell of London. We sat close, but I was not unhappy to be wedged betwixt Mr. Franklin and Peter. I felt safe, though how I should feel at Charles Ravenden's isolated country estate might prove another matter.

William, Mrs. Stevenson, and Polly bid us Godspeed, and we headed out of town for the third time in a fortnight. A great jam of traffic—an overturned carriage—held us up by Glasshouse Street for three quarters of an hour, but at last we reached the Knightsbridge Turnpike. The storm still teased: gusts of wind and fitful scatterings of rain that promised a deluge; but it was just as well the skies did not open, for then we might never arrive at Chalton House. The road was little traveled today; we met few others: a parson on a spavined nag, a dray hauling rough-cut logs. Did only fools venture out with such a storm brewing? The sky was a low, black threat.

Mr. Franklin fell to reminiscing. He recalled how as a boy in Boston he had devised a pair of paddles for his hands and feet to help him swim faster, and how he had once used a kite to pull himself across a pond. He recalled being apprenticed to the printing shop of his older brother, James, and how, hating his brother's tyranny, he had run away to New York, then Philadelphia. He recalled his first trip to England aboard the *London Hope* with his friend James Ralph. "I arrived on Christmas day, near penniless, at the age of eighteen." But he had survived, he had prospered. Now he was back in England.

Yet his stories did not prevent me from brooding. The gentleman had sent a note round to Soho Square this morning to bolster Tom Elstree. He had asked for some reply, but none had returned. Why?

The weather darkened the Buckinghamshire landscape. Its long grasses seemed to flatten in fear, and even the oaks and yews ducked their bushy heads. But we traveled smartly, and two and a half hours from Craven Street brought us to the looming stone gatehouse that marked the entrance to my lord's grounds. It was unoccupied, no one hailed us. Then the long drive on the chalk-

and-gravel road, past the rows of elms shivering with autumn's tattered leaves. Here, too, we met no one, though we glimpsed the top of Ravenden's tower, *Fay ce que voudras* in somber gold at its apex; I had come to despise the phrase.

At last the trees gave way. Chalton House appeared below, and misgiving took my breath; I felt safe no more.

We descended the curving drive.

❧ 25 ❧

IN WHICH the Power of the Heavens Meets the Might of a God . . .

Chalton House had not changed: a gloomy mass amongst twisted oaks. It was near five o'clock, the day rapidly sliding toward night, but few glimmers showed in any of the old arched windows. Were guests not expected? Furthermore, no figure stirred to greet us as our coach stopped on the graveled circle before the manse. Getting down, we were whipped by a stinging bluster. We gazed about. There lay the artificial lake, wrinkled by wind, there the temple, there my lord's tower flung up into the sky. But the Dionysians had vanished. No pursuits. No lewd tumbles. The grounds appeared tenantless.

A sound made us turn, and the door of the house opened to reveal a man standing there: Simkins. He glided toward us wearing his hooded look. His eyes narrowed at Peter.

"You have brought your manservant, sir," said he to Mr. Franklin.

"I have."

"I do not believe my master expected your servant."

"Your master was not very precise what he expected. Are we to stay the night? If so, I cannot do without my man."

Some doubt seemed to ruffle Simkins's demeanor. He appeared to quell it. "You are indeed to stay the night," said he. "I shall show your man your quarters. But I am ordered to tell you to dismiss your coach. And to join my lord at his temple."

"Now?"

"If you please, sir. With your boy."

I did not like this. Glancing at Mr. Franklin, I saw him peer at the distant marble columns, ghost-pale in the dying day. Did a light flicker betwixt them? Thunder growled in the west as the gentleman squinted at the waiting house, then at Simkins, who sent back his thin smile. Did Simkins long to add some adjuration of his own?

"Very well." Mr. Franklin drew Peter and me aside. "Go with the man," the gentleman whispered to Peter. "Look about. Study the disposition of the place: its rooms, its corridors. Seek the whereabouts of the other servants, too. Above all, talk to Simkins; see if you can draw him out—but do not be diverted. If Nick and I are not back within the hour, come uphill to seek us. Your pistol is primed?"

"It is, sir."

"I do not like this, but we must play it as it comes."

Peter went with Simkins. Just before they vanished, I glimpsed the turbaned black boy inside the door with a flickering lamp. Then the door thudded shut. Mr. Franklin turned to our driver as wind set leaves in a whirl. He seemed to debate whether to order the man to depart or wait out of sight—but he could not leave him to be trapped by the storm, so he dismissed him, though I was not pleased to hear the wheels crunch away.

Mr. Franklin sent me a look.

Wrapping our scarves about our throats, we headed uphill.

The leering statues still watched from the trees: frozen shapes of lust and rape. No one offered to dress us in chitons at the robing house—it, too, was deserted—so we passed on up the curving path. Treetops tossed. The wind rose to a banshee wail; surely the storm must soon break. In ten minutes we stood at the steps of the temple, capped by its processional pediment; and peering up I thought Dionysus' face resembled Charles Ravenden's, a mask of ruthless vanity.

I patted my coat pocket. The small, hard shape of my pistol reassured me, but I unbuttoned the flap, in case.

One last glance back over our shoulders at the dark green sweep of lawn, the moving trees, the lake with its forlorn beached barge (all about us was an agitated rustling); then we turned and mounted the steps. Inside the temple half a dozen flames flickered in glass chimneys set at intervals upon the broad marble floor to form a Dionysian hexagon near the tall rear door cut into the hill.

The door stood open.

No one was to be seen.

Mr. Franklin placed his hand upon my arm, glancing round before drawing me to the very center of the temple. On three sides of us rose tall columns, through which we glimpsed a tossing world of impending deluge; on the fourth, the wall of obscene paintings, with its door like a black mouth. The light from the lamps produced an unsettling effect, making our shadows loom and dart. Outside, rain began to scatter. The storm at last? But it was the open door I gazed at, exhaling its odor of earth.

"He wishes us to go into his cave, Nick," said Mr. Franklin. "He expects us to go."

"Shall we, sir?"

"I shall."

I turned in protest. "I must go with you!"

He shook his head. "No. He has read me well. He knows my determination; he knows I will see this through. I must stop him, and if 'tis to be by a battle on his own ground, I shall not hang back." He touched my arm. "It is not so easy to finish me. But I cannot take the chance you might be harmed. I need you here with your pistol. You will be safe if you stay alert. Peter is just downhill. He will come up if we do not return. Then you and he together—"

He meant that if something happened to him, I could escape under Peter's protection. John Fielding would then help us, and with him we might bring down the Earl of Chalton. But I could hardly bear to hear talk of such a pass. Staring into the kind, familiar face, I felt a great woe, but I yielded. "Very well, sir. I will wait." I had no choice.

"It is best. And now—" Bending, he gathered one of the lamps in his left hand. He gripped his strong bamboo in his right. I was not reassured. I had seen him fell dread brutes with that bamboo—but Charles Ravenden was no mere brute; he was a serpent, as Tom Elstree had said, a viper who might strike before that stick could be used.

Mr. Franklin went to the door. He peered in, and I saw by the glow of his lamp satyrlike Priapus amongst the gloom. Then he stepped in—I could see his face in a brief flicker, his voice echoing hollowly: "Keep watch, Nick."

In another moment he was gone.

I waited. I went to a back corner of the temple, and I waited. Whilst I shivered, the storm arrived.

A great cold gust swirled grit and leaves into the temple, knocking one of the remaining five lamps upon the floor in a crash of glass and burning oil. Then the heavens opened in a seething roar. I had been able to make out Chalton House below in the last light of day, but it vanished now, as did the lake, the path, the road; a whipping curtain of gray obscured everything. Rain swept in from all three open sides of the temple as wind blew willy-nilly, and a sheet of water poured across the floor, threatening the four still-burning lamps whose flames writhed like imprisoned spirits.

I felt helpless. Mr. Franklin might be in harm's way, but the storm must be reckoned with, too. I had not ever seen so fierce a downpour. Lightning cut the sky. In its flash I glimpsed a figure distantly approaching. The man was there, then gone. Cloaked. A blot of blackness trudging uphill from Chalton House.

Peter? If not Peter, who?

Thunder followed the flash, and in its aftermath I imagined the worst: seeking to vent his spite against Mr. Franklin through me, Charles Ravenden had guessed the gentleman would never take his boy into the cave. Thus instead of awaiting Mr. Franklin within, he marched uphill to finish Nick Handy with his knife.

I shuddered; and as if to affright me more, another bolt sizzled. Seeing the figure closer, behatted, advancing, I shrank back. I was vulnerable in the glow from the flickering lamps. Where could I hide? The lightning was capricious. Would I even know when the stranger drew near enough to enter the temple, reveal himself, do as he would?

Scurrying along the back wall, I tucked myself behind the last marble column on the right. Better. From here I could run out into the storm if I must, trust my fate to the dark and wet, where I would not easily be found.

Meanwhile, Mr. Franklin . . . ?

Another flash of light showed the man terribly near, at the top of the long, drenched sweep of lawn. In a moment he would be at the temple, mounting its steps, seeking. The lightning died, and I crouched, peering round the curve of the column, gathering myself to run. Only at the last moment did I recall the pistol, and frantically jamming my hand in my pocket, I pulled it out. A form appeared betwixt two of the forward columns, sodden, dripping. My fingers tightened on the handle. The figure staggered into the glow from the lamps.

It was not Charles Ravenden, not Peter, not even Simkins.

It was Tom Elstree.

I dropped the pistol back in my pocket. Bewildered, I stepped from behind the concealing column. "You, sir? What do you here?"

He swept off his rain-soaked hat. His square, stolid face was lined with dread, and his small eyes darted frantically. "Where is Mr. Franklin?"

I glanced at the gaping door. That was answer enough.

"He has gone in there?"

"Yes."

"With Charles Ravenden?"

"He entered alone."

"I was at an upper window. I saw you drive up, but when I came down to greet you, there was no one save Simkins and your blackamoor. Why—?"

"Simkins said my lord awaited us in his temple. He was not here, but the door was open. Lamps lit, too, six of 'em."

He peered at the four remaining. "In a hexagon?"

"Yes."

Elstree crushed his hat in his hands. "Ravenden plans one of his cermonies, then. With the knife and the altar. He loves the game. Whyever did you come to Chalton?"

"A letter commanding Mr. Franklin. Why are you here?"

"O, I promised your master I should not see Ravenden again, I know. But my lord commanded me, too. He said he had news to tell. Likely it was just a lure. No matter. I wished to break with him to his face. I wanted to tell him how I despise him. I wanted to spit upon him, do you see?"

I saw that the young man was so far gone in self-loathing that he would dare a murderer. "And did you tell him?"

More jagged lightning. A crack of thunder as the rain continued to whip. "I meant to. I arrived only half an hour before you, but Ravenden was not in the house. I was told to wait, and when I came down to greet you, Simkins said you had gone to the temple. I hung about, but when the storm began—" He flung his hat away. "There is no time to waste. We must follow into that cave. Charles Ravenden hates your master."

The altar. The knife. We must surely follow. Mr. Franklin had told me not to, but Tom Elstree was with me now. I had the pistol, too.

He scooped up a lamp, and we hurried through the shadowy door.

Tom Elstree had been here many times before, so he led the way. Passing Priapus with his mocking motto at his feet, we descended the sloping tunnel betwixt thick wooden beams. A musty dankness filled my nostrils. The scent of danger, too. We were out of the storm but in a chiller realm. We could not see far ahead, for our lamp lit only a pale circle about us, but Elstree hurried rapidly, his breath puffing. Did he know more of what Charles Ravenden intended than he revealed? The whisper of water came to us; then we were at the stream, clattering across its narrow wooden bridge. The way curved. The descent grew steeper and with it my gloom. Had I been foolish not to follow Mr. Franklin sooner? Had some terrible defeat been precipitated?

In five minutes we reached Harpocrates, the god of silence, with his closed eyes and his finger upon his smiling lips. "Ravenden always made us bow to the statue," Elstree murmured. " 'Obey Harpocrates,' he told us. 'Do not speak of anything you have seen or done here.' " He held up a hand; round the very next curve the walls would open into the circular chamber with the debauched mosaic upon its floor and the blood-stained altar at its center. My heart beat fast. Would we be too late?

Elstree set down his lamp—we did not need it, for light showed ahead, a soft sputtering which told us the torches had been lit— and we crept forward, breathless. Hearing voices, we slowed yet more as the ceremonial chamber began to slide into view, dedicated to the god of joy and madness.

In a great rush of relief I heard Mr. Franklin's voice. "You make it very clear why you murdered James Tandy and Jack Scratch. I thank you for being honest."

I heard Charles Ravenden's voice, too, prating: "It does not matter. You will tell no one."

"Did your man, Simkins, help you to do Scratch in by luring him to that tavern?" Mr. Franklin asked as Elstree and I drew nearer.

A laugh. "My dear sir, Simkins is why I was forced to finish the damned scribbler when I did. O, I would have seen to him sooner or later, but Simkins made it pressing by betraying me. He gave Scratch James Tandy's letter, which I had saved for years, to remind me of the first delicious death."

"Why did Simkins do that?"

"Because he has no gratitude! O, I will deal with him when I have done with you; he will suffer. Is loyalty dead?"

"Some men still inspire it."

There was silence at this, whilst we crept behind a mound of earth where we could view the whole chamber. There were the six evenly placed torches shedding light over the vile mosaic. There, too, was the stained marble slab where horrors had been done; a pair of filled wineglasses sat upon it. Yet it was Charles Ravenden who drew my eyes, for he was stark naked. Yet he had painted himself white all over, his hair an ebon thickness about his shoulders, His lips were scarlet. He wore a fillet of vine leaves about his brow. What a fantastical sight! His body was crisscrossed by vine leaves, too, and he held a rapier at the ready.

Mr. Franklin stood but a few feet from him; very still, one hand resting upon the head of his bamboo, his balding head tilted as if he merely attended some discourse at the Royal Society. Yet his eyes were alert. Ravenden's sword flicked in barely repressed fury, and I recalled how I had first seen him on that cloudy London night, masked, holding just such a weapon.

I recalled, too, what he had done to Jack Scratch.

"I shall make you suffer for your insolence," said the earl now.

Mr. Franklin faced him squarely. "I proclaim what I think, nonetheless. You do not inspire loyalty. How so, if you must murder to gain it? And your deeds fail in their purposes. You murdered Hester Ward to keep Tom Elstree's loyalty, but you have lost that. You murder to punish betrayal, but in doing so you only close the door on what has already fled, which is neither clever nor useful. There is something lacking in your methods and your wisdom, sir."

These were provoking words; I trembled.

As if to confirm my fear, my lord swung his rapier so hard it sang. "You dare!"

Mr. Franklin stood his ground. "Why did you murder Tuesday Marrowbone?"

"Ha, that does not fit your fine theories! For pleasure, sir, pure pleasure. Dionysus demanded it. I felt the need here"—he clutched his groin—"and so I dispatched her."

"To see her blood?"

"To hear her begging cries."

"With no qualms?"

"She was a whore."

"She had a soul."

"She was a *woman*!"

The torches sputtered. The mosaic seemed to twist and dissolve.

"But why cut out her heart?" Mr. Franklin pursued.

"Dionysus!" A ringing pride in the name. "Dionysus must have the heart!"

Mr. Franklin tutted. "I have not read that in any ancient lore."

"There is new lore, sir."

"Dionysus tells you so?"

Ravenden strode back, forth. "Perhaps he need not tell me. Perhaps *I* am Dionysus." He stopped. "What do you think, Mr. Franklin?" He spread his arms, as to display some wonder. "Am I Dionysus?"

"There is no Dionysus."

"You blaspheme."

Mr. Franklin shook his head. "There never has been a Dionysus. He is a creature of men's imaginations; he is a figment of yours. He is a convenience to you, sir, a toy."

"The god will have revenge."

"He shall not. Come, the masque is done. Let us leave this place. Chalk was dug here, it is no temple, and nothing sacred is accomplished upon your 'altar' save trickery and murder."

Ravenden held his sword tip under Mr. Franklin's nose. "Do you know what those words will earn you, sir? Death. I shall puncture you. I am an excellent swordsman, you will not escape. You shall die, and so shall your boy. How dare you doubt Dionysus? The god is wise, despite what you say—*I* am wise—for you will be found upon Hampstead Heath, along with Tom Elstree. You will be thought the victims of highwaymen, and I shall take your paltry purses to prove it. The law will never touch me."

"Tom Elstree?"

Ravenden smiled. "You see, you do not know ev'rything. I have lured him here, too, the weakling! He waits in my house even now. Waits for his own death, if he knew it."

My whole body tensed. Would Ravenden stab now? He seemed to ready himself, his smile like the rictus I had seen at Bridewell; he would take joy in murder. Frantically I scrabbled at my pocket, reached, pulled out the pistol. I cocked the flint.

"No!" cried I, pushing past Tom Elstree, and Ravenden's white-painted face turned toward me. Stopping a scant six feet from him, I aimed as Mr. Franklin had showed me, though my hands shook. "I shall fire! I swear that I shall!"

My lord's eyes took me in, leaking fury and contempt, and I trembled the more. Could I truly kill a man? Then Tom Elstree was rushing past me. He placed his hand upon Ravenden's sword. The two men's gazes met, and I saw Elstree flinch. But with a calculating look at him, at me (did he see I *would* fire?), the earl released the sword, and Elstree stepped back with it. He glared at Ravenden. "I did not murder my dear Hester! You told me I had done it, but I did not. *You* murdered her, sir! You! You!" I thought the young man would slash and cut, then, but he only stood with his chest heaving as tears of anguish squeezed from his eyes.

A white-painted savage with thick black hair, a scarlet mouth, and vine leaves for garb, an apparition from the land of demons, Ravenden took us in. But he showed no signs of defeat, and I misgave.

After all, was he not the Earl of Chalton and (in his mind) a god?

"I see," said he. Turning, he strode to the altar whilst I kept my pistol upon him. Lips pursed, he gazed at the two glasses of red wine resting on its stained marble top. What did he ponder? Touching one glass, running a finger round its rim, he picked up the other. "To Dionysus." Smiling, he raised it. "To myself." He quaffed it, the grape staining his chin as he swallowed. Then he tossed the glass away to shatter upon the mosaic where Maenads tore at human flesh.

"It is time to leave this place," said Mr. Franklin sternly.

The earl looked at him. "O, I shall leave it, sooner than you think."

"What do you mean?"

Ravenden leant upon the altar. One hand clutched his heart. "Ah, it is swift!" His eyes closed, and when they opened they appeared glazed. "The poppy," he slurred. "A powerful distillation. One glass for me and one for you, if I chose not to use the sword. But I have drunk your glass. In small doses, the poppy brings rest; in large doses, death. So, you see, you have not got me after all. Yet I shall never die." He flung up a hand. "Charles Ravenden, die? Dionysus? Nay, I shall be resurrected when your flesh is dust. I have beat you, Benjamin Franklin. And thus . . . and thus . . ." Stumbling, he sank to his knees. "So soon . . . ?" He drooped. He fell upon his back. His eyes rolled up. A great sigh escaped him, and a trickle of saliva reeled a silver thread from those scarlet lips.

Tom Elstree stood over him. "I am glad! I am glad! I am glad the devil is done!"

"But is he?" Mr. Franklin knelt by the body, feeling of its limbs. "I shall not miss the man, but we must save him if we can, for he breathes still. Better he stand trial. Some emetic may cure him— Fothergill has taught me the antidotes to poisons." He looked up. "You must help me to get him from this cave."

Plainly Elstree would rather leave his nemesis to rot, but he tucked the sword into his belt, and he and Mr. Franklin wrapped an arm about the earl, raised him, began to drag him up the tunnel. Releasing its flint, I thrust my pistol in my pocket and scooped up one of the lamps to guide us. I glanced back only once, at the mute marble altar where mock death and real death had met. How glad I was to see the last of it.

We proceeded past Harpocrates, then over the wooden bridge, slowly, ponderously. Ravenden sagged betwixt the two men.

"He is heavy," puffed Mr. Franklin.

"Damn him for murdering my dear Hester! Damn him for blaming me!"

"And damn you for being a fool," came a voice.

The Earl of Chalton?

I had glanced down to avoid stumbling—and when I looked up the earl stood facing us, alert, his sword in his hand. My heart sank. Why had we trusted him? He had drunk no drugged wine, merely pretended. He had waited. At his chosen moment, when our guard was down, he had pulled free and snatched his sword from Tom Elstree's belt.

I had no time to think more, for he thrust the weapon's tip against my throat; I felt its sharp prick. "Drop your stick, sir," said he to Mr. Franklin. "Drop it, I say, or I shall take the boy's wind."

Mr. Franklin's eyes smouldered, but he let his bamboo fall. My pistol—could I pull it out? I made a small movement, but Ravenden's sword bit deeper. "Nay, boy, do not think it. I shall take your sting." With a deft movement he slid the pistol from my pocket. "That is better." Suddenly his sword lashed out, and Tom Elstree staggered back, a hand to his face, where a cut cheek oozed blood. "You puppy!" the earl growled. "You think you can defy me and pay no price? You shall pay worse than that." The sword flicked again, and Elstree stared at a bloodied hand. Another slash, and his shirtfront opened in a line of red.

"Sir!" protested Mr. Franklin, but the earl kept at it. Eyes glittering, he struck again and again, and blood flew about, Elstree flailing his arms, falling back under a flurry of blows that sent buttons and shreds of cloth flying. Ravenden might easily have killed him, but that was not his aim; pain was his aim, punishment, and he smiled as he inflicted it.

Mr. Franklin stepped betwixt them, taking one of the blows himself, upon his right arm. "Sir, you cannot . . . This must stop . . ."

Ravenden paused. "You, sir?" he keened. "Shall I reprimand you, too?" He expertly swung.

Mr. Franklin's spectacles flew from his face, and a thin red line appeared in the brow above his eyes. He blinked as blood ran into his face.

"The eyes, the eyes," Ravenden breathed. "First your eyes. Then your heart, your heart for Dionysus. Afterward your boy will die, too—but first I shall have him how I like. I shall bugger him, sir. I shall bend him. I shall make him groan."

I felt cold all over. This was my father he spoke to. Blind my father's eyes? I little cared how Charles Ravenden threatened me. I only knew I must save Mr. Franklin, and as my lord readied his sword, I used the only weapon I had.

The lamp.

I flung it at the Earl of Chalton. It made a whooshing sound; then its fragile glass struck the hilt of his sword, shattering, splashing the flaming oil on his naked, vine-wreathed skin and black cascade of hair.

Charles Ravenden screamed.

In an instant he was aflame. He dropped the sword. He flew about, slapping at himself, piteously yelping. He wore wings of flame: orange, red, yellow feathers that hissed and sang.

He fled up the tunnel.

The storm, thought I. *Rain. It will put out the flames and he will escape!*

He took our only light with him—he *was* our light—and wiping blood from his brow Mr. Franklin scooped up his spectacles. He grasped Tom Elstree's arm. "Come!"

Together he and I propelled the wounded young man up the tunnel's ascent behind our will-o'-the-wisp.

A new smell filled the loamy dankness: the stink of roasted flesh.

We panted, we pressed on. Ravenden drew away. And then he vanished, winked out; he had passed through the door, its shape emerging from the darkness ahead, illuminated by the lamps that remained outside. Had he escaped after all? Extinguished himself in the storm?

Tom Elstree moved sluggishly, but we urged him on. The door drew nearer, and I had a horror that Ravenden would slam it, bolt us in. If he did, would Peter find us?

Where was Peter?

We lunged past Priapus, and I sucked wind-wracked air as we stumbled out into the great rectangle of the temple. Beyond its columns the storm still blew, a thrashing of wind and trees, a driving rain. We were half blinded by a flash so near it seemed to sear the air, followed by a crack of thunder that shook the marble floor. Had Charles Ravenden escaped? No. He lay amongst the remaining three beleaguered lamps. Had he sought safety in his hexagon? Believed Dionysus' magic could save him? In any event he had gone as far as he could before an ungodlike mortality overtook him. We stood, stared. He was not dead yet. He stirred, he groped, a blackened thing, croaking, stinking, smouldering.

"Dear God . . ." murmured Benjamin Franklin.

And then Charles Ravenden died.

An unmistakable stillness came over him. A relaxation. Peace. The clawlike fingers froze, and a glazed gleam faded in the blackened hollows of the eyes, making me recall Hester Ward's vermineaten orbs. Whether or no this were justice, it was the end of Charles Ravenden, the end of the Dionysus Club, the end of the earl's mockery and murder. Tyburn had been cheated of his hanging.

Another crackling flash. The almost simultaneous clap of thunder made me jump. "We must get away from here," muttered Benjamin Franklin, and I knew why: Ravenden's tower thrust into the very heavens beside the temple where we stood, a point to draw the power of the god of storms: Zeus.

At that moment two figures dashed through the columns into the temple.

Peter and Simkins.

I was amazed to see their mismatched forms, Peter broad and strong, Simkins narrow-shouldered and pale. Yet they appeared comrades. "I pray you are well, sir?" Peter cried.

Mr. Franklin touched the blood upon his brow. "Not perfectly. But I live and breathe. More than I can say for this poor thing." He pointed at Charles Ravenden.

Simkins's eyes fixed upon his master. He cocked his head solemnly at Mr. Franklin. "He did not take your measure, sir. I knew he did not."

"And I did not take yours—but that must wait." Mr. Franklin waved his hands. "For now, away. The storm—"

Peter understood, and turning Simkins round he propelled him out betwixt the columns. Then he hurried to help Mr. Franklin with Tom Elstree, still dazed. In a moment we were all stumbling down the broad marble steps into the rain. It lashed my face, it ran down my collar; in seconds I was drenched, but I did not care. I wanted only to escape. We eschewed the sidelong path; instead we pounded straight downhill. I fell twice on the slippery grass but scrambled up. We must get as far from the tower as possible, for my lord might yet triumph by means of it. Reaching the lake, we skirted its sheet of roiling gray. Lamps had been been lit in the house, beckoning pinpoints, and I longed for their warmth and light. I longed for sweet safety, too.

Moments later we stumbled upon the graveled circle before the house. The blackamoor boy stood in its front door holding a lantern. Would he joy to learn his master was dead?

"In, in!" urged Mr. Franklin, still helping Tom Elstree.

But first: a deafening blast. We whirled upon a jagged finger of light. It was anchored in the sky but played its crackling force about Charles Ravenden's tower. The golden medallion with *Fay ce que voudras* writ on it smoked, melted. Then the whole tower sundered, marble sheathing broke, stone crumbled. The shaft tilted and, with a groaning inevitability, crashed upon the roof of the temple, which likewise could not hold. The pediment cracked, the roof gave way. The lightning winked out. The rain sighed. Charles Ravenden lay buried under the ruin of his creation.

26

IN WHICH Truth Is Told and Our Adventure Ends . . .

Two weeks to the day from the Great Storm (so London called it, for none like its fury had struck in years), I stood on the cobbles beside Benjamin Franklin as he gazed up at the roof of number 7 Craven Street. It was the eighth day of December, 1759, brisk but cloudless, an icy blue sky stretching like a ribband of promise over the city. Other rains had fallen in the fortnight, other winds blown, other lightning flashed, such was Nature as the days shortened toward winter, but none to compare with the Great Storm.

Extremity had taught us to bear up under the quotidian adversities of life.

The Thames flowed at our backs. At the top of the way the Strand churned with commerce at a quarter past noon: the clatter of iron wheels, the song of the balladeer, the cry of the coster.

Mrs. Margaret Stevenson stood with us in her white housewife's cap, but Polly did not, for a week ago she had returned to her aunt in Wanstead. Polly had hated to leave—life quickened for her in Craven Street—but she must go, and I missed her. Had she stayed, would she have tickled me again so that we tumbled upon the sofa? Would I have tasted her warm breath?

Other things had changed, too. I had got my razor, as Mr. Franklin had promised, he presenting it with great ceremony one morn at breakfast. It made me inordinately proud, and though there was little as yet to shave, I practiced the art every three days, never cutting myself more than seven times each try—"No gains without pains," as Poor Richard says. A home had been found for Susan, the child we had met at Mrs. Goodbody's. A place had been found for William's milliner, too, where she could lie in till she delivered her babe; and lodging had been found for the child afterward, so the mother might go back to her hats. Though he had resumed his busy town life, William seemed soberer, chastened; his father hoped he had learnt some lesson. The Board of Trade had met in the meantime; and as the Committee for Plantation Affairs reported against the Penns, the bill to tax their lands was allowed. Mr. Franklin smiled at this victory after two long years. "We have won the right to tax the True and Right Proprietaries! The King himself pays taxes, Nick. Bit by bit, even millstones are ground to dust."

As for Charles Ravenden, he was truly dead. No more tricks. No resurrection—though twice he bobbed up in my dreams to haunt me with his white-painted face and haughty eyes. Standing in the storm, we had stared at his tower and temple: rubble swept by lashing rain. We had gone into the house by the lamp which the blackamoor boy, Prince, held up. Shivering, we had gathered round a fire in a cavernous hall to dry our clothes and gather our wits. Tom Elstree had been laid upon a sofa, and the housekeeper had brought hot water and bandages to see to his wounds. Though numerous, none proved critical; all would heal.

His wounded soul? It must heal itself, if it could.

Simkins had explained much that eve. He was as shaken as any of us, and I reminded myself he was but a few years older than I. Charles Ravenden had got him from one of London's houses of boys, he told us whilst the old manse creaked. He had been sixteen; he was nineteen now. "I was grateful at first; I could hardly believe my luck. I was growing old for the buggering game—they toss most boys of sixteen into the street. I did not expect much from my lord—I knew another boy had come and gone before me, so my new master'd likely use me only 'til I grew stale. But I was not starving, so I did all he wished. He set me some tasks about the house, and I learnt quick. He liked that—'a clever pet,' he called me. He had fits, ranting and smashing, and one day he threw out his butler, a good old fellow who'd served him for years. He made me head butler in his place. I didn't know why; I was only eighteen. But he liked to do things to shock people, and he laughed to know the other servants hated it. But they didn't dare say anything, and I worked hard—I liked having food and a bed, and if my lord got rid o' me, it'd be the streets. Things got better after a while. He left me alone, I mean. He was always seeking something new, other boys, other men. And he started building his temple and tower.

"Yet I hated him! He made me crawl like a dog. I could bear that, but I could not bear what he did to others." Simkins gazed at the blackamoor boy. "I could not help seeing how he treated his Dionysians, taunting 'em so they'd push old men down in the streets. Why? Did he want to bring others low, too? He lured street boys to his house and used 'em and cast 'em off. He brought girls as well. At first I couldn't think why, but when I heard their screams I knew it was to hurt 'em."

We were silent whilst the storm raged against the old stone walls. "Tuesday Marrowbone?" proposed Mr. Franklin.

"Poor girl, one o' the troop that came here to the country sometimes, to be used in his tricks on the altar. In his orgies, too, where he made the gentlemen like Mr. Elstree roger 'em so he could watch. One time he did not let the one with the mulberry mark leave; he brought her to St. James's instead. In the last year he'd taken to painting his face and carrying on about Dionysus. He frightened me, and I used to cover my head at night so I would not hear the cries from his chamber. But I heard 'em that night, one in particular, awful. And then when I came there in the morning"—Simkins's mouth worked as if he could not go on—"I found blood on the bed, red soaking gouts of it. The counterpane was missing. Had he killed the girl? Had he wrapped her up and carried her from the house? He was gone, but when he came back he made me burn the bedclothes in secret, so I knew that's what he'd done. He caught me looking at him. 'She was a whore!' he yelled. 'A whore!' He started hitting me. I knew, then, he must be stopped."

"You did not go to a constable or a magistrate?" Mr. Franklin asked.

"What would I have told a magistrate? A servant with no proof? I would've been dismissed by the law, and then my lord could do me in, too. I must find some other way."

"Jack Scratch."

A nod. "I knew he watched the house. I read the newspapers, too; I found out who he was. I heard my lord curse him, and I saw that for all his vanity, he feared the man. So on my afternoons off—or when I was sent on some errand or other—I took to meeting him. I was scared, for my master has eyes in the back of his head, but I had to do it. I told Scratch all I'd seen and heard, and he scribbled it in his book. He was a spiteful little man—I never liked him—but he wanted to bring my lord to justice. We must have real proof, he said, so I began to go through my master's papers. That terrified me, too, but when I found the letter from James Tandy (Scratch had told me about Oxford), I was glad. I gave the letter to Scratch. 'This will finish him!' he crowed. We met on a foggy night two weeks later to make plans—and only hours after that, Scratch was dead."

"The devil, the murdering devil!" moaned Tom Elstree from his sofa.

"Your master had eyes in the back of his head, indeed," said Mr. Franklin. "He followed you that eve, so you have been living on borrowed time ever since."

Simkins's mouth flattened. "I guessed as much. As to tonight, I felt sure some sneaking plan was afoot. I almost didn't send you to the temple, but you were a man who could take care of himself, I thought. Yet when your servant began to question me, when I saw how much you knew and that my lord had to know you knew it, I decided we must go uphill despite the storm." His look found me. "He meant to finish your boy, too?"

"He could allow no witnesses."

Simkins turned to the blackamoor boy standing silently in turban and dog collar. How solemn a face. Was he even twelve? Simkins placed a hand on his shoulder, and the boy's large eyes turned up. "The master is dead," Simkins said reassuringly. "No more shouts. No more blows. No more of any of it." He shook the boy, as if to release him, set him free. How often had he had to watch the child maltreated? How often had he had to restrain his anger? But he had bided his time, and now both of them were free.

"One thing more," put in Mr. Franklin, "how did you know that Tom Elstree was 'innocent,' as you told us?"

"Because I followed him and Miss Ward and my master to the cave. I hid. I watched. I saw Mr. Elstree swoon. I saw my master drive his knife into Miss Ward's heart. I heard his lies afterward, too. I had crept in the cave secretly before; Jack Scratch asked me to, to learn what happened there. I followed that night because it seemed strange, just the three of 'em; it had never happened before. I was sick at what I saw, but I stayed and listened and heard my lord say they must take the body back to London. When I met Scratch in the Running Footman, he wrote it all in his book, so if my master got his hands on that book—"

"As he did."

"—he had good reason to wish to finish me."

There was little more that eve. The servants must be informed; and when they learnt their master was dead, they looked amazed, as if he *had* been a god (surely gods did not die!), but their expressions showed no sorrow, only bewildered uncertainty as to what would become of them now the earl was no more. Little could be done for his remains in the storm, buried under marble and stone, so he must keep till next day, when workmen could be summoned.

We stayed the night, sleeping in strange beds in that cursed house.

The storm was spent by morn, eves dripping, the world new-washed; I heard birdsong as I awoke. Simkins agreed to stay behind to deal with the local authorities: the constable, the coroner, the undertaker, whilst Mr. Franklin obtained the name of Ravenden's solicitor in London, so that he might inform him of the death.

We departed Chalton by half past ten, Mr. Franklin and I in one coach, Tom Elstree in bandages, aided by Peter, in another.

Reaching London by one o'clock, I stopped in Craven Street to tell Mrs. Stevenson and Polly the story of how our adventure had ended, whilst Mr. Franklin went on to Charles Ravenden's solicitor; afterward he conferred with John Fielding. The solicitor was the Honorable Samuel Parfitt-Jones, of Gray's Inn, and the upshot of his protracted labors, we learnt after many weeks, was that the estate and title would pass to the next in line, Mr. Dobbs Ravenden of Bristol, Charles Ravenden's cousin. We met the new earl briefly. He proved a man of scholarly habits, surprised at his change of fortune but happy for it. He had always despised his cousin, and that cousin's remains having been interred in an out of the way corner of the estate, so no one could be reminded he had existed, the new earl set about planting vines about the ruined temple, adding a charming series of waterfalls leading to the lake. Picturesque ruins were all the rage, and many a traveler came to see them, we heard—though no one, to our knowledge, visited Charles Ravenden's resting spot, which seemed to have been forgot.

Hating town life, Dobbs Ravenden closed up the St. James's Square house, but he removed most of its servants to Chalton, including Simkins and Prince. He was unmarried, of a retiring nature, with but one eccentricity: the study of butterflies; so Mr. Franklin and I had good reason to believe Simkins and Prince enjoyed a well-deserved regularity under his reign.

As for Tom Elstree, he betook his wounded self to his father in Soho Square. I do not know how he explained his injuries, but we heard he studied the business, learnt it well, and two years later married Miss Elizabeth Cray of Chandos Street, whose father owned a thriving porcelain manufactory in Stafford. They had three children.

Mr. Franklin busied himself. With Mrs. Goodbody's aid, he prised Nelly Skindle from Mother Cockburn, finding a place for her as underhousemaid with a respectable family in Portsmouth Square. Though she still sorrowed for her murdered friend, the girl was grateful. "I wish her well," Mr. Franklin said.

For my part I longed to help in like fashion, so I told the gentleman all about Birdy Prinsop. He appeared unamazed to hear of my secret life. "Might we do something for her, too, sir?" asked I.

"Talk to her," said he.

I did.

We met in her little crib above the alley off Covent Garden, in the narrow room, breathing the compromised air of that house of paid love. "What?" she flashed out when I made my proposition. Her blue eyes glinted. "You wish to ruin me, boy? I shall not lie with the likes of you forever." Her pert nose lifted. "I will find me a *gen'leman* someday. I knows many girls what have done so, and

243

the gen'lemen sets 'em up with a house and a maid, and they buys 'em clothes and jewels. Go be a serving girl?" She laughed. "I shall never be no servant."

I stared. I argued to no avail, and when I left Birdy, with her fists upon her hips and a trembling about her mouth, I knew I had been some sort of fool. But she had been a worse, for some months later I caught sight of her from our coach window, standing on a corner by one of those dismal, soot-blackened warrens near Blackfriars, in ragged clothes with stringy hair, no creature any gentleman would want. A brutish fellow plucked at her elbow, and I saw her turn into his rough, grizzled face a sketch of the smile that had once made me burn. Hearing gin-soaked laughter as she allowed him to drag her into the shadows, I felt sick at heart.

As for truth, Mr. Franklin laid all our evidence before John Fielding. It was damning, the strongest being Simkins's tales of Tuesday Marrowbone's blood and the murder of Hester Ward, both of which he deposed with his hand upon a Bible. But the Earl of Chalton was dead; he could not be tried. So, though London learnt of his guilt (the story spread like plague; it would have been Jack Scratch's greatest triumph) and many gossips smiled to know they had been perfectly right to despise the mad earl, nothing came of it in a court of law. Hester Ward's uncle, the Marquess of Bathurst, went on his profligate way unencumbered.

And justice? A species of it had been done when I flung the lamp in the cave, but the act haunted me. I had not intended to harm Charles Ravenden, only to stop him, so I shuddered every time I recalled his screams. In imagination I smelt his burning flesh. Did I pity him a little, too? He had not chosen the path of wickedness; some quiddity drove him to it. Had it secretly tormented him? Had he longed to die? Seeing my remorse, Mr. Franklin said, "You did what you must, Nick. You cannot blame yourself." And, gazing into his gray-brown eyes, I saw I must agree: if Ravenden had escaped, more innocent women like Tuesday Marrowbone might have died. Nonetheless, I had been struck a blow in life's forge, and I waited to see how it shaped me.

But I felt no sorrow, no confusion, that bright morn before number 7, with Benjamin Franklin and Mrs. Stevenson. Peter joined us. At our backs lay the little alley where Polly had glimpsed Jack Scratch spying, but I did not think on that. All our attentions were fixed upon the slender iron rod which workmen, instructed by Mr. Franklin, expertly affixed to the sloping slate roof of Mrs. Stevenson's house.

The lightning rod.

Having placed it, the men descended their tall ladder, unreeling the wire which would carry any perilous electrical discharge harmlessly into the ground.

Mr. Franklin watched them. "It will keep you safe," said he, turning to Mrs. Stevenson. "It will keep all of us safe."

Safe, thought I. Truly safe from the perils of the past few weeks. Time now to think on my drawings and notes, from which (long after those years with Mr. Franklin) I have told this tale. Might I fashion from them something for Mr. Tisdale? For London? I would try.

But for now a breeze freshened the air. Now Benjamin Franklin rested a hand carelessly upon my arm, and I was content to breathe free, beside the best and wisest man whom I have known.